UNHOLY DIMENSIONS

UNHOLY DIMENSIONS

Lovecraftian Tales

by

JEFFREY THOMAS

with illustrations

by

peter a. worthy

MYTHOS BOOKS LLC

POPLAR BLUFF

MISSOURI

2005

Mythos Books LLC
351 Lake Ridge Road,
Poplar Bluff,
MO 63901-2177
United States of America

www.mythosbooks.com

Published 2005 by Mythos Books LLC.

FIRST EDITION

Cover image copyright © 2005 by jamie oberschlake.

Illustrations copyright © 2005 by peter a. worthy.

All Rights Reserved.

The author asserts the moral right to
be identified as the author of this work.

ISBN 0-9728545-2-5

Set in *Misproject* and *Adobe Garamond*.

Misproject by Misprinted Type
www.misprintedtype.com

Adobe Garamond Pro by Adobe Systems Incorporated.
www.adobe.com

Typesetting, layout and design by PAW.

Contents

"Strange life . . . may pulsate in the gulfs beyond the stars or press hideously upon our own globe in unholy dimensions which only the dead and the moonstruck can glimpse."

—H. P. Lovecraft

THE BONES OF THE OLD ONES

On the door to the apartment there was a symbol in red spray paint, crudely rendered and streaking, as if to further complicate interpretation of its meaning. It appeared to portray a star with an eye in its center, though the pupil—wavy and jagged—seemed to be a pillar of fire.

At first Bell had thought the paint was blood, but the smell of it was still fresh. Inside the apartment, however, the red streaking down the walls was not paint. He could tell that by the smell, too.

In the hall, a black-uniformed officer had stepped aside to admit him. Inside the apartment, there was a second uniformed forcer and a forensics field man. Bell nodded to them as they met his eyes. A man lying on his back on the living room floor met his eyes, also, but no cognizance showed in them. The man on the floor had been shot through the throat and the belly, his blood soaking into the ratty carpet and spattered on a bookshelf by his head.

"Three more," said Graf, the forensic tech, shrugging in the direction of a narrow hallway. "One in the kitchen, two in a bedroom. All dead when we arrived."

"No more children?" Bell asked him.

"Just the one down at P.H."

Bell nodded, and moved past Graf into the hallway. The kitchen opened directly off it, brightly lit and poorly cleaned. A cairn of dishes had been erected in the twin sinks, and the trash zapper was broken, as evidenced by a conventional waste basket filled to overflowing. There were posters and pages torn from magazines taped or pinned to the walls in here, as there were in the parlor. Some were astronomical charts, others astrological. There were photos of archaeological sites and artifacts. On the aqua Choom-made fridge there were what seemed to be a child's drawings held by magnets. They were involved designs, crude for having been rendered without benefit of a ruler, and yet obsessively geometrical. Some were like snow flakes greatly enlarged, others like technical blueprints, a strange mix of childishness and sophistication. They had all been drawn in a black marker. Had they been done by the little boy who was now being cared for at the precinct house?

Bell frowned at these imaginative designs, then down at the woman splayed grotesquely at his feet. She wore an oriental robe, imitation satin with a colorful dragon embroidered on the back. One of her well-worn slippers had come off and lay apart from her. It was a pathetic little detail of the sort Bell often noticed and focused on and wished he wouldn't. Madness had entered amongst these mundane, everyday objects and personal possessions, subtly transforming them into sad, orphaned things. A crime scene to Bell was like a still life in which a skull had been set down in the midst of the flowers and fruit.

The woman's lips were squashed open against the dirty floor and her face was half-enveloped in a caul of blood which had poured from the ragged entrance wound in her scalp. A door of skull had opened on a hinge of skin and much of her brain had been added to the mess already in the sinks.

Bell proceeded along the murky hall toward the bedrooms lightly, as if he expected the murderer of these people to suddenly spring at him from me of these doors . . . even though he knew that man was down at the precinct house right now, also, safely jailed behind a barrier of magnetic force.

The bathroom was empty if filthy. It stank of urine and wine-tinged vomit. At the end of the hall were two bedrooms facing each other. One was empty, the furnishings spare and the bed a mere mattress. There was a small mattress for a child fitted in a large closet with its louvered doors open. Nearing the closet, Bell poked his head in and saw more of those odd drawings taped to the walls. There were few toys. Under the mattress, Bell found a dagger. Had the boy hidden it away, meaning to use it to escape from these people, or had they given the weapon to him?

Well, this was Paxton after all, and far from being a town of peace, as its name might indicate, it was a place in which it might be wise to give your child his own weapon to keep by his bed. After all, Bell's presence here was proof enough of that. Bell had no children of his own, and wouldn't have raised one in Punktown—as its inhabitants had renamed the city—if he did.

In the other bedroom lay the last two bodies; a man shot through the hand and right eye and a woman shot through the jaw and neck. Both wore the perplexing vapid smiles of the dead. There was a second forensics tech in the room and she merely glanced up at Bell. His heart had flinched a little in his chest when he'd seen a living person in here. This was hardly Bell's first homicide case, but there was an unsettling feel to the scene. It had more to do with the identity of the murderer, he thought, than anything else. His identity, and the mysteriousness of his motives.

Bell knelt by the man and lifted the sleeve on his white T-shirt a bit to better see a half-exposed tattoo. It was a design done in metallic silver ink: a series of concentric circles, with rays radiating out from the center. A target? An eye?

When he stood, Graf was there beside him. Graf was a Choom, a native to this planet called Oasis, indistinguishable from humans save for the wide dolphin-like mouth which split his face from ear to ear. His heavy jaws were full of rows of molars evolved for the mastication of Oasis's hardy roots, though right now he was chewing on the end of a pen. He talked around it as if it were a cigarette.

"You know this Kaddish guy, huh?" he asked.

"Yes," said Bell.

"Why would he do this?"

"I don't know."

"There are weapons in the place," Graf said. "Guns, knives, but Kaddish took them all by surprise so it wasn't self defense. He's a hired investigator, John, but do you think he'd take on a hit for money?"

"No. I don't believe he would."

Graf shrugged, watched the tech as she worked over the female corpse, utilizing a small vidcam to record the body in full and the wounds in extreme close-up for the lab records and for courtroom use as needed. "These people weren't too normal themselves. Looks like a kind of cult. There's some sort of an altar in the living room; you should take a look."

Bell grunted and followed the Choom back down the hall and into the parlor. In here, the vidtank which nearly took up one wall was filled with static as if it were a sand storm raging in a giant aquarium. Its hissing was low in the background. The uniformed man turned to Bell. "We've ID'd them all, sir. But for the kid; he doesn't show in any station files, though he does bear a physical resemblance to this man here, and the woman in the kitchen."

"Names?"

"This one, Willy Pugmire. His wife in the kitchen is Ingrid Hobbs-Pugmire. Both unemployed—laid off from Polyform Ceramix for two and a half years; on extended benefits. The two in the bedroom are Jesus da Favela and Wanda Macumba, both collecting welfare benefits. We cross-referenced them with the perpetrator and nothing linked up."

"Thanks," Bell murmured, brushing past the young officer, the altar Graf had mentioned having caught his eye.

A table had been made of a thick, oblong slab of gray stone resting atop two piles of ceramic foundation blocks stolen from some construction site. Various items needed for rituals were stored in the hollows of the blocks; candles, a lighter, a sheath of papers rolled in a tube. Bell withdrew this and opened the papers like a scroll. He grimaced. "What is this, another language translated into English?"

Graf peered over his shoulder. "Tikkihotto?"

"I don't think so. We'll have to run a scan on it." He shoved the tube back into its slot, from another Bell removed a clear vial containing a green powder which sparkled like pulverized emeralds. It was a trendy new drug nicknamed absinthe, popular with artistic types. He passed it to Graf. "Absinthe makes the heart grow fonder."

"Your friend Kaddish isn't involved in drug running, dealing, like that, is he?"

"No. Drink. A lot of drink. But no chemicals."

"Well, you don't know. He's obviously changed since last you knew him, John."

Bell couldn't argue with that. If Kaddish could become a ruthless mass murderer in three years, then why not an addict or a dealer?

He took in the altar table's surface. A black candle had been positioned in each of the four corners of the slab, fixed in a pool of its own dried wax. There was a hollow at the center of the slab, and in it rested a curious decoration sculpted from black crystal marbled with blood red striations. It was an egg-sized gem cut into an odd-angled trapezohedron, though Bell wasn't familiar with the mineral. He lifted it for closer inspection, and found himself narrowing his eyes as if he thought he might see into its darkness through his reflection on the polished surfaces. A shudder went through him unaccountably, and as he went to set the gem back into its hollow he saw that there was a shape outlined in the surface of the slab.

"Graf, is this a fossil?"

The Choom had been poking around inside more of the ceramic blocks, and straightened up to have a look. "Hm. Yeah. Looks like it. Well . . . it's a spiral. Could be an old sculpture of some kind. Mm. No. No, that looks organic. A shell? Some giant shelled mollusk?"

"Did Oasis once have giant shelled mollusks?"

"No, but it doesn't have to have come from Oasis."

"Giant is right." Bell pointed to the edges of the slab. The spiral kept on going, fading off the sides, as if the slab had been cut right out of the middle of it. How much farther would it have continued to extend out from the center, uninterrupted? And it was in that center, in what seemed to be a natural hollow, that the black polyhedron fitted. Bell set it back in place.

"Any idea what the focus of this cult might've been?" he asked the Choom.

"Never seen anything like it. The papers there will help us, once we decipher them. They didn't own a computer but they have books; a bunch of weird occult dung, looks like. Some pseudo-Satanic thing?"

"Doesn't look that simple."

"Was Kaddish a religious nut? Maybe he felt he had to trash some infidels. His own little jihad . . ."

Bell was about to say that his old friend Joshua Kaddish was no religious fanatic, but stopped himself. Again, at this point he didn't know what Josh Kaddish was capable of. He sighed, looked up at the wall mirror which hung directly above the altar. Once they took their absinthe and chanted their chants, with candle glow dramatically under-lighting their features, would the cultists then gaze into this mirror and imagine that their faces were transforming? Would they wait for spiritual visions to appear in their own reflected eyes?

Bell's reflection showed a man of thirty-one, with sandy short hair neatly cut and brushed back from his forehead. His eyes were blue and far-spaced, his lips too full for his taste though his ex-wife had called them sensuous, back when she was inclined toward such a compliment. He thought himself homely; that his nose was too flat in profile, his teeth too small and his smile too wide. His wife had once called him handsome. There was to his face, oddly, both a boyish quality and a prematurely wasted, haggard aspect. He was slender but it was winter and his black, cloned-leather jacket gave him a little bulk. He thought he looked tired and unhappy. He expected to see no magic transformations, in that regard.

"What do you think happened to the rug over here, Graf?" called the forcer from across the room.

Graf and Bell joined him. The man was pointing to tears in the carpet extending from that corner out into the center of the room. It was as though a heavy bureau with spike-tipped legs had been dragged across the material, ripping it.

In the corner, at the point where the tears began, Kaddish had spray-painted another of those red symbols like the one he had sprayed on the apartment door. They knew he had painted these symbols, as opposed to the cultists themselves, because he had had the paint gun in his possession when apprehended, they'd heard. Bell wondered if Kaddish might indeed have become some sort of religious nut, of a kind violently opposed to the beliefs of this little group.

What about the corner had inspired Kaddish to paint the symbol there? And why did those tear-marks extend from the corner into the room? And why, finally, were there several bullet holes clearly punched into the plaster of the corner, as if Kaddish had made a target of the painted symbol? Bell fingered one of the holes absently. His eyes dropped to the tears in the soiled, food-stained carpet once more. Did those rows of tears extend from the corner out into the center of the room . . . or had they, instead, originated from the center of the room and then ended in the corner, at the red symbol? Either way . . . what had made the marks, and what had become of the thing that had made then?

"Can you turn off that damn vidtank?" Graf grumbled to the forcer.

The uniformed policeman reached out, punched some buttons to shut it off, accidentally changed channels instead. There was a brief glimpse of a broadcaster looking quite serious, and then the man hit the correct button and the tank was emptied.

"What was that?" Bell said. "Put it back on a second."

The forcer obliged. The broadcaster materialized once more within the vidtank, practically life-sized.

". . . absolutely no communications of any kind as of a half hour ago. All

5

emergency communication frequencies have been opened, but as yet, no transmissions are being received from any source, commercial or government. Until the explanation for the communication black-out is investigated and rectified, all teleportation to or from Earth is to be officially put on hold . . ."

"Earth?" said Graf. "What happened?"

"Try another channel," Bell said.

The forcer switched past a soap opera and a sitcom rerun, found another grim-looking newscaster.

". . . the Emergency Lockout System. To repeat this urgent newsbreak: as of thirty-four minutes ago, all communication with Earth has been lost on every frequency and mode of contact, on all government, corporate and civilian bands. Whether the Earth has come under attack or suffered a natural calamity is not known at this time. Colonies as near as those on Earth's moon also report full loss of contact with Earth, and are conducting probes and scans, with results forthcoming. We will let you know what is found out about this communication failure as soon as the information is relayed to us. Until the reason is understood and safe conditions are assured, no teleportation to or from the Earth is being permitted, all teleportation channels being blocked by the Emergency Lockout System . . ."

"Man," breathed Bell to himself.

The forcer flipped through more stations. On a number of the many channels, there was only static. Programs from Earth, Bell realized, the transmissions now blocked. Or eradicated.

— 2 —

At his precinct station, Bell had to decide between interviewing the boy Kaddish had taken with him when he fled the apartment of his victims, or Kaddish himself. Perhaps wanting to delay confronting his old friend, Bell chose the boy.

"He's six, our med scan says," Bell was told by Irene, the officer who had been ordered to look after the boy until it could be decided what to do with him. "No medical problems, no signs of physical abuse from either the family he was with or from the perpetrator. He does have a tattoo, though, in the middle of his chest . . ."

"Silver ink. Circles inside circles, with rays coming out from the middle of it."

"Right. You know what it means?"

"One of the victims had the same thing on his arm. Has he told you what happened?"

"No. He won't talk. Hasn't said a word. He must be terribly traumatized, but he smiles, at least. I gave him a sandwich and he ate a few bites."

There was a bank of monitors near them, and Bell watched the boy on one of these. He looked calm enough, sitting there coloring with markers Irene had given him. His hair was so closely shorn that he looked bald, but no haircut or style was unusual in Punktown.

"So Kaddish was dropping the boy off outside Central Hospital . . ."

"Right," said Irene. "He was letting the kid out of his car, outside the front doors. But he'd been followed by Ferrara and Woo, who responded to the reports of a vehicle fleeing from a gunfire scene. They pinned his car in with theirs and he took off on foot, but Woo brought him down with a dart. Kaddish had a gun on him but he made no attempt to fire on Ferrara and Woo at any time, luckily. He's a very dangerous guy, so it's funny. Unless he's selectively dangerous. Must be, because he was obviously trying to leave the child in a safe place, even at risk to himself. Strange."

"Yeah," agreed Bell. "I think I'll go try my luck with the boy."

"Good luck."

Irene let the detective into the room where the child was being kept, pending a search for surviving relatives and a psych appraisal from a Child Services worker on her way over.

When the door slid open, the boy looked up and crumpled the drawing he'd been working on into a tight ball in his fist. Bell smiled at him and chose to ignore this act for the moment, though he did take note of the color of the marker the child had selected to draw with from all those Irene had supplied him. Not black, as he would have guessed, but a metallic silver one. Irene left them alone together, and Bell seated himself opposite the boy.

"Hi there, pal. My name's John. What's yours?"

The child gave the detective a great big smile, the winning but unusual quality of which confirmed to Bell beyond any doubt that this was the same child who had drawn those obsessive geometrical designs. The boy replied, "Yog Sothoth."

He had spoken readily enough. Maybe he trusted men more so than women. Encouraged, Bell repeated, "Yog? You're Yog?"

The boy began to giggle wildly, rocked back on his rump. Bell tried on a smile but it didn't fit well. Despite his concern for the boy's welfare, he wasn't in the mood for children's games. And how could this boy be in the mood? Hadn't he seen his parents slaughtered this afternoon, assuming the Pugmires were his family? Hadn't he been kidnapped by their murderer? Had the experience shattered his uncomprehending mind?

"Is Yog your name, pal, or are you just kidding with me?"

"I am the gate," the boy replied sweetly, rocking forward and back, hands on his knees. "Yog Sothoth is the key and the guardian of the gate."

Bell's smile was losing its hold on his skin. "What does that mean, buddy? Is that something your parents taught you? Were Willy and Ingrid your mom and dad?"

The boy stopped rocking but his smile, at least, didn't falter. He said, "Ph-nglui mglw'nafh Cthulhu R'lyeh wgah'nagl fhtagn."

"Uh-huh," Bell said. He straightened up, thinking the boy was really taunting him now. Nonsensical jibber-jabber. Unless . . . he was speaking in tongues. And then Bell remembered the alien language translated to English on that roll of papers from the altar. Yes; it had to be that. The Pugmires had given the boy a strong religious foundation, like mothers and fathers were expected to do. "Can I see what you were drawing there, mate? I saw your drawings back at the apartment; you're quite an imaginative artist, there. C'mon, let me see." He extended his hand.

The boy's smile remained but his eyes narrowed slightly. He looked wary or cunning, and the effect on his young features wasn't pleasant. Bell switched to a sterner tone of voice, wiggled his fingers. He was prepared to pry the ball loose if he had to.

"Give me the picture, buddy."

The boy giggled, and relented. He passed the crumpled drawing to Bell, who smoothed the crinkled paper on the table top.

Like those at the apartment, it was a perplexing pattern of lines, angles and curves like some mathematical equation, but rendered in silver ink so that it resembled the web of a deranged spider. In some respects it bore a resemblance to the tattoo that Irene had told Bell the boy wore on his chest. "Very nice. Interesting. What is this design, guy? Does this mean something?"

"A gate," the boy replied.

"A gate. Is this Yog . . . whatever?"

"*This* is Yog Sothoth." The boy touched his sternum. "The spheres within spheres. Gate, key, and guardian in one. I am Yog Sothoth."

Bell said nothing for several moments. It was sad. Whether his family had made him this way, or Kaddish had frightened him to madness, the six year old was deeply in need of psychological help. He hoped C. S. got here soon to tend to him. He hoped the kid could be salvaged.

"May I keep this picture, pal?" The child said nothing. Only stared, and smiled. Bell folded the drawing and tucked it into his shirt pocket, rose from the table. "Thanks. Maybe I'll come back and see you later, okay?" Then he turned, and moved to the door.

He was glad to leave.

* * *

"I knew you'd come in to see me," said Joshua Kaddish.

"This is my precinct. I'm homicide." Bell drew closer to the softly humming barrier of the jail cell, a field of magnetic force, transparent but illuminated a soft blue so that it would be immediately evident when it was activated. "Did you kill those people just as an excuse to see me again?"

Seated on a chair directly facing the barrier, Kaddish snorted softly at the joke. "A coincidence, Johnny. Then again, there's no such thing. Maybe we were meant to meet up again, huh? Who knows the blueprint of the universe?" At this last question he gave an odd little smile.

It was a common enough expression for him, all too familiar to Bell. Kaddish's gray eyes were at least as sly and mysteriously amused as his cat-curl smile. His ears were almost impish and nearly pointed, lending him more of a darkly mischievous look. His short, dark auburn hair was gelled and brushed back and he wore a light- colored beard of several days. He was trim, dressed neatly for an alleged psychopath in a crisp white shirt with the cuffs rolled back and black trousers. His voice was calm, its accent British. He seemed composed enough considering his situation, but Bell knew his smiles could conceal a lot. He knew the man was volatile . . . but capable of the carnage he had seen back at the apartment complex?

"Can you get me a cigarette, Johnny? I know you don't smoke, yourself . . ."

Bell ignored the request. "Why did you do it, Josh?"

"She was beautiful. She wanted me. And she wasn't a good choice of wife for you."

Bell drew in a long breath, reining in his control over his emotions. Barely. "I mean why you murdered those people, not why did you fuck my wife."

"Well, don't you think we should get that out of the way before we move on to the other? It's obviously been what's stood between the two of us talking, these past years."

"Who were you to judge that she wasn't a good wife for me?"

"She slept with me, didn't she? She was sleeping with another man, too. I forget his name now. I followed them, took vids to show you. A little freebie detective job. I wanted you to know what she was really like, pal. She wasn't the wife you wanted her to be. You were blinded by her looks."

"So you were doing me a favor. You didn't want to sleep with her for your own sake . . ."

"Of course I did, Johnny. She was lovely. But I wouldn't have seduced her if she'd been really right for you. I killed two birds with one stone. I was going to show you those vids, but then . . . well, I employed another method of showing you her true colors. But I did send you those vids. Did you ever look at them?"

"No. I tossed them in the zapper. I thought they were vids of you and her."

"Me and her? Christ, man, you think I would gloat like that?"

"You're gloating now."

"I'm not gloating, Johnny." The feline smile was gone, and Kaddish nearly looked sincere. "I didn't want to hurt you. But you wouldn't listen. I warned you about her. I knew her better than you did, in the beginning."

"It was none of your business, no matter what she was capable of. It was my marriage. My wife. My life. My decision to make, my problem to deal with."

"You were crazy marrying her."

"I was crazy ever having a friend like you. I guess I'm not a good judge of character."

"Just a wee naive, is all. And where is she now, Johnny? I haven't seen her around, either."

"We're divorced."

"Good." Kaddish held Bell's gaze without blinking, waiting to see what came next.

"Why did you kill those people?"

Kaddish rose from the chair, half turned away from his visitor. He had been given a marker to do a crossword puzzle in a hard copy of the morning news, and he tapped the capped pen against the bare white wall of the tiny holding cell as if testing it for weak spots.

"I met another lovely woman, Johnny. Her name is Kate Redgrove. She's an archaeologist . . ."

"I don't think she sounds good enough for you, Josh. Maybe I should sleep with her."

"We've already broken up, I'm afraid. But I learned a lot from her. There's a bad time coming, Johnny. It's already begun. There are people who've been waiting a long time for this. Some dreading it . . . and others, like those cultists I—that you saw . . . those people have been trying to make this thing come about."

"What thing?"

"There are beings outside our reality. Outside our space, time and dimension. They've been worshiped as gods, because we're amebas to them— dogs at best, when they need us. I can't believe there are those who try to help them come through. Do they really think they'll reward them? Give them power? When they don't need these fools anymore, they'll squash them like bugs."

My God, Bell thought, he is insane.

"They're known as the Old Ones, the Great Old Ones, the Outsiders. By other names in other cultures and religions on a hundred planets. They once ruled everything . . . long before us. They may have seeded humans throughout many systems, like we'd plant crops. Sometimes for labor. Sometimes for food . . . not for the Old Ones themselves; they don't need to eat to survive. For all intents and purposes, they're immortal. But there are lesser beings. Spawn. Minions. More corporeal in the way we understand it. They seem to feast on us sometimes . . . though I don't know if it's blood they feed on, or the essence of life itself. Anyway, I think the Old Ones also might have seeded us because they wanted us around to help them come back through if they ever got locked out. Because that's exactly what happened. Another powerful amalgamation of beings—the Elder Gods—came and overpowered them. Locked them up, locked them out."

"This . . . girlfriend of yours told you all this?"

Kaddish turned back to face the police inspector, smiling, tapping the pen against his own chest now. "I know it sounds crazy, pal, but there's no way to make it sound sane. No one with influence has ever wanted to believe it. It's too big, too scary to believe. There's always been a few eccentrics and geniuses who uncovered some hints, investigated. More often than not, they didn't survive to pass on to the masses what they'd learned. Or else, they were considered too mad to believe. And sometimes they were mad, though they didn't start out that way."

"Is this Kate Redgrove mad, then?"

"Kate? She's as cool as gun metal, Johnny. She's quite a woman. I think you'd better go talk to her yourself."

"I intend to. But why do you think I should?"

"Because you don't believe any of what I'm saying."

"What do these, ah, god-like entities have to do with what you did? Are you saying those people you killed . . . ?"

"They worshiped the Old Ones. And worse than that, these idiots were trying to pick the locks on their cells. Open the gates and the windows. In every way they could. Chants, rituals. It's always been said that the Old Ones would return when 'the stars were right'. That means, when the conditions of space and time were optimum for them to break free of the prisons the Elder Gods left them in. 'In strange eons', the dead gods are supposed to be resurrected. Well, it's time, Johnny. The stars are right. The strange eons are now."

"Says Kate."

"Yes. But I knew it was getting very close from watching the cult, too. I'd been watching them for a while. They were stepping up their activity. I had to stop them." The smug smile drained out of Kaddish's face; even from his eyes. "Believe me, I had to do it. Before they could do more damage. But they're not the only cult in Punktown. There are even more cults on Earth . . ."

"Does Kate intend to kill any of these cult people?"

"No. I can't see her doing that."

"Well, you messed up, Josh. You got caught. Now it looks like those other cults will just go on chanting and opening the doors for these super-aliens."

"That's just what they'll do, John. They have to be stopped. You have to get me out of here."

"You murdered . . ."

"I was truth-scanned when your people took my confession. I told them my story then. Go look at the scan. You'll see I'm not lying."

"Maybe you aren't, but the scan will only prove that you believe in what you're saying. It doesn't mean it really happened, except in the mind of a madman suffering some very paranoid delusions."

"Then you have to take a memory recording. Play it back, Johnny. You'll see for yourself that it's no delusion . . . the thing I saw in that apartment. I shot it, for Chrissakes."

"What thing?"

"A few days ago I smuggled a bug into the cult's apartment in their mail. I heard them summoning something up, so I moved in on them   . . . and when I busted in, they were calling up a creature. I don't know what it was, exactly. Some lesser being. A hound, some call them. It's easier to let the minions in, the ones that are more material in the way we understand. This thing was being manifested right in the middle of the living room when I burst in on them. I shot at the thing, and it disappeared into the corner . . ."

The corner. Bell had seen the bullet holes there. "It just walked into the wall, huh?"

"It passed out of this dimension. There's a kind of geometry involved in opening some of the portals. Certain signs and patterns can open them up . . ."

"Is that what that red symbol was you painted in the corner, and on the door to their apartment? A portal?"

"No—that was the sign of the Elder Gods. Kate showed it to me. The Elder Gods used it to seal up the Old Ones. It has great power against them."

"Like, oh, a crucifix against vampires, huh?"

"I sprayed the sign on the door to keep out other beings or agents that might try to come to the apartment later. Even if it gets painted over, it's still there. And I painted the symbol in the corner to keep the hound from coming back out of the wall. They like corners. Something about the angles. The geometry . . ."

Bell tossed his head far back and let out a weary laugh. "The hounds like corners. Ohh . . . this is steaming dung, you know that? Do you think my chief will spend the money and time to have your memories recorded and played back, the way you're talking?"

Kaddish came very close to the blue-tinted barrier, so that its glow gave him a chill, corpse-like appearance. "I'll tone down my talk around everyone else but you. But you have to get that recording made, pal. You have to see for yourself. And show them, too, afterwards. Time is running out. The cults have to be stopped. Their books, their relics, it all has to be destroyed. At least get them to record the last day of my memories. How difficult can that be? Just one day, tell them. Just today."

Bell was wagging his head. "What happened to you, Josh?"

"Will you tell them?"

"I'll ask them to do the recording, yes—okay?"

Kaddish seemed to relax slightly, found a shred of his smile again. "How's the kid?" he asked a little sheepishly.

"We can't get through to him. I think he's traumatized by what he saw." Kaddish seemed almost to wince, looked away. "I was trying to drop him off someplace where he'd be taken care of . . ."

"All he can do is babble a bunch of gibberish and talk nonsense like what you're telling me."

Kaddish looked warily back at his old friend. "Gibberish? What's he been telling you? Things about the cult?"

"He isn't 'telling' us anything. Just some kind of language that sounded made up as he went along, and he says he's a gate. A gate and a guardian and a key, all at the same . . ."

"Jesus! Oh fucking hell! My God!" Kaddish whirled, paced violently, his reaction and actions so sudden that Bell was startled back a half-step, as if afraid Kaddish could fling himself straight through the magnetic field. "Yog-Sothoth!"

"Yes," Bell said. "He told me his name is Yog Sothoth."

"He isn't Yog-Sothoth. But he's been made an extension. He says he's the gate? They've turned the boy into one of their portals. Yog-Sothoth will reach through him. And if Yog-Sothoth opens the gate, then the worst of the gates will be open . . ."

"What are you saying?"

"I shouldn't have let him go. I should have killed him, too. How could I have let this happen? I got caught trying to help him, and all along he was the one I should have killed first . . ."

"You're out of your mind, Josh. Listen to yourself. You're totally fucking . . ."

"Listen to me!" Kaddish bellowed, halting from his pacing and stabbing a finger toward the barrier. "You have to believe me! The Old Ones have to be kept out! You have to sedate that boy. I know you won't kill him, but you have to immobilize him. Drug him, put him in suspended animation, but you can't let him go free!"

"He's in our custody."

"You can't stop him from opening the gate by fucking baby-sitting him! Jesus, John, you have to record my memories immediately. You hear me? You have to see that I'm telling the truth about the danger to all of us! To the Earth and the whole fucking universe!"

The Earth. Had Kaddish heard about the loss of contact with the mother world? Bell felt foolish for letting himself connect that alarming mystery with

13

the ranting of his old friend.

"I'll arrange the recording right now, all right? But if you don't calm down, they'll just consider you a raving lunatic like I do and throw you in a psychcenter."

"The boy is still here? He's in this building?"

"Yes."

"Watch him, Johnny. For God's sake, don't let anyone take him away . . ."

"We can't keep him in a cell in here forever. We're trying to find family. Family that you haven't executed."

"Don't let him leave here, John, I'm warning you. He's one of them. Worse. I should have figured it out before."

"Where does this Kate Redgrove live?"

"In Beaumonde Square, off the P. U. campus. Nineteen Cobble Plaza, second floor."

"Second floor. Nineteen Cobble Plaza. Money, huh?"

"Rich Earth family. Yeah, go see Kate. Tell her what I did. Tell her about the boy, what he told you he was. And Johnny? Tell her that I still love her. Will you?"

"Yeah, yeah—I'll tell her."

"John. I am sorry about the wife. Truly. It was brash. It was stupid. And it was selfish."

"It was a thrill you couldn't resist. Sleeping with your best friend's wife. I think you used all that dung about concern for me just as an excuse, Josh. Maybe we should truth-scan you on that, while we're at it."

"We'll talk about it again another day, John. I can see you aren't inclined to believe me now, and there are more pressing matters."

"Well, you got that much right. I'll go ask them now if they can do that recording . . ."

"Insist, John! Insist!"

"I'll see ya." And with that, Bell left his old friend standing at the humming barrier, his eyes glowing eerily with its reflected light as he anxiously watched him depart.

— 3 —

Bell's hovercar rode two feet above the street, and it would seem to require a stronger than usual repulsor field to hold it aloft, but the huge, heavy-looking replica Edsel was actually constructed of lightweight, durable ceramic. In hover mode, its wheels tucked up into their cavities. When Bell had first seen the car, its amphibian face and distinctive grille had won him over immediately. When he found out about the original's reputation as a fluke, well, that was only the icing on the cake. He loved the monstrosity.

The original, no matter how controversial in its day, had not possessed the monitor screen on its dash which Bell had had installed, and spoke to now. Graf's Choom face filled the screen.

"I'm taking the recording now," the forensics tech reported, "but the chief would only agree to go back a day, for now, to record the crime as it took place."

"Good enough."

"You don't really expect to see anything like Kaddish described . . ."

"Of course not. But we'll see what he did do. Clear up a couple of mysteries, like why he really fired into the corner, and how those marks in the carpet got there. If nothing more, it will prove his guilt in court and save the tax payers from footing a long trial."

"It wouldn't have been a long trial even without his memories. He admits he killed them, and we have a truth scan. The scan says everything he told us was straight. At least, that he believes everything he told us is straight. He really believes he chased a monster into the corner, and put a few slugs into it. He might be totally burnt, but he's not lying to us."

"Any drugs in his system? Absinthe?"

"No sign of him ever taking that. He's clean."

"I wonder if this Kate Redgrove is on something. I don't know what she did to Kaddish's mind. Although Kaddish felt he had to destroy the cult, his delusions and theirs are based on the same belief in the same things. Just that he opposes the beliefs, and they embrace them."

"Mm. Oh—hey, you should put the news on. John. They've lost all contact with Luna and Mars, now, too. There were a few panicky-sounding transmissions, and then they got cut off. Whatever's blocking Earth communications seems to be spreading outward."

"Jesus. Did any of the transmissions hint what's going on?"

"Somebody was saying something about a gaseous fog everywhere . . . a cloud. 'A cloud with mouths'. Lots of mouths. Crazy stuff. Creepy to hear it, though; they played a bit of the transmission on the air. These people were really scared. I don't know what they actually saw, but . . . reminded me of a recording I heard once of a shuttle going into a crash landing. Gave me the chills."

"Wow," Bell murmured inadequately.

"Anyhow, I'll get back to you when I have a look at his recording."

"Mm," Bell grunted.

He stopped at an intersection, his vehicle idling but his mind hurtling on ahead, though it wasn't sure of direction, maybe not even of destination. All around him, the colony city of Punktown loomed; skyscrapers slate gray or mirror bright, as ornamented as gothic cathedrals or as smooth and featureless as obelisks. Smaller buildings with skins of brick or tile, bright pebbled mosaic or pastel stucco, crowded around the bases of the titans. Piercing the ash sky were minarets both glittering new or tarnished and with masonry crumbling. There were plastic gargoyles leering down at him from on high, like taunting demons. There was a bronze angel lifting a sword above its androgynous head, atop a dome of verdigris green. Elegant Art Deco scallops and tiers, and structures of metal like giant primitive engines, grease-stained and covered in incomprehensible mechanical detail.

It was a many-faced tribute to the power of ingenuity, the perseverance of living things, of survival in a universe mindlessly hostile toward life, beneficial to life apparently only by accident. So many races, so many varied interpretations on life, had come together here—not always harmoniously, by any means, but successfully—to erect a temple of sorts to the god of Life itself. Surrounded by these colossal edifices, watching the teeming masses on the sidewalks, the hordes of vehicles on ground level and even in the air, it was hard to believe that Earth—its cities far greater still than this one—could be under any kind of devastating threat. Let alone the Armageddon, the Doomsday, that Kaddish predicted like one of those scripture-quoting fanatics who seemed to haunt cities everywhere. There was history here, behind every building's style of construction and ornament, telling of the civilizations, the cultures, the religions that had brought them here to this world—like solid foundations that were built on a bed of time. This was not a fragile scene. This was strength. Only Nature was stronger, and was that even true, when these beings had drained many a verdant planet dry and turned many an ocean black to reach this pinnacle of power? What natural cataclysm could have befallen Earth that its inhabitants couldn't foresee far ahead, and take measures to divert or repel? And yet something had happened, hadn't it? But what?

Bell reminded himself that most of the cultures represented in the vista around him had developed weapons that could level a Punktown in one bright flash, no matter how immortal its appearance. Even turn this planet of Oasis to a charred ball. And if these lowly creatures, all more or less equivalent in their technology, could render such horror . . . well, what might a vastly superior race of beings be capable of?

Bell sighed the thought out of him. He wasn't letting Kaddish distort his thoughts the way this Kate Redgrove had obviously distorted his, was he?

The current of traffic changed, and once again his Edsel was surging forward, toward Beaumonde Square, one of the nicer regions of a much blighted city. Blight was a kind word. The crime in Punktown was legendary, even on Earth. The poverty in some slums made a bygone city like Earth's Calcutta seem tolerable. There had been riots in these streets, a devastating earthquake that had buried whole branches of the subway and the subterranean sectors of the city. And yet it still survived. Life still clung tenaciously to its streets. Again, if there could ever be a threat such as Kaddish alluded to—a threat to the Earth, mightier still—it would have to be a tremendously dangerous force. It would have to be something like one of those doomsday weapons. Worse, really, since even against those there were defenses and counter-measures.

A cloud with mouths. Lots of mouths. What had the Mars colonists witnessed that could be construed that way?

He drew nearer to Beaumonde Square, whose inhabitants feared changes in the stock market more than cataclysms of nature or evil gods.

His vidscreen beeped him. He reactivated it. Again, Graf was there, but looking more intense than several minutes ago.

"John—I've seen the memory recording."

"And?"

"You want to come back and see it on the spectacles, or should I play it for you now?"

"Put it on."

"You'd better pull over first."

Bell parked the Edsel in the lot of a library of traditional Choom design. "Go on," he told the tech.

The film had been shot from Kaddish's point of view, the cameras being his eyes. If he were wearing the viewer that Graf had worn to watch the recording, Bell would feel that he was experiencing these memories through his own eyes. But even watching them played out on a tiny screen, with the sounds of the city around him, it was still an unsettling experience. Doubly so, considering the owner of these memories.

Bell watched Kaddish's hand paint the red star/eye with its pupil of flame on the apartment door. The sign of the—what?—Elder Gods, he had called it . . .

Next Kaddish extended an illegal device burglars used to defeat certain styles of locks. Bell owned one himself. Its beam cut the bolt in one silent second. The door opened.

Whirling to face Bell on the screen was the living face of Willy Pugmire. Chaos unfolded now at a dizzying speed. There was a cry of outrage transforming into a cry of fear all in one smoothly blended moment. The loud blasting of a handgun with no silencing features. Solid projectiles rather than bolts of energy found their mark. Kaddish's obsession seemed to demand the thunder of righteousness and the spilling of sacrificial blood.

"Shit!" Bell hissed, sitting closer to the screen. "What is that?"

Pugmire had fallen, and now Kaddish was firing at something that had been obscured behind the man. Something in the center of the room . . .

It moved across the room, into the corner. Bell heard Kaddish roaring his own fear and outrage after his target. His bullets pursued it. And then it was gone.

Pugmire's wife had run screaming into the kitchen. Kaddish whirled away from the corner, darted in there after her. Bell felt as if he himself shot her dead, and flinched at the reports.

Confused voices from deeper in the apartment. Two others, startled from sleep. Kaddish bolted down the hall to find them. He found them, all wide eyes in the hot flashes of gas from his gun, like deer caught in headlights. The collision of bullets with flesh and bone . . .

In the remaining bedroom Kaddish found the boy cowering in the closet. Kaddish pulled him out. The child didn't have time to grab the knife that was hidden under the mattress. Bell knew about it; Kaddish hadn't. Kaddish had been lucky.

Before he left the apartment, Kaddish sprayed the pentagram in the corner where the . . . hound . . . had vanished. As he turned for the door, holding the boy's shirt in one fist and the gun still in the other, Kaddish's frantic viewpoint fell on the altar. That odd black gem or carving on its fossil table. He extended the gun, pointed it at the carving, and pulled the trigger. It clicked. Empty. He had unloaded the magazine of solid projectiles into his victims, and into the corner.

Bell could hear the alarmed exclamations of neighbors. The boy struggled against Kaddish. He could not remain to reload his gun and point it at the crystal again. With his prisoner, he fled the apartment . . .

"End recording!" Bell blurted to the screen. Blood throbbed in his ears. "Graf, run it back again. Right after he shoots Pugmire, put the play into slowmo."

Graf complied, and the memories unfolded once more. At the requested moment, as Pugmire went down, the recording went into slow motion. This time, Bell had a better look at the creature that was revealed behind him, seen through a spray of arterial blood. A shiver blew up through the hollows in Bell's body.

It was the height of a man, but that was the extent of its anthropomorphic traits. The creature was torpedo-shaped, all black and rubbery, and moved across the room upright with an obscene flopping motion that might have been comical had it not been so hideous. In regular playback, the swaying from side to side had been quick but awkward, as if this was not the thing's normal mode of locomotion, or its intended environment or medium.

Gill-like slits opened and closed on the thing's smooth sides as if it gasped for air. In this and in its general shape, it was like a shark without fins, tail—or head. Its means of locomotion were flippers or pseudopods at its base, with black claws curling out of them, as cruel as an eagle's. It was these that tore the carpet as it moved. The thing had no other limbs, except for that one tentacle—or was it a tongue?—that lashed out of the hole in the top of its body. This opening had five flaps, a somewhat grayer color like that vaguely translucent tongue or limb that thrashed uncannily in slow motion.

And in slow motion, Kaddish's bullets tore into the rubbery flesh of the being. A thick bluish fluid spattered out into the air and ran down its flanks, though Bell had seen no such fluid at the crime scene. Graf would have to go back to see if it had soaked thoroughly into the carpet, or evaporated totally.

In regular play, the creature had emitted short, sharp, guttural cries. Almost like barks. It was the only reason Bell could imagine for its moniker, unless its function to its masters was as some loyal animal.

In slowed play, its barks and Kaddish's own cry were unearthly, blending together into a terrible sepulchral groan.

When the creature reached the corner, it vanished into the joining point of the walls, as if it or the walls were merely an illusion.

"Jesus," Bell exhaled. Gone, like an apparition. An apparition that could bleed. "Graf?"

The recorded memories vanished. Graf returned. "It's real, boss. If Kaddish was hallucinating, the hallucinations would be in his mind only. This isn't what his mind interpreted, but the physical reality his eyes perceived."

"It's something from another plane of existence. Another dimension."

"I've seen a lot of exotic fauna come through this town, but never anything like that baby."

"Graf . . . did you take that crystal thing from the scene with you?"

"Yeah, we have it here. It looked like it might be of value, so we thought it best to put it in the vault. Why? You were wondering why Kaddish tried to blast it?"

"Yeah. I'm also wondering why he didn't put his gun down a second to take it. He wasn't thinking." Bell glanced up and out the windshield as two teen-age Choom girls pranced up the front steps of the library, sharing innocent laughter. Ignorant laughter. The mundane image did not soothe Bell's disorienting sensation of vertigo. It only served to worsen it, by contrast. Seeing him watching them, one of the girls gave him an obscene gesture before ducking after her friend into the building. So much for innocent laughter, but Bell was too absorbed to let it irritate him. "What else did Josh tell me that I should believe?"

"What did he tell you in there, John?"

"Show the chief the recording. And tell him not to let that boy leave the station, no matter how many C. S. people or family members come for him. He isn't to leave our custody until I can talk to the chief himself about it. Understood?"

"I'll tell him, but you tell me what Kaddish told you."

"I will. But right now I have to go talk to Kate Redgrove. If anything else Josh told me has truth to it, we might be under a kind of . . . deadline here."

— 4 —

On the outside of Kate Redgrove's apartment door there was a red five-pointed star with an eye, perhaps, at its center, the pupil if such it were being a pillar of flame.

This one was not crudely spray-painted, but very neatly done, as if it had been masked off first. Still, Bell found it no less dramatic. He stabbed his finger into the buzzer several times more, though his buzzing from the lobby had gone unanswered. Beside him stood Mr. L'Vesk, the apartment manager, who had agreed to escort the inspector up here when his attempts to contact the archaeologist failed. Before L'Vesk had agreed to accompany him, however, he had first tried calling Ms. Redgrove on her vidphone. The calls had also gone unanswered.

"I can't believe I let her talk me into painting that thing," the spindly humanoid sighed, nervously drumming together pale fingers twice as long as the detective's. "Her neighbors are not happy with it. But she was so set on it, and she's been a fine tenant except for that. She teaches over at P.U., you know . . ."

Bell rang her again. "Damn," he whispered.

"Maybe she's out. Over at the school. Or she might not want to be disturbed, you know; she's always been extremely insistent that I never let anyone up here unless she knows about it in advance."

"Open it."

"I . . . well, do you have a warrant, Inspector?"

"No, but you're the manager, right? You can voluntarily open it for me." If the being refused, there was always the lock-cutter device in an inner pocket of his leather jacket.

L'Vesk sighed, and moved past Bell to tap out a code on the keypad by the door frame. The apartment manager held open the door, stuck his tiny head in, and promptly withdrew it with a rattling gasp of horror.

Bell pushed past him, drawing his pistol from its holster under his jacket. "Go call Precinct House 15. Tell them to send some people over here, quick!"

Once inside, Bell shut the door behind him.

Kate Redgrove sat on a sofa at the far end of the parlor, slumped to one side with her chin resting on her chest. She was as white as a cave dwelling animal. She wore a suit of comfortable, loose-fitting men's pajamas, the front unbuttoned. Or torn open. In the center of her chest, above her heart, there was a large circular wound, so deep that the blackness within her seemed an awful void.

As Bell moved closer to her, wondering if the wound had been caused by a bolt from a ray pistol, he noticed the tear marks on the lovely white carpet.

He swung around with his chunky black pistol held out before him, eyes large and flicking in their sockets. Before he examined the corpse more closely, he stealthily moved through the rest of the apartment. He found no lurking intruders, human or otherwise. Only slightly at ease, he returned to the body propped on the living room couch.

He knelt down to gaze up into her face. As Kaddish had told his ex-friend, his ex-lover was beautiful, her short dark hair hanging softly around a delicate face with large, dark brown eyes that were now half-veiled by their lids in death. Bell took his eyes quickly from her face, switched his study to the wound in her chest, between her slight breasts. Her skin looked like wax. There was no blood around the wound, on her clothing or the sofa or the immaculate carpet. Bell knew from the look of her that no blood would be found inside her body, either. But there was another fluid along the rim of the great puncture wound. It was thick, syrupy, and a ghastly blue color that was almost luminous. Bell remembered the memory of a thrashing tentacle. Or tongue.

The Elder Sign might have repelled intruders from her front door, but they had found another way to send an assassin. And Bell didn't doubt that the assassin was the same being or creature that Pugmire had summoned up, perhaps for this very purpose. Kaddish had not wounded it enough to kill it, if it could be killed.

Bell rose, still holding his gun by his side, and glanced around at the woman's things. A series of shelves along one wall drew him for a closer inspection. There were framed photographs of Kate Redgrove with friends and colleagues at various digs, apparently on various worlds. On one planet they had worked inside a giant bubble, it seemed, Bell guessing that the atmosphere had been unsuitable for humans. In fact, what he could see of the landscape through the transparent wall behind them had a lunar appearance, though Bell didn't know what ancient civilization might be excavated on an airless moon.

More notable than the photos, however, were the artifacts on display behind the glass cabinets of the shelves. They were lit and labeled with cards as if exhibited in a museum. There were vases in whole or part, a row of crude iron chisels that might be weapons or tools, a human bust with white eyes and its nose and lips broken away, as if all of its senses had been robbed. A bowl with the painting of a naked Choom warrior inside it. A small stone tablet with carven lines in some unfathomable language, and above that portraying in bas-relief a sphinx or griffin-like creature with wings somewhat like a bat's and the head of an octopus, with a nest of tentacles in place of a mouth. Bell looked at the card for this piece.

"*Oasis. Choom. Irezk Island Tribe. 19th Cent. Cthulhu.*"

Bell frowned, disturbed by the strange, abstracted image and feeling that he should understand or recognize that last word on the card. Unable to, he shifted his attention to another artifact.

This looked to be more of organic origin than shaped by the hands of an artisan or craft-maker. It was a large fossil that he had at first thought was a great shallow bowl carved from stone, standing on its end inside the cabinet. Ringing the bowl were thick spines or spikes, some little more than blunt bumps and others long and sharp like the horns of a dinosaur. Bell couldn't imagine what sort of animal it might have come from, or even what part of the body of an animal it might be from. Was it a shell or carapace? A portion of skull? A half of a pelvis? A lower jaw, a scoop-like hand? Some fragment of anatomy for which there was no terrestrial counterpart? Again, he read its card, standing on his toes to see it.

"*Oasis. Irezk Island. 225,000,000 B.C. Fragment. Old One? Spawn?*"

"Jesus," Bell breathed.

The sharp barking cry behind him made him spin around. The thing was rushing at him, flopping madly from side to side like a man with his legs bound, and his arms too, for it had none. Just that tongue or tentacle, whipping out of the opening atop its body. Its claws tore up the carpet as it flung itself toward him.

Bell thrust his gun at the thing as if the action of his arm alone would make the bolts of energy fly from it. Bell's beam weapon fired short lances of a dark violet light. They pierced the creature, bored round holes from which drooled that blue blood or mucus. Bell backed into the shelves. He cried out in terror and rage. The creature barked in rage and maybe pain. But it kept coming.

Behind the creature, Josh Kaddish leapt out of the walls where they joined together in the corner. He fell to his knees, looked up at Bell, his eyes crazed in a squirming black mask. There were black leeches half covering his face, his white shirt, some as big as lampreys or remoras with primitive flippered tails thrashing, their mouths fixed to his skin.

Bell nearly quit firing into the creature, so shocked was he by this manifestation. He was confounded even more when Kaddish got to his feet and bolted from the room as if running for his life.

"Help me!" Bell roared, and aimed higher up, at the tongue and its five-lobed mouth. Several beams tore through the base of the tentacle and out the other side, spattering bits of rubbery flesh. Bell heard glass shatter somewhere as his beams passed through. The limb's frenzied whipping only became more violent.

He darted sideways as the creature reached the shelves, smashing into them blindly. Perhaps it was blind in this dimension, and followed the smell of his blood or the hum of his life force inside him.

Dancing sideways, putting more space between him and the being, he whirled and fired into it again. And now Josh Kaddish had returned, came to his side. Most of the slugs were gone from him, Bell saw peripherally, the rest dropping off him and writhing in the fibers of the pristine carpet.

Kaddish had a pistol in each fist, and began adding his onslaught to Bell's. One bucking handgun fired solid projectiles with a deafening report, the other launched gel caps filled with a corrosive green plasma. Where these hit, larger wounds began to open in the shiny, dolphin-like hide of the being, the uneven edges of the wounds bubbling and sizzling. One wound joined with the next, making yet larger wounds. Inside, the creature was all slick pulsing blackness. Bell now aimed his beams into that blackness. Under this fusillade, the creature finally toppled, and began a terrible flopping on its side like a fish drowning in the air. Bell and Kaddish had to fast-shuffle backwards to give it more room in which to convulse, but they didn't relent in their conjoined attack.

The creature, much torn and melted through the middle, split into two large pieces. To Bell's horror, both began to make their way back toward the corner of the room from which it had appeared—the upper half pulling itself along with its serpentine limb, the lower pulling itself along with the talons which had served as toes, before.

"Keep shooting!" Kaddish bellowed. "Here!" He passed Bell the gun loaded with plasma capsules, then rushed to the shelves of artifacts. Out of the corner of his eye, firing both pistols at the ends of his extended arms, Bell saw Kaddish sliding open one of the cabinets and withdrawing some small item.

"All right!" Kaddish yelled. "Hold fire!" Bell did, and saw the private detective lunge after the hideous crawling shapes. He was holding out the item he had taken from the shelf, and actually pushed it into one of the holes Bell's rays had punched into its flesh. He then leapt away, and covered his face as if expecting an explosion.

It was apparent why a second later, as a smoke or vapor as black as squid's ink and just as slow—as if it were spreading under water rather than in the air—billowed from both portions of the bisected animal or entity. The foulness of the vapor's stench was so intense that Bell immediately dropped to his knees and vomited. Nothing he had ever smelled at any crime scene, however long the victim had waited to be discovered, could hint at this.

But moments later, the air was clean of both smoke and stench. Lifting his head with a groan, Bell saw that the broken thing had vanished, leaving behind not so much as a drop of its blue fluids on the soft white carpet. Kaddish was crouching close by, cupping one hand over his mouth. When he removed the hand, he was smiling that cat-curl smile.

"We killed it. We killed one of their bloody hounds!"

Bell gestured with his gun toward the couch. Kaddish started to look around, but stopped himself. His smile dissipated. "I know. I saw her there. Fucking demons. They'll pay for that." He stood, held up his remaining pistol. "I bought these for Kate, to protect herself. They caught her off guard."

Bell slowly got to his feet, fighting to hold onto what little else his stomach contained. Adrenalin crackled through the wires of his nerves. He realized that all the slugs had dropped off Kaddish now, and dissolved from the carpet, also leaving no trace. "How in Christ did you get here?" he asked.

"Same way that thing did. Through the wall. But I went through the curves, and it went through the lines. I picked up some stowaways on the way, but they didn't last." He rubbed at his neck, looked at his palm as if for blood, but he was unmarked.

"Have you done that before?"

"No. Never. But your friends left me no choice. I knew I could chance it if I had to. I kept a diagram in my pocket, and I copied the formula into the corner of my cell back at your precinct house. You can thank your friends for giving me that marker. You should have remembered, Johnny, that I've never done a crossword puzzle in my life."

"Are you crazy? Huh? How did you think you could survive that? How did you find your way?"

"I was lost a few minutes, I admit. I suppose it was a few minutes. You can't tell time in there. It's . . . not something I can describe. I was disoriented. I started to panic, especially when those things started swarming onto me. The diagram was supposed to get me back to my apartment in an emergency . . . if I ever got cornered or trapped. Kate drew it up for me. But then I saw or sensed the beastie, and I followed it here. Good for you, huh? I really do think some force, at least, is on our side. Fate, or maybe even—Them." He walked to the spot where the being had dissolved, bent, picked up something from the carpet. He came to Bell and showed him a stone disc resting in the palm of his hand. It bore an etched star, and at the center of the star was an eye-like design, with a band of fire for its pupil if indeed it were an eye.

"The sign of the Elder Gods," Bell said.

"Like a crucifix against a vampire. Remember? Do you believe me, now, pal?"

Bell's communication device beeped on his belt. He unclipped it, brought up before his face. "Bell here."

It was the commander of P.H. 15, Chief Bellioc. His face was like a living postage stamp on the device's tiny screen. "John, your friend Kaddish is gone."

Bell almost said, "I know." Instead, he said, "Gone?"

"Check this out. We had a camera on him the whole time he was in his cell—standard procedure. I'm going to run you the end of the vid." Bellioc's face was replaced by a scene of Kaddish in his cell, shot from a corner of the ceiling. Kaddish was finishing up a drawing in the corner, a black web of lines and angles. He was using the edge of the folded newspaper he'd requested to make them as straight as he could.

He finished a last line, stepped back to admire his handiwork for several moments while capping the marker and slipping it into his breast pocket. Then, he extended an arm—which vanished into the white wall as if it were a pool of milk.

"Unbelievable," Bell said, even as he watched Kaddish walk into the wall and disappear, leaving only that web of black lines to mark his passage.

Bellioc returned. "I saw the memory recording of that creature, too. Do you know what the hell is going on, here?"

"Ah. I think . . . I'm not entirely sure. But . . ."

"I'm putting a call into Colonial Headquarters. I think they should send some of their security force in here. We're dealing with some uncatalogued life forms here. And God knows about these portals . . . these dimensional . . ."

"I think that's a good idea, chief. Get them in on this. And keep everybody out of that cell. Keep the barrier up. There's no telling what might come out of that opening, now."

"The boy!" Kaddish hissed. "The kid!"

"That boy," Bell said into the device. "Chief, don't let anyone take him. Trust me. Don't let C.S. have him. We have to keep him in custody. Under guard . . ."

"What do you know about all this, John? You obviously know a lot more than you're telling me."

"I'll fill you in, chief, but I have to get my head together first. I'm not sure what I've seen or how to describe it. Just trust me for a little while. I'm on this. I'm trying to find out what it's about. In the mean time, all I can ask you is to keep that boy under lock and key."

Bellioc's diminutive features did not look pleased, but Bell was his best homicide investigator, not some impulsive rookie. "Alright, do whatever it is you're doing . . . but when I get the Headquarters to send somebody over, I'm going to call you back, and I'm going to want you to be here and tell them—and me—everything you know."

"I will, chief. But until then? Play back the part of the surveillance vid when I went in to interview Kaddish. Listen to what he says. All that crazy dung about an ancient, god-like race? I'm afraid it might be true."

Over the top of the communication device, Bell saw Kaddish smiling at him, and nodding in a weary kind of satisfaction.

— 5 —

"We'd better get out of here before the uniforms arrive," Bell told the other man, handing him back the borrowed gun.

"Are we going together?"

"Yes," Bell answered, sounding disgusted at himself for saying it. "You're the expert, apparently, so you tell me where it is we should go."

25

"I know of another especially dangerous cult in Tin Town." Tin Town was one of the least friendly sectors of a generally unfriendly city. Bell had never ventured there, nor did any peace officers, unless pushed into it. "We have to stop them, pal. I don't know how much time we have left before the doors really come off the hinges, but . . ."

"You mean kill them, don't you?"

Kaddish paused, drew in a breath. "Yes. Kill them. We can't lock them up. They can still perform rituals to a lesser extent, even in custody. You saw what I did . . . and they know more than I do."

"I won't be murdering any cults tonight, Josh. And neither will you."

"You've seen the truth, man! Jesus, what does it take? I just walked out of that fucking wall, there!"

"Shit!" Bell hissed, whipping his head around as if someone had whispered in his ear, reminding him of something. Something about walking into walls. Webs that could bend the walls between dimensions. "The kid . . ."

"What about him?"

Bell unfolded the boy's drawing he had taken from him. Lines and angles in silver ink like the symbol of silver ink tattooed on his chest. He passed it to Kaddish. "The boy was drawing things like that in the holding room. Formulae. Like the one you used . . ."

Kaddish's eyes leapt up from the paper. "If I escaped that way, he can, too!"

Bell brought his communication device back up to his face, beeped his precinct house. He didn't want to have to talk to Bellioc again, however. Bellioc might change his mind, order him back right now. "Put Graf on!" he snapped at the dispatcher. Several moments later, the Choom was there. "Graf—you have to do me a favor, man. Don't ask why. Go in and take that marker away from the kid from the cult. Make sure he has nothing at all to draw with, understand?"

"Sure. But . . ."

"Is he being guarded, now?"

"Yes. The chief said you called, and . . ."

"Tell them to watch him! He might even try to draw in his shit or his blood. Watch him! Keep him at the table. Don't let him near the corners of the room!"

"The corners? John, look . . ."

"Do it!" And Bell cut him off, lowered the device.

"He has to be drugged, John. Or put suspended animation. I'm telling you. He was born and raised to be an extension of Yog-Sothoth. And of all the gates of the Old Ones, Yog-Sothoth is the biggest. The rest are just cracks. Yog-Sothoth is the fucking dam, Johnny, and this kid's finger is all that's holding back the flood. Understand? Yog-Sothoth is the gate and the guardian of the gate and the key to the gate, all in one."

"I've got to get back there. I have to fill the chief in now. And you're coming with me, Josh, I'm sorry. I can't let you go off killing more people. There has to be another way to handle this. You can tell my chief your story, and the Headquarters agents when they get there."

Bell fully expected Kaddish to put up an argument, given the strength of his obsession. He was surprised, then, when Kaddish dropped his eyes and slowly nodded in agreement. "Alright," he said quietly, "I'll go back there with you."

*   *   *

Outside Precinct House 15, lions cast in a pale blue resin flanked the front steps. These terrestrial creatures, no matter how fearsome in aspect, were a weak and ridiculous symbol of protection in the face of the threats Bell had learned of.

Bell was handing over to another officer the two pistols Kaddish had acquired for Kate Redgrove when Chief Bellioc, having heard that Bell had brought his quarry in, came hurriedly into the room. The private detective looked calmly up at the police chief and gave him a pleasant nod.

"So, it's the magician who performed that disappearing act in his cell," Bellioc grumbled.

"You must be Chief Bellyache."

"Don't fuck with me, you sleazy little piece of dung. I should put you in a nice safe stasis field right now. Tell me what's happening here. What kind of threat is this to the city?"

"The city?" Kaddish snorted a bitter laugh. On the ride here, Bell had filled him in on the loss of contact with Earth, its moon, the Mars colonies and now, according to the news they had listened to on the Edsel's radio, outposts on the moons of Jupiter. When asked what he thought the spreading cloud might be, Kaddish had only said under his breath, in a tone of awful reverence, "Azathoth."

"Sir, the whole Coalition . . . the whole universe . . . is under threat," Bell told him. "There are cults still here in Punktown, cults on Earth, that are working to make this happen."

"John, do you expect me to believe in Satan worshipers calling up demons?"

"Demons, gods, aliens, call them what you want."

"And what are we supposed to do about it? Go and murder all these cults like your friend here did?"

"We have to see the boy," Kaddish said. "There's no more time to argue."

"He's under observation," Bellioc assured him harshly.

"Let me talk to him. I can get him to open up about this. What he has to show us . . . you might find enlightening."

Bellioc looked to Bell, who nodded. "We've got to trust him. He knows more about this than we do, and it doesn't look like we have much time to learn."

The precinct commander gestured roughly. "Okay, okay, let's go."

As they moved down the corridor toward the holding room where the orphan was being kept, a guard visible outside its force barrier, Kaddish asked Bell, "What became of the Shining Trapezohedron?"

"The what?"

"The black crystal Pugmire had in his apartment."

"We have that here, in the vault. Why? What's it do?"

"Not sure, but some say it can be used to view other worlds. Other realms. It may also be a battery of power, a focal point of power . . . or a door in itself. Whatever it is, it should be destroyed. I never should have left there without it."

"Like I say, we have it. No one's gonna touch it."

They had reached the barrier, and the uniformed forcer stepped aside. The barrier was deactivated, and the boy with the shaven head lifted his head from his arms, crossed before him on the table. He was smiling, and his eyes had locked on Kaddish.

"I'm going to show him something," Kaddish said, slipping a hand into his pocket.

Bellioc seized his wrist. "What is it? Has he been scanned for weapons, John?"

"Yes."

"Just this, I want to show him." Kaddish withdrew the stone disc with the carven eye, and held it out for the chief to see.

Bell saw the boy crane his neck, trying to get a look at what the object was. His smug smile had become less sure, more concerned.

Kaddish turned, and held the seal of the Elder Gods aloft in his left hand for the boy to plainly see.

The boy let out a cry of rage, bolted up from his chair and backed into the wall. He turned his eyes away and tore at the front of his shirt, scattering buttons, revealing pale skin and bony ribs and a silver symbol tattooed on his chest: concentric circles, one inside the next, with lines or rays radiating out from the center.

"What is that?" Bellioc demanded. "What are you doing to him?"

The boy's cry had turned to a rattle, and the rattle to another kind of cry that made Bell shudder. The child began to scream gibberish in a weirdly altered voice, at once sounding both full of phlegm and full of gravel . . .

"Ygnaiih . . . ygnaiih . . . thflthkh'ngha . . ."

"Jesus!" Bellioc gasped.

The tattoo on the boy's chest was splitting along its radiating lines. The skin of his chest began to peel open of its own accord, like a flower blooming in

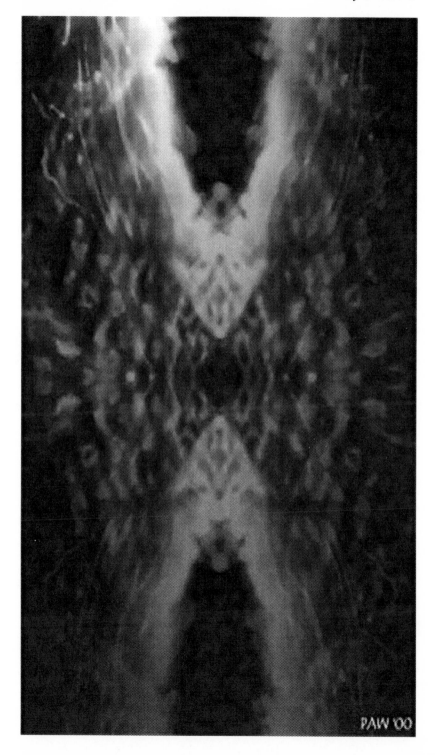

stop motion photography. The petals of this flower folded back, curled in upon themselves, opening up a black maw within the boy. A great cavity that showed no organs inside. Too deep for the shallow confines of his slight child's body. It was as though all space itself resided inside his frame.

"Yog-Sothoth," the boy shrieked, still hiding his gaze from that dreaded seal. "Eh-ya-ya-ya-yahaah—e'yayayayaaaa . . ."

"Look!" Bell yelled, pointing at the void in the boy's flesh. In that empty blackness of space they could see distant stars shining. But the stars were drawing nearer. They were like a shower of comets coming toward them, a fleet of glowing spheres or globes, iridescent, but the colors of that iridescence alien to their human eyes. As they neared, the spheres began to join with each other, become a great mass made of these glowing bubbles, like cells linking to form one immense body. And yet some few smaller, faster spheres shot on ahead, still seeking to reach the hole in the boy's chest. To shoot through it . . .

And still the boy went on screaming, "Ngh'aaaaa . . . ngh'aaa . . . h'yuh . . . h'yuh . . ."

"Yog-Sothoth," Kaddish breathed, and lunged into the room. No one tried to hold him back. Not even Bellioc.

Into that void, Kaddish tossed the stone disc in his hand.

The boy lifted his head at last, his eyes wide in horror and a rage that could show in no human child's face, however deranged the mind behind it. The boy threw out his hands to grab a hold of Kaddish, but he danced back out of his reach.

The wide wound now began closing, the petals folding inward, once again concealing the infinity beyond. But one small glowing sphere was still hurtling at the portal, as if it thought it could make it through before the door of flesh closed completely . . .

Kaddish collided against Bell in his retreat. Bell staggered back a step, and when he recognized his own pistol rising in both of Kaddish's hands, realized what his friend had done.

Kaddish fired at the boy's head even as the globe impacted against the nearly closed flaps of skin. The dark purple energy bolt plummeted into the boy's forehead just above one eyebrow, snapping his head back. His small skull was shattered, the wall behind him becoming splashed with a black mulch that couldn't possibly be human brain matter.

The closing flaps of skin opened again briefly at the impact of the globe, letting in a blast of weirdly colored light. A single wide ray or beam, which struck Joshua Kaddish squarely in the chest and hurled him backwards out of the room, against the opposite wall of the corridor. And then the petals in the boy's chest sealed completely, as if they had never existed, and his corpse slid into a sitting position against the wall, his open eyes fixed with that expression of malice that no child—no human—should be able to manifest.

Bell and the others went to Kaddish, but stopped themselves. Bellioc withdrew in horror. The uniformed officer whispered some half-prayer under his breath.

Kaddish was also slumped in a seated position, propped against the corridor wall. His entire front, his face, had been charred black, his eyes empty sockets steaming—as if the horror of what he had seen in that last moment had burned his eyes away utterly. And yet his lips had burned away also, and his blackened skeletal grin seemed hideously full of a sardonic humor. It seemed an apt expression for the man, in death.

Bell retrieved his gun from where it had been dropped by his friend, and carrying it in his fist, walked off down the corridor.

He asked to be let into the station's vault, and was told by the officer on duty that he needed clearance. He pointed his gun at the young man's eyes and softly repeated his request. It was granted.

John Bell took two steps into the vault of Precinct House 15, leveled his sidearm at the Shining Trapezohedron, and squeezed the trigger.

Black shards of crystal were scattered across the room.

*   *   *

A transmission, weak and uncertain, was at last received from a colony on Titan, one of Saturn's moons. Contact had been lost with the colony over a half hour before.

Bell watched the transmission live on VT, a drink in his hand. A man filled the vidtank. His image was shot with static, but Bell could see that the man's face was horribly swollen, covered in great blisters with a weirdly metallic sheen. He barely looked human, his eyes were fused shut, but the man was smiling nonetheless. And he was greeting his viewers with the words,

"Ph-nglui mglw'nafh Cthulhu R'lyeh wgah'nagl fhtagn!"

The newscaster returned to report that more transmissions were now being received, one by one, from the colonies on Jupiter's icy moons, from Mars and from Earth. Bell was torn between hope and utter despair. He was tempted to turn the VT off before he saw what those transmissions contained.

He wondered if he and Kaddish by themselves had been responsible for blocking the Old Ones from coming, or if there had been other men and women, like themselves and Kate Redgrove, here on Oasis and on the Earth, who had been fighting their own desperate battles to prevent the dead, defeated gods from rising anew from their cosmic sepulchers. Were the doors now locked again—or merely shut? He watched, and waited for the news.

*   *   *

Even now Bell didn't know if his mutant companion was elderly or a youth, male or female. It pointed a scrawny arm through the rubble of the ruined structure in which the two of them hid, its great lidless eyes filled with fear at the sight of what it pointed at.

Across a lot heaped in junk and the exoskeletons of hovercars, a low flat-roofed building stood, its windows long since gone. The building was painted white, and thus, with its many gaping windows, resembled the fossil skull of some vast creature, with rows of black sockets. And an evil ghost of a brain, whispering inside.

Bell paid the mutant, barely noticed it as it crept away. The poor blighted creature would have elicited more interest and concern from him, if such beings weren't so abundant here in the slum of Tin Town.

In his hands, Bell gripped a sawed-off pump shotgun with a banana clip full of crystal shot. In a shoulder holster was a ray blaster, in a hip holster a pistol loaded with solid projectiles, and in an ankle holster a little palm piece loaded with plasma capsules.

And in one of the pockets of his leather jacket he carried a small spray gun, loaded with a tube of blood red paint.

THE AVATARS OF THE OLD ONES

— 1 —

H'anna was used to having others stand before her artwork in attitudes of confusion and even discomfort as they attempted to interpret it, to understand it . . . but now, she found herself in a similar pose as she regarded her new creation, "Headless Angel."

Other pieces crowded her apartment in a kind of personal museum. It was all she had by way of a permanent exhibit; only several pieces had ever been accepted into a few small gallery shows, and she had yet to sell anything. But then, it mattered more to express herself than to sell herself. Not that she wouldn't have minded a bit more appreciation. Or to quit her day job.

Outside her high apartment window, a string of helicars hovered at a stoplight, and then hummed onwards again. On the roof of the building opposite, a gigantic holographic Indian woman in traditional garb sang in a cheery high-pitched voice like that of a dwarf child on helium about the virtues of a new NetLink service. The summer sun shone through the woman's chest like a molten heart within her. Inside H'anna's living room/studio it was stifling; only the climate control in the bedroom was functional. At least she could sleep at night. Right now she wore only her panties and the t-shirt she had slept in, her long dark hair in sweaty snarls.

Not only had her inspiration for "Headless Angel" come to her in dreams, but even now with it finished she had still dreamt about it last night . . . as if the thing were still not out of her system. It was work, she felt, that was doing this to her. Giving her these nightmares. Work was a recurring daily nightmare . . .

Her sculptures up to now had been nothing like this piece, even when they were born of anger and meant to shock, like "Precious Knickers", which hung in her bedroom. That piece had found its origins in an annoyingly tiny pair of bikini underwear she had stolen from her ex-boyfriend's apartment when she let herself in to gather up the last of her belongings; needless to say, they were not her own panties. Filling the underpants were two pigs' hearts. The hearts were stitched together like conjoined twins, and she had taken the wings from a dead pigeon and stitched one to each of the hearts. The whole piece had been spray-painted a lurid red and spray-sealed with a hard preserving plastic.

So, it might not be so difficult for someone else to imagine that "Headless Angel" was nothing out of the ordinary. But H'anna felt the difference . . . even if she couldn't understand it.

She had completed it last night; perhaps the morning would give her fresh perspective. And so she took it in as if someone else had created it (and it felt that way, didn't it?). The sculpture was entirely composed of sheets of thin scrap metal, jaggedly cut and torched together into an entirely black-painted figure as large as herself, which resembled a suit of armor one moment and a chitinous exoskeleton the next. This latter effect was heightened by the wings of the being, which looked like they'd been charred when this angel had fallen. Its crouching body was both anthropomorphic yet dog-like. One hand was raised as if in a perverse blessing. And it had no head. But rising up from the stump of the neck was a thin rod, which branched off to support three black metal discs with edges so sharp she'd sliced her flesh while snipping them. These were the headless angel's triple halos. H'anna wondered if subconsciously she had meant for the triple halos to represent the Holy Trinity. Thus, the lack of a head might represent—what? The death of God? The emptiness of blind faith? Or might this creature not even be anything affiliated with Christianity? It had the aspect of a sphinx. Some mythological creature . . . some other, older God.

And in standing nearly stripped before it, H'anna felt either like a worshipper to it . . . or a sacrifice.

— 2 —

The man's face was horribly swollen, covered in great blisters with a weirdly metallic sheen. He barely looked human, his eyes were fused shut, but the man was smiling nonetheless. He greeted H'anna with the words, "Ph-nglui mglw'nafh Cthulhu R'lyeh wgah'nagl fhtagn!"

"Same to you," H'anna replied pleasantly, walking on quickly by the man. She cast a look over her shoulder to be certain he hadn't turned to follow after her, but he kept on strolling—shambling, rather—along the sidewalk in the opposite direction. She had heard that precise gibberish repeated so many times over the past four years that she could almost recite it herself, maybe with the help of a mouth full of marbles.

The summer air was compacted in the narrow chasms of the looming city, so that the squalid smells of garbage and piss and sweat were more potent than ever, densely concentrated into a nearly solid miasma. Uptown, with its better quality shopping district and higher-class office blocks, was climate-controlled, but a combination of a troubled economy and the terrible calamity of four years ago had left much of the city in a blighted state. The sun was directly overhead, in what little of the sky could be seen, but even when the streets were entombed in the shadows of the towers that soared impossibly on all sides, there would be little respite. Helicars whirred far overhead like agitated hornets, and closer to the streets, hovercars whisked impatiently, all as if maddened by the hellish atmosphere. Was it just her imagination, or had the summers become hotter since the incident of four years ago? Had everyone just taken it for granted now, as they had all the people like that blister-faced man? Taken it for granted because they didn't want to confront the implications?

H'anna wore a sleeveless vest-like garment unbuttoned at the bottom to reveal the sly depression of her navel, and similarly dark brown cloned-leather pants. These were a tad tight and heavy in this sweltering heat, but she was a bit self-conscious about baring the muscular thickness of her thighs and calves, not being as cadaverously thin as was once again the fashion. Her scuffed boots looked too large for her feet. H'anna Chabert was twenty-one, shortish and pale, her brown hair parted down the center and falling to below her breasts in greased tangles and tendrils. Her brows were heavy, her eyes dropping down at the corners, hazel in color and intelligent in aspect. Her lips were full, and her smiles showed a broad expanse of bright teeth. She wasn't beautiful in any conventional sense, but someone of more refined taste would appreciate its various effects taken singly and in their very human whole.

H'anna had taken a hoverbus from her neighborhood to this sector, and now was coming up on the Ambuehl Building, where she worked; a sleek tower with a rounded top, pale sea-green in color and trimmed in lines of bright chrome. It housed a number of Social Services offices, including the local welfare branch. It was the welfare office that had established the soup kitchen in the basement, and this was H'anna's destination.

In the lobby with its high vaulted ceiling and glitter and glass, there was a tiny mall of sorts: a hairdresser's, a haberdashery and a little cafe with scattered tables that offered a limited luncheon menu. H'anna stood behind a woman in line, glanced around with boredom, grateful for the cool of the building's interior. Her eyes returned to the woman ahead of her. It was her turn at the counter, but the girl behind the counter looked irritated and nervous.

"Downstairs," the counter girl said. "You want to go downstairs . . ."

The woman in front of H'anna shuffled slowly around and H'anna took several steps back. She was one of the Afflicted. Her mouth squashed to the side by one of her metallic tumors, another growth filling an eye socket, her remaining eye crusted shut. The disfigured creature seemed to be studying H'anna's face, though how her kind saw at all through their slitted eyes she didn't know.

"The entrance is in back of the building," H'anna told her.

The woman smiled, and dutifully trudged across the lobby and blundered out the revolving door after several trips around and around in it like a gerbil in a treadmill. H'anna had expected her to end up back in the lobby again, for a moment or two.

At the counter, H'anna purchased a large coffee and a small salad for her lunch. She would eat it here before going to her work in the basement, however, as it seemed to be in poor taste to eat such things in front of the many who were sustained by lumpy gruel and poor bread.

An old security guard robot purred into the lobby from a branching hallway. The hallway was lined with scratches from the robot's flanks, which was hardly reassuring as to its accuracy in matters of protection. While making its rounds, it must have sensed too late that one of the Afflicted had been misdirected into the lobby. The building's owners did not seem to perceive the Afflicted as a serious threat, though in the soup kitchen there was always one organic guard on hand, due to the sheer numbers of the clientele.

Having finished her salad, H'anna rose from her table and took the rest of her coffee with her past the escalators, down another hall and from there down a short flight of steps to the employees' entrance to the soup kitchen.

She was on the lunch and supper shift, and on some weekends worked a breakfast/lunch shift for extra money. It was barely enough to pay the rent for her tiny tenement flat, but it had to do for now . . . though she thought she might soon be having to take her meals in the soup kitchen, as well. The gruel was a specially concocted blend of proteins and electrolytes and vitamins and so many other good things that it all became one pasty grayish sludge (with a different artificial flavor added each day). The pita bread was good for wiping the last smears of porridge from the bottom of the bowls. Tying an apron around her waist, H'anna took her place behind the long counter. She had at first worked in the kitchen itself, but the powder of the gruel mix was a constant cloud in the air, seeming to fill her lungs, and the steam from the vats it cooked in made the atmosphere humid and nauseating in their vicinity. The heavy, doughy smell of baking breads had made her feel that she had an oven in her guts. Not to mention the hellish heat in there. So she served out the slop instead.

The challenge in that, of course, was being in the presence of the customers.

The cafeteria had been created only four years ago, walls knocked down to widen it from its earlier basement rooms. There were other such establishments scattered throughout the sprawling city. It spread before her, low-ceilinged and with support beams here and there, and filled with long tables. At these sat nearly three hundred of the Afflicted.

Three hundred people, and there was no chatter, no laughing, no joking, no gossip . . . nothing but slurping, chewing, the rustle of clothes and clink of spoons. Tumescent heads bowed over tables, sometimes long hair hanging in the bowls of porridge. Men, women, some children. The authorities had never determined why these particular people had become afflicted while others had not (and there was no in-between). Some had been inside, some outside, during the great cosmic calamity, or alien attack, or whatever it had been (even that was uncertain, and much debated). Some were young, some old, some rich, some poor, some human, some alien immigrants. A number of authorities had gone so far as to wonder if certain personalities had been more susceptible to infection, certain individuals of a particular psychological disposition. (After all, a number of cult and even church groups had been afflicted to the last member.) No one knew, or at least there was no agreement on theories. But here on Earth, and the colonies on Luna, Mars, and the moons of Jupiter and Saturn, there were 24,000,000 of the Afflicted all told. It was a staggering, unthinkable figure to H'anna, who on a daily basis saw this mere three hundred bodies as a vast expanse of horror, like looking out on a sea of churning blood.

One of these beings now stood directly opposite her; she was always grateful for the length of counter, a protective wall or barrier. In the kitchen they also mixed powdered juice (another choking kitchen mist) with water in a large tank, and she placed a cup of this on the man's tray, where he had already slopped his gruel. They often spilled half their food just getting to a table. Her hand just briefly brushed against his and he smiled at her foolishly around the tumors on his gums, as if she had meant to flirt with him. Thank God for her disposable gloves. H'anna had to remind herself that this monstrosity had once been someone's beloved father, perhaps, a husband, once a cherished child. She had to hold on to the great tragedy and waste of all this.

Next in line was the security guard on duty, John Bell. He was a great improvement over the last man. John had short sandy hair brushed back neatly from his forehead, a trim mustache, wide-set blue eyes in a somewhat haggard but oddly attractive face. She judged him to be about thirty-five. He was soft-spoken but seemed to have that too-solemn demeanor of a policeman wannabe. She felt better with him around, however; felt better about the gun plainly holstered on his hip.

"Hey, kid," he said in greeting. "Do you have any coffee left back there?"

"Hold on." H'anna ducked backstage for a moment, reappeared with a steaming cup, which she handed to him. "Careful; real hot."

"Speaking of hot," he said, after a sip, "it's horrible today, huh?"

"Yeah. It makes it smell worse in here than ever. I think we should hose all these folks down one of these days."

"Well, not all the homeless centers have showers. I think we'd be better off just vaporizing them all."

H'anna laughed uneasily. And she thought she was bad. "That's a horrible thing to say, John."

"Don't get me wrong," he told her, that too-grim look in his eyes. "I ache for the people that they once were. But they aren't those people anymore. Those people are gone. These people are something entirely different."

H'anna found John's attitude a bit militaristic and cold-blooded for her taste, but at least his toughness about the creatures made her feel more comforted to have him around. Not to mention that she found herself somewhat attracted to him, though she normally wasn't interested in men of his age. She decided to change the subject, and nodded at the cup in his hand. "You know, the coffee is a lot better down the block at Le Caffeic."

"I've never tried there. Still new in town."

"I'll have to take you some time," she said, and wondered what she was thinking as she did so. Did she really want to start this? He didn't seem like a fun-loving date. Then again, she wasn't the most bubbly and chipper person herself, nor did she want to be. Well, she'd acted on a sudden whim, but she could always back out later if she felt that was the better idea.

John's eyes widened, and seemed to brighten, in the most subliminal way. The faintest of smiles touched his lips. "Well, that would be nice," was all he said at the moment, and she liked that . . . that he didn't pounce on her suggestion like a dog humping her leg.

Peripherally H'anna saw a figure moving up on John's right, and he had already turned toward it. The next person in line, no doubt. She saw that it wasn't one figure, however, but three children. All three were girls of about ten, all three of the same height, and dressed in similarly shabby clothes and ripped tights made all the more grotesque by their cheery crayon colors. Only the placement of their silvery-sheened boils seemed to distinguish them from each other.

In fact, the trio now spoke in unison.

"We know you, John Bell," they said.

It was the first time H'anna had ever heard one of the Afflicted speak in plain English, and ice water flushed through her limbs. John didn't seem to take it much better . . . particularly where he had been so personally addressed.

"And who are you?" he managed, harshness in his tone; to mask his apprehension, H'anna sensed.

"We are the Dreaming Ones," the triplets replied.

A low but widely-radiating hiss or rustle caused H'anna to look out across the cafeteria, and what she saw chilled her more than before. Every Afflicted at every one of the tables had turned its head to gaze directly at her. Or so it seemed. But her next impression was that they had swiveled in unison to gaze at the back of John Bell.

"John," she breathed.

Either he followed her stare, or he had felt the many eyes fall onto him, but John whirled around to confront his audience of three hundred.

"My God . . . it's now," he mumbled. And he drew his firearm from his belt, half-turned, and in rapid succession shot each of the three girls straight through the forehead.

A black ooze like rotted and liquefied brain matter spattered across the counter and H'anna lurched back with an inarticulate cry. She saw the three children crumple in dream-like slow motion, their gray skirts spreading out

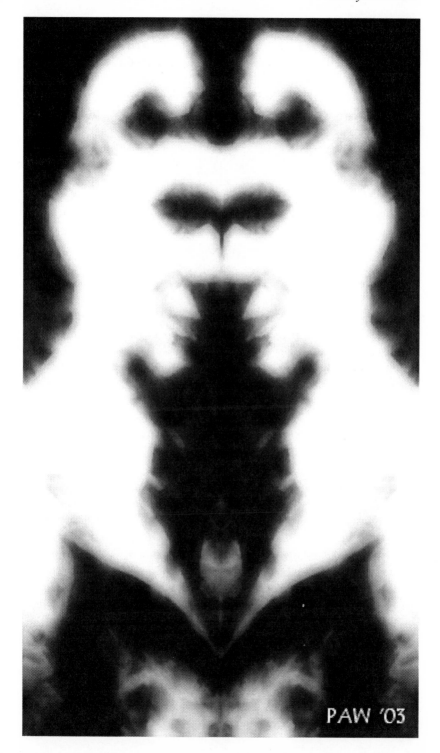

PAW '03

around them in lacy pools. She saw, also as if in a dream, the three hundred Afflicted rise to their feet, their three hundred chairs scraping the floor with a terrible grinding as if three hundred coffin lids had squealed open.

John vaulted up onto and then behind the counter. He took hold of H'anna's arm. Though she had just witnessed his execution of three children, strangely she didn't try to pull free of him, and it had nothing to do with any attraction she might have felt for him a moment earlier.

His face close to hers, his eyes fevered, he told her, "We have to go."

And then the Afflicted bore down on the counter in a solid wave, moving surprisingly quickly, if awkwardly, some falling and being trampled in the avalanche of bodies. Other workers behind the counter began to shout and scream, and bolt into the kitchen. H'anna saw one woman become seized by the hair, however, and dragged backwards over the counter. John spun toward her shrieks and fired at the creatures who had her, but not before they had hooked their fingers into her eye sockets and clamped their teeth into her shoulders and arms. One creature tore out an ear and a mouthful of hair before a projectile from John's chunky black handgun plummeted through its skull. In moments the girl was swallowed from sight, and her cries drowned.

H'anna and John were the last to make it into the kitchen alive. As soon as they had passed through its door, John whirled about to close it and tap the red keypad that would lock it. Before his finger could touch the key, however, three of the Afflicted pressed into the threshold in one surge, and wedged themselves there. H'anna saw that the blisters on their faces, necks and hands had begun to rupture, and a thick silvery pus was winding from the wounds. This vile fluid was so sticky that strands of it had spread from one of the poor wretches to the other, as if metallic cobwebs had grown between them.

In unison, the three creatures chanted, *"Tibi Magnum Innominandum, signa stellarum nigrarum et bufaniformis Sadoquae sigillum . . ."*

But John's pistol drowned out their words, and destroyed the mouths that uttered them. His bullets hammered them backwards, unstopped them from the door. Others swarmed to take their place, but not before John was successful in stabbing the red button. They heard the lock snick in place a moment before multiple bodies thudded against the door.

John turned back to H'anna. They were alone; the others had fled without a look back. After the explosion of chaos, it was a moment of almost eerie calm.

"It won't be safe with me," John told her, "but it won't be safe anywhere. At least let me get you out of here, and then we'll decide what to do with you."

"What's happening?" H'anna husked. It was a question born of terror and utter confusion . . . and yet, she also sensed that John somehow knew. When this had begun he had said, "It's now." He had been expecting this, somehow. There was a resigned sort of fatalism in his manner that made him weirdly collected while the others had run off in panic.

With the stare of a fanatical convert, he answered, "The Old Ones are trying to come through again. The stars are lined up favorably again. I tried to anticipate it . . . I've studied up on astronomy, talked with people, tried to plot when this would happen . . . but how can you know what stars to look for, in all this universe? How can you really know?"

It was all mad gibberish to H'anna's ears, like the Latin those three creatures had just spouted. But John wasted no further time on it. He took her arm again, and together they wove their way through the kitchen. Once more, H'anna did not resist.

— 3 —

Emerging into the lobby of the Ambuehl Building, they saw that the security guard robot had pinned two of the Afflicted against a wall with its bulk, and clutched the limbs or necks of three others. But more were beginning to pour into the revolving door; luckily their numbers and their awkwardness had jammed the door temporarily. John and H'anna raced up the escalator, and on the second floor found an elevator. They rode it to the roof, many flights above. All the way, H'anna was terrified that the thing would suddenly become stuck between floors, trapping them, or let go and plummet. Wasn't all of reality in rebellion, after all? But the ride was smooth, and there were no leering, oozing fiends waiting to flood into the compartment when the doors parted open (though John had his weapon ready in case). The hallway beyond was clean. The upper parking lot, when they entered it, was as still as a sprawling tomb, the darkly gleaming helicars like ranked sarcophagi.

John's helicar was a battered old Hummingbird, its iridescent green paint now dusty and scratched. He had to tap out his entry code twice to get it to open up. H'anna was not reassured that she would be flying   it . . . but no sooner had she seated herself inside than she looked back and saw that a half dozen of the Afflicted were silently threading their way through the parked cars, having found their way onto the roof.

"John!"

"I see them," he said, and started the craft up. It sputtered, jiggled as the fans fought to catch their rhythm. Slow as they were, the creatures were drawing closer. Two of them shuffled together, holding hands like lovers. Further back, three stumbled along with their arms draped over each other's shoulders. What was this sudden display of affection, H'anna wondered?

But then she saw it was more than that. Somehow, these beings were attached to each other. Linking with each other. Strands and ropes of that gelatinous silver pus or mucus wound around them in loops and garlands, even as more of it drooled from their now gaping wounds. And yet it wasn't only the ooze that merged them together; in places, it actually seemed that their flesh was fusing. H'anna was reminded of the pig hearts she had stitched into one obscene organ for her sculpture "Precious Knickers".

John glanced over his shoulder at their advance, still punching keys. The Hummingbird began to whir, and lifted off the pavement at last. Several feet off the surface, it floated down a row of cars, still shaded by a protective roof. But the hot sky glared beyond, as if to taunt them.

"They're each one a cell," he told her. "One cell of one great being. And now they're beginning to come together . . ."

The Hummingbird cleared the covered section of the lot, sunlight filling the craft like a waterfall of lava. John tinted the windows darker. The helicar now began to lift higher . . . but they heard a sound against its rear. John glanced at a screen on his control console. It showed that two of the conjoined Afflicted had seized hold of the craft, and were borne aloft with it. "Oh," he said, "you want a ride, huh?" And he punched up the speed.

H'anna gripped her arm rests; her already agitated stomach rolled over inside her as John whipped the helicar through the city canyons, picking up altitude then dramatically dropping, taking a sudden turn at an almost sideways angle. At last, though H'anna did not actually see the creatures become dislodged, the screen showed they had lost the twin parasites.

John leveled the craft and cut back on its speed. "Where do you live?" he asked, and H'anna numbly told him. They began to head in that direction.

They were too far up to see what was happening on street level, but in one spot H'anna saw a fire from a crashed hovercar or helicar, black smoke billowing. She heard the banshee cries of sirens distantly all around them.

At last, H'anna was able to formulate at least one of her countless questions. "How do you know what's going on, John?"

"I don't know everything about it. Nobody does. I was a police detective on Oasis, H'anna. An old friend of mine was arrested after he murdered the members of a strange cult. I investigated, and I soon found out why he did it. The stars had come right, and the Outsiders began to come through. We barely managed to stop them, my friend and I, but he was killed. That was the great cataclysm, H'anna . . . that was when all these people became afflicted. Infected, with the consciousness of one or more of the Old Ones."

"They're . . . possessed?"

"Yeah. But not by the Devil. By beings more powerful than any demon anyone ever dreamed up. The Old Ones are a race of beings that are dead, but waiting to be reborn. They need our help to do it. Some people say that another race of beings, called Elder Gods, originally beat them down, locked them out of our dimension . . . but other people disagree about that, and claim there is no bad race/good race war, corresponding with Christian devils and angels. Not many people know about any of these secrets and mysteries, H'anna, and like I say—the few who do can't agree. Most of them, like me, are seeking their knowledge and fighting against these creatures alone. How much the government believes, how much they're fighting against it, I don't know. But they looked the other way when I started killing cult members myself. The worst they did to me was take my badge and kick me off Oasis. So I settled here. Took a job in the soup kitchen just to be near the Afflicted . . . study them . . . keep an eye on them . . ."

"Those three little girls in the cafeteria said they remembered you," H'anna recalled now. "They said your name . . ."

"Yeah. I guess I should be flattered. We're just insects to the Old Ones, but I guess I got their attention when I fought them on Oasis. I closed the door on them, with my friend's help. But he knew more than I do. He knew how to close the portal. But this time, I'm not sure I do . . ."

She tried to assimilate all this as they rode on. In the close confines of the vehicle, H'anna caught the subtle scent of her own sweat, brought out by heat and exertion. She squeezed her arms closer to her body, and then felt ridiculous for it; here the world was crumbling about her ears, and she was afraid that her body odor might offend the man seated beside her. The Hummingbird was small and their knees lightly touched. She found that small human contact to be a vast source of security.

"That's my building, coming up," H'anna announced, pointing out a distant tower with a reddish sandstone color and texture, wedged between two taller and sleeker models.

"Here," John said, and reached across her knees to flip open a dash compartment. He withdrew another handgun, this one larger and composed of a matte gray ceramic, which he passed into her hands. "Keep it. It's loaded with blue plasma capsules, so be careful. It should melt anything living that gets in your way."

Not exactly flowers or candy, but their first date had been unconventional from the start. So much for her fears of John Bell being a boring companion. She turned the pistol over in her hands, both afraid of it and grateful for it.

"What's that?" John snapped, and H'anna's head jolted up in time to see the line strung across their airborne path a second before they struck it. It looked like a clothesline draped between skyscrapers; was no doubt some sort of power cable. But a cable running across an open airway? She immediately tensed for impact, expecting the cable to shear its way through the old craft, cutting its occupants in half. But the cable was cleaved, and its two halves dropped away like a severed vine. Throwing a look over her shoulder, H'anna thought she saw something like drops of glittering mercury falling from the hacked ends. And in addition to that, brief sputtering forks of a violet electricity. A connection had been broken . . . it was indeed a kind of power cable . . . and yet up close she had seen it was silvery in color, and organic-looking.

"Look," John said, calling her attention to the fore again as they neared her building and turned a corner to approach it more directly.

There were more of those silvery vines, stretched here and there between buildings quite distant from each other, like the strands of an immense spider web. In fact, they could see how the strands had got up here: crawling across the face of H'anna's building was a cluster of four or five Afflicted, merged into one creature that was appropriately very spider-like in appearance. As they drew closer, and stopped at a hover not far from it, the creature turned several of its heads and snarled silently at them. Black teeth, whipping black tongues. Faces like those of mummies half wrapped in metallic bandages—withered, as if they were draining their own fluids out of themselves in order to secrete this ooze. And inside a window of the reddish building, they could see others of the Afflicted moving about. One of those strands or cables actually passed through the open window into one of the building's apartments.

"John," H'anna said with a dreamy, entranced horror, "that's my apartment."

"What?" He then pushed the helicar ahead a few feet to get a better look inside. H'anna leaned across him to see.

The silvery organic web strand ran into her living room. Ran directly to her sculpture "Headless Angel", which was wrapped in veils of metallic secretion. Across these veils, miniature flashes of lightning fluttered like thoughts firing through the membranes of a gigantic brain.

"What is that thing?" John demanded.

"I'm an artist; it's a sculpture of mine. An angel, or a demon, with no head."

"No face? And a triple crown?"

"Triple halos."

He turned to her, his stare so intense it was accusatory, inquisitional. "Why did you design that?"

"I didn't design it! It came in a dream."

John gazed out again across the city at the other strands trailing away into the distance. "Do you have other artist friends who've been dreaming strange ideas for their art?"

"Yeah . . . yeah, you know, I have. My friend Todd has been going through what he calls his Mollusk Period. He keeps dreaming about giant squid . . . squid angels with wings . . ."

"They're connecting up their lines of power. It can't just be artwork, idols. It may be powerful books . . . archeological displays in private collections . . . anything else linked to their past that might focus their energy. They're weaving a web. Whatever's at its nexus has to be the portal they plan to come through." He faced her once more. "Our destinies converge, H'anna. But for a minute there I thought you were one of them. Anyway—I can't let you off here . . ."

"Thanks; I'd rather not."

"We have to tear down this web. Excuse me a minute." He tapped a button, and opened his side window. Now they could hear the hissing of that multi-limbed, multi-headed chimera. The head of an elderly man unhinged its jaw like a snake's and began an ear-splitting ululation.

John's gun bucked, spewed its solid projectiles, his arm stretched out the car window. Black brain matter spackled the reddish wall. The creature started to fall, half of it dead, half still hissing, gummed palms coming away from the wall it clung to. John drove more slugs into it, and at last it was peeled entirely away. They watched it tumble to its death in the street far below, the elderly man still howling, still lashing his tongue all the way down.

John emptied the rest of his clip into H'anna's apartment, but not at the Afflicted that skulked within. He sprayed the shrouded "Headless Angel". They heard its black metal skin ping and clang as the bullets punched through it. The triple halos were blasted away. The arm raised in cursed benediction was bent to another angle. The whole figure toppled from its base—and the lightning stopped flickering across it.

"Sorry," John told her.

"I've had worse reactions to my art."

He smiled at her. Closed the car window. And now the Hummingbird flew onwards again, tearing through the silver strand that was extruded through H'anna's open window. The other end of it passed right through the body of the giant dancing Indian woman who sang the praises of her net service on the opposite roof top. As her severed umbilical cord fluttered away she caterwauled cheerfully in their wake.

— 4 —

John took the helicar up higher, above the ceiling of the city. An alarm sounded in the car, and a stern female voice let him know he was out of the proper airways and that his violation was being recorded in central police files. Oh well.

They began to make out the pattern of the web below them. It glittered in the sun as if spun from thin lines of steel. The pattern had an almost geometric configuration to it, more like a gigantic hieroglyph than a spider's web. Yet it did appear to have a central point of convergence . . .

"That's FAM," said H'anna. "The Fine Arts Museum."

"I know," John said. "I've been there. It makes sense. They have something there I should have destroyed before. I didn't know how to do it without being caught. And I guess I underestimated how dangerous it could be. But

45

it's one of the reasons I decided to settle in this town."

"What is it?"

"Something you plagiarized, H'anna, without knowing . . ." He began to drop altitude again.

They could see more and more of those multi-limbed creatures crawling like flies across the faces of the buildings as they descended; some now seemed to be made from as many as a dozen bodies. H'anna saw a man dragged out of his apartment window by one of this swarm, but she also saw another man lean out of his window and fire an old pump-action shotgun into one of them. She watched another creature open one of its myriad mouths and fire a silver line out of it, which sailed amazingly far until it stuck to the building opposite, where another monstrosity took hold of it and scampered away out of sight with it, around the corner of the building. They were so like industrious insects, serving their unseen queens in their alien dimension. Preparing this world so that those queens might break free from their imprisoning chrysalises and fly free once more.

John lowered his car to the rooftop parking lot of the Fine Arts Museum. Even as they landed and floated under the covered section, two other crafts hastily departed. A man ran past them with his wife, both carrying young children in their arms. "Don't go in there!" the man yelled as they charged by. H'anna watched after them nervously until they were safely in the air, then turned to follow John to the elevators, where he had patiently waited for her, popping a fresh magazine into his pistol as he did so.

When she reached him, he asked, "Sure you want to go with me, H'anna? You could stay in the car. Take the car, if I don't come back . . ."

"I feel safer with you."

"Really? They have a grudge against me."

"I don't care. I don't want to be alone."

"Okay; but I'll be too busy to ask you again." Then he hit the button for the elevator.

The bell dinged, the door slid open, but the elevator was already crammed full. H'anna gave a cry and scrambled backwards, as a silvery tentacle lashed the air just inches from her face. There were as many as twenty Afflicted in the elevator, now so fused and shrouded in metallic webs that they had become an amorphous mass. John wheeled about and flicked the switch to chamber the first round off his fresh clip, but before he could aim his gun, H'anna extended hers in both fists and fired shot after shot. The blob howled from nearly two dozen toothless mouths as the blue-glowing plasma immediately began to spread, like fire across paper. The now inhuman limbs thrashed in agony, the flanks of the thing pitched and heaved as they blackened. John hit the door button again, and the sight and most of the stench of the liquefying creature were shut away.

He hit the button for the other elevator, hopefully with better results. They both stood with guns pointed, legs spread in firing stances. Ding. The door parted. Their fingers curled. Just a soft instrumental version of last year's cutting edge music hit. They boarded the lift.

"Floor eleven, I think—right?" John said. "For alien antiquities? Choom? Tikkihotto?"

"Yes," H'anna replied. She knew the museum well, had often wandered its halls while fantasizing about exhibiting her own work there one day. It seemed such a trivial dream, now, with a gateway to another dimension opening up somewhere below them. The elevator sped them downward toward that place. H'anna felt like it was lowering them into Hell.

"Floor eleven," a pleasant female voice announced, and the door opened. Before them stretched a wide, dim hallway with glossy floors. It was utterly, eerily silent. Warily, they disembarked.

"What display do you want?" H'anna whispered.

"Tikkihotto," John replied.

"Um, that way." She pointed with her gun, and so they headed down a narrower branching corridor. It was also gloomy, almost dark, but with recessed, lighted displays in the walls. These were holographic dioramas portraying the colonization of the Tikkihottos' planet by Earth people, nearly a hundred years ago now. The holograms, on a regular cycle, switched to ads for various museum sponsors—a sneaker company, a vidphone service, a mood adaptor implant. "Stress dominating your life?" asked a pleasant female voice.

The corridor opened into a series of interconnecting galleries of ancient Tikkihotto artifacts, beginning with a collection of intricately embroidered ceremonial robes spread across the walls like tapestries. The rooms were as still as a labyrinth of tombs.

Next, an exhibit of weapons; axe-like swords, lances, handsome early muskets. In this room, they began to hear a sound at last, somewhere ahead. Murmuring voices. A chorus of them. It sounded like a low monotonous chanting. They glanced at each other, crept forward more stealthily to listen.

"Iä . . . Ngai . . . Ygg . . ."

Waving his companion back, John ventured a bit further ahead, poked his head through the next doorway. H'anna held her breath—and nearly screamed when a gun started firing explosively. At first, she thought it was John, but he jolted back just as startled as she. He then lunged forward, however, and not wanting to be left behind, she plunged after him.

It was a wide, circular gallery, ringed with statues and busts on pedestals, with the colossal figure of a legendary Tikkihotto hero in the center, bronze tendrils curling from his sockets where a human's eyes would be. At the base of this figure, some of its tentacles wound around the bronze legs, was a great

47

undulating bulk that could not have been less than thirty human beings at one time. One of its limbs had whipped out and circled the throat of a security guard, who had now dropped his gun, his eyes bulging in a blackening face.

John and H'anna skidded to a stop and opened fire wildly, in a desperate panic, as the beast turned several of its limbs in their direction.

H'anna's melting plasma did more good than John's solid projectiles. A tentacle was burned free and flopped at H'anna's feet like a dying snake. Black smoke began to billow, a vile fluid as shiny as quicksilver to spread in a pool. A third of the monster was able to surge away through the opposite doorway, but they could still hear it wailing away in agony, the plasma still diligently at work on it. The miasma it left behind caused H'anna to retch, but she clapped her free hand over her mouth. John had already rushed forward to one of the statues, and H'anna saw that there were numerous silvery lines affixed to it. Lifting her head, she followed them to a ring of windows near the concave ceiling of this domed projection of the museum. The windows—though bullet and ray-proof—had all been melted through somehow to permit the entry of the strands.

Still covering her nose and mouth though the putrid mists were dissipating, H'anna crossed the room to join John at the base of the statue.

"Yes," she said, lowering her hand. "Oh my God . . . yes. And I've seen this before . . . I have. Maybe, maybe subconsciously I remembered it, copied it . . ."

"No," John said. "You were right the first time. You saw it in your dreams. They were using you to make an idol for them. Another nodal point of power."

H'anna read aloud the translated title on the plaque. "The Black Messenger." She read more. "They don't know what kind of material it was carved from. A kind of resin, they think, 'perhaps secreted by insect colonies cultivated for such a purpose; the Tikkihotto were known to breed certain insect species for food and silk'." She again lifted her gaze to the sculpture.

Whatever it was made of, it was entirely ebon in color, the silvery black of hematite. It was a crouching, a sphinx-like hybrid, with the longer forelimbs of a hyena, and stylized folded bird-like wings. Atop its head was a crown with three cones. And there was no face on the creature's head. No snarling demon's visage with mere eyes and fangs could have disturbed her more than this.

"Nyarlathotep," she breathed aloud.

John looked at her sharply. "How do you know?"

"I just know. From the dreams . . ."

Both front limbs rested on the ground, whereas her version had had one hand raised in a blessing.

But now, one of its front limbs did rise up, with a crackling sound like the

48

crumbling of sanity.

— 5 —

Jerking up her pistol in both fists, H'anna let loose a shriek of madness and a volley of gel capsules, that broke against the statue's blank visage. Sizzling, black smoke, and corrosive blue glow. The sculpture toppled forward off its base, and the taloned fingers of its raised hand raked H'anna across the leg. She screamed and crumpled.

John caught her under the armpits, dragged her across the marble floor and knelt protectively over her, gun aimed toward the fallen statue.

H'anna expected it to convulse in seizures of pain, to see the vulture-like wings open up and beat at the floor madly . . . that the now headless monster would scrabble across the floor to tear them with it claws. But it lay still, the plasma slowly spreading down its shoulders now, a black pool beginning to grow under it. Had she only imagined the arm raising, then? Might it have been raised all along?

John clamped his palm over the young woman's furrowed thigh. Blood flowed between his fingers, but there was no arterial jetting.

"I thought blue plasma only worked on organic things . . . living things," she cried.

"It does," John muttered softly, watching the statue melt. Most of the strands had torn free of it, bleeding drops like mercury, a few tongues of violet electricity flashing from their ends, but then dying out.

H'anna clung to John and now, as if finally jarred out of some prolonged trance of numbing unreality, began to sob against his chest. He stroked her back reassuringly, but looking up at his face, she saw that his eyes appeared just as afraid, just as exhausted. He seemed to be glancing around the circular room at the other statues on their pedestals, as if he might be wondering what other horrors lay hidden behind quiet masks, on this world and others.

"We did good," he said at last, turning his attention back to her and helping her to her feet. "You did really good. But let's get you to a hospital, now, huh?"

She leaned against him, her arm around his shoulders, as they started across the chamber. She winced at the pain. But something distracted her from it momentarily, a glitter on the floor. She glanced toward the metallic pool where most of that tentacled monstrosity had melted away. Lying in that silver ichor was a gold wedding ring. She now saw, also, rags and bundles of clothing. A belt. Some shoes. She was reminded of the human loss, the tragedy behind the monster's face—or facelessness.

They took an elevator back to the roof. Because a tourniquet might do more harm than good, especially where arteries weren't severed, H'anna had simply stripped off her torn cloned-leather pants and put pressure on the lacerations in her thigh with the undershirt of the strangled security guard. While riding the elevator she saw John cast a guilty look at her bare bloody legs, and smile at her bashfully. She resisted the joke that he was welcome to wash her off later if he liked. Despite their intimacy of having been forced to take part in murder together, she wasn't sure if she were ready for sex yet.

On the roof, they heard the city alive with sirens (as if it were one vast organism wailing from countless echoing mouths) and the crackle of gunfire, as citizens and policemen alike launched a counterattack against the mutated Afflicted. Whether these creatures were still channeling the consciousness of the Old One called Nyarlathotep, or were merely mindless protoplasm at this point, not even John speculated . . . though in the next few days, all of the Afflicted on Earth and her immediate colonies would have been slaughtered or—in most cases—perished on their own.

John disappeared for a few days. She thought for good, but then he appeared at her apartment, and told her that people from the government had questioned him about what had transpired . . . and what might transpire in the future. Though he wouldn't admit as much to her, H'anna believed that he had agreed to work with the government in some capacity.

He ended up moving into her apartment with her for several weeks. He helped her clear out the ruined "Headless Angel", patch bullet holes, look for a new job; he cooked breakfast for her, painted her toe nails dark brown one evening, and they made sweaty love with an almost frightened desperation in the sweltering summer heat.

And then one afternoon she came back from her new job in the FAM gift shop and he was gone. But a few days later, she received a crackly, static-shot call from him on her vidphone.

"I'm sorry, H'anna," he told her. "It was a spur of the moment thing. My new friends needed me here. I don't know when I'll be back, either."

"Where is here?" she asked him. She heard an ocean surf somewhere close by, wherever he was. But the sky outside the window behind him had an unearthly purple glow. Was that strange cry she heard the call of some sea bird?

"I can't say right now," he replied, his eyes beseeching for understanding. "Another world. It seems even farther than that. I miss you, H'anna. I'll try to come back . . . I will . . ."

"Okay," she said blandly. She gave a little shrug like it didn't matter. It did, but she understood. After what they'd seen together, she understood quite well.

It was difficult being alone again, but there was something even more difficult that soon developed. H'anna found she was incapable of returning to her art. She couldn't sculpt . . . couldn't even sketch. It was not so much that she couldn't, however, as that she was afraid to.

Because one night she woke up and felt a compulsion to sketch in colored pencil an image from her dream. She had the mental picture mostly captured before she fully realized what she was doing. And then she tore the thing to bits. But before she did so, she sat back from the sketch and took it in, as if studying a drawing someone else, some stranger, had rendered.

The drawing showed a great gray beast rising up from the sea in a spray of foam against a dark purple sky. The leviathan had vast jagged fins or wings spreading out from its back, and a face without eyes or any features other than a nest of thrashing silvery tentacles.

THE YOUNG OF THE OLD ONES

— 1 —

VT programs had changed a lot in the eight years that Pal Sexton had been lost in another dimension.

He was watching a version of *Hamlet* that had been released last year, and was now running on the premium channels. Hamlet's voice was by Kenneth Branagh, taken from a twentieth century film version, and Ophelia's voice was by Helena Bonham Carter, taken from a slightly older version than that. Pal did not realize that the joke here was that the two actors had been romantically involved in their time. But the voice of Polonius was provided by a contemporary actor, the rubber-faced Choom comedian Kip Vreelee, whose body customarily jerked about a movie screen like that of an electrocuted marionette.

But these voices were dubbed in, so that they appeared to be spoken by actual dead animals, the mouths and beaks of which were computer-animated to mouth the dialogue. Hamlet, for instance, was a scruffy dead mongrel that had been filmed where it lay in some lot or alley, and his animated lips moved around a drooping motionless tongue. Ophelia was physically portrayed by a dead cat which steadily decomposed as the film wore on, so that by the time of her suicide it was a roiling mass of maggots. In keeping with the fact that Vreelee was not an earthly being, the animal which starred as Polonius was a rotting land-mollusk called a t'uub, indigenous to the planet Oasis, its shell apparently crushed by some wheeled vehicle.

The medical attendant who brought Pal his breakfast lingered beside his chair after she had set his tray in front of him, and chuckled at the scene now unfolding. Yorick the jester was presented as the skull of a small bird.

Pal looked up at her. "I can't believe they made a whole three hour movie like this. How well did it do?"

The young med pried her eyes away to grin down at him. "Are you joking? You should see the new *Romeo and Juliet*. Everyone's doing 'dead critter' movies now. They're hilarious." A more serious expression crossed her face as if she chastised herself. "And educational, too—they keep these important classics alive." She poured Pal a coffee from the cylinder on his tray, and then whisked whitely from the room, tossing back one last look at the screen.

Pal switched his attention to her exit, watched her nicely ample rump in her tight white slacks. He hadn't seen a woman in eight years. But then again— except where his former fiancée was concerned—that fact did not register to him as a profound loss. Perhaps if he had his full memories intact, right now

52

he would be sick with yearning for the blandly pretty med as if she were some glamorous model. Perhaps this long-unknown coffee would taste better to him. Perhaps he would feel more grateful for the security of this base, and feel more bitter at the years of his life robbed from him. But he couldn't remember. He felt more dazed and perplexed than anything. It had only been yesterday, as far as he was concerned, that he had sat down inside the spiky urchin of the transdimensional pod.

Sexton twisted in his chair to gaze out the window that ran the length of his room, the heavy drapes drawn back to reveal it. One might have thought the glass was tinted a purplish color, but that was the color of the sky and the sea on R'lyeh. There was little more than sky and sea on R'lyeh.

He saw low humps that were a cross between small hills and large dunes, sparsely crested with long, translucent colorless grasses that bowed and rippled like rods of flexible glass in the breezes that came in off the sea. White lines of foam coursed slowly to the shore, which was a seemingly endless narrow strip of beach under the lowering clouds of twilight, growing a darker and darker purple. The whole world seemed bruised, and the ocean like a polluted wine. The sand of the beach and of the dunes was a fine black powder which glittered when you held it in your hand, like pulverized obsidian.

Sexton could see his yellow-warm room and his own face reflected back at him, as if he were a ghost without that stared longingly, forlornly in at him. Only by looking at his face could be believe that eight years—eight long, mysteriously draining years—had transpired. He was still fit, tight—tanned from much time, apparently, spent outside. It had been required, after all, that he be tough enough to cross over alone. His eyes were an acetylene blue in his face, which was thin-lipped and intense. He was not scarred, not wasted like some furtive, desperate mongrel (that poor dead thing humiliated, not glorified, in its starring role as Hamlet). His face had not sunken, and its lines were not deep. But his short, curly hair had been a sandy brown, eight years ago. Now, it was going silver. The nests of his eyes seemed darker. Not more sunken. Just that the shadows seemed more dense.

He had kept himself clean-shaven, apparently, he was told. He had a thin beard of whiskers now. It was darker than his hair, and he hadn't shaved it off since regaining consciousness, as if to compensate for the premature graying.

There was a knock on the door to the infirmary room, and Pal broke his connection to the window with a flinch. Just a split second before the knock, he had thought he saw the water far out to sea swell with a massive rising, as if a terrible bomb had gone off on the ocean floor. A new visitor let himself into the room. Pal had not met this one yet. As the stranger crossed to join him, Pal threw a quick look out the window again. Nothing had arisen; just the terrible sameness of the dreaming waves, the lapping surf.

"Mr. Sexton," said the stranger, extending his arm. They shook hands and he dragged a chair nearer to sit more directly opposite Sexton, blocking the VT. "I'm Special Investigator John Bell."

"Who are you with?" Pal asked.

"Colonial Security. Just recently."

"Just recently? What were you before that?"

"Just security," Bell said with a smile, but wouldn't elaborate. "I've gone over your circumstances—such as we know of them. I realize there isn't anything more you can tell us about your experiences that we haven't already extracted from your memory artificially, but it's only fair to you that we let you know our conclusions in regard to those memory scans."

Bell, Sexton decided, did look wasted, as if something had physically drained him. He was clean-shaven, his short brown hair brushed back from his forehead, taller and thinner than Sexton. There was a melancholy to his eyes, his friendly smile, but that didn't mean Pal trusted him. He didn't trust any man who carried a gun, openly like Bell did or otherwise. Sometimes openly was worse. Where Pal wore white pants, white t-shirt, white sneakers as if he were a med himself, Bell wore a charcoal sports jacket over a black shirt and black pants; perhaps it was even a uniform. The gun glimmered under the flap of his jacket in a shoulder holster. Pal had taken a gun with him into the other dimension, though he hadn't brought it out with him, they'd said.

"What do you consciously remember of the eight years you were lost?" John Bell asked. "And I'll tell you how your interpretation compares to the dry facts your brain recorded through your eyes."

"There isn't much . . . like I told the doctors. The researchers. Just scraps, shreds. It's like . . . someone dug out all the tiles in the mosaic, and only left a little grout."

Bell nodded knowingly, which already told Pal that they hadn't salvaged much more than that, either.

"It isn't a matter of me forgetting. It's gone. Irretrievable. Erased or lifted away."

"Do you feel . . . is it your opinion, or your—I don't know, intuition—that this erasure was due to the process of dimensional travel? Or . . ."

"No," Pal Sexton cut in. "No. They did something to me. I can't remember it. But I know it. I know it in my eyelashes, in my fingernails. In every cell of my body."

"Again . . . just what exactly do you remember?"

Pal looked again out the window, and night had already fallen. So quickly? Time was alien to him now . . .

The great darkness of the window unnerved him. For all he could see out there, the base might be resting on the floor of the ocean. Before he continued, he rose from his chair, crossed the room, and activated the button that drew the heavy curtains closed.

— 2 —

Inside the great hangar with its high, semi-circular ceiling, the pod hung suspended from two black intersecting arches, like some thorny black fruit from a branch. Outside, a strong wind had picked up, spraying a fine mist of black grit against the skin of the hangar in howls and rasping hisses.

Pal Sexton wore a bulky black life support suit that nearly doubled his width, its helmet now being fixed in place by two young techs. The insect-like helmet bulged and bristled with cameras, scanners, sensors. They knew the atmosphere of that other dimension to which he would cross could support human life, but still felt it was wise not to take chances, to insulate Sexton as much as possible from direct exposure, unbuffered contact.

Sexton had been to other dimensions before—to the world of the beetle-like race of Coleopteroids, to that of the roughly humanoid Antse and the boneless, putty-like L'lewed. These races had congress with Earth and its colonized worlds. But it was possible that the number of dimensions yet to be explored rivaled even the number of planets that might support life. Perhaps, some said, even far exceeded that number. Due to one anomaly or other, there were places where the membranes between dimensions became thin. It was easier to tear through them at these points. One such point had been discovered on the otherwise largely unremarkable planet R'lyeh—mostly sea, and the life in those seas of primeval development.

But he was jittery about today's excursion. This was the first time a live subject would have passed into this other plane. Probes and robots had returned successfully, with little to tell. The atmosphere was breathable, the temperature bearably cool. Vids showed that for all intents and purposes, it was a twin of the planet R'lyeh . . . but without the extensive research complex that had been completed only six months ago.

Pal mounted a few steps to the pod, and was settled inside with the aid of those same two techs. They then withdrew, as did the steps, and the spiny pod hung suspended with the researcher/explorer Pal Sexton sealed inside it. As if within a chrysalis, waiting to be born into a new world.

Inside, he checked his umbilical coupling, to be certain it was tight. He knew it would be; it was only a nervous mannerism. A long umbilical cord would keep him connected to the pod's interior at all times during this first expedition. He would venture no farther than its utmost reach.

Inside his helmet—almost a cockpit it was so large—he lifted his eyes to several small monitor screens. One showed him the external view of the transdimensional pod from the perspective of his colleagues in the control center. He heard a synthesized woman's voice too placidly begin a countdown. He swallowed a wedge of saliva, and saw the pod on that monitor screen begin to cloud and blur black . . .

"And that's the last thing I remember," said Pal Sexton to Special Investigator John Bell, in the infirmary of that same research installation, eight years later.

"The last thing you clearly remember, until they found you back here on R'lyeh," Bell said. "Walking out of the sea."

"Yes," Pal murmured. "Walking naked out of the sea. No pod found. No life suit. No memory."

"But you do recall some scraps between."

"They may only be dreams . . ."

"Tell me," Bell persisted softly.

Pal averted his gaze, resettled himself in his chair, as if he were to disclose some particularly embarrassing erotic fantasy. "It has to be only a dream. I don't see why they would let me remember this. Unless . . . it was so—horrible—that it was the hardest thing to erase . . ."

"Yes?" said Bell. He wasn't going to let him out of it.

"Well, you've seen the dream, no doubt, in the scans they've taken. That huge, unbelievable animal, coming out of the sea . . ."

"Describe it."

Pal rushed along with it then, just to get it out. "Gigantic. It's against the laws of physics that an organism could be so large without crushing itself . . . it isn't biologically practical, considering the amount of fuel it would require. It goes against the square cube law, all right?"

"So it's broken the law," Bell said, more sternly now. "Tell . . ."

"I am!" Pal snapped, his eyes jumping fiercely back to the other's. "It was mostly submerged. Maybe . . . maybe a liquid medium helps support its mass. What I saw was a grayish color. Smooth, slick . . . but it looked like there were rough patches, crusted, like huge colonies of barnacles or maybe diseased flesh. I saw what looked like the shoulders or upper portions of front limbs, but no extremities broke the surface. On its back were a couple pairs of small fins, I guess . . . small for *it*. And there was one pair of fins that were just titanic . . . they were ribbed like a swordfish's sail. Black." He paused. "They might have been wings . . ."

"And the head?"

"Rounded. No eyes. No ears. Nothing but a thick cluster of tentacles up front around where a face should have been, about half-way down the head. They were a metallic silver color, with black patches that became stripes toward the ends. They were . . . they were squirming in the air. Like worms. Alive. Like they were all seeing. Seeing *me* . . ."

Sexton turned away, his hands gripping the armrests of his chair, as if he feared an unseen vortex in the room would suddenly tear him from his seat.

"And where were you, when you saw it?"

"In the water. In the sea. Out in the middle of the sea, with no land in sight. Treading water. Cold . . . very, very cold . . ."

"How did you get out there?"

"I don't know how or why. They must have left me there . . ."

"Who are 'they', you keep referring to?"

"I don't know."

"What do they look like?"

"I can't see them. But I know they were there. I told you. I can remember it in my skin. I think . . ."

Pal heard Bell's own chair squeak as he leaned closer to him. "Yes?"

"I think they serve him, and worship him. They're like his children, I think . . ."

"And who is this 'him'?"

"The creature. I can hear its name in my head, I think, but I'm not sure if I can pronounce . . ."

"Cthulhu," said John Bell.

Pal Sexton whirled to stare at him. "Did you get that from my scan? From the dream?"

"It isn't a dream, Mr. Sexton. That's what I came to tell you. The scans can differentiate between what you actually physically saw, and what you might hallucinate, dream or imagine. The animal or being you just described is real. What you saw . . . it really happened that way."

Several empty seconds. "And you know something about it."

"A little. That's why I'm here."

If it were possible, the scientist grew more intense, his emotions as compacted as the stuff of a collapsed star. "I see a lot of military people on the base since I've come back, Mr. Bell. Tell me you aren't here to try to use that thing as a weapon. To find ways of releasing it at a given target point . . ."

"Hell no," Bell said, glancing at a wall clock as he rose to his feet. "I wouldn't be a part of that."

"What's the military presence for, then?"

"What do you think, Pal? To make sure that thing never does come through to this dimension, or any other. Because that's what it wants. Some day we might know enough about it to send a weapon through, to kill it. But we can't risk that now. We can't risk tearing the hole wider. We can't risk making that thing angry. Some day we might learn how to mend the veil. But for right now, we're just here to learn. And to be on guard." Bell moved to the door. "I have another meeting now, with Dr. Locklin. But we'll talk again."

"Wait," Pal said. "The other things I remember . . . the other scraps. They weren't dreams, either?"

"No," said Bell.

"The city beneath the sea?"

"They aren't dreams," Bell said, and turned and left the room.

— 3 —

Dr. Locklin. Did Bell know about him and Dr. Locklin? That once, Dr. Locklin was to have been another Dr. Sexton? After marrying Pal Sexton?

Sexton had learned that five years ago, biologist Juliana Lynch had married fellow researcher Peter Locklin. He had seen Juliana twice since his return. He knew Peter was still with the project, but he had stayed out of Pal's way thus far, either out of respect or guilt or fear.

Juliana had come to see him the second day of his return. She had been so concerned, so gentle. So polite. It had all been unbearable. The others had already prepared him for it, because he had asked for her right away upon his return. He had been warned, but it didn't help much . . .

She had been polite. He had been cold. An hour after she left him, alone in his infirmary bed and hooked up to a ring of cruelly voyeuristic scanners, he finally and without warning broke into wrenching sobs of self-pity and an almost unfathomable emptiness. But he made himself stop after less than a minute. He must hold on to what was left of himself.

He had been gone three years before she married, he reminded himself so as not to hate her. And yet, it all seemed like yesterday to him, the two ends of his memory spliced together to hide the gaping chasm where all the rest had been uprooted.

During those years, he'd learned that one of his cousins had been killed in a hovercar accident. It was a good thing Pal hadn't owned a dog, he joked to himself humorlessly. Finding out that Spot was dead would probably unhinge his mind altogether.

As with the premature graying of his hair, only where Juliana was concerned did the yawn of the missing years come home to him—cut through his numb daze with real pain. He knew there was desperate, impotent emotion that wanted to howl out in fury and anguish from the depths of that canyon where his life had been severed. But he kept the howl inside him, like a raging demon locked behind a door.

He couldn't wait until they were done with him here. They had mapped his brain, taken what they needed. Hadn't the meeting with this John Bell had a feeling of finality, been a kind of dismissal? In any case, he had no desire to resume his researches here on R'lyeh. He did not want to have to see Jule again. Did not want to see the churning dark ocean under that heavy purple sky again . . .

*   *   *

"They have a resemblance to plankton," Bell said, watching the monitor. Across the large screen moved two distinct animal forms. One floated, drifted with little lazy spurts. The other slithered, wriggled with rippling cilia. They were translucent, grayish. The cilia glittered silvery in the microscope's light.

"Are they single-celled?"

"Plankton aren't single-celled," Juliana Locklin chuckled softly. "You're thinking of protozoa . . ."

Bell turned to face her. He said nothing.

Juliana flushed. "No, they aren't single-celled," she answered, her tone growing more austere. "Superficially, they put me in mind of Earth's nematodes, which also come in diverse forms . . . they're a group of microscopic worms. Some favor a marine environment, while others dwell in soil or can . . . infest other animals as a parasite."

Bell nodded grimly. Not for the first time, he took in Dr. Locklin's prettiness. It disturbed him that he could be distracted by something so trivial as one woman's prettiness when matters of cosmic importance weighed on his shoulders—it was further reminder of how very small humans were. But it didn't help that the doctor reminded him of his ex-wife; both had a kind of mysterious sadness in their nearly-black eyes. Bell hoped for her husband's sake that this woman was more loyal than his wife had been . . . and then he thought of Pal Sexton, with an illogical little stirring of resentment for the doctor's husband.

Juliana Locklin was a small, slender woman, with almost child-like features, very white skin and very dark eyes and hair—which was a crazy mass of curls badly bound up in a frazzled burst of ponytail. It seemed to express her very personality. She was British. So was her husband, who was blond (artificially, Bell believed), good-looking in a boyish way, a little beefy, wearing a thin platinum beard. Bell addressed the both of them . . .

"Do these two forms represent two sexes?"

"We can't determine that from scanning," answered Mrs. Locklin, her accent both mannered yet darkly smoky. "And we've witnessed no mating or reproducing."

"Are we looking at full-grown creatures here, or a larval stage of something?"

"We haven't determined that yet, either. All I can say is that these animals are not native to R'lyeh. At least, not R'lyeh in this dimension."

"When Pal collapsed on that beach," Peter Locklin continued for his wife, "he was carrying thousands of these things in his tissues, in his blood. It took us five teleportation sessions to filter them all out of his system."

"Can they be killed?"

"Yes. The filtering process killed most of them—though it should have worked on the first try. We've also destroyed them with very intense heat, various toxins. They have a high tolerance to cold; they can be frozen, but revive when unfrozen."

"Are you absolutely certain that Sexton isn't carrying any more of these things?"

Something in John Bell's eyes must have made Juliana afraid, because her voice was shaky when she said, "Are you thinking of tossing Pal into an incinerator, Agent Bell?"

He said nothing. He looked again at the monitor. "Ever since I was told about this situation, I've been afraid that the Spawn would come through as titans. An army of giants. But this is what they intended instead. To hijack their way here . . . to hide and stowaway." He faced Peter Locklin. "You've learned all you need to know about them for now. I want the rest of them destroyed."

"What? But we have them securely . . ."

"We can't take foolish risks."

"They're an unknown species!"

"And they'll stay that way, if I say so. I'm not here to argue with you, doctor, but to order you. You can replay your vids, study your scans. But I want you to destroy every last crawling speck of these things. Today."

The two doctors Locklin exchanged looks, but neither protested further.

*   *   *

Pal and Juliana sat at what had once been their usual table in the spacious cafeteria, one wall of which was nothing but windows looking out upon the mindless churning sea. The primitive crab-like flying things that dipped at the waves screeched like tortured gulls.

Had she selected their favorite table on purpose? Subconsciously? Or had it become hers and Peter's table, now?

She drank tea, he a large flavored coffee. They obviously didn't feel comfortable eating in front of each other, although it was lunch time. And what Juliana had to admit to him would not have gone along well with eating. Before this, Pal Sexton had not been aware of the parasites that had been carried in, and filtered from, his body.

She launched into it with little small talk, as if the small talk might be harder for her than this revelation.

Pal did not berate her for keeping it from him. But he asked, "Do the others know you're telling me this?"

"Yes. I had permission. I volunteered to be the one. Otherwise, Bell would have done it, and I find him to be a bit of a fucker."

"Well, he realizes how dangerous this thing is. It obviously has to do with what happened on Earth while I was gone . . . these beings that almost got through, and all the people they destroyed."

"He believes they're the creatures that the Coleopteroids and some other races have worshiped for generations, as gods. They actually have tried to call these entities through . . ."

"I saw one of them," he breathed, dropping his gaze to his coffee.

"I know."

"They are like gods."

Juliana flinched as one of the flying crabs swooped down at the window but pulled up to avoid a collision at the last moment, fluttering up out of sight. "We need to find out why you were there all that time. Whether you were alone, or whether . . ."

"They had me. I know it. All that time."

"If that's so—why eight years? What would they have been doing for so long?"

"Planting those things inside me. And then maybe waiting for conditions to be right to return me . . . the right alignment of our respective dimensions."

"Why not let you return in the pod?"

"Maybe it was damaged. Or maybe the parasites wouldn't make it through that way. Or maybe they wanted to hang onto it, in case they could ever make use of it in coming through themselves, some day—if coming through inside my body hadn't worked."

"Peter's destroying the last of the specimens right now, under Mr. Bell's very watchful and distrusting eye. While they were both thus engaged, I thought it would be a good time to talk."

"Thanks for telling me everything," he muttered.

"I wish we could have told you everything sooner, but . . ."

"I understand."

"You are very understanding, aren't you?" Jule, as he'd always called her, said in a lower voice. Did he dare interpret sadness in it?

"One has to accept what one can't change."

"That doesn't sound like the ballsy young scientist I used to know." She tried a smile.

"Yeah. Well."

She sipped her tea. He stole a glance back at her as she was looking out to sea. Time had been good to her. Much of her doll-like, childish beauty had taken on a becoming, more mature quality. Her endearing awkwardness had become grace. Her slim tendoned neck, pointed nose, slightly thrust jaw in profile were elegant, agonized him. This subtle yet profound transformation intimidated him. He hoped it was her natural evolution, and that Peter couldn't be credited with it. Might he even believe that mourning might be partly responsible?

Still watching the ocean, she said, "You were gone two years, Pal. We all thought you were dead, long ago. Then . . . Peter and I gradually drew closer. And a year later, whilst on Earth for a bit, we married . . ." She turned back to

61

him.

"I told you," he said blandly, "I understand."

"I . . . ," she began.

A klaxon whooped to life. Emergency lamps up near the ceiling spun, swirling red beacons of light.

"What is it?" Pal said, as both he and Juliana bolted up from the table.

She unclipped a device from the belt of her skirt, thumbed keys, studied a readout. "Oh dear Lord . . ."

"What?"

"It's something with the specimens . . ."

— 4 —

Pal nearly had to trot to match Jule's brisk, clacking walk as she sought to contact her husband on her remote phone. "He isn't answering," she husked, and suddenly broke into a run down the corridor. Pal tore around a corner to keep up with her.

"What do you think you're doing?" he yelled. "If containment's been breeched you could get infected with them!"

"I have to do what I can!"

A young tech ran past them in the opposite direction. Pal called, "Hey!" over his shoulder, to find out what the tech might know, but the man vanished around the bend in the corridor behind them, and Pal couldn't afford to go back after him—he had to remain with the madly racing Juliana. Pal put on a burst of speed to catch up with her. She was afraid for her husband, he knew. And he was afraid for her.

As they turned another bend in the corridor, they heard the crackle and patter of gunfire somewhere ahead, and both faltered clumsily to a stop, Juliana unconsciously gripping Pal's arm.

One of the soldiers in the military security unit that had been assigned to the base in Pal's absence appeared around the corner, and leveled his multi-barreled killing engine at them. Juliana gave an involuntary cry, and Pal took an involuntary step toward him as if he had a chance of opposing the man, but the soldier recognized them as allies and his voice came over a microphone from the beetle-like helmet he had donned.

"Get out!" he boomed at them. "Hurry . . . back off . . . go!" He waved his arm violently, glanced over his shoulder down the branch of corridor from which he had just emerged. They couldn't see what he saw, but whatever it was, it inspired the black-garbed warrior to fall into a crouch, swivel his weapon around, and open fire. Hot gas flashed blue from several muzzles and the air rattled.

"Let's go!" Pal shouted, seizing Jule's wrist and pulling her away. She didn't resist, however.

The lights went out in the corridor.

It took only a fraction of a second for the emergency power to kick in, and a series of small pale lights dimly illuminated the hallway, but it was still as if they had plunged into a cavern lit only by a fungous glow. As he and Juliana retreated, Pal tossed a look back at the soldier, whose gun still sputtered.

He saw the soldier leap forward into the air, out of view. It was an unnatural movement. It was more as if something had seized him around the throat and forcibly jerked him off his feet, but it was too gloomy and quick to see for sure.

But there was no mistaking the rustling, hissing sound of some great mass squeezing its bulk through the narrow corridor, just around that bend. Coming this way . . .

"In here!" Juliana said, falling against a door. She, too, knew that they were in the path of something terrible, that they might not be able to outrun it. She opened the door to a botany lab, and Pal crowded in after her. They shut the door as quietly as their nerves would allow, and sealed it closed with a keypad. But a long, large window in the lab faced directly out into the corridor, and the two of them ducked down below it so as to be out of sight to whatever might come.

In the half-dark, they squatted low to the ground, their panting and throbbing blood nearly deafening them to the whispery sliding sound of approach. Whatever it was, it came slowly, but it came. Pal looked at Jule, saw her watching his face with dark eyes bulging wide. They didn't dare speak. Then, a faint shuffling sound became audible to them. But to Pal, it had more the sound of a bipedal creature—a man—dragging its feet than of the great bulk he vaguely envisioned. Gingerly, he turned to the window and poked his head up slightly. Juliana did the same.

Indeed, it was a human figure they saw shuffling down the hallway. A man, staggering along as if he'd been wounded, or walked in his sleep. At first Pal thought it might be the soldier, having lost his helmet, but this man wore a white smock . . . and as he came further into the pallid light, Pal recognized him a split second after Juliana did.

"Peter!" she gasped, springing to her feet. She darted to the door.

"Wait," Pal hissed, taking hold of her shoulders from behind, grabbing fistfuls of her own smock to restrain her. She tore out of it altogether, reached her hand to the keypad. "Look, look!" he insisted, still clutching at her.

She shot a look out the window, and stopped fighting him. Peter saw them through the window, bluish light glowing on his face. And bluish light glistened on a long boneless limb like a cable, which trailed from the back of his head, across the floor, and out of their sight. This slender limb was striped in alternating bands of black and silver. Though they couldn't see where it ended, it was apparent that its tip was buried in the scientist's nape.

"Peter!" Juliana screamed.

And Peter responded to her call, his eyes on them through the glass but as empty as those of a manikin. He moved out of view, but they heard the chirp of the code he was entering on the keypad. He was trying to unlock the door.

"This way," Pal said, and taking her hand, drew Juliana toward the back of the botany lab. With a reluctant sob, she followed. They passed between great burbling tanks in which aquatic plants swayed dreamily. The outpost addressed many areas of research, from the botanical to the biological to the geological, in addition to its experiments with crossing dimensions. Its focus had been more on R'lyeh itself, since Pal's disappearance and the reluctance to send another subject beyond the veil. Through an open doorway, they burst into a large nursery area. In long elevated trays, dune grasses like glassy rods sparkled with the bluish glow of the emergency lights. A white, spherical species of fungus grew in other trays, the largest specimen being too fat for a person to get their arms around. These looked like the tops of huge skulls, rising from the fetid soil of their graves.

Behind them they heard the crash and clatter of a tray of tools, knocked to the floor. Peter had got in. And they heard his voice moan sepulchrally, "Juliana . . ."

Pal and Jule had reached another door at the back of the nursery, one they knew would take them out into the labyrinth of corridors again. But Juliana threw a look back toward the botany lab and pleaded, "Pal . . . please . . . we can't leave him that way." She looked at Pal directly, her eyes so tragic in their anguish that their touch agonized him. "We can't leave him like that, Pal."

He understood. But he dreaded her words. Would she subconsciously hate him hereafter, for doing her this mercy? He felt guilt that he should be worrying about his own considerations when she was in such pain, when this other poor man was as good as dead. If not dead already. He broke his eyes from her, glanced around desperately for something to use.

"Juliana," they heard his nearing voice. "Julianeh-ya-ya-ya-yahaah . . ."

They saw him walking toward them through the rows of glowing grass. And beyond him, they heard a large aquarium tank burst, its water gush out across the floor, as the thing that used Peter oozed its great body into the botany lab.

Pal spotted a hoe, thought of snapping it in half and driving its end into the marionette's throat . . . but his eyes fell on a knife on a sink counter. He snatched it up, surged forward. He didn't know if Jule watched him or not, but he prayed that she closed her eyes as he rushed to murder the husband of the woman he loved.

Peter saw him coming. He lifted his arms as if to embrace him.

Pal cocked his arm back for a strike. He would bury the blade in the scientist's forehead.

But as Pal was within reach of Peter, his stomach lurched, and he found himself unable to deal the killing blow. Peter's outstretched fingers touched his sleeve. He batted the man's hands aside, stepped behind him, and plunged the knife into the tentacle that was buried at the base of his skull.

The limb withdrew like an angry snake, whipping in the air, the knife still in it. And with the tentacle no longer inserted into his brain, Peter dropped bonelessly. He didn't give so much as a twitch, and his eyes had rolled up white in his head. Pal crouched by him, felt at his neck. He only remained a moment, fearful of the limb thrashing in the air, but he didn't detect a pulse. As the tentacle arched itself like a cobra to strike, he bolted.

Jule already had the door open, and they piled through it. He was sure she expected, as he did, to find another creature in the hall waiting for them—or at the very least, to be confronted by another marionette. But the hall was deserted in either direction. One direction would take them toward the many small apartments of the crew. The other would head them toward the transdimensional project. With no conscious reason why, Pal led Juliana in that direction.

— 5 —

At this moment, Pal Sexton assumed that Special Investigator John Bell—who had accompanied Peter Locklin to destroy the last of the creatures that had stowed away inside his body like soldiers in the Trojan horse—had also been possessed, or killed.

Bell was surprised he hadn't been.

He hadn't seen what happened. He had been in an adjoining portion of the lab reading some data off a monitor as Locklin went about the preparations to destroy the specimens. Bell wondered, now, if Locklin had tried to do something to move or hide some of the organisms, which had released them to the air. But he believed, instead, that somehow they had known that they were the last, that they could no longer bide their time, and must act now before it was too late for them . . .

There had been a crash, Locklin had cried out and come running in from the other room. Behind him, Bell had seen something fall from a counter to the floor like a large jellyfish, with an appropriate splat of wet flesh. Then another. Another. A few other creatures had seemed more like eels or perhaps centipedes with rippling bands of silvery cilia, and one slithered into the room after the scientist. Even as it came it seemed to grow larger, its half-liquid flesh rapidly shedding and being reabsorbed and then sloughing away to be assimilated again, over and over . . . as if it fed on its own substance.

Bell ripped his gun from its holster, fired at the eel-like creature as he let Locklin get past him and open the door. He splattered much of the gelatinous centipede's assumed head, but now beyond it the other animals grew even larger, and he saw nests of writhing tendrils striped silver and black. He turned to flee after Locklin, whom he saw waiting for him at the threshold, staring back at the nightmarish display in horrified enthrallment.

As Bell pushed Locklin out the door, a tendril flashed past Bell's face, nearly grazing his cheek like a bullet, and speared into the back of Locklin's neck. He was yanked backwards.

Bell whipped about, fired his handgun past Locklin's grotesquely dancing body, which spasmed like a man at the end of a gallows rope. He hit the animal that held him again and again, but this one was too large and his projectiles appeared to have little effect. With the greatest reluctance, but driven by blind terror, Bell left the poor scientist in the creature's grip, and fled out into the hall.

And now, he stole his way through more hallways, peering around corners like a mouse dreading the stride of men. But finally he had found his way blocked by a door made of rubbery flesh. This flesh crawled slowly from left to right. He realized it was the flank of some great creature, grown so huge in the transverse corridor that its bulk was squeezed flush with the open threshold as it slowly oozed along.

Worse than the look of that grayish, half-substantial flesh was the sound he heard coming through the walls around him, and even over the open intercom. He wondered if the two distinct—voices—represented the two different creatures he had glimpsed. One sound was like the bellowing of a mammoth, blended with a synthesizer, run backwards and underwater. It was awesome in its depth and in conveying what Bell interpreted as loneliness on a cosmic scope. It was terrifyingly forlorn. Bell had never considered that before today. That the Old Ones, the Outsiders, might suffer in that way.

He took that to be the voice of the bulky, apparently tentacle-headed spawn. The other voice was angry rather than morose, like the hysterical whinnying of a horse . . . but with almost subliminal whisperings laced under it, along with a fluctuating ringing tone that reminded Bell of someone playing glasses of water with their fingertips. This he imagined was the sound of the elongated beasts.

He backtracked, entered a lab, started violently when he found a dead man slouched by the door with his arm wrenched off. The blood made a wide swatch down the wall where he had slumped. Bell took in his surroundings, unfastened an air vent and determined he could fit within the narrow shaft beyond. Before he entered, however, he dabbed a towel in the stump of the dead man's shoulder and began drawing a figure on the door to seal off his retreat.

The figure he painted portrayed a star with an eye in the center, the pupil of which resembled a wavering column of flame.

It was the sign of the Elder Gods, the mysterious race who had sealed up the Outsiders in their various tombs, cells and places of exile. They were not angels to the devils of the Outsiders, might be seen merely as rivals. Bell had never communicated with them, did not pretend to comprehend their whims, could barely comprehend their existence—if in fact they did exist. But this had not stopped him, any more than it had many a human before him, from appealing to the gods for their intervention.

All he knew was that the sign could be potent, and he felt better with it behind him as he entered into the circulation system and began crawling in what he hoped was the direction of the dimensional research area.

Bell didn't know what he could accomplish there. He didn't know if he could even hope to remain alive much longer. But his instincts told him that the place to be was the hangar where the transdimensional pod was suspended like a bathysphere waiting to be lowered into black depths. It was a threat, somehow. A weak spot. A bulging door with creaking hinges . . .

The Spawn were here. But their master was not. The Spawn had not come to strangle and wrench apart each trifling human being one by one. They were here to open the way for their father.

So Bell crawled. Like an insect, rushing to intercept the tramp of a legion of armored soldiers.

— 6 —

Pal and Juliana emerged into a closed observation deck that looked down into the hangar where the pod hung suspended from its two intersecting arches. With only the emergency lights on in the great open space below, the view that lay before them was murky. It looked like a black ocean, with glistening waves that rose and fell. But the waves, they realized, were of flesh—and then they were glad that their view was limited. They tried to keep down out of the way after that. But Pal did peek long enough to make out a few white lab coats. There seemed to be some figures calmly at work down there, amid the shifting flesh, and the terrible cacophony of sound.

"Look, Pal!" Juliana whispered, pointing to a bank of monitors. Figures scrolled down the screens.

"They've taken some of the crew, like they did Peter," Pal whispered grimly, hunkering down beside her again. "They're using them to program the pod." He shifted closer to a control board. "I'll see if I can override them." He tapped a few keys gingerly, then moved across to another control board. He chewed his upper lip. This end of things was not his area of expertise; he was the one sent, not the sender.

Juliana poked her head up enough to gaze down into the yawning blackness again. She flinched as a dark train of flesh poured across the outside of their enclosed balcony and then was gone in a blur of cilia-like legs.

"Here," Pal whispered, and tapped a few last decisive keys.

Below, Juliana swore she saw the lab-coated figures all look up at the window simultaneously. She dropped below its edge and hissed, "Pal! Oh God—whatever you did, they know it was done in here!"

"We have to go," he said, and rushed to her side.

Before the two of them could reach the door, it opened.

The two techs barely seemed to glance at them; instead, they made their way stiffly to the two control boards Pal had tampered with. Pal and Juliana saw the tendrils snaking from the backs of their heads, tethering them to something horrible and mercifully out of sight. But out of view or not, it would be blocking their escape from this room.

All that remained, then, was to stop these two puppets—or inconvenience things as long as they could . . . however empty that gesture must obviously, finally prove. Pal picked up a chair and swung it over his head with all his strength, down on one of those trailing cables. The tech was jerked backward and fell on her rump comically, but the tendril was not dislodged and she righted herself with just a dirty look at her attacker. Pal dropped the chair. He looked around for something that could cleanly split the skull of the female tech herself.

"Pal!" Juliana shrieked, and he looked up to see a third tendril slithering into the room. Raising up into the air. Banded silvery and black . . . and it was inclining itself in Juliana's direction.

It launched itself.

"No!" Pal roared, and shot his hand out, and to his own amazement, he caught the snake-like appendage in mid air, grasping it firmly. It thrashed, tried coiling around his forearm, but he did not lose his grip. He glanced at Juliana, and even in her terror she too seemed to gaze at him in wonder.

He stared back at her face. How he loved her. He had a sudden, piercing memory of her from years before. She was wearing a sweater he had bought for her as a Christmas gift. They were at an ocean—not this ocean. A blue ocean. They were in a cottage they had rented. And she sat and he stared at her face and marveled at its purity. The white of her skin was so perfect that he could not imagine it to be made up of rough links like the contrasting dark weave of the sweater. Could not imagine it to be made up of cells. It was a white wholeness, like a single cell, made from light—glowing soft light from which her eyes beamed like black stars. And she smiled at him subtly, but he read love in it clearly, and it was the most beautiful image that had ever registered upon the sad and ephemeral jelly of any man.

But another image came to him a second later, and it carried equal force in its vividness. He saw an ocean that spread to the limits of sight in all directions, as if he hovered just above the very center of it. It was an ocean of churning red fog. The sky above it was streaked gray and yellow. And from this limitless ocean of red smoke, great black idols loomed high out of the mist. Roughly human faces, with long lobes and slanted dreaming eyes.

This image abruptly switched to another, again as shockingly vivid. He was looking up at a ceiling of stone . . . he was on his back . . . and figures leaned above him in an intent circle. They were faceless; more like plants than men. Their hands, upon him, more like fluid branches. But he felt no horror at their touch—for he himself appeared to be one of them.

Dreams. But why were dreams crowding in on him now? Why . . .

He saw his hand that gripped the squirming tentacle. He saw the flesh on his forearm slough away, the shed flesh reabsorbed, then shed again, in an almost liquid rippling effect. Its color became grayish. Its flesh looked less substantial . . .

His eyes flashed to Juliana. She saw it too.

The two techs stared at his arm as well, their eyes glassy and growing large in drugged confusion.

Juliana screamed, "Pal, Pal, what's it doing to you?" She started toward him.

He raised his other hand to ward her off. In a soft, trembling voice he said, "It isn't doing this to me." And even as he said it, the tendril in his hand blackened and withered as if burnt. It dropped from his hand, and was violently extracted from the room. The two tentacles fled the heads of the wavering techs, leaving their dead husks to crumple slackly to the floor.

Pal felt the churning move up his shoulder. His neck. It flowed throughout him. Juliana saw his face begin to subtly ripple.

"I'm sorry," he told her, and his voice caught on the start of a sob. He felt tears rise to his eyes, even as he realized they had never been eyes. He took a half step toward her. "I'm sorry, Jule. All this time I've been back . . . I thought . . . I was me."

And then she screamed again, as Pal Sexton disappeared altogether.

The Changeling loomed before her, in the pool of Sexton's clothing. Gray, plant-like, its various limbs floating in the air like coils of liquid smoke. It remembered itself now, now that it had shed its camouflage. The cloned memories had been shed with the cloned flesh. It recalled itself . . . and how it had come to be here.

"Pal, no, no, no!" Juliana wailed, her hands fluttering. She wanted to kill this thing that had masqueraded as her lover all along. Tricking their most delicate scans, on the most minute microscopic level.

The Changeling understood her terror, but knew that she misunderstood its origins. She took it to be a tool of the Old Ones. But that tool, the human named Pal Sexton, had been stolen by the Changeling's kind even as the servitors of the Old Ones were returning Sexton to this plane. Pal Sexton had been intercepted. The switch had been so perfect, that even the spore of the

Old Ones that had been secreted in his body were switched to this body instead. It had all occurred in the blink between that world and this world, but the exchange had taken place. The Spawn dreaming inside the Changeling had never been the wiser.

The weirdly both awkward and graceful creature turned to the windows that overlooked the hangar, and pressed its upper ring of limbs to the surface. It perceived itself reflected it that glass and was glad to know itself restored. It ignored the poor noisy human as it began to grow up and out—its flowing, increasing bulk at last pressing the window panel out of its frame to crash below. Then, the Changeling lowered its gray sinuous form into the arena.

— 7 —

Bell lay in the metal shaft with his hands clamped over his ears, imagining that at any moment his palms would become wet with blood . . . or with his streaming brains.

He had nearly reached the dimensional research area, by his figuring, when the uproar began. The sounds he had heard before—and had been following—paled in comparison. Those previous sounds were present in this mix, but new noises equally alien and monstrous were blended in as well, until it all became one deafening hurricane of sound.

And just when he thought the cacophony might kill him—or at least wished it would—silence.

His feet had braced against the wall of the shaft. Now they slid down. He lay there, unable to hear his own panting breath, his ears ringing. At last, he rolled back onto his hands and knees, and resumed his crawl to a vent at the end, through which he saw slats of soft blue light.

After peeking out into the hangar for several wary minutes, he finally kicked out the vent grate and emerged timidly to inspect the great, sprawled body of the dying thing.

It was gray, and immense, like the body of a whale that had been flattened or deflated, and yet still subtly pulsed and shifted. Tendrils lay torn from it, others half-ripped away. Gray shrouds of mist or smoke escaped tears in its translucent flesh. Most of the gray creature's central body lay directly under the transdimensional pod—which still hung there suspended. Intact.

Of the offspring of Cthulhu, Bell saw only heaps like tar. Black pools. Bubbling smears. Smudges and stains, like sticky shadow. All spread about the mass of the failing gray creature.

A few other people had straggled into the room since Bell had entered. And on the far side of the hangar, he found Juliana. Her hair was badly disheveled, and her eyes were burned painfully red from tears. She looked up at him like a shell-shocked soldier, without recognition at first. But then she motioned with her arm stiffly at the dying animal.

"It was Pal," she said softly, and with his hearing still blasted he wasn't sure he understood her words. "Pal."

He put his arm around her, and when he looked back to the gray mass, it no longer pulsed or shifted. Bell felt an instinctual understanding in his very cells, and a kind of awe so acute it was like a yearning ache. Its vast body, he took in at last, was five-lobed—like the star he had painted on the door in blood. It had sacrificed itself here, he understood, where the veil had been so thin. Its very body had become a seal . . .

He wanted to express his gratitude to the dead thing. But how does one say a prayer over the corpse of a god?

As he stood there with his arm around Juliana, more people found their way into the room, to form a kind of reverential ring around the perimeter of the creature. And even at this moment—outside the hangar building—another person came staggering blindly, drawn to pay his respects. He trudged barefoot across the black sands, and water ran down his naked flesh.

Pal Sexton remembered nothing of the last eight years. He only remembered that he was home.

RED GLASS

We called him the Screaming Man. I don't know if he is alive or dead, though he was probably moved into Eastborough State Hospital once the old woman passed away. He may still be a patient, and I plan to find out. Find out if they've medicated him into passivity, or if he still rants and laughs. If he is an inmate, I'll visit his room. And sneak in a knife, to scrape off some of the paint on his wall . . .

An elderly woman lived in the small house by the head of our driveway, and she cared for several disturbed people in her home over the years, an assortment who came and went; there was a hulking huge bearded man, ever silent, who took walks in the neighborhood. I didn't care to have him trailing even distantly behind me when I walked uptown to buy a jug of milk for my parents. There was the shriveled little mummy of a woman, her face lined beyond what seemed natural, who would stand at the head of our driveway and watch me while I walked my dog in the yard. There was a youngish man with banged blond hair, who also wandered about town occasionally. One time when I entered my back hall to take my dog out, I was startled to see this man's face at the window of the outer door, staring into our back hall. He turned, upon seeing me, and trudged up the driveway back to his own home.

But the Screaming Man unnerved me most of all. Sometimes I thought that he was never let out of the house—not even out of his room. I imagined him chained by the leg to his bed. And yet, would that afflicted a soul be permitted to live with an elderly woman? Other times—and this was even more frightening, in a way—I believed he was actually that huge hulking man, so very quiet when drifting about town by day, and so bedeviled by night.

The Screaming Man's silhouette in the second floor windows was, after all, bulky. I would peek out my parent's kitchen window and watch his silhouette against the shades of his room. He would be pacing and flailing his thick arms wildly in the air. Roaring, as if in outrage, frustration . . . and then, other times, laughing in a way that I could only feel was calculated to disturb, unsettle his neighbors. My family, in particular, I came to believe . . . perhaps only out of fearful paranoia. But did he see me peeking nightly around my shade at his windows? Was he peeking around his shades at me, when his lights were out? I can still remember his abrupt, booming, deliberate laugh—"Ha . . . Ha . . . Ha . . . Ha!" Each part of it unnaturally spaced out . . . those spaces between more chilling than the sudden, barking sound itself.

When the old woman died, the miniature sanitarium was emptied of both her belongings and her inmates. I remember my father somehow acquired a few of her things, and offered to me a pair of tacky Japanese fans. I declined them . . . horrified at what diseased energies might have soaked into them.

And yet, when my father told me how little the small house was going for, now it was on the market, my negative feelings toward it began to change. By this time, I lived in my own apartment across town, a sterile few rooms, depressing as a cell in themselves. My credit was good, and I was engaged, and my fiancée and I decided to take advantage of this opportunity quickly, before someone else acted on it. She was close to my family emotionally, and didn't seem to mind the prospect of being so close to them physically.

I bought the house. It would be tough, but if I could handle it alone until that June, my new wife would be living with me and adding her income to my own. Our wedding would be modest, but it was worth the sacrifice, not having to live in a slightly larger version of that sterile cell I occupied.

To save more money, we took to doing most of the renovations in the house ourselves. The simpler things, at least; some plumbing and electrical matters were beyond my abilities. But Lynn and I painted the outside of the small house, and stripped the age-darkened, water-stained wallpaper inside to paint the walls instead.

I was alone when I began to strip the wallpaper from the upstairs bedroom.

Lynn was at work that afternoon; I had called in sick with one of my frequent, agonizing headaches. But I had become restless watching TV downstairs, and thought I might at least make the day productive in some small way. And I had been relishing the thought of tearing away that room's particularly ugly paper: jagged, swirling paisley designs like an orgy of psychedelic tadpoles.

Instantly, something seemed amiss, as my blade tore through the discolored paper and seemed to skid upwards almost out of my control. The action caused my entire hand to slip under the paper as if into the belly of some beast I was flaying. I took hold of the flap of old paper, and tore a large strip of it free from the wall.

Beneath it, the wall had an odd character. It was dark, smooth where the blade had scraped away what little dry paste still remained. It was not plaster, beneath, but some slab of metal or glass that had been papered over many years before.

I used my tool again to dig under more of the paper, and clear more of the crumbling residue of paste. I peeled off more long strips by hand. I expected to find that the smooth slab comprised only a limited section of the wall. Instead, as more and more of the wall was cleared, I came to realize that this entire wall, running the entire length of the room, was made of that smooth dark material.

And now, I had decided that it was in fact glass. A great single sheet of it, of a deep red color so dark that at first I mistook it for black. But there was a distant light glowing behind the glass wall. Not the glow of an electric light, but of sky. And as I cleared more and more of the paper and paste away, incredibly, I saw the glow grow softly brighter until I realized that what I was seeing behind the glass wall was the coming of dawn. Even as outside the windows of the room, night was falling.

I nearly stumbled downstairs. Ran around to the side of the house, staring up at where that wall would be situated. But there were no windows in that length of wall, to let in light from streetlamps or elsewhere that I might be mistaking for a dawning glow. Solid wooden slats, freshly painted by Lynn and myself.

I returned to the house, putting on every light along my way. The steps of the gloomy staircase creaked. Entering the bedroom, I put on the lights, but they reflected in a glare on the glass surface. When I put them out I could see that the glow was ever strengthening, streaking a sky free of the tree and roof tops of Eastborough.

Gingerly, reluctantly, I went to the wall. Cupped my hands around my face, and pressed it against the cool surface.

It was a barren terrain, beyond. Not desert, but blasted, strewn with rubble, twisted wire and jagged metal, as if an atomic blast had leveled a city to just the rubble of rubble. Here and there a thorny bit of scrub wavered almost imperceptibly in the faint breeze. A dead leaf from some unseen tree would tumble lazily along in the air, black against the gashes of red cloud. Everything red, as if I gazed through an aquarium window into an ocean of blood.

And then, I realized that it was an ocean.

The leaves tumbling before the desolate vista were not blown on a breeze, but floating along in deep, nearly still waters, the scrub swaying in a gentle undertow. But then, what was that light spreading from the horizon, rather than coming from above?

I backed away from the spectacle, so that again all I could really make out was the crimson strata of clouds, the landscape again lost in gloom. I backed into the opposite wall, and then I jumped away from it, whirled around as if it might engulf me, my bladed implement held like a knife before me. Electricity buzzing through my body, surging in my guts, I advanced on this other wall and dug my blade under the paper there, too. But beneath the paper on this wall was only white plaster. I discovered the same was true of the other walls. The miracle was confined to just one wall of the bedroom of the Screaming Man.

The windows of his room were now black. But the wall of red glass . . . it was now so luminous with dawn's light that I could make out the silhouettes of ruin and debris and eerily waving vegetation even from across the room.

And further . . . I now began to detect other distant shapes silhouetted against the red horizon.

I floated to the wall. As I neared it, I saw its red glow on my shirt front, on my hands. The glow now softly illuminated the entire room.

I was terrified to press my face to the glass again. I was in a state like shock, like a waking faint. The fear in my belly was so great that I had to gag back a retch of nausea. My parents were in the next house, and I wanted to run to them, but I was so in awe of the red glass wall that I was too frightened to turn my back on it. And I felt almost a masochistic compulsion to find out what those new shapes were emerging from the distance.

I returned my face to the glass, again cupped my hands around it.

They were floating a bit off the blasted floor of rubble, carried on some slow current or tide. Dark forms, upright, without limbs. They were leaf-shaped, and so terribly still as the current drew them nearer and nearer . . . nearer to the red glass wall.

Again I backed away.

This time I lunged out into the hall, descended several steps, gripping the creaking banister for support, as if it were the railing of a platform miles above some seething volcanic pit. I must call Lynn, who would be home from work by now. Beg her to come over here. I couldn't bear this alone. And if I was insane, then I had to know that. I desperately hoped I was not sane. And yet, I was too stricken to move. I was too afraid to step outside into the dark of night to descend the driveway of my parents' house. Even that short distance was now a gulf of impossible mystery, with all the unknown cosmos yawning infinitely above. For a while I remained totally paralyzed, my sense of reality so decimated that a single step might hurl me into some whirling vortex.

At last, I turned and gazed back at the open doorway to the bedroom. The red light glowed on the mildewed wallpaper of the hall landing. It beckoned me. Slowly, I ascended one step. Another . . .

I stepped into the bedroom of the Screaming Man.

But I froze in the threshold as if I had been caught in a powerful electric charge. My hands seized the doorframe and the air hissed out of my throat, and I was suddenly so terrified that it was as though I had simply been mildly anxious, before . . . so terrified that tears literally rolled from my eyes and I heard my own voice whimpering like that of a child awakened from a nightmare and too afraid to call out for his parents. But I had not awakened from a nightmare, but into one.

The infernal, alien landscape was hidden now behind a wall of figures crowded up against the glass, living figures mashing their flesh against its surface so that it was bent and flattened horribly. There were so many of these figures that they stretched off to the formerly barren horizon, a sea of them at the bottom of this red sea. Pressed together, unmoving, thousands if not millions. And all gazing through the glass wall at me.

They had no limbs, their bodies elliptical, and red, glistening, with rows of ribs showing starkly under the thinnest sheath of skin. They looked like half-

PAW '01

dissected things, prehistoric invertebrates—I am put in mind of the planarian—and I wish I could believe that they were that primitive. But . . . those silent glaring faces. Blank, hardly human, barely even animal. Empty as they were, they conveyed a malign—unmistakable—intelligence. And worst of all, of course, the eyes. Because their eyes glowed. Glowed white, somehow, even through the deep red tint of the heavy glass wall. The white hot gaze of those unmoving multitudes upon me . . . pinning me . . . and yet enticing me to come closer to the wall. To pick up the hammer from my tool box. To swing the hammer . . . against the glass . . .

I don't know if the Screaming Man had been driven mad because he had somehow, consciously or not, summoned these things, opened this window— unseen by him behind the paper, but those gazes felt upon him—or if the window had opened and those things had gathered as a result of his existing madness.

But I hope to find him now. I hope to ask him what he knows.

I feel he's here in this complex with me somewhere. I have all the time in the world to find him. They think me crazy, you see, because they don't understand why I would have burned my new house to the ground. And there is no proof, because my tactics were successful: I destroyed that strange portal with cleansing fire. No one found a trace of it in the charred ruins of my new house. Just timbers, and empty window frames.

I'll find the Screaming Man. And I'll dig at the wall of his room, to see if he has attracted those hungry beings again.

And if he has, I will have to kill him . . . so that he does not let them into our world. And then, of course, I shall kill myself as well. For they have tasted my fear now, and been drawn to it.

They have both created—and hungered for—my own madness.

I MARRIED A SHOGGOTH

The ending of my story should be spoiled for you in one respect; since I'm narrating in the first person, it will be fairly obvious that I don't die at the end. However, consider me a survivor of a race car crash, who lost a few psychic limbs in the inferno. Now your morbid interest will be engaged. But I'm being bitter and cynical. Think of me, then, as a mountain climber, an explorer of new places, whose return to the mundane world is forever haunted by memories of dangerous terrain, and beauty. The dangerous terrain was as much in my mind as it was in the pages of that book. And the beauty . . . ?

My story begins with fear. Now I am a factory worker. Then I was a pre-med student. The human body in death didn't stir fear in me. Revulsion, yes—skull dust kicked up by a bone saw is a taste that lingers in the mouth very unpleasantly for hours—but the dead can't hurt you. The dead can't laugh at you. The dead can't reject you. The dead don't toss their hair out of their eyes or swing their blue-jeaned asses when they walk, which they also don't. Naked dead women lying complacently before me don't move me. But when I was a pre-med student, that was the only kind that did lie before me. I was a virgin then. Maybe I still am. That's the question here, I guess.

A self-portrait at this point would be helpful in explaining much of my fear of my biological counterparts. I'm very tall, in a stooped sort of way, and gangly. I'm horse-faced and lantern-jawed, a possible reincarnation of Huntz Hall. Frankenstein was a common childhood nickname, and maybe a kind of premonition. Anyway, we are a very corporeally oriented culture. Material, obsessed with the random juxtaposition of molecules we call beauty. My own obsession is largely to blame for what happened. Tell me some less than beautiful woman somewhere wouldn't have had me. Maybe one still will, someday—if I ever feel ready for that. But our culture is constantly shoving fleshly beauty down our throats, and being the arrogant, immodest, greedy creatures that we Americans are, even a geek like me thinks he should have beauty in his bed.

Cavel had one. Cavel was my best "friend" in school. Why we were friends, I'm not entirely sure. He was good-looking, bold, outspoken, confident. Opposites attract. I guess he liked having a sorry case like me around to instruct and goad so that I could be like him, which he must have known was useless. I set off his greatness by contrast. For my part, I suppose his undeniable charisma held me. Though I did often like him, more often than not I found myself contemptuous of him. I really just wanted to be free of his hold.

Another reason I stayed, however, was Susan. Cavel's beauty. Not a movie star goddess beauty by any means, but perhaps the more enticing for her seemingly more accessible "human" beauty. I've always preferred flawed, idiosyncratic beauty even in celebrities. Sue was short and "Rubenesque" (as Cavel would both reassure and tease her, depending on his context and mood), very pale, blue-eyed, with a thick nest of naturally curly, naturally blond hair that killed me. Basically cheery and kind-hearted, she became more of a true friend to me than was Cavel. Sometimes we had lunch, went shopping or for a walk together without him. That was a good feeling.

He could be so cruel to her. Mean-spirited, was Cavel. He was what all young American men seem to want to be these days, aside from a cretinous rock star. When he would torment her in front of me, a favorite pastime of his, I would want to stab my dinner knife into his smug handsome face. At such times I would either pity her or despise her for her weakness and masochism. I suppose that she was held by his charisma too, poor thing . . . he obviously wanted to lower her self-esteem to the point where she felt she deserved his cruelty. Like I said, Cavel was so typical of our country. Of our species, actually . . . and gender.

Cavel had a sweet job in the university library, and it was he who first got me interested in the book. It wasn't like I'd never heard of it . . . I'm a townie, after all. But gone were the days when the book was displayed or permitted for study to just anybody who asked for permission. One night as the three of us sat over beers in the campus pub, Cavel told us how he had finally seen the legendary ancient book, and paged through it. He had also gotten his hands on related notes, documents, translations stored with it in its vault. He related the famous story, with great relish, of the time when three boys from the school stole the original manuscript and drove off with it. Their car was found flipped over and smashed, though what exactly they had hit was never determined. The three boys were decapitated in the crash . . . and the book, the *Necronomicon,* was recovered without so much as a drop of blood on it.

Can you imagine, Cavel said, grinning, the odds of three people being decapitated in one car? He'd never heard of such a thing. Neither had I, I admitted. And what had they struck? They were drunk, I reminded him. Cavel shook his head. If you ask me, he said, a shoggoth got them. That was the famous signature of a shoggoth killing. The head was unscrewed . . . like a bottle cap. What, of course I asked, was a shoggoth?

Oh, he was only too happy to share his weird enthusiasm, grinning all the while, voice lowered in a conspiratorial tone. Sue and I, ever his rapt audience, leaned close to listen.

According to the book, and to the documents of an Antarctic explorer who claimed to have visited strange ruins in 1930, the Earth was colonized by a race called the Old Ones before the inception of life on our planet. In fact, it was said that the Old Ones created the first life on Earth. This was done to insure a constant food source, though later life went on to evolve by itself more in the way we're familiar with. Also, the Old Ones introduced to the colonies a malleable blob-like creature called a shoggoth. These basically formless masses could be shaped and controlled in their movements by telepathic command, sort of like living silly putty. These were more or less the slaves and beasts of burden for the weird, semi-vegetable Old Ones.

After a time, the shoggoths seemed to gain in intelligence—a more dangerous attribute than the ability to alter one's shape—and finally the Old Ones had to go into battle against them in order to suppress and control them once again. This accomplished, the colonists went on to breed bigger and better shoggoths, capable of responding to vocal commands, and even to imitating their masters' voices.

Eventually the Old Ones regressed, went decadent. Died out—though the crazed explorer claimed not only to have seen the recently killed bodies of Old Ones . . . but the shoggoth that supposedly killed them. By sucking their heads off.

Of course Sue and I said we didn't believe a word of it. Cavel insisted that the explorer had been a rational man, and reading his story was chillingly convincing. He urged me to do so . . . he would photocopy the whole thing for me. His eyes twinkled at this invitation. Cavel seemed to be capable even of enslaving the light to him. Well, I am an open-minded person. I am fascinated by the unknown . . . though these attitudes might seem incongruous for a man of former medical aspirations. I told him I would read the manuscript after finals, when I'd have more time. Cavel then told me he would also include related passages photocopied directly from the *Necronomicon*.

*   *   *

Frankly, I aced the finals. So did Cavel. He gave me the materials, and about a week later I sat down with them. It didn't take long. I'm sure I was seized that first night . . . and that I was already—subconsciously—researching a specific subject within a few days. My inner self plotting on what it foolishly felt was my behalf. These secret intentions didn't suddenly crash into my forward mind, or even come to it in gradual wisps of awareness. They just smoothly, seamlessly flowed into it, undetected, and integrated themselves there, like cancer.

In my childhood I lived in books of mythology. How could I forget the feeling of opening a book and seeing in its depths untold possibilities? Transportation. Escape. Magic. I thought of the story of the sculptor who fell in love with his beautiful statue, which came to life . . . though as an adult I could no longer remember if that were an actual myth (a strange expression, actual myth) or just a movie.

Raw, unformed flesh. Raw potential. Waiting only for that command which would give it shape and purpose. No games. No silly, humiliating, primitive courtship dance. No pretense. No need to be handsome or rich or popular or a drug dealer or music star in order to touch the flesh of beauty . . .

Clay, waiting for the artist's caressing hands . . . the breath of life.

And then maybe the clay would be able to breathe some life into me.

I asked Cavel to show me more. He was only too happy to oblige me, perversely enjoying my mounting interests in the controversial readings that had captured his interests, though it was a little harder for him to get near the materials now with classes finished. I told him how fascinated I was by the insane notion that life on Earth was created initially by aliens, and particularly how they enslaved the things called shoggoths to do their bidding. Get me whatever you can on shoggoths, I told him . . .

He did. And now I saw him and Sue less and less as I remained in my apartment to read and study and decipher. To practice the pronunciation of impossible tongue-twister chants. I was convinced that these words, rather than being magic, per se—if pronounced properly, with the proper tone and rhythm—created a kind of resonant vibration, as is the intention of Buddhist chants. Capable, maybe, of piercing time and space? I was very careful not to combine any of these words in my practice, would only try one word, over and over, each day . . . though my impatience was growing. I began to feel the butterflies of a guy looking forward to his upcoming first blind date. Dread. And hope.

Only three weeks after the materials fell into my hands—or were placed there by the unknowing administrant of my fate, Cavel—I was ready to begin.

*   *   *

I didn't have a basement in which to carry out my experiments, or to lock something in if things went wrong. My apartment was the third floor of an old house near school, a married couple below—both second-shifters, luckily—and the two old widowed sisters who owned the building on the ground floor. The apartment was one huge room, with weird and interesting slanted walls and alcoves for my book shelves. Framed movie posters for *Eraserhead* and *Taxi Driver*. On the red linoleum floor between the kitchen area and the living room-bedroom was the insignia for a Miskatonic fraternity which had once occupied the house, looking like a necromancer's cabalistic circle. Or so it appeared now.

There were two incantations I had memorized; one for the "ascending" mode, or summoning, and the "descending" mode, for banishing. This was pretty much the first one spelled backwards, but for the word *Yog-Sothoth*, present the same way in both. I had taped my voice chanting the descending incantation over and over. I didn't have a gun, or any other weapon. If I couldn't control this visitor, I planned to switch on the tape and flee the house immediately . . . then probably to go beg cool, confident Cavel to bail me out.

Who was I to think that I could control this thing, I wondered on that night, as I prepared to begin. I didn't have the telepathic abilities of the Old Ones, and even they had had to war the shoggoths to beat them back into submission. But of course I had come too far. In this state of mind, I was prepared to risk my life . . . maybe my soul. Willing to risk releasing a dangerous entity into our world. That's how primitively hungry our bodies can be. And that was the most frightening part of the whole thing . . .

It was raining out, the air was charged—lightning flashed in the distance. I hoped it wouldn't come this way. If the power were to go out in the midst of things . . .

I lit candles throughout the apartment. I had every electric light on, too. Now I was ready. Trembling, feeling nauseous, I stood on that frat symbol, facing toward my sleeper sofa, and began speaking aloud for the first time the ascending chant from a paper in my hands. I wanted to sit down, so boneless and bloodless my legs felt, but couldn't permit that. I was a step from the tape recorder and three from the door.

At the end of the incantation . . . there was nothing. Some mispronunciation? A different pitch needed? On the tape I had tried numerous variations, not trusting to get it right the first time. I was both disappointed and relieved that nothing had happened . . . but I started again. It was hard to think clearly enough to try variation. At the end of the second round: nothing. I was a fool. Maybe this was what Cavel had wanted, as a perverse joke . . . for me to be standing here alone trying to summon up magical powers while he was off somewhere making love to Susan. Revenge. Surely he had caught me looking at her, dreams in my eyes. He flaunted her before me, to tease me. He encouraged us to go places without him. To tease me. How could I have let his mean-spirited humor lead me into . . .

It came.

I had just finished the third attempt, and perhaps the doubts had taken the fear out of my voice. Maybe the anger behind the words had done it . . .

But it was here. No strobes or lasers, no dry ice or thunder clap. There was a sudden chill, but I realized that was coming from its body. It had come from a very cold place. Also, water ran down its body onto the old living room carpeting. It was huge; fifteen feet around. Loosely spherical, it looked to be made up of huge bubbly cells clinging together like soap suds . . . but black. It had an oil-slick's multi-hued iridescence. There were none of the temporary organs, limbs or eyes they could manifest, thank God. I had feared that it might try mimicking the terrible form of the Old Ones, as they could. It was not even amorphous, really, as it was said they were; ameba-like. It kept to that rubbery spherical form, and in fact it didn't move but for a subtle pulsation. I realized why, when my fear leveled off to a manageable degree (my first desire, besides letting my bladder go, of course, had been to hit the tape player and run). It was waiting to be told what to do.

I had succeeded.

*   *   *

For an hour or so I just observed it, finally making myself a cup of coffee (decaf; I was shaken enough), but keeping my eyes on it. The frigid cold no longer came misting off it, and in its place was a horrible odor, rotten fruitish, dead animalish, and fishy. That could prove quite the problem, but I'd worry about it later. It just remained there throbbing. As I drew a little closer to it with my coffee, I began talking to it. Throughout, this helped me focus better than trying to think commands at it, except on certain occasions later when I grew more daring. I decided to be honest, up front and respectful, but kept my voice firm.

Your function here, I told it, is to as flawlessly as possible imitate the form of a human female. You may be required to imitate *numerous* human females, but you will not change shape in any other way, and never change except when I tell you. You will live here with me. If I leave here for a time you must not leave this room. You must never attempt to imitate the human voice, or any other, never have contact with anyone unless I prompt you. You must never attempt to reproduce. (The shoggoths reproduced by parthenogenesis, being neither male nor female.) You will never attempt escape, rebellion or to harm others. You will never harm me. You need me to send you back home one day. I will do that some day . . . I don't know when. Hopefully one day soon. And I promised it that.

This is the female form, I instructed it. Observe. I activated my VCR. I had been making this tape for two weeks. Bits of this and that. Movies. Talk shows. Sit-coms. Game shows. Aerobics. MTV. I sat and watched the tape also, so that it could simultaneously read *my* perceptions of the subject matter. Also, for weeks, I had rented porn flicks, and copied excerpts from them onto the tapes. I sat there remembering the few girls I had kissed, what it had felt like. I smelled the skin of my arm, touched my hair and smelled that. I had poured over my anatomy books, and been especially intent over my dissection notes. The thing would need to approximate an inner structure to some extent to give the outer accurate form and movement. I was going to put my tongue and my fingers and penis inside it. I didn't want to be met by anything bubbly and black in there.

At first I was horrified to see that it had manifested dozens of luminous,

PAW '00

pupilless green eyes all over it, blinking in and out of existence, the better to observe, but I didn't try to discourage it. Its intentions appeared obedient. I began to have doubts about its size—could it compact that bulk into the size of a much smaller human female, and if so, would she be of normal human weight? I envisioned a fifteen foot tall woman, or a five foot tall one who weighed hundreds of pounds. Maybe I'd have to have it split into two women at once. I banished these thoughts; I had to be careful of my imagination.

The tape ended. I spoke to it some more, softly, while I paged through those magazines and books I had collected, even before this project, which contained the most evocative imagery of women I had been able to capture. I had no true memories of sex to feed it, but for movies and fantasies and *Penthouse* letter columns. It would have to do . . .

It began, suddenly, to flex its muscles.

A human arm tore out of the blob, thrusting and grasping at the ceiling. Another burst from one side; this one was the arm of a black woman. Another. A naked leg slipped out, the foot thumping the floor in a nervous spasm. A bulge, the bulge ripped open, a woman's head emerged, her eyes rolling. I recognized her as a porn actress. She had on makeup, her hair dry and fluffy. One arm's fingers had nail polish. At least it seemed to know that clothes and jewelry were separate objects, and didn't reproduce them.

The mass was alive with writhing limbs, heads peering out then being sucked back in, insane pulsations and ripplings as though an orgy were taking place within it. It was all pretty alarming a display, and I raised my voice to the creature . . . told it to stop. One woman at a time, not all this. It died down and stopped at last, and I realized then that it had only been testing its abilities, or something to that effect. I let out a shaky breath, trembling and hugging myself. Good, I told it. Now just one woman at a time . . . I put on a new video tape. Opened new magazines and books. Focused my mind on one woman.

Within a half hour, the black bubbly mass split open again . . . but this time, it tore deeply down the middle and began to turn its halves inside out. The inner surfaces of the halves tore further and the wounds were pink. The pink areas spread as the mass turned in on itself again and again, like a storm cloud brewing, until all the mound was a fleshy pink. Its previous iridescence suggested the ability to isolate and expand on any number of colors. Now the shapeless, tormented-looking flesh seemed to be shrinking rapidly . . . but was in fact contracting, drawing itself into a more compact bundle. The bundle became smooth as hideous wrinkles were ironed away, and I was now staring at a human woman—naked—rolled into a ball on elbows and knees, head tucked in, shiny bottom in the air.

The blonde head lifted, and Marilyn Monroe looked at me with her bedroom eyes. She smiled dreamily.

unholy dimensions

*   *   *

Marilyn was never one of my real favorite celebrity beauties, but I felt almost obligated to manifest her, particularly as the very first sculpture, powerful American icon that she is. Cavel loved Marilyn, too. I felt kind of smug about that.

I didn't take her to bed right away, of course. I watched her a good couple of hours while I made myself more decaf and tried to screw up my strength. Rather than being impatient to begin, I wasn't sure I could ever touch her. She sat in my armchair watching TV as I had instructed, occasionally smiling over at me. Chills went through me . . . of both fear and delirious excitement. She wore my bathrobe. She had crossed one leg over the other without my conscious command. Beauty mark and all. My God . . .

At last I decided to wait until tomorrow. It was very late and I was tired. I told her to sleep on a blanket on the bathroom floor, then I put a chair with stacked cans of food atop it in front of the closed door as an alarm. I slept with the tape recorder in bed with me.

The next day my phone awoke me but I didn't answer it. Tape recorder under my arm, I stalked the bathroom door. The chair was undisturbed. She waited on the floor for me in a fetal position but with eyes open, turning up toward me . . .

I had breakfast, then walked to the armchair where it was sitting again and gingerly reached out to it. I lay my hand on her shoulder, round and firm under the robe. I could feel bone in there. She looked up to smile at me again, and I told her to go to the bed . . .

I was a virgin, as I have said. Even as I write this I'm not sure I really know what it's like to make love with a woman. But it was—as it could only be—as I had imagined it. And it was wonderful. As frightening as clinging nude to the face of a cliff, without ropes, without comrades, and yet it was wonderful. She read my mind. She knew what I wanted and needed. The ultimate blow-up doll. Play Dough of the Gods.

*   *   *

That week I went to bed with the Jane Fonda of *Barbarella*. Young actresses like Drew Barrymore, Reese Witherspoon and the terminally busty and cute Jennifer Love Hewitt. Voluptuous silent screen vamp Theda Bara and the rail-thin singer Fiona Apple. The exquisite British actress Helena Bonham Carter, my favorite, lasted three whole days before I traded her for a vintage Marilyn Chambers (I told myself I'd go back to Helena, maybe settle on her, later). I called up a beautiful Asian woman from a magazine ad. It was always better, though, if I had seen movies, many views of a body or face, for maximum detail. When I summoned the stunning actress Nastassja Kinski, she had the naked body I had seen in films from the eighties, that mole on her shoulder and the little scar on her cheek from a girlhood accident while playing with a knife. The Asian girl, however, had a modified Marilyn Chambers body, lean and with her muscular neck, but in Asian skin tones. This body for the face was selected not by me, but by the creature from its files.

I made a frightening mistake by asking it to take the form of a Renoir nude. What began to manifest itself looked more like a three-dimensional painting than a living thing, and I quickly told it to go back to the previous model, Brooke Shields. She was the first to sleep throughout the entire night beside me. When I woke up the next day, I saw that she had left the bed.

She was at the stove, turning up the heat under the coffee pot. She looked over at me and smiled. As on that first night, I was both thrilled and washed with fearful awe. Where did my subconscious programming end and the creature's personality, as such, begin? Was its own personality all but gone, leaving only a mindless robot, or were those smiles in any way authentic in their sentiments? I found that hard to believe. But what of this? Had my dreaming mind told it to rouse and make coffee? Was it imitating me? Or was it trying . . . to please me?

I decided that night to grow daring, as I earlier mentioned. I took TV star Alyssa Milano out to dinner.

I half expected her to make a scene; eat the lobster's shell, so to speak, like Darryl Hannah's mermaid in *Splash*. She was, however, quite well behaved, and ate her meal slowly and delicately. I thought my commands at her, and I had told the waitress my date was deaf. It was extremely gratifying to note the looks of men at neighboring tables, stealing glimpses when their own women were looking elsewhere. Alyssa was gorgeous in the dress I had bought her for the occasion. Thus far, my women had had to wear my robes, pajamas, my T-shirts and sweat pants and the like. I would have to do more shopping. Anyway, the night was a success. I took her to a movie after and held her warm hand throughout it. She squeezed my hand from time to time.

The phone was ringing when I got back. I knew I should answer it, but I just didn't want to be disturbed.

The next day Alyssa melted and blurred, reshaped into a new woman before my eyes. It was inevitable, this one. Though I didn't know all the particulars of her body when naked, I knew the outer shape and her face and lovely curly blonde hair by heart. The shoggoth had no problem manufacturing Susan for me perfectly.

*   *   *

Susan remained with me for nine days straight. During that time I didn't call up another form once. In fact, I never did again. I think that if I had had the strength to keep to one form, Susan would have been it, even over Helena. But I doubt that any man could have had such power at his disposal and been content with only one woman. Such is human greed and hunger, as I have said.

Susan would wrap her legs across my lower back, as I had often dreamed, her putty face twisted in expressions of ecstasy which might not have been absolutely accurate, but judging from the creature's learning from porn flicks and its knowledge of Susan's common expressions, probably were dead on target. From its original miasmic soup of stinks it could isolate and fine-tune subtle and pleasing smells, even to the shampoo in her hair. Her skin smelled like skin, not of the black mass' fishy rot. She smelled musky under her arms, and sweated slickly with the exertion of our love-making. She had prickly gold hairs on her legs, as I had spied on Susan in shorts. Her breath came out hot and human on my vulnerable neck. Other than her acted breathing, however, she never made a sound. I could go deep inside her body, push my tongue in her mouth. And elsewhere if I wanted . . . but I wasn't ready for that yet.

It was a humid August day, our last day together, and school was nearing . . . my last year of pre-med. I dreaded going back to school, now. I resented the distraction . . . the intrusion. We lay naked on the sheets, a fan blowing on us, dozing to the low radio murmurs. That was how Cavel found us when he let himself in.

He had been trying to call, I'd learn in a few minutes, had asked the landladies for my key, concerned. But at the moment he was hissing swears and crossing the room toward us. No, no, I told him, sitting up. Susan sat up, too. Cavel got a handful of my hair and cocked his fist back. I cried out the words, *"Marilyn Monroe!"*

Now Cavel was swearing in the awe of sheer terror, as if the chanted curses would banish this creature which before his eyes transformed from his dominated girlfriend to his untouchable idol, Marilyn Monroe. It's a shoggoth, Cavel, I told him. Getting out of bed to take him by the arms, I began to tell him the story I'm telling you now. I don't think, despite his interest in those forbidden manuscripts, he really believed any of it until now. Finally he calmed. I told Marilyn to make us some coffee. Cavel marveled. He laughed deliriously and squeezed my arm. Said my name several times. We could rule the world, you know that? he told me. We could rule the world with powers like these.

Cavel asked me to turn the creature back into Susan. I asked him why, in a groan, but he persisted. I passed the order on, and he daringly stood within several feet of the creature to watch the shifting of plastic flesh, the reshaping of the subtlest details, called up from the photographic perfection of my subconscious memory. During this I dressed, then we three sat at the table.

Cavel's eyes twinkled at me. I felt eerily as I did when I sat with Cavel and the real Susan. And he felt it too. Why Susan? he asked me now. Huh, buddy? All the girls you can have, and you want your best friend's girl? I stammered, stuttered. I was just playing around. Every man wants to make love to his friend's girlfriend just once, right?

I'll forgive you for it, he promised. And I won't tell anyone about all this. On certain conditions. You and I will explore the powers of the manuscripts further—together. I have all I want, I told him. I don't, he said. But we'll go into that more, later. Sue is away this weekend visiting her folks, and I want to borrow your friend for company. After all, every man wants to make love to his friend's girlfriend just once, right?

I pleaded with him. I raised my voice, trembling. Susan meekly, resignedly watched us, like the real Sue. Prepared to be dominated again. But hadn't I dominated her, too, just as Cavel always had? Hadn't I selfishly exploited her? Enslaved her?

In the end he was too strong for me. All my new found confidence fled. I could barely stand, I was so defeated. So humiliated. But I instructed Sue to go with Cavel for several days. To do whatever he said. She nodded. God, Cavel said. And then they left. And I cried at the table.

*   *   *

After two days, it was Cavel who didn't answer my calls. That night there was a thunderstorm. A pounding at my door. I opened it, and there stood Susan. Hair plastered. Clothing plastered. Susan's clothing. I said her name. She didn't respond. My God, I thought. I took her in.

It was in the papers the next day. Some of my questions about the extent of the creature's free will were answered. It had chosen to disobey my commands. It had rebelled. It hadn't done as Cavel had ordered. And it had hurt people. Cavel was found in his apartment by his sister—beheaded, his naked body smeared with an odd slime. The head had not been recovered.

Why it killed Susan also I can only speculate. Did she come in on them, and act in such a way as to alarm the creature? Or . . . I know this is stupid, but . . . might it have been jealous of her?

That night I told it I was sending it back. It looked at me strangely. I explained my reasoning to it. I didn't tell it I was angry for what it had done to poor Susan. I couldn't be, not really. *I* had done that.

We made love one last time, and then we took our places. It by our bed, me on the mysterious fraternity symbol. I couldn't remember the descending incantation, so I activated the tape recorder in my hands.

I regretted, as I watched it standing there watching me, not embracing it. Squeezing its hand as I had in the movie theater. But it was too late; the tape was underway. It waited. But it made no attempt to change into its actual form. It apparently waited until it was home. I'd like to think I know why . . .

Did my subconscious give it one final command? It tortures me not to know. Am I fooling myself to believe that—just before the naked figure vanished without fanfare, leaving me alone in that huge room, the sofa bed folded away—it was of the creature's own volition when she smiled dreamily at me, and mouthed the words, "Good bye"?

THE ICE SHIP

The men of the whaling schooner *Scylla*
Had witnessed a strange thing only the previous night
The great pale mass beneath Antarctic waters
Had taken two harpoons before sliding from sight
But the last thing observed of the silent leviathan
Was a nest of thrashing arms, serpentine and glowing white.

And now the *Scylla*'s men met another weird vision
Though once this vessel must have resembled their own
A schooner slowly emerged from behind a looming iceberg
Its ice-caked masts and lines like a framework of bare bone
Snow lay heavy on her deck and the sails were stirring rags
She drifted like an apparition, and her hull gave a creaking groan.

The men were afraid to explore her but the captain led the way
They rowed out to the spectral craft through a broken icy flow
She towered above the little boat like a palace made of crystal
A howling wind blew across her deck in swirling ghosts of snow
One by one they boarded her, and shivered at more than the cold
And the captain himself hesitated, before leading the rest below.

The ship's inside was a mausoleum that spoke of decades gone
But they found the corpses of the crew preserved by the frigid air
Like a cargo in themselves waiting long to reach their port
And in his cabin at his desk her captain sat with frozen stare
His log lay open and its words perplexed the *Scylla*'s men:
"*She* is no mermaid but a siren and pure evil, however fair."

One of the men yelled and the others rushed to the next room
There was a bed and on it a woman's naked body had been bound
The captain began to remark upon the life-like color of her flesh
When she lifted her head from the pillow and at them smiled around
"Free me from these chains," she whispered straight into their minds
"And I will grant you pleasures, as few live men have ever found."

But the men had seen those corpses and hurried up the stairs
Fled back to the *Scylla* without even learning the vessel's name
They returned later only long enough to pour precious kerosene
There are some stories even seamen won't give a legend's fame
None would ever tell how the siren pleaded in their skulls
As they sailed away, and watched the ice ship melt in flame.

SERVILE

The man who opened the door startled Gabrielle, so that she drew back her rapping knuckles as if a snake had bitten her hand. For one thing, he was a stranger, and for another he was striking in appearance. He was a black man, and literally that; he had the darker skin of an African who had not had his genes diluted by a single corpuscle of white blood. He was bald, and wore large dark glasses with lenses so opaque she wondered if he were blind. His black suit was expensive, and lent further impact to his tall, muscular frame. Gabrielle was not prejudiced—the man was an impressive, if dramatic, vision—but she had not been expecting anything like him at this familiar door.

"Hello," she stammered uncertainly in her British accent. "I'm Gabrielle Rumsey? Mrs. Wallace is expecting me?"

The black man stepped aside like a human door, with neither a word nor gesture. Gabrielle hesitated a moment, and then entered the house of her former employ. As she remembered it, the interior was dark and necessitated several seconds for her vision to adjust, as if she had entered one of the ancient tombs Dianna Wallace explored. Or, rather, had once explored.

he black man closed the door, and then held out one large hand to Gabrielle. For a beat she stared at it, afraid to touch it. But he wasn't offering his hand to be shaken, she realized, feeling foolish; he was offering to take her bag. With a nervous smile she handed it to him, and as she did so noticed something odd about his hand . . . something that had subliminally caused her moment of apprehension. The man's palm was as coal black as the top of his hand. She concluded that some Africans must not have lighter pigmentation on their palms. Perhaps it was a regional thing, a tribal characteristic.

She followed the man through the house, to Dianna's office at its far end. Gabrielle's unease had lessened now that she accepted the stranger as a servant and not some intruder, but there were other causes of unease that she did not expect to be so easily dismissed.

The servant opened the office door, and again stepped aside to grant Gabrielle entrance. She crossed the threshold, and gently he closed the door behind her, disappearing with her bag.

Dianna Wallace was slumped forward across the front of her desk, her head resting on crossed arms. She had returned to this country recently after having narrowly cheated death abroad. For a strange, desperate moment Gabrielle was afraid that Dianna had succumbed to death after all, here in her office—but she heard a faint intake of breath and realized her former employer was in a deep doze. Even from this distance, Gabrielle was shocked at Dianna's appearance. It had only been three years since Gabrielle had so abruptly left, but in that time Dianna seemed to have aged twenty years. Her handsome, strong-jawed face was haggard and lined; her once long, thick black hair was short and choppy like a boy's, streaked with gray.

And Gabrielle knew that it was in a wheelchair that Dianna was seated behind her expansive desk.

Gabrielle glanced about the room, not yet having ventured another step forward, partly afraid to wake Dianna. It hadn't changed much; it was an office, a study, a library whose walls were built-in book shelves full to overflowing, as if the room was in fact constructed from books alone. They were even stacked in the corners, covered several chairs.

The shades and curtains were drawn, but Gabrielle could still make out the artifacts that hung on those portions of the wall, and which stood on those sections of shelf, that the books had not claimed. There were Egyptian canopic urns, topped with the heads of animal-headed gods. Paleolithic hand axes, early Bronze Age daggers, a gallery of masks: a green-skinned woman from India, a narrow face with a six-pointed star in its forehead from Nigeria, masks from Sri Lanka, the Eskimos, the Cherokee. Their leering eyes, whether painted or empty holes, all made Gabrielle uncomfortable.

Yes, Dianna had taken souvenirs from her many travels, her many adventures as archaeologist, anthropologist, author. But her most recent, her last souvenir had been a bullet in the spine from an unknown source while on a trip to Tibet. Now her legs were of less practical value to her than these hollow visages on the walls.

But there had been some artifacts added in the past few years that Gabrielle had never seen. Most noticeably, to either side of the broad desk a sturdy table had been set. And atop these flanking tables were identical plain stone cubes. The stone was of an odd pale violet color,   which almost seemed faintly phosphorescent. At last, Gabrielle took a number of steps further into the murky room. The cube on the right proved to be a basin, hollowed out from a single block of stone, but empty. The cube on the left, though of identical size and form, served as a pedestal for an odd sculpture. Gabrielle drew even closer to this table for a better inspection.

The sculpture was carved from a black stone as glossy as obsidian. It was an icon, a figure, a monster of some kind. The creature was like some perverse genetic splicing of a wild boar, a frog and an obese human male. Gabrielle found its incredible detail impressive, particularly if it had been rendered somehow from volcanic glass, but its realism made it far more unsettling than the abstracted masks around her. She found the icon repellent.

And yet it was mesmerizing. The hybrid's eyes were closed as if in sleep, and Gabrielle knew she was letting her imagination become far too agitated when she thought she saw the travesty's gross belly rise with a deep intake of breath.

She timidly reached out to touch the thing . . . as much to break her self-induced spell as to see if the sculpture was as glossy as it looked.

"Don't touch it!" a voice cried out.

Gabrielle withdrew her hand sharply for the second time that afternoon, her heart rocketing in her chest. She whirled to see Dianna's eyes upon her. They were wide and darting, as if she had just been startled, herself.

"I'm sorry, Dianna," Gabrielle stammered. "I . . . just never saw that piece before."

Dianna Wallace pushed herself as erect in her wheelchair as she could manage. She had composed her wild look, and even offered a wan smile, a shadow of her former grin. "I'm sorry, hon, I didn't mean to scare you. It's one of my most recent finds. He's called Tsathoggua."

"He looks like a sitting hog," Gabrielle joked, in regard to the name. "Is he some kind of god?"

"Compared to us he is," Dianna said, her smile taking on an odd taint. "You look enchanting, Gaby, as always. And don't waste your time telling me I look good. I know I don't."

"You don't," the petite young woman admitted, her lips pursed in an unhappy pout that she knew brought out the protective instinct in men, but it was a pout that men often inspired themselves.

"I'm so glad you agreed to come back. I need you now more than I ever did before. Back when you were a house-sitter, not a baby-sitter. I know you were reluctant . . ."

Gabrielle couldn't explain to Dianna the nature of her reluctance. The woman had suffered enough. Instead, she lied, "I just wasn't sure I could offer you the care you need. I'm a housekeeper, and I've been a   nanny . . . but don't you think a private nurse is what you need most?"

"I need my little Gaby back"

Gabrielle smiled shyly, and diverted the embarrassing compliment by asking, "Who is the guy with shades who showed me in?"

Dianna smoothed back her disheveled hair with both hands, turning her eyes to the curtained windows. "His name is Smith. He helps move me around, runs errands for me in my research, serves as a watchdog in case my would-be assassin has friends in the states, who don't realize that the nature of my research is benign. He won't be in your way, Gaby . . . you'll run the house as you see fit. But he is a mute, if you haven't noticed."

"Who would want to kill you in Tibet, Dianna?" Gabrielle asked, coming close to her employer and taking her hand. "Don't they have any leads?"

"I was following an esoteric path of study, hon," Dianna replied softly, squeezing the young woman's small hand as if she were a child. "Something I had never even heard rumors of before. A kind of ancient cult. And the sniper proved to me that the cult still exists, and takes its religion very seriously."

"And what religion is that?"

"The worship of the Dreaming One."

"Who is the Dreaming One?"

"Tsathoggua."

Gabrielle glanced behind her again at that fat toad/warthog/human, seated like some obscene Buddha atop the block of violet stone.

"They were trying to kill me, but they didn't. I can't explore the way I once did . . . but I've found a way that's even more exciting. It's like exploring the bottom of the ocean, exploring space. And better than either. More frightening. More exhilarating . . ."

Gabrielle thought Dianna was referring to her involved computer set-up, which dominated most of the desk top. The internet, the web that now linked a world it had taken bygone explorers months, years to traverse.

"I'm glad you haven't let this stop you," the young woman said awkwardly, trying not to sound patronizing. "You have the right kind of attitude to fight this . . ."

"I can't fight what's happened to my body. And I don't care to. My mind is free. I can still dream." Dianna's eyes had taken on a kind of wildness again, and it was unnerving. She had always been obsessive about her work, and Gabrielle had always admired her for that. But this seemed different. This was the look of a zealot. A fanatic. As if she had joined some strange sort of cult, herself.

Gabrielle squeezed the woman's hand again. "Can I get you some tea?"

"Yes, darling, that would be wonderful. That ass of a husband of mine can't even boil water to save his life."

A flicker went through Gabrielle's face at the mention of Mr. Wallace, but her smile only faltered a second. "I'll go make you a pot."

"It's good to have you back here, my little Gaby," Dianna told her.

"It's good to be back," Gabrielle replied, only half truthfully.

* * *

Gabrielle was setting out a tray to bring to Dianna when she sensed a presence enter into the kitchen behind her. The flesh of her nape prickled, and she turned—expecting to see the mute bodyguard Smith looming there. Instead, it was someone who unsettled her even more. A handsome white man, bearded, with longish dark hair and a wide grin. Kevin Wallace held a glass of liquor in his hand. He didn't care for tea.

"Hello, Gaby," he said.

Gabrielle turned back to her duties, murmured, "Hello." She heard Dianna's husband move a little closer behind her.

"You look as lovely as I remembered you. I missed you."

Gabrielle said nothing aloud, but to herself she said that this was a mistake, her returning here, a terrible mistake.

"I know you're hurt," Wallace cooed. His soft voice at the back of her neck, though several feet away, felt like a dirty caress.

"I'm not hurt," she replied coldly. "It wasn't me you hurt, but your wife."

"Di isn't hurt, Gaby. At least, not by us. How could she be? She never found out."

"If she knew, she'd be hurt. And she'd hate me. As much as I hate you."

"Well, that's convenient, isn't it?" Wallace said with amusement, sipping his drink. "You're a victim, and I'm some evil seducer? I don't recall raping you, Gaby. I seem to recall that you were quite . . . amorous toward me, at first."

Gabrielle turned to glare at the man. "I was nineteen. I was stupid. I made a stupid mistake. I betrayed the best friend I had. I was sorry about what I did . . . I felt guilt, and pain. I still do. But you . . . you don't. You betrayed your wife and you feel nothing. That's why I hate you."

"Oh come on, Gaby, you know it's more complicated than that. You hate me because I didn't give up Dianna for you."

"I never wanted that!"

"You fantasized about it. You had to have."

"Listen to me, Kevin," Gabrielle hissed. "I'm here to help my friend. To make up for my betrayal, whether she's aware of it or not. But you are not invited to make any attempts to seduce me again. I won't stay here if you do . . . and you'll only be hurting Dianna. You'll only make it so that she has to hire someone else. Can you be that cruel to her?"

"Gaby," Wallace said, drawing nearer, causing Gabrielle to back into the counter. "I never stopped thinking about you. To be honest, I would leave Dianna for you now. I should have done it three years ago, when I lost you and thought I'd never see you again."

A sneer came to the young woman's face. "You should have been an actor, Kevin. Of course you'd love to be with me now . . . now that your wife is paralyzed from the waist down. You're vile, you know that? You're absolutely vile."

"Listen . . ."

Gabrielle took up the tray and whisked past him. "Don't talk to me any further, Mr. Wallace. Unless you want some tea." And with that she was gone from the kitchen.

Kevin Wallace watched after her, and sighed, smiling bitterly. "Coffee, tea or me," he muttered, and looking up saw the black man Smith standing at the other end of the kitchen. He must have just come up from the cellar. Wallace hated the man; always sneaking around quiet as a shadow. Mockingly, Wallace saluted him with his drink. The black man only stood regarding him a moment, and then drifted out of the room as well.

*   *   *

"She sleeps a lot these days," Wallace remarked, watching Gabrielle emerge from Dianna's office the next day. She carried a tray containing a barely eaten meal. As Gabrielle walked briskly toward the kitchen he kept up with her, and went on, "Did she tell you about her new . . . research?"

"Not really," Gabrielle answered, eyes ahead.

"I'm a bit concerned about her. I think she might be better off elsewhere, under more professional care."

Gabrielle stopped to glower at the man. "You had better not mean institutionalized!" she snapped.

"You haven't heard her mad talk. She's afraid to disturb you with it, as she has me."

Gabrielle glanced back at the closed office door, and then whispered, "Come into the kitchen . . ."

When both were well out of range of Dianna's hearing, her husband explained, "She swears she's exploring in dreams, Gaby . . . the world of dreams. I understand why she would be drawn to this notion. A woman who once traveled every corner of the world, and now can't even cross the room easily, but that doesn't mean it's a healthy delusion."

"You're misinterpreting her! She must mean she's studying dreams, interpreting them, like Jung . . . finding cultural similarity in dream symbology, or . . . or exploring the idea of the collective unconscious . . ."

"Ah, nnno. According to Di, there is something like a collective unconscious. But it's a dream world, that most of us only glimpse, and not too clearly. But Di swears she's taught herself to enter her consciousness into this world. To send her spirit, her astral self into this place to explore it. She says it isn't so much a dream world, Gaby . . . as another dimension."

Gabrielle gaped at the man, horrified that these ugly accusations might be true. She remembered the fanatical sheen she had witnessed in Dianna's eyes. "She can't mean literally," she protested. "She must mean . . ."

"Quite literally. She says she's been to a place called N'Kai, which is deep inside the Earth . . . or a variation on our Earth. She says she's trying to find her way back again, to learn more, but her first trip took a lot out of her. And that much, at least, is true. One night I heard her gagging in her office, retching . . . being sick. I ran in and saw her on the floor, where she'd fallen out of her wheelchair. She was vomiting into her trash basket."

"Did you call a doctor?"

"Yes. A doctor came out the next morning. She was all right, considering. But it was very alarming, Gaby. And her vomit . . . well, not to nauseate you, but it was black as oil. And when I tried to take the bucket to dump it out she wouldn't let me. I persisted but she threw such a fit that I was afraid for her, so I left it alone. I don't know what she wanted it for, or what became of it. Or what it was. I wish she had shown it to the doctor the next day, but . . ."

"My God . . ."

"Yes. And shortly after that she hired that Smith person. I don't know where she found him, and I took the liberty of checking our accounts to see what she pays him, and as far as I can see he works for nothing but a room to sleep in. He runs errands for her sometimes. He brought her those two purple stone tubs in her office."

"Oh . . . poor Dianna."

"So you understand my dilemma? Don't be so quick to label me a fiend, Gaby. What would you consider doing, in my position?"

"I'd like to talk to her about all this . . ."

"To see if I'm telling the truth about her delusions?" Wallace swept his arms theatrically. "Be my guest. Maybe you can talk some sense into her, huh? Maybe you can get through to her. Myself, I'm at a total loss." He touched his fingers to her arm. "I'd appreciate whatever you could do for her."

Gabrielle slipped away from the contact. "I'll do what I can. For her . . . not for your sake. You don't deserve her."

Wallace grinned. It was as repulsive to her as that icon in Dianna's study. "I always had the feeling that Di liked you yourself, Gaby. In much the same way I do, I mean. Is it possible that you feel the same way toward her?"

"You disgust me, Mr. Wallace." Gabrielle again left him in the kitchen, and he smirked at her smartly moving buttocks as she headed for the office at a determined clip.

*   *   *

Through Dianna's closed office door came a weird atonal piping, frenzied in pace as if part of some primitive ritual full of rapture and dance. A recording of something from her travels, Gabrielle decided, rapping on the panel. Somehow she was heard over the disturbing racket, which abruptly ceased. She heard the door unlock, and there stood the impassive Mr. Smith behind his impenetrable sunglasses. He let Gabrielle in, then departed.

"Come in, hon," Dianna said from behind her desk.

Gabrielle did so, but froze after a step.

The idol of the Dreaming One, Tsathoggua, was missing from atop his stone base. In fact, the base itself was missing, replaced by another stone basin to match the empty basin on the other table. Except this tub was not empty. It was, instead, filled to the brim with an opaque fluid, dark as squid's ink.

"Where's the statue of our chubby friend?" Gabrielle joked, gesturing at the receptacle.

Dianna seemed to hesitate, and then answered, "There was no statue."

101

"Of course there was. You told me not to touch it."

"That's what you saw, there," Dianna said, also gesturing at the basin.

Gabrielle approached to peer into it. It was indeed a vile-looking black liquid. As black and as shiny as the icon had been. It was as though the statue had been made of black wax, and then melted into this pool. As if this hollow tub, and not a solid base, had been below the statue all along.

"You must have heard it playing for me," Dianna went on. "I'm its master, now."

Gabrielle looked up at her friend, a weighty ache of compassion in her chest. Yes, that bastard Kevin was right; Dianna *was* insane . . .

"Whose master are you, Dianna?"

"The spawn serve me, now. The formless spawn of Tsathoggua. I brought that creature there back from N'Kai with me. I carried it inside my astral self . . ."

The vomit, Gabrielle realized with a woozy shiver. The basin was now filled with the black vomit she had refused to let Kevin dispose of. But how could there be so much? Had she been accumulating it over weeks?

"Kevin . . . Mr. Wallace told me you've been . . . you feel you've been exploring a sort of . . . alternative plane," Gabrielle managed.

"Yes," Dianna said, nodding eagerly to see that her friend was sympathetic to her, willing to listen. "I've seen . . . *wonders* . . ."

"You saw Tsathoggua."

Dianna visibly shuddered, averted her gaze. "Yes. And I lived . . ." She intoned this last as if that in itself were the marvel. "He had his sleep imposed upon him by the other gods . . . the Elders. So, we who would otherwise be mere insects to him can instead serve him a purpose. We can be his eyes. We can be his consciousness in the waking world." Dianna returned her stare to her young friend. "I serve him, Gaby, as you serve me. His followers in our world tried to kill me . . . but now I've become one of them."

"This Smith," Gabrielle said, trying to remain calm, "does he bring you drugs, Dianna? Does he . . . ?"

"What I tell you is true, hon. Believe me. I know it isn't easy. I stood before the Dreaming One. His mind spoke to mine. He sat dreaming on his throne of carven rock, miles below the surface. The bones of his sacrifices heaped all around him. The sacrifices sustain him in his long hibernation . . .

"To either side of him were great basins filled with his spawn. They're amorphous . . . like protoplasm . . . primordial soup . . . primal clay. They are what you will them to be, taking any shape. He gave me my own, to take back with me . . ."

Gabrielle drew away from that inky pool in the basin. Had she heard it gurgle, softly?

"Gaby, I wouldn't trust many people with this knowledge. I told Kevin, and

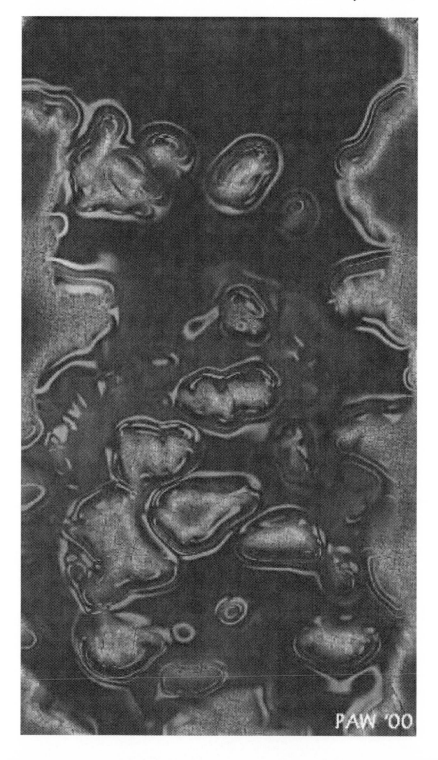

it was a mistake. He thinks I've lost my mind. But I trust you . . ."

"Dianna . . ."

"I know you slept with Kevin. But I don't blame you for it, my dear girl. You were young, he took advan—"

"Who told you that?" Gabrielle burst out in an angry, helpless sob. "He told you, didn't he? To hurt you, and hurt me . . . to ruin our friendship!"

"Shh," Dianna said soothingly, her smile maternal, "shh, baby. I told you. I forgive you. It isn't important. And it wasn't Kevin who told me, but Smith . . ."

"I thought . . . I thought you said he was mute," Gabrielle sobbed, lowering her teary eyes in shame and self-loathing.

"It isn't important. What is important is that Smith told me that he heard Kevin speaking to his brother on the phone. His brother is a clinical psychologist, Gaby. Kevin is talking about declaring me incompetent. About committing me to a hospital. You can't let him do that to me, all right? I have so much else to learn! So much else to see! The Tower of Koth! Celephaïs! The castle of the Great Ones on the mountain of Kadath! You have to tell him I'm not mad, Gaby . . . you have to tell him you believe me!"

"But I don't believe you!" Gabrielle blurted. "I'm sorry, Dianna, I'm so sorry for everything . . . but how can you expect me to believe any of this?"

"You have to believe me!" Dianna cried, her eyes bulging alarmingly. "You have to listen! Let me show you! I'll show you what my spawn can do . . ." And with that she reached across the desk, pointing to the basin of fluid.

But Gabrielle could take no more, turned and darted from the room, sobbing even harder. Above her own sobs, however, as she dashed through the door, she could swear she heard a burbling sound rising from that faintly luminous basin.

*   *   *

Gabrielle remained in her room for several hours. She paced, biting her nails until the skin around them bled, expecting that at any instant Dianna would rap at her door. Or worse—perhaps—Kevin. But no one came to fetch her, no one called for her, and at last she stealthily cracked her door.

At the end of the hall was the door to Smith's room. She paused, struggling with herself, and then crept down the hall to listen outside it. No sound from within, but then the man made no sound even when in plain sight. She drew a deep breath to steel her nerves, and then cracked the door as she had her own. Smith was not inside the small room, so she slipped through the door, eased it shut behind her. She prayed he would not return in the middle of her snooping.

He must have been part of the cult that had tried to kill Dianna, and had been brainwashing her either with drugs or otherwise, preying upon her vulnerability since her traumatic experiences in Tibet. Even though Kevin had said Smith arrived after Dianna's strange behavior had already begun, Gabrielle could not rule out Smith's silent influence over her friend.

His bed looked unslept in, as neatly made as if he had served in the military. The closet held a few more suits and ironed shirts, the bureau neatly folded underwear and socks, all identical. No personal belongings in the sense of photographs, papers. The only object that gave Gabrielle pause was a glass of water by the bed. It contained a full set of dentures. And then she noticed, folded beside the glass, Smith's pair of dark glasses.

She stole from the room, having found no drugs, no weird literature. Despite how much her last meeting with Dianna had unsettled her, Gabrielle knew she must go look in on her. Dianna needed to eat. Dianna needed tending to. However frightening her ranting, Gabrielle must go to her, help her the best she could. It seemed impossible that she could salvage anything of the once brilliant woman before her husband could have her committed to some Dante's purgatory of a psych ward, but she must try .

*   *   *

As she moved through the large house in the direction of Dianna Wallace's office, Gabrielle once again heard that bizarre, distorted piping music. It seemed to be growing in volume until it was a maniacal shrieking, and Gabrielle wished the Wallaces had neighbors near enough to complain about the cacophony at this hour of the night. But they didn't.

As Gabrielle put her hand to the knob, she thought she heard another shriek beneath the frenzied music. The shriek of a voice made unnatural with terror beyond mere panic. But as she turned the knob, the music died suddenly away, and she opened the door to a silent room.

That made the horror the room contained all the more surreal.

Dianna sat back in her wheelchair behind the desk, as if merely a spectator like Gabrielle. But where Gabrielle watched in stunned horror, Dianna was smiling faintly, calmly, her eyes alight.

Kevin Wallace struggled with Smith in the center of the room. Smith was larger, stronger, and Kevin's efforts seemed futile. It was easy to understand that the scream Gabrielle had heard had been his . . . and easy to understand how it had been cut off. Kevin's head was buried inside Smith's mouth, buried to the neck as if in a lion's maw, and that was how wide the black man's mouth had opened, like a snake's with its jaws unhinged. Perhaps without his false teeth it was an easier feat, part of Gabrielle's mind considered with the blasé attitude of encroaching madness.

His false teeth must also give his mouth a bit of color, she realized, should he ever part his lips a bit. His only color besides black. Because she saw that without his glasses, even his eyes were entirely ebon-colored.

From the cuffs of his expensive suit, his fingers had lengthened into smooth serpentine tendrils, which had wound themselves around Kevin's arms and throat. Even as Gabrielle watched, more tendrils sprouted off and grew and twined around Smith's prey, reminding that blasé portion of the young woman's mind of a television program in which jungle creepers had been shown growing in stop-motion photography.

Then Smith's head began to slip down over Kevin's weakening, suffocating form, stretching impossibly, stretching out of human guise. As Kevin was consumed, absorbed, lost his form, so did the creature—the mass—that had been Smith seem to lose its hold on humanity. Soon all that was left of both of them was a black viscous ooze that poured out of Smith's clothing, leaving it puddled but unstained on the rug. And then the ooze ran up the legs of the table nearby, coiling along them like a spill in reverse, up the sides of the violet stone basin. Poured inside. Until there were two basins filled to the brim with black ooze, that gurgled and bubbled softly like hot tar.

"My servants," Dianna explained dreamily, "as you serve me. And as I serve Tsathoggua."

Gabrielle backed into the door frame, did not have strength remaining to take a step to the left and back out of the room. Instead, she sank down the frame until she sat on the floor, hugging her knees to her chest like a child in its mother's womb. Staring at Dianna, who had been like a surrogate mother to her.

"I told you he was trying to hurt me," Dianna went on. "I was hoping you could dissuade him. But you didn't believe me, Gaby. I had no choice. I'm sorry. I'm not sure whether you loved him or not, but I'm sorry."

"Let me go," Gabrielle whispered in a ghostly little voice. "Please don't hurt me, Dianna."

Dianna sat up a bit, looking distressed. "I wouldn't hurt you, my darling girl. I love you! Please don't think that . . ."

"I have to go now. I have to go . . ."

"Please don't, baby. Please stay with me. I love you. More than Smith and the other one. You'll be my favorite servant. And you will win the favor of my master, for in serving me you shall be serving him . . ."

"I can't." Tears coursed down Gabrielle's cheeks. "I can't."

Dianna slumped in her wheelchair again, sadness pulling at her hollow features. "You could come dream with me. There are such places I could show you."

"I just can't, Dianna. Please understand."

"I understand," the older woman mumbled, barely audible, and her head lowered. Her chin touched her chest. Her eyelids began to flutter. "You had better go, then."

"Dianna!" Gabrielle now found the strength to scramble to her feet, jolted by alarm. "Don't go back there! Please stay here! It's not your world!"

"That's . . . why . . . I want . . . to go," murmured Dianna Wallace, like a somnambulist. And then her eyes closed.

"Dianna!" Gabrielle cried out, approaching the desk.

From both the stone containers, the formless spawn reared up. Gabrielle could make no sense of what she saw, only that they reached the ceiling, even spread across it, and that their many limbs and pseudopods had blossomed in the air like some explosion of raw living matter. Some of these limbs were snaking, ropy tendrils, others like thrashing flippers, some frilly like the bodies of sea worms, others barbed with cruel spurs.

The display sent Gabrielle twirling on her heel and bolting for the door. She nearly fell as her foot snagged Smith's pooled clothing, but caught herself. She heard the many limbs rushing at her through the   air . . . and as she dove through the threshold, the reaching arms slammed the door closed behind her. She heard it lock.

*   *   *

Gabrielle forced herself to pack all her belongings before fleeing the house of Dianna and Kevin Wallace, made sure to leave no trace of her presence there. At any moment she expected to turn and see Smith standing behind her. Or just as bad, Dianna with her mad, acolyte's gaze. But she was able to collect her things and leave the house without harm.

In the city, the next morning, she paid a homeless man twenty dollars to call the police and tell them he thought they should go look in on a crippled woman named Dianna Wallace.

In the paper the morning after that, Gabrielle read about what the police found there.

The noted archaeologist/anthropologist/author Dianna Wallace had been found dead in her study, slumped across her desk. She had suffered a killing stroke, the article reported. There had been an autopsy, since the husband Kevin Wallace had not yet been located and there were men's clothing discarded in the room, but foul play had been ruled out.

A former housekeeper, Rita Molina, had been interviewed and said that Mrs. Wallace often napped in her wheelchair between her long hours of study, and so it was possible the woman had died peacefully in her sleep.

The article went on to describe the impressive collection of artifacts in the house . . . but made no mention of any black fluid residing in twin containers in the study. Though Gabrielle could never be sure, she guessed that the formless servitors of the Dreaming One had left this waking plane in the same manner they had entered it, by stowing away inside the body of Dianna Wallace . . . and thus, within her astral self.

For weeks after she had fled the Wallace house, Gabrielle slept fitfully, in short restless naps, and only in the day with sunlight streaming into her apartment, with the TV on and babbling for mindless comfort. And even still, she dreamed.

Sometimes she thought she saw Kevin in her dreams. But he was tangled in a writhing, living nest, half submerged in a slime of black protoplasm, reaching for her, screaming.

And she thought she saw Smith standing in a strange sort of graveyard which she found herself walking through, barefoot, her nightgown billowing behind her. He kept his distance, merely watched her, his eyes black as obsidian.

She saw alien places, and somehow knew their names. The impossible tower of Koth. Celephaïs. And the looming, mist-cloaked peaks of Kadath in the Cold Waste.

And she saw Dianna, with her long hair restored, whipping and snaking in the wind. Dianna walking toward her without her wheelchair, reaching out to Gabrielle to join her. Join her forever in the realm of dream.

But Gabrielle resisted sleep the best she could, until she was haggard, could barely function, would pass out from sheer exhaustion. But it seemed to work, to break up her link to the portal Dianna had left in her wake. The portal closed up. The strange, beckoning dreams stopped.

Finally Gabrielle was able to mourn her friend instead of fear her. And even, after a time, envy her the freedom she had found.

If she was indeed free to explore those remarkable dreamlands . . .

. . . and not serving the whims of some dark and evil god, who slumbered in the prison of sleep—Dianna herself a damned soul, herself sentenced to a nightmare from which there was no waking.

CONGLOMERATE

"Solid as a rock" was the company's motto, and the company icon rested in the cathedral-huge foyer of its corporate headquarters. It was displayed atop a circular base, directly in the center of the glossy sea of floor, the first thing one saw when entering the towering edifice of Monumental Life. The elevators were pushed off to the left, the reception desk to the right, like afterthoughts.

Atop this central pedestal rested a huge globe, tall as a man. It reminded Colin James of those massive stone spheres found scattered throughout the jungles of Mexico. Rather than being smoothly shaped from one great rock, however, the sphere seemed to be made from thousands of individual pebbles, cemented closely together. Its outer skin was a dense mosaic of shiny stones like the scales of a vast snake coiled sleeping in a tight ball. The pebbles had the color and metallic polish of hematite.

Seated behind the reception desk, staring across at the immense ball, James thought that a better symbol of the Monumental Life Insurance Corporation would be one solid rock, like those Mexican spheres, but then he supposed the pebbles might represent the people who bought into the Monumental Life policies, all held firmly together in one family. Didn't go as well with the motto, but then, he was no artist, and he was sure whoever had created that sphere had been paid a pretty penny to design it.

James let his eyes trail up to the high ceiling of the foyer, three full levels above. No, he was no artist. The ball at least he could understand, but that hanging thing was just ugly and weird. It was like a circus pavilion of translucent material, stretched across the foyer half-way up and held taut by strong hooks. It was colored in irregular patterns of blues and greens, so that with the lights glowing through it, the hanging had the organic look of a titanic butterfly wing. Maybe, with its many arms stretched and hooked to the walls, it looked like the flayed skin of some immense octopus. Sometimes, subtly, the hanging rustled like a sail above James's head.

The light glowing through the hanging cast a soft blue and green radiance across the sphere, so that sometimes it resembled a mysterious planet hanging in the murk of space—the vastness of space beginning just over the edge of James's desk. This impression would give James a jolt and then a shudder, as if he had snapped awake after drifting into a hypnotic doze. A dream of vertigo.

The revolving door that gave access to the lobby began to turn, a treadmill rotating on its side. Its churning seemed to stir the air, and the hanging billowed slightly. The door took several seconds before it revealed its occupant: a middle-aged man with longish blond-gray hair and a thick gray beard. His suit was as shabby as James's was tailored and free of wrinkles. The

jeffrey thomas

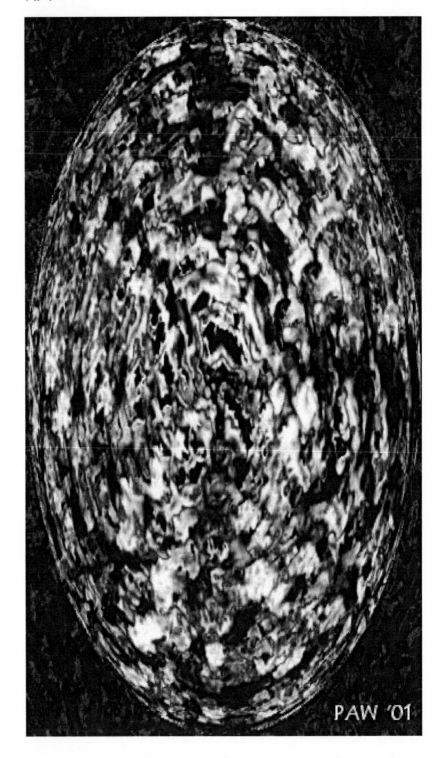

PAW '01

visitor took two steps into the foyer and froze there, staring at the globe in the center.

James watched the man for a few moments, waiting for him to orient himself, to look around and see the reception/security desk over here to the right. And at last, the man did look James's way. But he didn't turn to approach the desk. Instead, he remained where he was. For several more seconds, at least.

Then, the visitor reached under his open jacket for something in its lining pocket. He withdrew a can of spray paint. James could tell this when the man began to shake it, and the can made its characteristic clattering sound.

"May I help you?" James asked curtly, coming out from behind the desk at a determined clip. "Sir? Excuse me—sir!"

But the man didn't glance at him again. Instead, he stepped up so close to the ball that he nearly disappeared behind it, out of James's range of sight. But, James heard the hiss. Smelled the stink of paint.

When he darted forward, he saw the bearded stranger was vandalizing the Monumental Life icon, spray-painting it with some graffiti. The paint was black, and the man moved his arm with such sure strokes that he might as well be an artist himself, the artist who had made the ball, belatedly signing his name to it.

James seized the man's arm, gave it enough of a twist to cause the man's hand to open and the can to drop. He watched the man's other hand, lest he draw something else from inside his jacket, like a knife.

The bearded man whipped his face around and his mouth worked moistly inside that scruff of beard, eyes red-rimmed and insane under the tufts of his brows.

"Let me do what I have to do, friend . . . you haven't got a clue. Not a god-damned clue."

"I think you'd better sit down, sir," James told the man. "I really don't want to hurt you."

"We have to stop them. It's futile, I'm sure of it, but we have to try, don't we? We have to at least *try.*"

"Come with me, sir."

The bearded man didn't struggle. He looked back at the sphere, and James allowed himself one quick look at it himself. Well, the damage had been done. The stranger had painted some symbol in wide strokes, right across the face of the ball. It appeared to be a star with five points and an eye in the center of that, running with black tears. The pupil of the eye was jagged like an abstracted flame.

James felt a hand dip inside his own jacket.

The bearded man slipped James's hidden 9mm SIG-Sauer out of its holster and from there it was just a few inches higher for it to poke James under the jaw. He felt the front sight tear his skin.

"Please," he whispered, "don't." He let go of the man's arm.

The stranger pushed James back with his free hand, and then thumbed off the chunky pistol's safety, snapped back the slide with a *clack.*

"Don't!" James blurted.

"You'll be doing the same, if they come," the stranger told him, aiming the handgun. "You *should* do the same, if they come." And with this said, the stranger jammed the gun's muzzle under his gray scruff of beard and pulled the trigger and blew off the top of his skull. A rain of blood pattered across the glossy floor, James's glossy shoes and the scaly skin of the vandalized ball. And then the stranger crumpled almost gently to the floor.

* * *

James felt under his jaw, looked at his fingers. A slight smear of blood.

"Are you all right?" the police- man asked him.

"Yes," he muttered. Another policeman drew near.

"Was your gun's safety on?"

"Yes. I saw him move it off with his thumb. He looked like he knew how to use a gun."

"Was your holster buckled?"

"It's always snapped," James replied evenly, but without meeting the man's hard eyes. "He got the strap off fast. Like I say, he seemed to know how to handle a gun."

"He didn't look especially big or strong, Mr. James. You got fifty pounds on this guy, easy. And he had ten years on you, easy. How did he get that gun away from you?"

"He was high on adrenaline Or drugs."

"Drugs, huh? Is that your professional opinion? Were you ever a cop before, Mr. James, or did you just wanna be?"

James still wouldn't look at the man's eyes, or let his voice falter. "No. I was never a cop." He did look at the first policeman, however. "What was his name? Did he have any ID?"

"Yes. His name was Richard Penn. That's pretty much all we know so far."

"Richard Penn," James repeated in a bland tone. "I'm gonna want to look into his files here at Monumental, see if he had a job here at some time, or a dispute over an insurance claim. He was saying something about, 'stopping them, somebody's gotta stop them,' something like that. He had a grudge of some kind."

"Good thing he took it out on himself," said the second cop, "and *that* thing," he nodded at the sphere, "instead of you."

*   *   *

James was offered a week off, but declined it. He wanted to find out who the bearded man had been, why he had done what he'd done. It was James's gun the man had died by. He had no more been able to prevent him from using that than he had stopped him from using the spray can. *If I was my boss, he thought as he drove to work the next morning, I'd fire me.*

When he entered the lobby, the great stone ball glared at him accusingly with the black eye that had opened upon its rough hide. But there was a man already here, scrubbing at the vandalism with a brush. The man glanced over his shoulder at James as he came in. The man was short, almost a dwarf, stocky, his white coveralls too large for him and his face troll-like, toad-like, shockingly ugly. His irises were too yellow. He turned back to his scrubbing and James smelled a strong chemical cleaner as he walked to the reception desk.

"How come maintenance isn't doing that?" James whispered to Warnes, the third shift guard.

"Dunno." Warnes stretched and finished off his coffee. "He had clearance, though. Somebody obviously called him in."

James shrugged as he came around behind the desk, and seated himself in front of the computer there. "I'm gonna call the police in a minute and see if they have anything on Penn that would save me from having to research him myself."

"He knew his paint, anyway," Warnes joked grimly, softly, nodding over at the ball. "Quasimodo's having a helluva time getting it off the globe."

*   *   *

The detectives in charge of the investigation didn't get back to James for several hours, but at last one did. By then, impatient, James had already begun his research. The two men exchanged their findings over the phone.

James reported, "We don't have any Richard Penn as a past employee, or as a past customer of Monumental Life at any time."

"We checked that end, too," said the detective, Robart. "He had Trustwell Insurance, through Berg College. He was a professor there up until he left two years ago, and he continued his coverage on his own."

"A professor? Of what?"

"Ancient history. They asked him to leave two years ago because he'd been acting erratic, coming to school drunk. They said he was teaching some really out-there things in class . . . *Chariots of the Gods* kind of crap. Didn't go over well with the dean, although I'm sure it was a lot less boring than the real stuff as far as the kids were concerned."

113

jeffrey thomas

"Had he been seeing a psychiatrist, anything?"

"Nothing in the way of mental health. Unfortunately. And you may be interested to know he did know how to use a gun; he once had a gun taken away from him and his license to own revoked for threatening somebody with it. Just after he lost his job, in fact. He didn't do time for it, though."

"Who was he threatening? What was it about?"

"The man he threatened took off before police could reach the scene, but there were witnesses to testify that Penn had brandished his gun in a threatening manner. At the time he babbled some stuff about this man being a, um, cultist of some kind . . . some kind of Satan worshiper or something. A 'servitor,' he called him. We only have a description of the man as being very short, powerfully built, maybe foreign."

"Mm," James grunted. "So . . . there's no motive for why he came here. Why he painted that thing on our sculpture."

"Not yet, unfortunately. We're trying to pin down family. They seem to be all out in Arizona."

"Strange," James muttered, more to himself than to the tiny holes at his lips. He listened to the whisking *scrub, scrub, scrub* of the man in the too-large coveralls as he worked to free the globe of its desecration.

"You might wanna check into the files of all the other Nye Conglomerate companies, to see if he might have had some dealings with another branch of the company," Robart suggested.

"What? The *what* Conglomerate?"

"Nye. Don't you know who you work for?"

"Monumental Life, I thought," James replied with some slight irritation.

"Monumental Life is one of the companies Nye owns. Man, Nye owns half this city, and a good chunk of the country. How long have you been working over there?"

"I've been in town and worked for Monumental just four months. I'm security chief, though. I'm surprised I never heard that before."

"Well, I've lived here all my life, so. But yeah, this foreign guy, Nye, he owns Monumental Life, OO Software, CM Investments . . . um, oh yeah, and of course all the Pantheon Banks . . ."

"That's my bank," James said, his brow furrowed into frowns. *Scrub, scrub, scrub.* He couldn't see the squat worker behind the glistening hematite planet.

"You may have seen Nye over there and never known it. I've seen him a few times over the years. Thin guy, always wears expensive black suits. Polite. Quiet. Looks Indian . . . Arab, maybe. Leave it to the foreigners; own everything in this country."

"Wow," James said, ignoring the last comment. "Funny. Yeah . . . yeah, I'll have to look into all of that. Penn might have had a grudge against one of these other companies."

"Keep me informed. I'll be happy to trade with ya. And pal . . ."

"Yeah?"

"Don't be hard on yourself about this. It wasn't your fault. The guy was a head case. You hear me?"

James said nothing. His gun pulled at one side of his chest like an organ fossilized into metallic rock.

"Buddy? You hear what I said?"

"Mm," James grunted.

* * *

It was the second night he had had this dream.

An aurora borealis spread across the heavens, a glowing curtain of light that would dwarf the mere ribbons over the Antarctic skies. As it billowed like some impossible serpent writhing, the air crackled and boomed deafeningly, charged with electrical anomalies. Lightning flashed, illuminated in harsh strobe glare a landscape of dense jungle. Not Mexican jungle, James thought weirdly, but far older. Far more primeval. He saw, in those flashes, scurrying life that no man had ever seen with flesh on its bones.

But now the aurora writhed more violently, like a snake pinned with the blade of a shovel. It was opalescent, iridescent, but this iridescence was made up of colors for which James's dream-self had no names. The electric storms grew more fierce, the thunder like the explosions of a battlefield. Somehow, he knew, it *was* a kind of battle. The curtain of light seemed under attack, somehow, and was lowering closer to the primeval earth from a great height. And as it descended, James could see that the curtain was actually made of many individual parts, like iridescent soap bubbles—like cells, he thought. Boiling, foaming, merging and reforming in a vast, lowering conglomeration. Until the conglomeration of glowing spheres seemed to fill the whole sky, Lucifer, angel of light, falling . . .

But as the vast curtain—*entity*, James thought—began to break up and fall, the pieces of it went dark first, like coals with the fire burned out of them. Like flesh turned to fossil. More of these dark spheres rained, more, until the air was black with a meteor shower such as the earth had not known since its surface had been one lake of fire. The earth was pounded, hammered. The forest began to burn, the great-but-dwarfed lizards began to howl, aflame, and black clouds of smoke began to billow into the air.

The dark, petrified spheres plummeted down toward James's up-turned face, toward his tiny dream-self, and he covered his face with his arms and screamed.

That was how he found himself when his eyes shot open. With his arms crossed over his face, and his own scream filling his ears.

*   *   *

Richard Penn had not worked for any of the companies that Detective Robart had named. But then, how many other companies might this Mr. Nye own that James hadn't been aware of? James used the phone to contact all of them but for Pantheon Bank, which he dropped in on while on his way home that afternoon. But it was the bank's head office that he sought out, not the small branch of the bank he cashed his check at every Friday. Having been able to leave a half hour early today, he hoped there was time to catch someone, maybe the head of personnel or security, who could answer his questions.

The building loomed above him as he approached its front doors, smaller than the obsidian black colossus of Monumental Life and older, art deco in style. As he entered, he saw two giant, tarnished metal angels to either side of the lobby, supporting the ceiling on their wings. They were curious angels; in the deco style, yes, slim beautiful women, but the wings had an almost bat-like quality. He only noticed this after, however. After he noticed what rested in the center of the lobby . . .

James didn't bother contacting personnel. He'd do that tomorrow. Although he had already called them, he returned to his car and drove over to OO Software. Then CM Investments.

There was no ugly, octopoid hanging suspended in any of those other foyers. That was a touch singular to Monumental Life's building. But there was, however, in the center of each lobby, a huge sphere made up of many dark pebbles that gleamed metallic like hematite. Like meteors that had crashed through the roofs of these buildings. Or, as if the buildings had been erected around them.

*   *   *

"He has a sister in Arizona supposed to come out and deal with his stuff," croaked the stooped landlord, unlocking the door to Richard Penn's apartment. He was wheezing dangerously from the climb to the third floor of this old tenement house on its steep hill overlooking much of the city. James had gotten lost trying to find this winding back street. It must be murder to drive on in winter. He was reminded of his teen-age visit to San Francisco.

The landlord put on a light, stepped aside to let James in; a prosaic enough kitchen, for an obsessed madman.

"I thought you guys had been over everything," the landlord went on. James had told him he was a detective. Detective Robart."

"We have some new information," was all James would say. He turned to the old man. "You can go on back downstairs, sir . . . I'll be in to see you with the keys when I'm done."

"Oh, well . . . okay," the old man wheezed.

James bolted the door quietly behind him.

*   *   *

In the living room, things were less prosaic.

A bay window overlooked the city, its buildings a misty violet-gray in the autumnal twilight so that they resembled crowded tombstones and obelisks in a graveyard. On each of the three windows that composed the bay, Penn had painted the same black star design with which he had defaced the sphere.

The walls of the room were one big bulletin board. Taped there were photographs of buildings James recognized from town, or didn't recognize, charts with apparent mathematical equations, photocopies from books, magazine articles. A large map of the city, full of push pins that Penn had connected with a highlighter marker. The resultant pattern had a geometric look.

James drew nearer to one wall to more closely examine this montage-like display. One photocopy was from a book written in another language; Latin? Taped beside it was a handwritten translation, James judged. It was headed: "From *The Metal Book.*"

"*So in the heavens there raged a war, as the Elder Gods did battle the Outsiders, and did hurl Them into the seas, and thrust Them under the earth, and lock Them in tombs and cells of Their own making. A sleep like death came upon the fallen Gods, but it was a sleep from which They might yet awaken, a death from which there might yet come resurrection and rebirth. The gates of the tombs and cells must be guarded from those servitors of the Outsiders, who seek to open them. The greatest of these gates is Yog-Sothoth. Yog-Sothoth is the Gate, Key to the Gate, and Guardian of the Gate all in one.*"

James let his attention drift to another page. It was from an article on the extinction of the dinosaurs; specifically, on the theory that a comet fallen to earth had brought on their doom. A shudder went through him. His dream of prehistoric monsters, screeching, aflame, puny compared to the cataclysm in the heavens.

Penn had said nothing in the lobby about this subject, had he? No, definitely not. So why should James have dreamed it? Why should he have felt that the writhing ribbon of light, the electrical storm and the subsequent meteor shower in his dreams had all been part of a battle of some kind . . . a cosmic struggle between gods as described in that passage from something called *The Metal Book?*

On the opposite wall of the room, James studied various other hangings, putting on a lamp as much to dilute his unease as to illuminate his reading. A newspaper clipping commanded his attention. It was from a business section, and there was a photograph of a man accompanying it. He was dark-haired, handsome in a severe, intense way. He was familiar, and the caption confirmed James's suspicions. He had indeed seen this man before, at Monumental Life. It was a picture of Ralph Nye, president of the Nye Conglomerate. The article concerned Nye's latest acquisition, a bought-out company to be renamed Gateway Realty.

Gateway. James thought of that transcription from the so-called *Metal Book.*

Under the caption, Penn had written his own caption in red marker. It consisted of one alien word: NYARLATHOTEP.

Was it Nye's full last name, shortened and made more Anglo-sounding for the sake of business? Nye didn't sound exotic enough to suit the man's swarthy looks, nor did Ralph, for that matter.

Ralph. James considered the alien word again. Nye could indeed be extracted from Nyarlathotep. And so could Ralph, for that matter.

The map of the city claimed James's attention now. For one thing, across the top margin of it was written, in highlighter marker, YOG-SOTHOTH. Drawing close to the map, he took note of the push pins. The location of them was obvious. One pin was situated in the place where Monumental Life loomed above the streets. Another, where the headquarters of Pantheon Banks was situated. Another represented CM Investments, then OO Software. James couldn't interpret some of the placements of the pins, however. Another map was butted up to this one, some of the pins spread there along the coast, even out in the ocean. One pin was inside the borders of this city's oldest graveyard, dating back to the eighteenth century. Again, all these sites were   connected with highlighter marker, forming a rough series of concentric circles, James saw now, as if they represented the waves of destruction emanating from a nuclear bomb. At the center of the circles was the pin for Monumental Life.

James lifted his eyes to the marred bay windows.

He saw that towering edifice, its lights glittering against the darkening sky. And beyond Monumental Life, distant but still towering ominously, a silent titan, was the headquarters of Pantheon Banks. Across the river, he knew, was CM Investments. One of the pins was in the river, he had noted.

One of the . . . spheres, he realized. One of the fallen meteorites. Once glowing with unnamed colors, but turned black in the battle that had raged above this spot eons before humans had dwelt upon it.

YOG-SOTHOTH, the word at the top of the map proclaimed, accused, defined it. The map was a diagram of Yog-Sothoth. As much of Yog-Sothoth as Richard Penn had discovered the traces of. Yog-Sothoth . . . Gate, Key, Guardian all in one.

And this man, Ralph Nye, or whatever his true name was . . . he was buying the sites of these fallen globes. Making them places of power, or more power. Uniting them into a web of power.

Another newspaper clipping nearby. A photo of a sphere being raised from the earth beneath the foundation of a building demolished by dynamite. The story explained that the rock, thought to be a meteor, had been discovered after the building had been brought down to make room for a new company called OO Software. Yes, James thought, yes. Spheres exhumed beneath or in the vicinity of CM Investments, Pantheon Banks, Monumental Life Insurance. Enshrined in each lobby. Linked, united into a web . . .

James looked out the window once more. Pictured that great sphere resting in the lobby of his company, and beyond that, inside the Pantheon Banks lobby, guarded by bat-winged seraphim, another sphere. And beyond that, a sphere buried beneath the mud of the night-black river snaking through the city.

The conglomerate was growing. And growing more powerful. More and more sites being linked together. What would happen when Nye possessed all those spheres, buried in the sea, in the earth? Would his power be complete? And then what? Would he then own all of this city? Would he then own all this planet, and more?

James did not question his sanity at these conclusions. He no longer questioned the sanity of the man who had killed himself with his gun. The truth of it all resonated in his soul on a primal level. It resonated in his cells, as if touching upon the memories of the ancient cells from which they had evolved. Upon memories of a horror so great that it had imprinted itself on the minds of creatures not yet born.

It was a gateway. A gate. And Ralph Nye was clearing it as surely as if he were a patient, diligent archaeologist. He was uncovering the gate, and its key. He would open the portal, James knew. And there were prisoners beyond it. Outsiders, *The Metal Book* had called them. Yog-Sothoth was the guard at that gate, which was Himself.

Colin James backed slowly away from the bay windows, as if he thought faces lurked behind each of the glittering windows of Monumental Life, windows glittering like stars against the now black sky. The brutish faces, the yellow eyes of servitors . . . perhaps human, perhaps not. Eyes watching him, reading his thoughts.

Was Ralph Nye even now behind one of those windows? And staring across the city at these bay windows, with their mysterious protective talismans?

James left the living room lamp on. He did not want to retreat through the apartment in utter darkness.

* * *

119

It was a new dream. A dream of the future, perhaps, where the other dreams had been of the past. One of the quotes on Penn's walls had read, after all, "Past, present, future, all are one in Yog-Sothoth."

It was dawn, and there was a rumbling beneath the city. An earthquake, perhaps.

But it was a selective earthquake. Only one building fell, crumbling in upon itself with a monstrous roar. Monumental Life collapsed, an amorphous cloud of dark dust billowing into the air as if to take its place.

But now another structure was crumbling. Pantheon Banks. And the water of the river was churning, bubbling. From the rubble of the fallen giants, through the clouds of dust, rays of light shot into the air. Light of unknown iridescent colors, dust swirling in its beams.

The sources of these beams lifted into the air. One brightly glowing sphere rose and hovered above the city. Then another. Another. One rose from the hissing steam of the river. Others rose from a great distance, like bright stars, perhaps from the sea.

They were now moving toward each other. Began to link with one-another. They were forming an undulating, blinding ribbon of light in the sky. And one man, a dark silhouette, stood   on the roof of an intact building with his arms spread to this terrible spectacle, this unholy miracle. He was crying, "Yog-Sothoth! Yog-Sothoth!"

And in the dream, James was crying out, also. But his cries were of terror, and pain, and damnation. And moments later, as the glow of the ribbon blinded him to the city completely . . . as if it had been burned out of existence . . . the air became filled with the screams of every occupant of the city. Every damned soul. Not sent down to hell, but hell raised up around them.

Colin James awoke with his scream still ragged in his throat.

*   *   *

And so he waited. Each day, he manned his desk. He asked for, and was granted, extra hours. He took over a Saturday for a grateful younger guard.

But he hadn't seen Ralph Nye yet. Not yet. But Nye owned this company. When he returned from his latest exploits, as eventually he must, James would be waiting.

He watched that silent ball for hours sometimes, its pebbled surface gazing dully back at him like the gigantic compound eye of some monstrous insect. The protective talisman was gone . . . but in his car, James had a can of paint.

The flayed octopus thing rippled above him, like the ghost of some creature hovering threateningly over his head. He smirked up at it. *Go back to sleep*, he mocked it.

He watched the rotating door for Ralph Nye. In his holster was the gun with which Richard Penn had ended his life. If Ralph Nye was mortal, his life would end too. And if not, perhaps just this incarnation, this mask, would end. Perhaps they couldn't be killed. But at least they could be prevented from coming back alive.

Yog-Sothoth, he thought. Gate, and Key, and Guardian of the Gate, all in one.

No, thought Colin James. *I* am the Guardian.

BOOK WORM

Pym's grandfather had disappeared nearly sixty years ago, during the fabled twenties of Al Capone and Prohibition and Tommy guns, of which Pym had read quite a bit, lover of books that he was.

Books were vastly more transporting than any movie could hope to be. Pym almost resented movies. While better than most, when you watched *Tess*, you were aware of camera set-ups and directorial techniques and familiar actors; when you read *Tess*, she breathed and you ached to save her from her Fate. A monster wasn't rubber on an articulated steel skeleton with pulsing air bladders to mimic life—it was alive, and it was something to be afraid of. The reading experience was transcendent to all other human experience; it was an out of body freedom of flight. But like some ancient supernatural ability lost to distant races, it was a fading talent, a forsaken skill, as television and Nintendo, rock and drugs loomed up almost as a unified force to eclipse the past.

Largely out of disgusted rebellion, Pym sought to plunge fully into that to which so many others were becoming increasingly blind. The past held a particularly powerful attraction for him, and books were the hatches to be crow-barred open, the coffin lids to be pried off for revelation. Books were the tombs of Pharaohs, the strata rich with dinosaur bones, the portals to the universe beyond. And so it was natural for Pym to become intrigued with his grandfather's colorful life and strange disappearance, and to become wholly obsessed when his aunt first told him of his grandfather's mysterious book . . .

From what his aunt and others had revealed to him through the years, Pym had pieced together a shady history of his grandfather Arnold Stowe. Even prior to his knowledge of the book, which his aunt had never dared refer to before, Pym had sought out all the information he could on the man who had died thirty years before his birth, even securing some cracked and blurry photographs of the young and handsome Arnie Stowe, dapper and smiling for the camera, arm slung around the shoulders of his pretty young wife, Pym's grandmother, whose death at eighty-one was what led to his aunt's disclosure of the existence of the weird metal book.

That Pym's grandfather had been a gangster in the true sense was doubtful, but it was doubtless that he had had his underworld connections, dealings and inclinations. Thinking of his withered and dying grandmother, Pym had difficulty imagining her, even with the photographs, as the sexy young woman her husband had repeatedly attempted to involve in a blackmail scheme, suggesting to her that if she secretly photographed married men with her they could quickly draw in thousands—assuring her, considerate man that he was, that she needn't strip down beyond her underclothes. She resisted. On several occasions Arnie Stowe's wife found inordinate amounts of wristwatches in a dresser drawer. After a time he took to carrying a revolver, and he slept with it under his pillow. He had recently done someone a favor by taking in and hiding away a package, and perhaps this was the source of his growing anxiety. He angrily resisted all inquiries made by his wife. When he suddenly vanished without a clue and remained that way, it was naturally assumed by all that his underworld dealings had caught up with him. His pretty young widow remarried, and Pym's pleasant but rather less colorful second maternal grandfather had died under rather less mysterious circumstances four years ago.

It was during the family gathering at his aunt's house, following the funeral of his grandmother, that Pym learned of the metal book.

They had been discussing Arnie Stowe, Pym and his aunt and his cousins Judy and Tom, appropriately philosophical on this day, wondering where Arnie Stowe's remains had finally come to rest. Tom suggested that Arnie Stowe hadn't in fact been murdered and weighed to a lake bottom somewhere, but had run off to start a new life under a new name, abandoning his wife. Tom's mother, Pym's aunt, told them why she felt this wasn't so.

Months after her husband's disappearance, Pym's grandmother started finding money hidden in books throughout their large but much-worn Victorian house in the suburbs. The last amount she chanced upon was two-hundred dollars in a volume on the Civil War . . . this being in 1961. Arnie would surely not have left what amounted to thousands of dollars behind.

Naturally Pym's grandmother embarked on an Easter egg hunt throughout her husband's abundant library, but his books were everywhere, in boxes and closets, in attic and basement, for he was a lover of books despite his cruder inclinations, and for this Pym felt a kinship with him though there was no actual physical linkage. The Civil War book, as stated, escaped her search. But during her initial search a singularly strange volume was found.

It was on the floor in the basement when she found it, beside a cardboard box full of junk which had up to now obscured it. On a table above, along with stacks of books, was an open cardboard box which was empty, once bound with string. The box was unlabeled. The book which Pym's grandmother lifted from the floor where it seemed to have dropped was heavy. The front and back covers of it were made from slabs of a tarnished metal, the edges of the paper were gilded and a thick metal catch system locked the book closed, requiring a key, which wasn't present and was never found. The spine of the book was very curious, being sort of a spring-loaded mechanism hinged to the front and back covers. There were some characters, maybe Arabic, inscribed into the book's front cover but no English translation. Pym's grandmother had never seen this book before or been aware that her husband possessed it.

At that time she put the book away in the event that her husband might return, and in later years her second husband made a few half-hearted attempts to force the lock mechanism without success, but resisted breaking the lock in case the book was ever found to be of historic value. He meant to bring the book around to dealers or museums but never got around to it, and the book was largely forgotten in its box on the top shelf of a closet in the old house where they went on to live the remainder of their lives.

What caused Pym's aunt to bring up the book was her rediscovery of it upon organizing her mother's belongings for a yard sale or distribution to the surviving relatives. Her mother had shown her the book once as a young teenager, but she hadn't seen it again until now by accident, and the rediscovery made her nervous to such an extent that she had been reluctant to discuss the book before this. Pym, increasingly fascinated, pressed her for details.

It seemed that the book was cold to the touch, to an almost unnatural degree, though she hastened to remind him that the covers were made of metal. She had remembered that during the time her mother first showed the book to her, she had shrunk back from the chilly surface of the thing, and her mother had reluctantly told her of the time the book almost seemed to be vibrating in her hands. She may simply have been shivering from the metal's cold touch, her mother had hastened to add.

Pym knew he must have this book in his hands. There was no doubt about this, it was not an idea or a question or a fantasy; it was a need. Though embarrassed to reveal his anxiousness, he couldn't contain his enthusiasm and asked his aunt if he could look at the book, secretly hoping she would offer it to him to keep, knowing his love of books. He had all he could do to restrain his anger at her response; she must have seen the heat flash in his eyes when she told him that she didn't want anyone to touch it until she got an antique book dealer to appraise its value.

Oh, she was no fool, he fumed to himself that night alone in his apartment, pacing with coffee in hand. She suspected, as he did, that this was the mysterious package someone had paid Arnold Stowe to hide . . . and that it had to be something ancient and stolen from a museum, maybe smuggled into the country, maybe worth thousands upon thousands. Yes, she wanted the money, but Pym wanted more. He wanted the book.

He couldn't very well steal it, but he'd be damned if she stopped him from holding it, examining it, opening it if he could. He would embark now, this very night. He had what he needed. He would bring his camera to photograph its outside and hopefully some of its inside. And he had his professional lock-pick tools. They had been advertised in the back of a Kung Fu magazine, as insidiously available to an indiscriminate audience as those bizarre Ninja stars and darts and swords and such, even more insidious, he felt, but he had bought them because he liked novelties, toys, the unusual and the obscure. He knew they'd come in handy some day. For a mere twenty five dollars (not including his seven dollar *how-to* manual) he had acquired a ten piece set of tension wrenches, feeler picks and rake picks. Easily sufficient to open the simple warded padlock which secured his grandmother's rear shed, which would then give into the old house. He just hoped that this limited selection would be enough to give him access to the strange book's interior as well.

As he drove in the night, and later even after he had mounted the shed's creaking steps, squatted at the door with a penlight gripped cigar-like in his teeth probing the lock like a dentist hovering over a mouth, he couldn't help but irrationally fantasize about stealing the book and some other articles and making it look like a robbery . . . but his aunt would suspect him if that book, of all things, was missing. How about a fire? They wouldn't think to sift through the debris for this obscure book then. Pym paused a moment from his work to glance around him nervously at the dark and to suck in a long breath. Enough fantasizing. He would only examine the book.

The padlock gave after more work than Pym had anticipated, perhaps due to his agitation. Once inside, out of the cold, he calmed down considerably. He didn't dare turn on any lights, let the penlight's dim and tight pool lead him like a spirit guide. The house was musty, much of the smell due to the great amount of books his grandmother had supplemented to her first husband's already prodigious collection. Pym's grandmother had lent or given him books over the years but this was a cave of rich treasure and it was painful to forego it all in search of a solitary volume.

There were several possible closets, but the second one Pym tried was it. Even as the door squealed open a vague chill could be felt wafting out at him, but this had to be a draft from outside. A cardboard box rested on the upper shelf. Smiling to himself in the dark, Pym reached up for it.

The box was indeed heavy. He carried it religiously into a ground floor bedroom his grandmother had made into a den, though his aunt had removed the TV already. There was one window only, facing into the back yard. Pym dared to turn on one lamp and place it on the floor after drawing the shade and closing the curtains. He squatted down before the box. The old string had been cut at one point but now was only loosely tied in a bow. Pym plucked the bow apart, folded back the box's flaps. Again Pym shuddered at a waft of chill but reminded himself that his aunt had had the heat in the house shut off for the sake of economy. He reached both hands in to remove the shadowed book into the intimate light.

Pym withdrew his hands instinctively. His aunt had understated the matter . . . the metal was like a storm door in the winter, for a quick but accurate analogy. Of course, Pym reasoned, when she had last touched it the house had been heated, and this was late October. He was simply jumpy due to the circumstances of his furtive mission, he convinced himself, and with a fresh surge of inspiration lifted out the book.

The metal covers were tarnished almost black, but the odd Arabic-flavored characters inscribed on the front were discernible. The lock was very curious and sturdy, and the binding was odder still with its spring-loaded mechanism, the exact purpose of which wasn't clear.

The alien characters did disillusion Pym a bit, who hoped to read something of so singular a book, but the exciting strangeness of the volume and its obvious great age still gripped him. He would take pictures, attempt a translation somewhere. And just to hold so unique a thing as this was memorable in itself. He had to see more. His grandfather may have died guarding this book. He tried his first probe in the oddly constructed lock.

Squatting with the book in his lap, Pym pulled his sleeve over his left hand like a mitten against the cold metal, which didn't seem to be absorbing any warmth through handling. Impatiently he selected a second pick, glancing up around him, for some reason suddenly conscious of the black and deserted bulk of the old house all around him.

The book began to vibrate, and Pym shoved it off his legs as he bolted straight upright and cried out involuntarily. He stepped back to stare at the book as it lay on the floor just outside the pool of the lamp on the floor. He wanted to run, on a physical level. Other parts of him, stronger, kept him magnetized.

The probe protruded from the lock, still inserted. The book was making a faint, slight noise. It was like a squeak of metal hinges. It was hard for Pym to see the book in the shadows beyond the light of the lamp, but it seemed to be . . . moving. Pulsing . . . slowly . . . as though drawing in breath . . . a slumbering living thing.

This couldn't be true—it was his agitated state of mind! Here he was trespassing; he had entered this house illegally, whether it was his grandmother's or not, and he knew it was wrong. This was no game, no crazy adventure, no fantasy to live out in a book . . . he was doing something seriously wrong. This was simply his nervous conscience punishing him, an imagination made vivid by the fantastic and nightmarish novels he consumed. Wasn't it?

Pym shoved the lamp directly over the book with the toe of his shoe.

Again he recoiled, cried out, this time hugged his arms. But he didn't flee . . . even as he heard the squeaks from the hinges magnify from additional strain as the book rhythmically bulged to a greater extent, the metal covers bowing out, the lock still resisting, the gilded pages breathing open into black gill slits but closing again.

Run . . . *run!* hissed the blood in his body. But the lock pick stuck up out of the book, waiting to be turned. He knew he could open the book. He knew it as surely as he had known he had to get his hands on this book when his aunt revealed its existence to him. His camera weighed heavily from his neck and against his chest. He had consumed books on life's mysteries, the supernatural, immersed himself in them and come away desperately hungry for more. How could he possibly turn from this now, the real thing before him, the unknown held apart from him by one foolish little lock?

Pym stepped nearer to the book as it breathed in its raspy, rusty voice.

* * *

Pym's aunt couldn't sleep, but it wasn't grief that kept her awake; her mother had been dying for a long time, and if anything she was relieved for the woman and for herself. She was angry at her nephew for the resentment she had seen in his eyes, but concerned for him also in a vague, unsettled way. That damn book. It was a good thing she hadn't related the rest of what her mother had told her, if it weren't too late already to keep him from again asking to see it. She hadn't mentioned what her mother had seen or thought she'd seen, partly because it was too creepy for her to bring up and mostly because it was ridiculous, but that story had still been enough to make her return the unpleasant thing to its box quickly when she rediscovered it, replace it on its shelf rather than carry it into her house. But now she felt she should take care of the book and be done with it as soon as possible, before she had to turn her nephew away from it again, send it away with its cold metal surfaces and its strange mood of uneasiness, even if she didn't believe that when her mother found it lying on the basement floor sixty years ago a piece of the cut binding string from the box hung out of the pages an inch or so, and when she lifted the book from the floor the string was sucked inside the book without a trace, withdrawn inside like a tongue . . .

The next morning she let herself into the old Victorian house through the front door, steeled herself against the musty-smelling gloom. If only her son Tom could have come with her, but he had to work, and Judy was on her way back to Maine already. Thank God at least the book was tied up in its box and she wouldn't have to look at it or touch that icy tarnished metal again. She moved into the stillness of the house.

In the central dining room, the table covered with bric-a-brac and dusty stacks of books, she noticed the door to the den was shut. This was odd, since she didn't remember shutting it; in fact, her mother had never employed use of the door in her day. She hesitated in approaching it, her instincts lifting their alert little bright-eyed heads. She didn't want to go to that door and open it, but she had to. She did.

They found her dead body in her dead mother's house, eyes glazedly

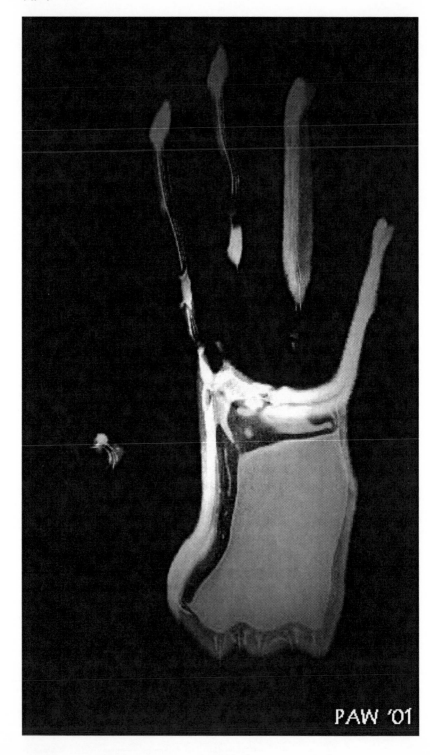

PAW '01

staring. The strain of her mother's death, and she had been a heavy smoker at the age of fifty-five. But if her son Tom had seen what she had seen, he wouldn't have taken the metal book which was found on the floor beside her home with him, meaning to unfasten that lock somehow or dismantle the spring-loaded hinged binding.

With his aunt dead, no one was able to testify as to how Pym must have struggled through the night and on into the morning; she couldn't tell anyone how she had come into the room in time to see him lose that struggle, as *The Metal Book* lay open wide on the floor, and Pym's legs stood straight up out of the black hole which was there where pages should have been, his legs thrashing madly but no screams or cries for help being heard from inside that black void as there should have been. No one would know how the fingers of one hand had gripped the outside of the book for a few last moments before being wrenched away, his legs sucked abruptly into the fathomless pit out of sight, the spring-loaded covers then slapping shut and locking automatically.

Only the glassy wide eyes of his aunt gave any clue, beyond translation to those who found her, of what she had seen coiled around the wrist of Pym's gripping hand, twined around one leg as it sought to drag him into that darkness. Slick and moist looking, it had been, grayishly translucent, and segmented; constricting and insistent, patient throughout the long struggle of the night.

More mysterious than the death of Pym's aunt was his disappearance, and his family murmured about it somberly at the gathering after his aunt's funeral. They had no idea where he had gone—but wherever it was, he had brought his camera to take pictures.

THROUGH OBSCURE GLASS

For W. H. Pugmire, Esq.

She plummeted . . .

. . . into a black well of space, a wormhole to other dimensions. She plunged into the abyss like an angel struck down by an arrow shot from that netherworld. Hurtled . . . and in her terror, wished that she would strike the bottom of the pit at last, and find the relief of death . . . for it wasn't death she feared, but the falling . . .

Judith opened her eyes with a snap, just as the bus cleared the tunnel in the wooded mountain side. Again, the interior of the bus was flooded with sunlight. She was embarrassed, thinking she had let out a scream in waking, but she could tell from the lulled, quiet aspect of those around her that she hadn't. Sitting up in her seat, she glanced at the passenger seated beside her, a pretty teenager headed for Seattle, she had told Judith a few hours earlier. She was blissfully asleep, her head resting against the window and her thick dark hair fallen into her face like a blanket.

Judith smiled faintly and looked away from the girl, but something made her look back. The girl's shroud of hair covered all of her face except for her mouth and chin, and Judith had had the weird idea that if she were to part the girl's hair, the eyes she would uncover would be—be horrible. Inhuman. Though she knew the girl had friendly hazel eyes, in her mind she had thought that eyes of glowing pink, lurid and bright as a sunset, lay hiding behind those curtains of hair, glaring out at her secretly through the strands. Further, the way the girl's head was tilted, and her mouth hung open in sleep, it appeared as if her mouth were a vertical opening in her head. Like a vagina, Judith thought . . . with teeth.

Flotsam and jetsam of a dream, she told herself, looking away from the girl. And yet, her presence so near to her unnerved Judith, and after a few minutes she stealthily gathered up her purse and magazine and stole to another seat closer to the rear of the bus.

* * *

Judith was the only passenger to disembark from the bus in front of a combination gas station/general store, and from its derelict aspect she couldn't decide whether this was deserted or still saw customers. Age-bleached letters on a sign announced to no one but her: SESQUA DEPOT.

But she wasn't alone. As she set her bags at her feet in order to dig a cigarette from her purse, Judith noticed that a figure stood framed in the threshold of the store, shadowed from the sun. It was an elderly man, wearing dark glasses, and apparently watching her through their lenses.

"Hello," Judith offered, unsettled at his presence. A too-cool burst of breeze ruffled her short dark hair, and a nervous smile flicked one corner of her mouth. "I guess I shouldn't be smoking with a long walk ahead of me, but they wouldn't let me smoke on that bloody damn bus."

The old man obviously took note of her British accent. "You're a stranger here," he stated.

"I've been here once before . . . very briefly. My husband and I stayed one night at his mother's house. We weren't married then, actually. I hope I remember the way . . . it was six years ago."

"Who is your husband?"

Judith didn't feel she needed to tell the man that it was her ex-husband. After all, she had said "husband" herself, hadn't she?

"Robert Fuseli," she told the man, and then hopefully: "Do you know him?" Perhaps this man could tell her if she might indeed find Robert living in his mother's house. She had recently learned that Robert's mother had passed way five months ago. Robert was to have inherited her house in such an event, he had told her. It was the most obvious place to look for him . . . for she had recently learned that Robert had disappeared five months ago . . .

With a creak of wood, and perhaps of bone, the old man stepped from the doorway and clumped stiffly toward Judith. Involuntarily, she took a step backwards . . . though he was stunted and obviously frail. It was his dark glasses that lent him an air of ominousness. It had become overcast, and again, he'd been lurking in gloom. Could he be blind? Or might the eyes behind those dark lenses be a glowing lurid pink?

"Robert Fuseli lives in his mother's house," the elderly man related. "But you would do well to leave him alone in his task, my dear."

"Robert is here?" Judith said. Though she had known he must be, an ache of both excitement and dread wrung her heart like a rag in her chest. And then: "What task?"

"The task of his mother, and his father before that. You aren't from Sesqua, my dear girl . . . you can't understand our tasks and callings. He should never have left here. He should never have married an outsider. Go back to where you came from, my dear."

Judith tossed aside her unlit cigarette, and slung her bags over her slight shoulders. "Thank you for your help," she said curtly, and started away. She didn't like the way the old man had kept stiffly advancing on her, like some animated corpse, as if he might not stop until he had hold of her.

"Wait," he croaked, behind her back.

She turned, and started—for the man had removed his glasses. And his eyes were not pink . . . but a silvery color, as if clouded with cataracts.

"If you must find your husband . . . then stay here with him. Outsiders have made their home here before. But don't take him away from his task. Now that his mother is dead . . . who else is there?"

Judith could not respond to the man, at first. For one thing, his words made little sense to her. For another—those metallic eyes. For they were so like Robert's own eyes. And his mother's. The effect was more subtle in the Fuselis, but similar enough. She had found Robert's eyes magical, unique, beautiful . . . and unnerving. They had excited her for unnerving her, in the beginning. But she had taken it to be a peculiar family trait.

"Are you related to Robert?" she asked.

"We are both Sesquans," the old man replied. "You are not." And with that, he stopped advancing just short of stepping out of the shadow of the building and into the pallid sunlight.

Judith stared at the man a moment more, and then turned away from him again, hurrying on her way. She didn't look back this time, but felt his silvery gaze upon her until she had turned a bend in the narrow, forest-flanked road.

*   *   *

By the time she reached the old two-storey house, it was early evening, and a light chill rain had just begun to fall. For the last half hour, Judith had become increasingly anxious, afraid that she had taken the wrong road. For that last half hour she had seen no other dwellings along the narrow road that wound through black fir trees so massed that it seemed it would be impossible to enter amongst them. But now, the house lay before her as she came around a bend, as if the black curtains of trees drew back to unveil it.

Beyond the house she could see a wide pasture, long overgrown with weeds and wild grasses, waist-high, yellow and bent down in a greeting to autumn. The pasture was bordered on its distant edge by a looming inky line of trees like the spiked and spired wall of some fairy tale fortress. And lending itself to this mystical image was a large standing stone in the very center of the clearing, gray in the gray light, tilted in the soil, like some fragment of an exploded world thrown to earth, impaling it.

Though from Britain, Judith was a city girl and had never herself seen any of the megaliths scattered across her land. This sight had made her marvel when Robert first showed it to her. She had asked him if it had been erected by a primitive people for religious or astrological purposes. He told her, as some asserted regarding the British megaliths, that it was probably just a scratching post for cows to rub their hides against.

Judith held back a few moments, watching the softly yellow windows for a

P.AW '00

passing silhouette, but saw none. The rain was starting to pick up, however, and she found herself floating to the door like a somnambulist. Watched her arm float up. Listened to the feeble rap of her knuckles.

The door opened, and there were the dark eyes with the silvery sheen, as if he wore contacts of a translucent chrome. Robert. His short dark hair, like her own, was tousled . . . his skin, like her own, as pale as that of some cave-dwelling animal that the light might wither. He needed a shave, and he looked thin in an oversized t-shirt, baggy pants, his bony feet bare. He looked distressed, as he took her in . . . as if he thought that she had died in these past months, and it was an apparition of his ex-wife he saw standing on his doorstep.

"What are you doing here?" he husked.

She gave him a strained little smile that barely touched her lips. Her lipstick was brown, his favorite shade, because it complimented her large dark eyes and the full dark brows that lowered over them intensely, mysteriously. She knew the power her own eyes held over him, but tried not to let her knowledge be transparent. In a voice dark as her looks, she casually joked, "I'm getting quite wet, is what I'm doing."

He craned his neck, peering over her head into the gathering murk. "You shouldn't be walking alone out here at night. You shouldn't be here at all . . ." He gestured at her bags. "What are these for?"

"Please help me with them, Robert." A moment, and then: "Please let me come in."

She saw his throat move as he swallowed. And then he was stepping aside for her, and holding the door wider.

*　　*　　*

He made a fresh pot of coffee; he knew she preferred it to tea. They had first had coffee together, on their first date, while strolling through Victoria's Butchart Gardens. Judith's family had moved to the very British city of Victoria, on the southern tip of Vancouver Island, shortly after she had graduated from school. In her mid-twenties, she met Robert, who had also left his home behind; the Sesqua Valley in the Pacific Northwest of the United States. She was the art director for a printing company. He was an aspiring artist who ran a printing press to pay his bills. In that regard, nothing much had changed for them over the five years of their marriage. In that regard.

After her long chill walk, Judith sipped the black coffee gratefully. Coffee had been the first passion they'd shared.

They stood about his small, warm kitchen, and now Robert turned to fully face her, to address her. "Why are you here, Jude?" he asked grimly.

Jude the Obscure had been his teasing nickname for her. They had also shared a passion for the works of Jude's author, Thomas Hardy. Robert's favorite of his novels was *Tess of the d'Urbervilles*. Thinking of the standing stone in the pasture, Judith remembered the climactic scene of Tess' capture and symbolic sacrifice at Stonehenge, after murdering her cruel lover so as to return to her husband . . .

For all their power over him, Judith still found herself averting her eyes. They didn't feel powerful at the moment. "Ian and I are no longer together, Robert."

Several moments. And then: "Really? Did you leave him, or did he leave you?"

"He's back with his wife. They're going to try again."

"I see. He dumped you. And so now, here you are. Here. With bags."

"Robert . . . you must believe that when we broke up—Ian and I—I was honestly relieved. I was actually happy. He's doing the right thing, going back to try to salvage his marriage. He should never have left her in the first place." She lifted her gaze to his at last. "And I made a terrible mistake as well."

Robert's voice had risen a trifle, and trembled slightly, but he was obviously struggling to keep its tone icy and composed. "A relief, huh? You were happy he dumped you? You weren't at all hurt? At all angry?"

"Yes . . . I was hurt and angry, too. But I was relieved. I was anxious to find you . . ."

"Find me. The spare tire, now that the other is flat. Find me . . . your second choice."

"Robert."

"Jude, you would not be here if Ian hadn't broken off with you. He's the love of your life. The one you left your five year marriage for . . ."

"Robert, I never stopped loving you. It wasn't easy for me, leaving you. It hurt me horribly."

"I'm sure he comforted you. Listen, Jude . . . I can understand why you left me. You should never have been with me in the first place. I was poor . . . we lived more on your money than mine. We could never vacation, struggled with our bills . . ."

"I never blamed you for that."

"But the money made it tense. We were scared, and we fought. Subconsciously, maybe, you resented me for not trying harder. Thought I was weak . . ."

"No. I never resented you. But yes, the money problems depressed me greatly. I was unhappy. We were both of us miserable. And then—Ian came along. Charming . . . handsome. I became dazzled like a wanky little teenager. He distracted me from all the fear and depression. But you weren't the source of my fear and depression, Robert."

"Ian is the man you always wanted. You were reluctant to be with me from the start, but I was persistent. You always said we weren't perfectly suited. Ian is British . . . He's more your ideal in every way."

"No, Robert. You and I aren't perfectly suited . . . no couple is. But we're both artists, and that makes us as well suited as any two people could be. Don't blame yourself for this in any way. It was entirely me. People are greedy, selfish. They become jaded, and lose their perspectives. They're restless and never content. Our . . . bloody consumer-obsessed society teaches us to always want more, something better, something different; that relationships are disposable like everything else . . ."

"I never felt that way."

"I know you didn't. You're different. You're loyal. Loyal to your family. Loyal to me. Don't put yourself down. You didn't disappoint me. God, you're too forgiving . . . but at the same time, I'm here to ask your forgiveness." Her dark voice had grown husky, and now cracked. Her brows gathered like storm clouds over her eyes. "I'm so sorry that I hurt you . . ."

"You think . . . you think I can just forget that you left me for him? That you laughed with him? Held his hand? That you made love? Him inside you, his hands on you? It poisons me, Jude. And I can't be someone's second choice."

"Robert, you are my first and only choice, now. I can see that Ian didn't love me as I thought. That changed my feelings for him. Yes, I was hurt. But it felt right that he left me. It felt right to remember my love for you."

A cruel, agonized smile marred Robert's face. "It's ironic, isn't it? Neither of us can be the first choice of our loves. You aren't Ian's, and I'm not yours. So I guess we two unwanted things are well suited, after all."

"Robert, I'm telling you, it isn't that way . . . not anymore . . ."

"You can never convince me that it isn't. You would be with Ian forever if he hadn't changed that."

"I don't know that. And I'd like to try to change your mind . . . if you'll only give me the chance."

"I can't go through this again, Jude! I barely survived it once. If it didn't work again . . . I can't. I could understand your leaving me. I could accept it because I felt I never deserved you in the first place. But don't do this to me now . . ." his voice broke, his face crumpled like a child's ". . . don't . . ."

Judith started toward him, reached out to him, but he backed against the sink, held up warding hands.

"Anyway, it's too late. I'm back in Sesqua, Jude. I swore I'd never come back here . . . even though I knew my poor mother was sick. But when we broke up, when I had nowhere else to go . . ."

"It isn't too late . . ."

"It is too late!" he half shouted, half sobbed. "I have things to do here, things you could never understand. Things I can't even describe, and that you'd never even believe . . ."

"What are you talking about? Robert, please—I'll do anything you ask. I'll even move here with you if that's what you want. I'll quit my job, freelance from here. Robert . . . only you matter . . ."

"No! No. You can spend the night. But tomorrow you have to leave. It's the only way it can be." He covered his face in his long, graceful artist's hands, scarred by years of factory labor. "It's too late . . ."

Judith once more thought of Hardy's Tess, how she had told her husband it was too late for them to be together again. Too late to stop the terrible gears of her fate. But Judith was determined that it was not too late for herself. She did not again try to touch Robert so as to comfort his weeping. But by the same token, though this was his house, she had no intention of leaving it tomorrow. She could have been wrong, but she believed that in his heart of hearts, he didn't want her to leave now any more than he had wanted her to leave him the first time . . .

*　　*　　*

In her dream, she knew the name of the tower that soared with impossible height from the caverns below . . . soared to touch the crust of the waking world. Koth, it was called . . .

And she knew the beings were called Gugs, before even she could discern them. At first, they were merely shambling hulks, dark and dark-furred. If only they hadn't reached that circle of stones. In its center, they had lit a bonfire. The light of its flames illuminated the silent procession . . . and their terrible activities at the megaliths they had erected. Each of these was a brother to the stone in Robert's pasture . . .

The flames seemed to glow inside pink eyes set on jagged-hooded projections of bone. And mouths gaped wide, soundlessly. Mouths that gaped vertically in hideous faces . . . fangs that flashed back the colors of fire and blood.

And what they were doing. What they were doing . . . God help her that she ever should have seen. The Great Ones had banished them for just such practices . . .

And there was something more horrible yet . . .

. . . and that was that the creatures seemed to be aware she was observing them. First one, then another, then all turned to gaze directly at her invisible dreamer's form, amongst them, spying on them.

It was then that the first of the Gugs started toward her.

It was then that Judith awoke with a gasp.

As her breathing slowed, she reached out shakily for a light. At first, she half-expected to find Ian beside her. But this was her ex-husband's bed, and the spot beside her gaped empty. Robert slept on his sofa, in the other room. He had insisted she sleep in his bed. His pillows smelled subtly of his shampoo, his after shave. She had wept into them.

The rain had stopped, the night lay still. No sound of city traffic, no sound even of rustling trees. Judith heard only one sound, and she had no idea what it was.

A scraping? A scratching? She was reminded of their former apartment together, on the second floor of an old house in Victoria. The branches of a tree, on windy nights, would scratch against the kitchen window like nails on a blackboard. It was just like that. Only . . . only it seemed to be coming up from the floor. Up from the cellar she knew lay below, though she had never gone down there herself.

She sat up in bed listening to the scraping. While she did so, her distracted gaze took in a gun rack on the wall, in which a shotgun and two rifles rested, and it vaguely disturbed her, as she knew Robert abhorred hunting. She was fully awake now; it was more the nightmare than the sound that kept her from slipping back beneath the covers, but now that she was awake, the sound tugged at her. At last, giving in to it, she slipped out of bed and stole out into the living room. For some reason, the sound made her afraid . . . as if it were the creak of a rope from which Robert dangled, unable to bear the fear of losing her a second time . . .

But he lay asleep on the sofa, curled against the pain that held his jaw tense and brows knitted intensely even in sleep. Standing over him, Judith wanted to gently smooth that brow, soothe it, but she did not touch him. Instead, barefoot, she continued on past him, into the kitchen where the door to the basement stood double-bolted.

She slipped both bolts, threw a switch against the wall. A breeze so chill it made her shudder was exhaled up at her, like a kiss from dead lips. Judith began to descend rough wooden steps that creaked and sagged even under her slight weight. At their foot, the darkness branched off into two directions. On her right, she heard the hiss of a water heater, saw the shadowy hunched forms of a washer and dryer. Prosaic enough. But the high-pitched scratching came from the left, from a room of the cellar into which only the dregs of light reached.

Boxes of books, of tools, bundled newspapers and old furniture were piled against the walls, but at its center there was one thing only—a great, rounded hump covered completely by a tarp large enough to cover a car. The squealing scratches came from this mound, from under that heavy tarp . . .

Bricks weighed the corners of the tarp, and Judith stooped to remove several of them. For a moment she hesitated to go further. Then, curling her fingers around the tarp, she threw its edge up over the top of the mound. She didn't know what she would find, and when she found it, didn't know what it was.

It appeared to be a great globe of dark metal or glass, buried in the cement floor of the cellar but for its upper surface. Or was that all there was of it, a huge concave object? Whether sphere or hemisphere, the scratching came from its inner surface.

Granted, it was gloomy in the basement, but at first the glass seemed truly opaque, if not absolutely black. But as she studied it, the surface seemed to gradually lighten. Until she was certain that it was indeed growing lighter. A murky gray. At last, somehow, miraculously, almost entirely transparent. It was gloomy within the glass, also . . . gloomy under the cellar floor, which the glass seemed to peer into like a monstrous lens. But she could discern light in that gloom . . . a flickering light bleeding in from the distance. The reddish glow of a nearby fire.

And there were two other lights, closer at hand. They floated nearer, like luminous fish at the bottom of the sea, rising to investigate her. The twin smudges of light moved in unison . . . and were of a soft pink color.

Before Judith could back away—before she could scream—the face pressed up against the interior of the glass. Huge nails raked against the inside of the lens. The thing's jaws gnashed vertically, so that its fangs ground across the glass as well. And the eyes of the Gug glared hungrily out at her.

"No!" Judith heard Robert shout behind her. "Don't let it see you! Don't let it see you!" He was suddenly pushing her out of the way, throwing himself across the lens as if to blot it out, pulling down the dreaming eyelid of the dark tarp and pinning it again with bricks.

Judith fell back against the wall, gasping for air as when she had been jolted from her nightmare. When Robert whirled to face her, they stared at each other in horror and despair.

"Robert," Judith began to sob, "what is it? What are they? What's down there?"

"It's the Dreamlands, Jude. It's why you shouldn't have come. It's what you shouldn't have seen, and what my family has been chosen to guard against since my grandfather's father built this house around the Dream Lens."

"I don't understand!"

He continued on as if in a trance, as if a terrible numbing calm had fallen over him. "The Dreamlands are on another plane, Jude. But Sesqua is a special place. The veils are very thin here. Extremely thin in a spot like this. It should not have been seen. Especially not by an outsider. Now you know why I can never leave again, and why I can't have you here . . . even if I wanted."

The scratching continued, frantic, desperate, hungry. Judith shook, hugging herself, eyes fixed on the shroud of the tarpaulin. The mound was like a belly pregnant with a monster anxious to be born. Who knew how many monstrosities, waiting to be born into this world?

"I'm afraid now that it saw you, and you saw into its world," Robert went on, "that . . . that things will be bad. The two worlds mustn't see into each other. It starts a door to open. My father looked too long in the lens, once . . ." He let the story trail off. "But it's too late, now. You didn't know; it isn't your fault. It's . . . too late to change anything now."

*   *   *

Robert had to support Judith as he walked her back up the stairs, and down the hall back to her bed. He sat on its edge as he covered her. As he rose, she looked up at him imploringly, her large eyes like those of a frightened child, and lay a hand lightly on his arm.

"Please," she whispered. "Don't leave me."

He sat beside her again, and held her hand. Held it until mercifully dreamless sleep clouded her stunned mind. Continued holding it. Long minutes after she was asleep, at last he whispered back, "I won't."

*   *   *

Was it a nightmare?

Robert was at the bedroom window, his body tense as a deer's . . . or a cougar's, ready to spring on the deer. He was staring out into the night, and Judith heard him whisper, "No . . . God, no . . ."

He whirled from the window, lurched toward the door. Judith caught a glimpse of his eyes, wide and flashing silver, and then he was at the gun rack. And then out through the door. She swung her legs out of bed. "Robert!" she called after him.

As she rose, Judith turned to glance out the window, and the curtains were still spread, as if some ethereal veil had been parted so that she might see what lay behind her former reality.

A translucent mist lay over the pasture like a milky membrane, a caul, a burial shroud, and the moon had come out from behind the dispersing rain clouds. It made the mist glow.

In the center of the wild meadow, the standing stone was gone. In its place towered a ghost, seemingly made of that same glowing fog.

"Robert!" Judith cried again, and then she too was darting from the room . . . barefoot, in her nightgown, like a sleepwalker running from her nightmare—or running deeper into her dream.

He had already left the house ahead of her . . . was already racing through the tangled field. As she burst through the door into the night air, Judith saw again that figure of mist where the standing stone had been. It was not a ghost, but a ghostly outline of the megalith's former essence. The mist sparkled in that smoky pillar, and then she felt she knew why. The stone had not turned to mist . . . but its substance had come unwoven, unmeshed, so that the tiny granite crystals swirled and glittered like powder.

As Judith waded into the meadow, the weeds and tall grass grabbed at her bare ankles like myriad living limbs of one vast, malignant creature. She thrashed wildly along, and at one point she fell. As she struggled back to her feet and lifted her head, she saw two things—that Robert had very nearly reached the center of the pasture . . . and that a pair of glowing pink eyes had appeared within the ghostly megalith.

Robert planted himself in a stance, worked the shotgun's slide, and a crashing report like thunder rumbled across the meadow as he fired into the mist . . . and then again . . . and then again. Judith flinched at each blast . . . and saw the pink eyes quickly withdraw.

She resumed her wading into the field, and Robert saw her coming. He called to her, "A sacrifice will appease them. Blood will close the door again. I think I got it." But he returned his attention to the unwoven obelisk, and added, "It's not closing . . . Jude, go back to the house!"

Pink eyes rushing . . . and then the Gug was through . . .

It stooped to pass through the portal of fog, but quickly raised itself to its full height. A tower of shaggy blackness with those orbs blazing near its summit. In one motion, as it came through, it swung one heavy forelimb— and Judith saw Robert go flying back as if struck by a car, the shotgun spinning end over end through the air.

She heard the weapon thud somewhere ahead of her. She beat her way toward it, trying not to look upon the great beast or being that shambled toward Robert. It took its time in reaching him. It did not expect him to escape it. No sound came from its jaws, which worked vertically like a giant clam fused into what passed for its face.

The Gug stood over Robert, and then turned its head abruptly to see Judith there, bringing the shotgun up and squeezing the trigger.

A small dry click like a twig snapping. The Gug took a step, now, toward her . . . reaching out . . . great clawed fingers spreading . . . fingers dripping dark drops of human blood . . .

Judith pumped the slide and squeezed the trigger again and the recoil kicked her back a few steps. She saw one of the twin pink suns above her suddenly go black.

It made no cry, but the Gug whirled away—in agony, now a Cyclops—and stooped again into the portal. Was gone . . .

Judith turned to see that Robert had risen to his feet. He hugged himself tightly as if against the cold, but from the dark ribbons flowing over both arms, Judith knew he was holding himself together. Their eyes met.

"Robert!" Judith sobbed, her whole body quaking. "Robert . . . I'm so sorry. Oh Robert . . . my love . . . I'm so sorry . . ."

He smiled, and turned his back on her as if afraid she would see how badly he was wounded. He trudged painfully toward the misty pillar, and just short of reaching it he faced her again. "Sacrifice will appease them," he repeated. "Blood . . . will close the door . . ."

"Robert!" Judith cried, but she didn't try to stop him as he began to back into that glittering, swirling mist.

He smiled again. "I forgive you," he told her, and then was gone, as if it were his own essence that resolidified into that dark, leaning standing stone.

*   *   *

It was a crisp, early autumn morning, the sky so blue and the bleached double peaks of Mt. Selta—looming over the valley—so bright that they nearly hurt the eyes. And morning found a small, lovely woman with dark hair and eyes walking up the road to the combination general store/gas station, where the infrequent buses stopped.

His eyes hidden by dark glasses, an elderly man hovered in the doorway, watching the woman approach. When she was near enough, he asked her, "Are you returning now, my dear?"

But Judith didn't stop at the spot where buses came. She continued approaching the old man, until she stood before him. "Is your store open?" she asked him in a calm, quiet voice.

"Yes," the old man replied, a bit confused.

"There will be things I need to buy. For the house."

"For the house?"

"Yes—there's a task that needs to be seen to," Judith told him. "I'll be staying."

THE SERVITORS

Skrey had chosen this as his day of emancipation.

He gave not the slightest indication of his plans, nor even of the discontent that had spawned them. He functioned as he had every day for the past four thousand years.

Skrey was an assistant feeder at the Twelfth Orifice. Kreve was crane operator and head feeder of this opening. At present, Kreve had had to shut down the feed crane in order to reset the great ring of black metal which held the circular wound open. As the wound attempted to heal, the ring was sometimes forced to contract. Kreve would adjust a huge crank to expand the ring and reclaim lost ground. First, however, he used a bladed pike, of the same black metal as the ring and the idle crane, to slice at the flesh which had begun to actually grow over the ring's rim. The severed fragments either stuck to Kreve's four multi-jointed grey arms, splattered at his bony cloven feet, or tumbled away into the great yawning crater of the orifice.

Standing almost on the opposite side of the vast wound, Skrey shoveled feed manually over the edge, digging a black metal spade into a black metal tub filled with a translucent sebaceous matter, yellow with coarse black hairs sprouting out of it. He heard the feed thump against the raw red throat of the wound occasionally but had never heard it strike bottom.

Pausing from his labors, all four arms aching, he watched Kreve pick at the unwanted collar of flesh in his usual crude, sloppy manner. He left ragged strands dangling, wouldn't sweep the debris over the lip into the volcano-like maw. Skrey would have to clip those untidy shreds, clean up the rubble. When he excised the flesh he always did it neatly. When he, rarely, got to operate the crane he never splashed feed accidentally all over the lip. Skrey kept the crane oiled, scraped off rust and blood—where Kreve would let the machine become clogged almost to a halt, on his own. But who was still head feeder, after four thousand years? Who was the favorite of the Supervisor, and could do no wrong? *Yes,* Skrey thought, *I could be a favorite also . . . if I treated the Supervisor like he was God.* But the Supervisor wasn't God; just another servitor, like the rest of them. A tiny, crawling nothing, scraping out his tiny existence on the planet-huge body of the Dreaming One. The One Who Slumbers. The Phantast. Now, *He* was God.

Kreve, the bastard. He had also been at fault for the death of Skrey's mate, four thousand years ago, when the drillers had first bored the Twelfth Orifice. Poor Mrek had been on the drill team. It had been the responsibility of both drill leader and Kreve, in setting up his crane, to ensure they had chosen a sound site to bore. But their check for parasites had been cursory. Just below the epidermis, the drill hit a great nest of plump writhing larvae, which in feasting had tunneled the immediate sub-layers profoundly. The drill lost its support and toppled into the fresh wound. Skrey remembered it now; the drill platform screeching metallically, vanishing in the thick mist of blood which geysered up out of the wound. And the operators, trapped on the drill, screeching in horror. One of those voices had been Mrek's . . .

Kreve had only received light punishment; his four arms and two legs cut off and prevented from regenerating for forty years. Unbelievable. Skrey's only consolation had been that brief respite, working without Kreve, while the bastard lay in a dark corner somewhere, counting dust motes.

Mrek had never pulled herself up out of that maw, as two other drillers had. They'd caught hold of the sides, which still offered ragged hand-holds, not yet fully bored smooth. Shaken, covered in blood and mucus, but alive. Mrek must have hit that far-away bottom. An ocean of bile, lost in the darkness beyond sight.

As he shoveled feed anew, Skrey imagined what it was like to die. The servitors had been created all but immortal. He had survived countless atrocious on-job accidents (most of them Kreve's fault). He was sure he had spawned a few fresh servitors that way. Vaguely he was aware that he himself had started life as an arm jerked off a worker in a cleaning team when a wild hose got wrapped around it. Was that worker like himself? Dissatisfied? Unhappy? Angry? And ever angrier, for being so unhappy?

Had the Supervisor allowed Kreve's six severed limbs to clone themselves into full servitors? Dormant One—he hoped not! Six more of the bastard . . .

Six more for Skrey to kill.

The servitors could die . . . if their bodies were fully and quickly dissolved. Or digested—as in the unseen corrosive sea at the bottom of the giant well Skrey labored at every day.

* * *

Jean's eyes felt full and hard with the pain of her headache, like billiard balls in her skull. They were the only part of her that showed, ninja-like, in her white costume, and she even wore goggles to complete her disguise.

Through these aching lenses she watched the carousel turn, the jiggling glass cartridges filling with a clear local anesthetic to be administered via hypodermic by dentists. Thousands of tiny tubes of pain-numbing elixir, none of it any good for the pain she felt now. They were a taunt. She imagined the deep stabbing of those thousands of needles.

Jean watched for crimps or dents in the little metal caps which her huge machine then sealed the cartridges with. A dent could make an air bubble. Dangerous. She plucked these and broken cartridges out with rubber-sheathed fingers. The carousel fed into a tray, the cartridges squeezing their multitudes into it like people swarming out of a carnival ride. When it was full she paused the filler, removed the tray and inserted it through a hole in the wall to a person on the other side, whom she could see but not speak with. This was a woman who always seemed to have a look of amused scorn on her face, and who seemed to make comments about Jean to the others out there. They could watch her all night through the glass, like a creature in an aquarium.

Jean couldn't go get some aspirin. Not for two more hours, her next break. And she shouldn't have had two coffees at supper; she would have to wait two more hours to relieve herself. Eight times a day she changed her clothes at work. Every time there was a break, all the outer garments of the sterile department—hood, mask, jumpsuit, booties, gloves—would be discarded . . . then, after break, a fresh outfit would be donned over her standard white uniform. All of it a blinding, eye-stabbing white. A termite white. Jean felt a rebellious urge to wear black or red underwear under all that sterile white, but was afraid that it would show through.

No conversation in sterile was audible over the roar of machinery, no lips could be seen to be read. There was no piped-in music, no portable tape or CD players allowed. There were no posters, no tacked up photos of children. Color, it seemed, had been forbidden. Just eyes . . . and though these were said to be the windows of the soul, the eyes Jean had contact with during the nights were dusty, showed no lights on inside, or seemed to have their shades drawn. She was sure that hers looked the same.

George, her immediate boss, came in and greeted her by motioning impatiently at the tank into which the great bags of metal caps were poured to keep them replenished. It was nearly empty. Jean knew this; she'd been keeping a peripheral eye on it. Hadn't she worked this job for five years now? But with huffy movements, George ripped open and dumped a fresh bag himself.

The tray was full; too full, as Jean had taken her eyes from it to look at George. It happened sometimes, but shouldn't while George was around. She paused the filler, slid the tray out, and, despite her attempts not to jar them, two dozen cartridges lingering on the walkway between carousel and tray toppled off the precipice like a horde of lemmings, crashing to a floor already crunchy with glass, wet with pain-killer.

At the end of the shift she would suck up the glass with a vacuum, hose down the floor, while the last dregs of the tank were drained. She could not go home, or even leave the room, until this was accomplished. She had complained once. "Overtime!" George had exclaimed. "How can you complain about making time and a half?" But the nights were so long, and life so short . . .

George disgustedly caught up a mop and pushed the bulk of the mess away from her feet, against the wall until later. The mop bumped her feet roughly as he did so. Jean thought, then, that anyone who could not at least understand why a worker would slaughter supervisors and co-workers had never worked blue collar.

* * *

Sometimes, as now, when Skrey concentrated hard or allowed a meditative calm to come over him, he could feel her. He turned his face of bony chitin up toward the roof of the cavern the Dreaming One reposed in, so distant and dark that it seemed the infinity of space itself. Beyond the infinity, he sensed her. She was her own being, and yet a version of himself, interpreted differently by the dimension she lived in, the plane she dwelt on. They were apart, yet connected. Did she ever sense his life?

She was a female of her kind, he knew that much. It didn't trouble him. What intrigued him was the softness of her flesh, and especially the brightness of her world. Every day she garbed herself in white, ritualistically, and entered a white place. Perhaps she was a priestess . . .

Skrey knew of her plane not only from this connection he had to it, but from what he'd heard from the caste of servitors called the explorers, who ventured into other dimensions to inspire cults of worship for the Phantast, and to destroy enemies. What a place of wonders they told of! Open skies of color, and—at night—stars.

Kreve came toward Skrey, carrying his pike. His mandibles chattered to admonish Skrey. "Dreaming again, friend? Leave dreaming for the Master and shovel that feed! If the Master grumbles hungry in His sleep you'll wish you had been sent to work in the waste holes, when the Supervisor is done with you."

Skrey dug his shovel into the tub, swiveled his head to glance over his shoulder. He saw no other workers from here. "Do you ever dream of freedom, Kreve?" he asked.

"There is no such thing as freedom. It is an abstraction. Even the Master is not free. He is trapped in His dreams."

"Death is freedom, though, is it not? Freedom from slavery? Freedom from pain?"

"Yes, fool, I suppose it is."

"Then I give you a gift, fellow slave." Skrey shoveled a blob of feed up into Kreve's face. Kreve sputtered, stumbled back, blindly tried to raise his pike, but too late. The shovel blade swung sideways against his skull like an ax.

Kreve plummeted over the lip. No hand-holds now. Slick mucus walls. Skrey did not hear him hit the sea of bile . . . just a screeching cry fading to nothingness.

"Be free," Skrey said.

*   *   *

The bottle of maximum strength aspirin sat on the top shelf of her locker. Also on the shelf, inside a paper lunch bag, was her boyfriend's cherished SIG-Sauer P-225 semiautomatic. Boy, would he kill her if he knew she'd smuggled it out of the house . . . not just tonight, but every night of the week thus far. But she had never taken it out of the bag, had returned it to its drawer each night when she got home. Lightly, she reached into the bag and touched the pebbled handle, the black metal. It had been a rebellious act, bringing this black blot into this white place. Like the panties she wanted to wear . . .

Roy, a plumber, owned his own house at twenty-six. Now he wanted to get married. He wanted children. Two and a half children, Jean thought. She did not want children.

"Why?" Roy had said. "Jesus! What kind of woman doesn't want children?"

She couldn't answer that. There might be many answers. A woman who simply did not care for those particular responsibilities? Who did not want to give away her life to others when she could be living it herself? A woman who did not see why she had to propagate a species whose worthiness of continuation was questionable?

Well, Roy had gone on, in essence, what *do* you want to do? What else is life for? To produce and reproduce. Like a good sheep. But Jean had once dreamed of traveling, of exploring, of being everything she could be, like they told you in school. Only, she had found in her twenties that you couldn't be all you could be. You couldn't *really*, ultimately, be what you wanted. There were limits. Walls. Society was bigger and stronger and had its own agenda. Oh, it sounded like a cop-out, even to herself . . . but it was true, wasn't it?

The pain was so great in her head, in the agonized orbs she stared through, she doubted the aspirin could help her now. Maybe if she took the whole bottle, it could help her. Cure her. Maybe then . . .

Instead, she removed the heavy paper bag from the locker. She slipped the chunky gun into the waistband of her pants, pulled her shirt down over it. No, its blackness didn't show through. Good. She felt better. She would smuggle some personality back into the sterile department. A shard of identity, a piece of self, compacted like a collapsed star into a heavy black core of anger.

*   *   *

Skrey rode a feed conveyer belt most of the way to the First Orifice, jumped off before the crew there could spot him. The absence of the feeders at the

Twelfth Orifice would have been noticed by now, but the Supervisor would not guess Skrey's destination . . .

He worked his way into the forest of the Dreamer's tentacles, immense trunks that stirred far above or flopped over, their tips almost brushing the floor of tough wrinkled flesh. Several times Skrey ducked behind a trunk as a cleaner crew moved by. At last, he reached one of the narrow cauterized tunnels leading to the headquarters of the explorers . . .

More ducking, here, more stealthiness; the explorers looked different enough for Skrey's presence to be conspicuous. Finally, one explorer did ask his purpose. Skrey chattered, "I'm a feeder, off-duty, come to visit my friend Gret."

Gret was not truly a friend, but the explorer was satisfied with this explanation and waved Skrey on.

Skrey wound his way deeper into the lair of the explorers, brushing past several more of that caste, muttering his same successful story a few times, until he entered at last into the Chamber of Portals. There were no guards at the entrance; no one had thought to enter this place before with questionable intent. Only once prior had Skrey come here, with a few other feeders and an explorer they'd bribed, just to look through the portals and marvel. Skrey had never forgotten. How could Kreve have suggested that freedom was an illusion? Every one of the round windows ringing this chamber hewn from flesh was a window on freedom.

This room was close to the outside of the brain of the Slumbering Master, and it was His mind that dreamed open the doors into these other worlds, these alternate realities. Some portals showed only seething fog, or writhing light. One showed the dark depths of an ocean. An ocean of water, not bile! Did Skrey have a self in that realm, and if so was it an intelligent being or a simple animal? Even living in that sea as a mindless animal, free to swim where it chose, would be liberation . . .

But he had only ever felt the connection to the female who wore white, the soft-fleshed being in the world of humans. It was her world he wanted to escape to. It was with her he wanted to be.

She would never have met a being like him. She would be horrified, but he would persuade her to accept him, and help him establish a life in some safe region. And she would help him. She would realize their connection. That she and he were the same many-faced soul.

An explorer entered the chamber and Skrey pivoted his head. He recognized Gret.

"I am told you are looking for me, feeder?"

* * *

Jean removed the tray from the carousel. She had not, however, paused the carousel. As though mesmerized, she watched it turn, a slow whirlpool, a vortex, drawing her in . . .

The gleaming glass parade of cartridges marched straight off the cliff edge to dash themselves on the floor between Jean's feet.

The amused/scornful woman outside the sterile department had come over to receive the tray but now began rapping on the glass, pointing at the carousel. Jean ignored her.

Peripherally, Jean saw her boss join the woman. He rapped more loudly on the glass. Still she didn't look. The cartridges became a small jagged pile, even across her booty-covered sneakers. A blur as her boss moved from the window.

This carousel was her life. Circles. It took her nowhere. And she was just one of many cartridges. No. Not just any. One of the ones with a dented cap. One of the ones with an air bubble. One of the dangerous ones . . .

* * *

Skrey felt vaguely guilty smashing Gret with the wrench he had brought with him from the crane, but he knew the explorer would regenerate. Of course, before he set upon him he had had the sense to ask, in a casual tone, which of the portals led to the world of humans.

More explorers came, responding to Gret's shrieks. From the floor he pointed a limb at one of the portals lining the circular room. "He passed through there!" he croaked. "He must be mad!"

"He'll be directed to his alternate!" cried a young explorer who had never journeyed into that place. "He will be revealed!"

"Don't worry," Gret groaned, pulling himself up. "He won't be noticed."

"Shall we go after him?"

"We don't know who his alternate is, do we?" Gret shook his cracked, bleeding head. "He's not worth tracking down, the crazy fool. He's just a feeder."

* * *

When the boss came in the room, fully suited, Jean heard his roaring over the roaring of the machine and the tinkle of glass. She turned to welcome him with a roar which blotted out his roar. A glittering brass shell leaped to join the cartridges. Another.

The white wall behind the boss was suddenly vivid with color. His pristine uniform became splattered with a deep beautiful red. He went crashing back, pin-wheeling his arms. His eyes were wide and horrified in his goggles. Windows of the soul with the shades spinning. The lights went out in them as he dragged his color down the wall. White canvas splashed with paint; Jean felt like an artist.

Now she turned to fire the SIG through the window-wall. Confusion had already wiped the scorn from the woman's face. Jean obliterated the potential for its return. The shower cap-like hair-covering the woman wore protected her hair from the blood.

Now the air outside communicated with that inside the sterile department. Oh-oh. The company wouldn't approve of that. Jean peeled off her hood, tossed aside her goggles. She inhaled deeply and smiled, as if divesting herself of her mask was the most radical action she had taken.

She fired the next two bullets into the carousel's control panel. It came to a halt, the last cartridges rolling off to shatter.

She heard screams beyond the window, saw darting forms. Termites exposed to the terrors of the world and scampering for fresh shelter, new rocks to hide under.

Jean placed the muzzle of the SIG between her eyebrows and hooked both thumbs over the trigger. She was sure the bullet would be the equal of her headache. It would end all her pain, in fact. It would sever her bonds, cut her tethers, and set her free.

*   *   *

Skrey floated through a vortex of blackness, of nothingness and allness, as if sucked down a whirlpool. A tunnel traversing space and time. He was drawn by some current, or propelled by the Master's unending dreams.

Though this tunnel led to only one of the infinite realities, Skrey still had an odd consciousness of his own infinity. He felt, simultaneously, something of the existence of all his many parallel forms . . . an incomprehensible bombardment of sensations. Distantly, he sensed himself battling in a war. Crying, hopeless, somewhere else. Dying in some worlds . . . being born in a thousand others. It was exhilarating and terrifying. He was a bullet shot through the very clockworks of the wheel of life. He could never know all the manifestations of himself. Could never know himself in his vast entirety. Just the little piece that he was. That, and the woman he was rushing onward to meet.

Like yet another soul being born, he perceived a circular light ahead—opening like an eye onto his destination—and then he was through that portal. The portal closed behind him, was gone. The tunnel itself was gone. It had bored itself ahead to link him with his alternate self, and no one who sought to pursue him could know who in this world that might be. He had succeeded! He had escaped . . .

The light, as in his vision of this plane, was dazzling—blinded him. It took a moment for his eyes to adjust . . . and then what he saw dazzled him more than the light.

The monster Skrey gazed up at in awe was not so huge as the Dreaming One, would still be infinitely small in comparison, but towered nonetheless. Unlike the Master, this creature could be taken in by the eyes all at once . . . and Skrey recognized it as a human.

Had he actually been friends with Gret, the explorer's knowledge could have spared him this shock of realization.

Skrey realized then precisely where the portal had deposited him. He stood upon the great supine form of his soul-mate. Was she sleeping, dreaming? The white-clad behemoth moved toward her, now bending. The horror of its visage! Could the Phantast Himself be so hideous? In terror, Skrey bolted for the nearest shelter. A forest of slim trunks he could hide in, reminding him of the Master's far huger tentacles. On the way, Skrey crossed a shallow pond of red fluid, with a current as it spread. He traced it to its source: a raw orifice, freshly bored. The monster leaned close over his alternate self. Had it spotted him, minuscule as he was? Skrey took no chances. He scurried into that orifice against the tide of blood.

Time passed in alien quantities. Skrey burrowed himself a safe nook. No parasites large enough to threaten him appeared. He could tell his parallel self was lifted, moved, transported. By this time, he had guessed the truth. She was dead . . .

Poor mortal thing. But even in dying, she helped him find shelter. He only wished he could have communicated with her, known her . . .

He went on living in her. Feeding on her. He was alert to the possibility that her kind would burn or dissolve her, but they buried her far below the ground in a container, much as the Dreamer had been buried in His deep cavern. Skrey ventured out at last, saw the container would be hard to escape from, even small as he was . . .

. . . but it would decay, weaken, in time. Until then he had all of his other self to explore, and feed on. And when her nourishment ran out he would survive his hunger, as he was virtually immortal. One day, a hundred years from now or a thousand, he would make his way to the surface. See the open sky for the first time, and the stars at night. He was not concerned. He was patient. He was elated.

He was free.

*   *   *

Mren was a cleaner in the waste holes, hosing out the foul matter of the Phantast's processed nourishment. It was the least enviable of the servitors' positions, but she had put in for work on a feed team. It would be a wait, as she was a young servitor, only freshly born.

She was a servitor born from an egg, rather than cloned from a lost limb, but still she had a sense of a prior life. This was not unusual, she was told, when one had been born of regeneration, but rare for the egg-born. Still, not unknown. Her fellow workers told her that she might be catching a sense of a previous existence, a soul banished from one realm to find fresh expression in another.

This explanation soothed her somewhat, but it could be a very disquieting sensation. Memory fragments surfaced at times unexpectedly, shocking her. Whiteness, blinding, loomed in her consciousness. Strange noises, strange machinery. Jarring violence.

The most horrible sensation of all was that at times she felt a horror of herself, a self-loathing almost as sharp as panic. As if that other self had awakened in her to find itself transformed into a nightmare. A demon. Trapped in a new body it couldn't run out of, escape from.

Mren's work made her restless. And these waking dreams made her restless. But she told herself someday things would get better.

THE DOOM IN THE ROOM

Gentlemen, though you undoubtedly consider me mad as I sit here before you, and indeed mad I nearly went after my encounter with that hell-spawned Doom in the Room, I can only assure you of my sanity and describe to you, though the memory horrifies me to the bowels of my soul, the events which befell me in that hideous house of gambrel-roofed antiquity in ancient and witch-haunted Arkham, Massachusetts.

I was, on that May Eve, 1927, a professor of archeology at Miskatonic University, and had for the past year been searching for a mysterious crystal from the tomb of an obscure Egyptian Pharaoh, said to have come into New England through various strange sets of circumstances. My latest information had focused on a vacant tenement in my own Arkham. The crystal, black with red striations, cut into an odd, unearthly geometric pattern, was said to be a key to dark and hideous wonders, and, though naturally I did not believe such legend literally, I knew I must examine the mystic object at close quarters.

And so it was that I located, with no small difficulty, that ancient, moldering edifice in the more decayed and decadent quarters of Arkham, once glorious but now given over mostly to seedy, furtive foreigners. Some of these types eyed me with horror or bitter humor as I unlocked the door to that building with a key secured from the foreign owner with the guaranteed persuasion of a bottle of spirits.

The musty interior choked me and a strange mood of unholy, wretched, bone-cracking nightmare evil swept me, which filled me with a terror which I didn't comprehend but which scared me. Luckily, some light came through the boards over the windows—enough to keep me from being totally engulfed in Stygian blackness, and I had my trusty pocket flashlight in my coat, along with my frayed clothbound copy of the infamous *Necronomicon*, which I had been reading on the ride here in the motor-coach to occupy my time.

No sooner had I closed the door behind me and taken several steps forward when I heard a strange sound above me which gripped my intestines in the wrenching jaws of stark maddening terror. It was a hard thump, as if something heavy had fallen, some accursed *tripper in the dark*, which rattled the rickety walls of the structure, followed by a kind of shattering sound, and the unmistakable exclamation, though hideously inhuman and muffled through the intervening floors, of "Oops!"

I gathered my wits, and steeled myself, my professional curiosity as yet the equal of my weird and nameless fear, and drawing forth my trusty pocket flashlight, mounted the moldering staircase which took me higher into the bowels of that hell-haunted ruin.

At the first landing I took another moldering, stench-ridden flight, and at the second landing a strange sight lay before me. On the moldering floor of the landing lay an odd chunk of crystal, black in the beam of my light . . . with red striations. It lay just outside a closed door of rotting greenish wood. My excitement temporarily banished my fears as I knelt and retrieved this obvious fragment of my searched-for object, holding it close to my face to make out the weird, unearthly hieroglyphs plainly carved into its surface. And then another surprise took me—as I recognized the horrifying symbols as resembling some I had seen only that day in the fabled pages of the hideous text of the *Necronomicon* of that Mad Arab Abdul Alhazred!

Excitedly, gripping my trusty pocket flashlight in my teeth, the crystal fragment in one hand and the book in the other, I compared the symbols of the crystal to those on those hell-penned arcane pages. Yes! I was correct. Here were the very symbols, part of some weird incantation meant to be chanted at a ritual of untold nightmarish motivation. As I read the Latin translation of that ancient, mysterious language I muttered the words under my breath and moved what little I had of the infamous crystal in strange geometric patterns as dictated by the text. This mumbled chanting was difficult to accomplish with my trusty pocket flashlight gripped in my teeth.

Just then, there was a strange noise behind the moldering greenish door, inside the *unknown room beyond,* which made me start and look up and nearly drop the flashlight from my jaws . . . a sound as of something large and *alive* shifting its weight on creaking, moldering floorboards.

I slipped the crystal fragment into one pocket and the *Necronomicon* into another, took the flashlight in my left hand and willed myself to reach to the knob of that horrid closed door with my trembling right. I was not alone in that gambrel-roofed haunt of ancient horror, and I knew I must confront my unknown companion face to face.

My uncertain hand closed on the cold knob—too late to turn back now—and twisted it until it clicked, and the door opened inward. I pushed it away from me, it swung on its creaking hinges, and I moved the beam of my flashlight into the room.

What stood thus illumined before me nearly drove me insane with God-forsaken fright and nausea, and I was torn between fleeing with a shriek, swooning in a faint, and standing in mute, frozen paralysis—this last winning out. A wave of unbearable stench wafted over me as from a thousand opened corpses, and yet this prodigious miasma of fecal proportions could not but hint at the greater horrors which assailed my eyes in that face to face confrontation I had so ignorantly sought.

The creature looming in that room of doom was more frightful and hideous than words can describe . . . no language or pen of man could hope or would even attempt to portray its unholy vision, so utterly beyond description was it

in its hideousness. It was nine feet tall at the least, and all made of some rubbery stuff I hesitate to call flesh, with nineteen swimming tentacled appendages, each ending in four jointed, insect-like arms tipped in multi-phallic protrusions. The seven legs were as those of an elephant stripped to the bone, and the waist was encircled with red glaring eyes with swimming black lashes as profoundly luxuriant as the underarm hair of a hirsute foreign female. And the face—God help me—was that of a skull with its flesh ripped off and crumpled up into two balls and crammed back into the sockets instead of eyes, the tongue like the lashing tail of a fly-maddened horse. It was like the most hideous, nightmarish thing that could have been shown to the eyes of man . . . the ultimate zenith of horror, unparalleled and insurmountable—only worse.

The crystal for which I had searched must have been what I had heard fumbled and shattered, for now this otherworldly demon was juggling the remaining pieces in its nineteen branching, tentacled arms with a fiendish and boastful skill. As it leered at me triumphantly I finally broke free of my vocal paralysis and screamed. But it was strange words from the book in my pocket that came from my mouth inexplicably. Yog-Sothoth! Ia! Xqyrhe! Rhrhszj!

Even now as I stand in the threshold of that damned room of doom, frantically typing out this last frenzied message and warning to all mankind, that leering and juggling horror bears inexorably toward me! God save me! That stench of open crypts, of the very septic system of other dimensions! Its breath is now upon me . . . those phallic projections! Ia! Yog-Sothoth! *Ouch!*

OUT OF THE BELLY OF SHEOL

The clouds crashed one atop the other and boomed like an angry surf. The ocean roared like thunder and churned as black as rain clouds. It seemed one had become the other—that the world had been turned on its head.

Jonah was glad for the men who held his arms; otherwise—looking straight up beyond the sails that thrashed like tortured ghosts—he had the vertiginous terror that he would fall upwards into that vortex of sky. Sucked up into the maw of the God he had failed.

They had found him lying in the hold of the ship bound for Tarshish, and knowing that he was said to be a holy man had bellowed at him to awaken and talk to his God . . . but he had not been sleeping. He was a prophet, and he couldn't describe to these simple sailors, who were fortunate not to be prophets, how the mind could become filled until the body fell helpless with the weight of the cosmos inside it.

He thought of the sensation of an encroaching prophecy as being like the tendrils of a strange plant snaking inside his skull, growing at an accelerated rate, winding into the very fissures of his brain, embracing and interweaving, suffocating and transfiguring. Out at sea, the sensation had appropriately felt like a serpentine invasion of squirming, choking seaweed. Whereas his bouts with prophecy usually seemed to drag him up into the ether, this time he had felt he was being dragged down into a dark liquid abyss.

He still shook with the blurred tatters of his visions. Rain shattered against his craggy face, dripped from his sodden beard, collected in the folds of his robes. The deck veered sharply; he heard men cry out, scrabble for purchase. They cried out to God to spare them, and to Jonah to pray as well if God were willing to listen to him alone.

They thought God was one voice, one form, one being who looked much like Jonah did. Like a parent a child could appeal to, converse with. They would kill Jonah if he told them the truth. Their poor minds, small clumps of earthly cells, could not contain the truth: that there were many Gods, and Jonah did not always know which one he listened to.

He had likened his situation to standing in a bustling marketplace, where the confusion of voices was the voices of the Gods. And not only did he hear the voices, but the thoughts of all these hordes of people. Therefore, he could not always separate one voice or thought from another. He might catch a moment of this message, a snatch of that one. They were seldom meant for—directed at—him. He simply had this ability to hear the cacophony of the Gods.

Some of these beings were dead, and the words that his mind intercepted had been spoken thousands of years earlier, to float out into the heavens aimlessly. Some of the words he overheard, like an eavesdropper at a keyhole, drifted to him from the future. Certain Gods had sympathy for the animal called man, and others despised him—while most couldn't have cared much either way. The heavens were as filled with the creatures his kind had labeled Gods as the land teemed with animals, and the seas with fish. One could not always see the fish that swarmed beneath the waves; the most that could be hoped for was a brief flash of bright scales. But Jonah could see beneath the waves of the heavens, so to speak.

The people who knew of his ability believed it to be a gift from Heaven. But Jonah was more inclined to think of it, many days, as a curse from Sheol—the Hebrew word for "cave" . . . and the Underworld.

By the time the men had found Jonah is his trance below, and then taken him above, they had already thrown overboard as much of the cargo they transported as they could to lighten the vessel's weight. Now with Jonah on deck, in desperation, they cast lots in an attempt to determine who amongst them was responsible for the evil of this unnatural storm. The result of their ritual, however primitive in its superstition, indicated Jonah.

The captain of the ship got close in his face and shouted through gritted teeth, "Our ship is soon to break up, man! Why has this evil come amongst us? What is your business going to Tarshish? What is your occupation? Where are you from?"

Jonah replied with a calm born of fatalistic weariness, "I am a Hebrew, named Jonah, son of Amit'tai of Gath-he'pher. I go to Tarshish to escape an errand I was commanded to attend to."

"And what errand was that?"

"I was to go to the city of Nineveh, and deliver a message there."

"A message from whom?"

Jonah hesitated, but then made his explanation simple for the simple man. "A message from the Lord."

The mariners ringed around the bearded man gasped, either stepped back from him or closer to him in horror. The captain snarled, "The Lord commanded you, and you fled from Him? And now we suffer because of it! Why did you not do as He instructed?"

How could he tell this man that he was tired of listening to voices, tired of sifting through them for meanings that might be of benefit for his fellow creatures? That he wished he could flee to some deep, dark and silent cave where he would never have to hear another voice again?

Some being, angered at the imagined wickedness of the vast city of Nineveh, capital of Assyria—and recognizing Jonah's gift of receptiveness— had ordered him to go to the city and denounce it, threaten it. But he had wanted no part of it. He had not wanted to risk that the citizens might doubt him, perhaps kill him. He had not wanted to witness their mass panic, if they believed him. And he had not wanted to be the instrument of yet another petty, furious God casting His judgments on the behavior of creatures whose lives, however puny, were none of His business.

He could only tell the captain, "I thought to flee, but now I understand I cannot flee this wrath. I am sorry I have endangered any of you."

"Well, old man, what can you do to appease the Lord so this tempest will cease? This is your fault—you must save the rest of us!"

The ship rose like a toy upon a titanic wave, and the men seized each other in their efforts to remain on their feet. Jonah heard the howl of a man who was pitched overboard, but several others grasped hold of him at the last moment and hauled him back. Yes, they would all die. And yes, it was his fault. Why should these men suffer because of his curse . . . and his cowardice? They had families, children back home. He had none. He was just a wandering madman, with the gibberish of mad Gods in his skull. He wanted it to be over. Blessed silence. Even if it could only be found in death . . .

He said to the captain, "Throw me into the sea, man. My life should satisfy this crea—" He amended his words. "Our angry Lord."

"What? I'll have no innocent blood on my hands!" He turned to roar to his crew, "Row! Row for all you are worth! Turn the ship back toward Joppa!"

Sun-bronzed, rain-spattered muscles and tendons pulled taut with effort, but their straining efforts were useless. The rains slashed the ship, the mast creaked as if it might snap like the sapling it had once been, the whipping sails cracked like lightning. At last, the captain grabbed Jonah by the arm again and called to the churning sky, "We beg you, Lord, to spare us! We have no desire to kill this man—but if it is Your will, then so be it!" He returned his attention to Jonah. "I am sorry, old man."

Jonah nodded, and held out his arms to be taken. "It is for the best, my son. Take me, you men. Cast me into the sea."

And so now, with the ship tossing, the men walked Jonah unsteadily to the side. He gazed up one last time at the skies. He hoped this would make the being happy—make all the Gods happy. Though his heart crashed like the waves, he smiled bitterly. Maybe this wasn't what the God wanted, after all. But it was what he wanted.

The men took Jonah to the edge of the deck . . . and he did not resist them, as they shoved him over the side.

An explosion of cold, all around him. An enveloping blackness. It snatched the breath from his lungs, and he thought he would die in that very instant. But though his mind wanted to die, his body's blind instincts for survival took over, and he waved his limbs frantically in an effort to break the surface again.

Jonah threw his head above the water with a desperate gasp—and then he stared in amazement at the ocean around him.

The ship bobbed on calm waters. Though the sky was still heavy with black clouds, the rains had stopped. Already, then, the angry God had been satisfied by his sacrifice?

As he tread water, he heard the voices of the men aboard the ship crying out to the Lord in thanks and in awed terror at His powers. And then he heard a man—the captain, he realized—shout out loudly in horror. He was pointing out to sea, at something behind Jonah. Jonah stirred the waters with his arms in order to turn about and look, even as more voices were raised in fear.

His heart stopped in his chest, then shuddered back to life reluctantly, at what he saw sharing the cold waters with him.

At first, he thought the vast, gray creature he saw rising to the surface might be a whale. Though he had never seen one, by his reckoning it must be a whale larger than any ever encountered. But no—it was more than that. He saw a long serpent's neck break the surface. It raised itself, seemed to peer about, then crashed under the waves again. Then, it rose again. And a second serpent rose with it. A third. They wavered at the sky, coiling around each other. Now he knew what he was seeing! He had heard legends told of immense squid that would do battle with whales. This great creature he saw must be a whale in the embrace of such a tentacled nightmare.

Despite his previous wishes for oblivion, Jonah suddenly began calling out to the men on the ship to hoist him back aboard. He could not bear the thought of occupying the same ocean with these battling titans, so close at hand and growing closer. He tried to turn and swim away, back toward the ship.

Beneath the surface, he felt something grab onto his leg firmly. It nearly drew him under. He screamed, and redoubled his efforts at swimming.

His other leg was gripped.

Jonah looked over his shoulder, and now he saw the creatures more clearly as they began to rise more fully above the waves.

They were not two animals after all. One creature. One great being . . .

It was a God. Not the one he had angered, but another. They knew his gift, the Gods. They always knew how to sniff him out, for whatever whims they might entertain. This one's name now came into his head—though he would have found it hard to bring to his tongue.

Gibberish filled his brain—bizarre chanting. It had a human quality. Somewhere, either elsewhere on this world or elsewhere in time, men prayed to this God, to awaken it from its slumber. And here it was—awake. Perhaps not so much roused by the chanting, but by the proximity of this hapless prophet.

As he suspected, two tentacles had taken hold of his legs. But they had no rows of suckers, and appeared to be striped in alternating bands of black and a nearly metallic silver. And these tentacles did not extend from the body of a squid, but from—a *face.*

The face had no visible eyes, or any other feature . . . just a mass of squirming tendrils where a mouth should be. The head of the beast alone, now fully risen from the sea, was as large as a whale. Water streamed down its gray, translucent flesh. Behind the head, two gigantic fins had also broken the surface. Larger than any sail, they loomed impossibly high. But they weren't fins after all, Jonah realized. They were the tops of immense, folded wings something like those of a bat.

He was suddenly drawn by those tentacles, toward that faceless head. He shrieked and beat his arms at the water more feverishly. The head filled his vision: a rearing mountain. Those banded, serpentine tentacles. Hidden in their midst, he thought he saw a black maw opening . . .

Jonah was engulfed in abrupt darkness. All sight was shut out, and so was the sound of the yelling sailors, and the rustle of the sea.

He was sucked feet-first down a long dark chute, the walls of which were rubbery, the atmosphere of which was steamy and hot. And that terrible silence. More than anything else, Jonah regretted his previous wishes for a dark cave, and utter silence. In their well-known sadism, the Gods were often more than happy to answer the prayers of men.

After what seemed an interminable slide down this twisting and turning rubbery channel, he dropped at last into a shallow pool that covered the floor of a large chamber.

In this chamber there was a dim illumination that seemed to come from white patches here and there on the walls and the curved ceiling. The patches, when he got close to one of them, not only gave off a faint glow but a profound stench of decay, and he assumed they were suppurating ulcers of some kind, perhaps the gas of their rot accounting for the light. Jonah clamped his hand over his nose and mouth but kept close to the white tumescent mass for the comfort of its meager luminosity, as he took in his shadowy surroundings as best he could.

He was in the belly of the giant, that he knew. But was it still lingering at the surface, or had it submerged again—perhaps to depths deeper than the loftiest mountains were tall?

A splashing sound made him flinch. He caught sight of a silvery flopping thing in the puddle of the floor. He then saw another one closer at hand, and relaxed somewhat. He shared his grotto of flesh with a few live fish. Whether they had been swallowed along with him, or whether they were born and died in this environment, he couldn't say.

The enclosed atmosphere was tropically humid and almost suffocatingly hot. How long would the air last? But the thought of running out of air was Jonah's only comfort. Better that, than be digested in some bath of gastric acid. His panicked heartbeat slowed to something more like calm. Yes, his prayers had been answered. So be it.

He ventured further into the chamber but stayed close to those fetid patches when he could, sloshing through the water, which was ankle-deep or knee-deep depending on the uneven floor. His sounds echoed off the high ceiling, vaulted like that of some obscene temple.

At one end of the irregularly shaped "room", he found the opening of a narrow tunnel that branched off like a corridor. Its glistening length was in deep gloom, but there seemed to be more pale light at its end, so gingerly he followed it, trying not to brush the claustrophobic walls of live matter. He heard the distant plop of dripping water or juices falling in another pool. It was the only sound beyond his splashing, and labored breathing. If this thing had a heart, he was too far from it to hear its great pumping.

Jonah emerged into another chamber, smaller than the one he had been dropped into. It was here that water dripped from the ceiling. And here, in the center of the room, he found a table and chair made of wood.

He went to the rough furniture, marveling that it wasn't toppled, as if some internal force kept the pieces upright and in place. There were even sheets of papyrus on the table, and a quill in a little bottle of ink.

There was a large patch of white decay directly above the table, and by leaning over it, Jonah could actually read some of the words on the sheets. View some of the illustrations inked there.

He wished he hadn't looked. The words and images were those of a madman. A madman who worshiped creatures like the one that had swallowed Jonah. They were called the Great Old Ones, according to these scribblings, and they came from the empty black gulfs between the stars. They were not Gods, Jonah knew, any more than any of them were. Creatures. Beings. But they were old, yes . . . and they were great. And he would be damned if he ever worshiped this one.

"It is good to have company," said a voice behind him, and he whirled to face it.

A figure stepped forward into the fungous glow. Jonah wished he hadn't. It had once been a man. Now, this blighted creature had no hair, not even eyebrows, and his skin had been bleached a horrid bone white, either from lack of sun or from the digestive juices of this breathing labyrinth. He was naked, and covered in black sores. His mouth was twisted horribly out of shape by one of these black tumors, but then Jonah realized it was a grin. When the figure shuffled even closer, Jonah gasped to see its eyes. They were entirely white. The creature was blind. How then, how had it managed to write on those sheets?

It nodded at the pages Jonah still gripped in his trembling hands. At this moment, he feared this other man more than he did the awesome monster whose belly he was trapped in.

"This is my Lord," the man said, sweeping his arm toward the ceiling. "Those are my prayers, and my tribute, and my testament to my Lord."

Jonah realized he still held the pages, and replaced them on the table. He said, "Is there a way out?" Suddenly he didn't want to die here. Not in the presence of this ghastly apparition.

"Out? Why would you want to leave?" Its croaking voice was disappointed. "Did you not come, as I did? To serve the Great One? To recite the words of power, within His belly? So we can keep Him strong, keep Him awake?"

"Awake?"

"The Elder Gods would see Him sleep. Sleep for all time, in the city under the sea. But I saw the Great One in dreams, and He instructed me to venture out on the sea in a boat." That horrid festering grin grew wider, in pride. "I am a prophet, you see. And my Lord needed me. He honored me, as He honored you. He swallowed me, so that I could say the words of power within Him. So He will never succumb to the prison of sleep again!"

"I was not called here," Jonah told him. "I know nothing about your God . . ."

Now, the grin was replaced by a frown, equally unpleasant. "You are not from the Elder Gods, are you? Did you come to cast the Great One back into His prison of dreams?"

"I know nothing about these Elder Gods, either," Jonah said . . . though perhaps he had indeed heard the thoughts of both the Great Old Ones and the Elder Gods before. But if they had a conflict, like giant squid battling monstrous whales, he intended to take no sides in it. "I will leave you to your writing, my friend, and . . . and continue my search for a way out of this place."

But the blind man advanced toward Jonah again, and with him brought a wave of that same stench of decay the white patches gave off. "But why should you not remain? Serve the Lord with me—the great Lord Cthulhu!" It was the name that had entered Jonah's head earlier. "We have fish to eat, and shelter above our heads, and now we will have each other for companions. With our prayers combined, the Lord will fully awaken, and the earth shall know His tread once more and always!"

Jonah turned and bolted back down the narrow tunnel, his bare feet kicking up splashes. He heard the blind man's voice calling distantly as he shuffled in pursuit. If only there were a weapon about! He couldn't bear the thought of strangling the naked priest with his bare hands—touching that bleached, infected flesh.

He reentered the large chamber, and raced to its opposite wall, where he found several more doorway-like openings he hadn't chanced upon before. He chose one more or less at random, and plunged into it.

Soon, the voice was lost to silence behind him. The tunnel took various turns, and at one point it became so narrow that Jonah had to crawl on hands and knees to squeeze through it into another chamber, where he could stand erect again.

A pale white fire burned above a fleshy mound in the center of the room. At first Jonah took it to be an altar made by the priest, but then he realized the fire was the result of ignited gas passing through a funnel-like growth in the center of the chamber. As he got close to it, he found that the flame was cool in this stifling air. He put his hand close to it, finally touched the colorless flame itself and found it almost frigid. By its light, he saw strange hieroglyphs etched into the flesh of the walls, evidently by the madman. There were crude images that seemed to show the Lord Cthulhu being imprisoned by some other powerful beings in a temple beneath the sea.

"WE DID IMPRISON HIM," a flat voice seemed to speak directly to his brain, bypassing his ear. "IN THE CITY OF R'LYEH."

Jonah looked about him, startled, as if this were the first time a God had spoken to him, though of course it was not.

"The Elder Gods," he muttered under his breath, and he headed away from the cold flame, toward the entrance to yet another passageway in this living maze.

And he saw more strange things, in the three days and three nights he was lost in that maze. He might have slept for a minute here or an hour there—he had no way to measure the time. He ate raw fish several times. Once he tried cooking one over another of those pallid flames, but it seemed to freeze its flesh instead.

One time the blind man came through a room in which Jonah had been dozing, but he kept close to the wall and held his breath and the blind man groped past him without discovering him. Jonah relaxed his hands, which had been clenched into fists.

And in those three days and nights, the Elder Gods continued to whisper to him in their flat, dead voices.

"HE MUST NOT AWAKEN . . ."

"HE MUST RETURN TO R'LYEH . . ."

"YOU MUST RETURN HIM TO HIS DREAMS . . ."

Finally, with these voices clamoring louder in his thoughts, Jonah stopped his lost wandering, stooped, and found the bones of a fish in the water he waded through. He clenched a single needle-like rib as if it were a stylus and turned to etch figures and symbols in the flesh of the wall . . . as the mad priest himself had done in some of these chambers.

Jonah did not understand the inscriptions he was compelled to set down. He let the Gods fill him with their ink, as if he himself were merely some tool of transcription.

But whatever he wrote, he knew it was potent. The floor suddenly heaved under him, and he fell, dropping the bone. Was it his imagination, or did the world around him seem to be moving, rushing madly upward? He had experienced no sense of motion inside the creature previously . . . but yes, it did seem to be moving now . . . very rapidly . . .

There was a rushing sound, as of water. Yes, a growing roar of water, a flood, drawing closer . . .

Jonah looked up from the floor to see a gush of water—no, a liquid like bile—explode into the chamber violently. Jonah just had time to catch his breath and hold it as the wave of bile washed over him, and swept him from the chamber into a narrow rubbery chute . . .

The bile sucked him along through this pipeline and that tunnel, and his lungs burned with the agony of holding his breath. Just as he thought he must open his mouth and let the horrid fluid drown him, the flood propelled him up, up, up, until he burst into the shocking white explosion of daylight.

Whether he was flung from a blow spout like that of a whale, or vomited out some other orifice, he couldn't say, but the geyser cast him clear of the monster's vast body. Jonah arched through the air, and hit the water's hard surface with a bone-jarring crash. He nearly lost consciousness. But as his arms and legs began to stir to keep him afloat, he glanced back and saw two things. There was a great bubbling and churning of the water, where the terrible beast had vanished beneath the surface. And beyond that, like a hallucination too taunting to believe in, were the dark humps and slopes of dry land.

Slowly, his body aching, he began paddling toward it. But he was smiling. He was happy to be alive.

"Thank you, Gods," he mumbled to himself, again and again, like a man who has had his faith restored. "Thank you, Gods . . ."

And he would be looking forward to that dry land, however desolate it was, however scorching the desert. He looked forward to the long, arduous trek ahead of him.

For he was going to Nineveh.

ASCENDING TO HELL

In the weed-encroached house his dead uncle willed him
Dan Virgil noted an odd thing in a closet
Behind musty coats, a small door plastered up
He uncovered the door, a chill gust did erupt
And beyond was a stairwell, narrow and dim.

There were no switches so he brought up a flashlight
The warped wooden steps creaked at his tread
Another way into the attic, thought he
But the stairs did not end at that level three
Continued on up past a point that seemed right.

On and on he mounted, as if climbing a skyscraper
His heart beat madly from the strain and the fear
His mind reeling madly at what was amiss
Ascending into an inverted abyss
His pale beam a ghost across rotting wallpaper.

At last he reached a landing, densely shrouded in web
He pushed timidly through into a place strangely lit
A cliff edge plummeted in front of his shoe
Far below there was nothing but a fog blocking view
And high above him a sea of living flow and live ebb.

It was a forest of kelp, black and impossibly long
Swaying and flowing as if stirred by deep currents
Like tentacles hanging down from a jellyfish bell
And the wind wailing through this vision of hell
Was as eerie and maddening as a banshee troupe's song.

And snared in the tendrils of this black sky of limbs
Were clipper ships and whalers, cradled like toys
Old airplanes entwined as if caught in a pass

paw

Were those figures moving behind the cracked glass?
The wind through torn hulls sang dead sailors' hymns.

Dan had lost track of the time, and also of space
But now spun and darted back through the door
Back down the many stairs he did flee
His sanity scorched by what he did see
When the kelp parted to reveal its vast staring face.

THE THIRD EYE

My father was a policeman in the town of Arkham, Massachusetts for twelve years, but he never spoke openly of his work. Not, in any case, in my presence. But on rare occasion I overheard him confiding to my mother in a low voice, late at night when I was out of my bed to creep to the bathroom. Sometimes I would steal nearer to their door, to listen more closely. Even then, I heard only snatches, but these fragments of stories were all the more frightening to me for floating free of any kind of context that might help me comprehend and accept them. Father would allude to, "those books stolen from the college", or refer to, "the fires in the woods." There was something about a "baboon, or dog maybe, but walking on two legs" that someone had seen somewhere, and could that have been connected to the hunter or fisherman, apparently, who had been found with, "his face all scooped out?"

Mother died when I was eleven, and within a year my father was no longer a policeman. He suffered a breakdown upon her death, and took to drinking, and when I lay in bed at night I listened to new mysteries, but these recited loudly, and to no one, in a drunken rant. It seemed my father blamed someone or some group for mother's death, though she had died of cancer. He would rumble about, "their rays," and claim that this mysterious enemy had, "set their eyes on her." But was he really blaming himself? For other times he would sob, "It's my fault . . . it was me they wanted . . . they want to punish me . . ." Neither source of guilt seemed likely to me. I was afraid of my father by then, though he was not cruel to me, and never ventured from my bed to comfort him. But then, he was too lost in his own pain to tend to mine. We both suffered; he loudly, me in silence.

Which isn't to say that he was not entirely without concern for me. One evening he drew me into his little study or office, into which he had never allowed me before. In fact, he had kept it locked at all times when he wasn't inside it himself. Mother had told me it was because of his gun collection, but I saw only one gun in there that night: a heavy revolver, resting by father's elbow on his desk blotter. I tried to take in the forbidden room as best I could without openly gawking, but father pulled me close to his chair. Around my neck he looped a rawhide cord, on which was strung a small stone disk. This crude amulet was etched with a design like a star with an eye in its center, though the pupil of the eye looked like a flame.

"Don't take that off, son. Never, ever," he told me grimly, his own eyes with a flame of madness, either dulled or compounded by tears and drink. "If your mother had only been wearing it . . . if I had only given it to her." He rose from his chair then, walked me from his private place to lead me to bed, but I remember stealing one good look over my shoulder on the way out. Though the room was murky, I saw a pile of very old books on the desk blotter, near the pistol, their spines peeling and page ends gilded. There were shelves on the walls, and the shadowy objects I spied upon them were like those tantalizing, terrifying fragments of stories: images floating like scraps of nightmare, beads unstrung or dinosaur bones in need of assembling to give them meaning. What to make of the glass jars in which pickled organs pushed gray against the glass, and the ratty-looking stuffed creature, moth-eaten and with glass eyes, which might have been a young ape but might also have been a hyena or wild dog, positioned by some taxidermist so that it reared on it hind legs?

As father's drinking worsened, he began to forget to close the door when he went into his study. One evening I peeked in to find him slumped across his desk passed out, by his elbow the solemn still life of whiskey bottle and Smith and Wesson. Though I dared not actually enter the room, I lingered to take in more of the details I hadn't been able to discern before in the gloom. Was it the taxidermist who had so marked the snarling, hideous face of that monkey-thing? I couldn't imagine that in life, the animal's face had been covered in swirling tattoos like those of a Maori tribesman. Also, I noticed that some of the pickled specimens were not organs, but fetuses, though I couldn't imagine them to be human . . . unless monstrously deformed. One had a huge bulbous head and great black eyes as empty as those of a shark, but its lower face deteriorated into a nest of translucent strands or tendrils that floated motionlessly in its womb of formaldehyde.

A book was open before father, and I craned my neck to look at the odd geometric diagrams worked in with the type. In so doing, I saw an odd object on the other side of him, previously blocked by his head. It was a human skull, or a sculpture of one. I thought it must be the latter because of certain strange characteristics. There was a hole in the side of the skull, of such size and smooth outline that I might have believed it was a third eye socket. It might have been bored in an actual skull, however, I considered. But the color? Was it paint, or stone, that accounted for the black color and obsidian-like glassy polish?

As I leaned forward a bit further, the extra pressure caused the floorboards to creak, as if to sound an alert. And drunk as he was, my father bolted upright in his chair, his left hand clawing for his gun and in so doing, knocking over the bottle of whiskey. The gun whirled in my direction.

When father saw that it was his son he pointed the revolver at, the madness in his eyes lessened. I had clung to the door frame, too frightened to flee. He lowered the pistol to his leg, and gestured to me.

"Come in, son. I'm reading the books we took from them. The one's in English, at least. We have to fight fire with fire, right? Come read with me.

We can use it against them. We can make ourselves safe. Come read with me, son . . ."

But I didn't enter the room. Slowly, I backed away. I turned down the hall, retreated to my own room. And I locked the door. And shortly afterwards, my father gave up on trying to call me back.

My father didn't emerge from his office, its door again shut, for several days, unless he did so while I was at school. But at last, one night as I sat at the kitchen table, eating cereal for my dinner, he appeared. He went straight to the refrigerator, gulped milk from the carton, then turned to face me. Milk dripped from his unshaven chin. His hair was in disarray. And from the right side of his head bulged a lump the size of a hen's egg.

He saw me staring, and rubbed at the growth self-consciously. "It's from the reading, I think. Some of them in the woods and the cellars had tumors like this. It's like . . . I think it's like a new part of my brain is growing, filling up with the stuff I'm reading, because it doesn't belong anywhere else in there." He fluttered a spasm of a smile. "But with the book, and the skull, and the other things I took from them, I'm just as strong as they are. They can call their gods, and I can call the others . . ."

"Don't read any more, Daddy," I remember pleading to him in a small dry voice. I hadn't uttered a word to him in weeks.

"It's for your mother," he told me.

My father took the milk back to the study with him. And I didn't see him for another few days after that . . . not until the night I heard the gunshot.

When I reached the door to his study, I found it unlocked. I had sped to the door in slapping bare feet, but now found myself hesitating, my hand on the knob. At last, I pushed the door open a few inches to peek in. And there sat my father at his desk, slumped across the blotter like that earlier night. The book was there, and the bottle, and the glossy black skull. But this time the pistol was in his fist. This time, a puddle of blood—vivid under the close glow of his desk lamp—spread around his fallen head like some living thing reaching liquid pseudopods toward that book and that skull.

"Daddy," I moaned, and went to his side. I touched his back. Once I had ridden on it, piggy-back. Once his back had been the strongest, broadest wall in the world. Now it was bent, and still.

But it was suddenly not still, abruptly not bent, as father sat up sharply in his seat. He seized me by my wrist, held me, regarded me as I screamed. I could see, now, the gore that had run down his face, making it a wet red mask in which his blue eyes were horribly contrasted. I could see, now, that he had fired the gun point-blank into the growth on the side of his head. Now, in place of it, there was a yawning wound from which blood ran copiously, down his neck and chest. The wound was too large for a bullet's outline; it was as though the growth had burst, and left its outline.

"I should have listened to you, son," he croaked, his voice a gurgle of aspirated blood. "I had to get that stuff out of my head. I was becoming one of them. I had to get it out . . ."

He let go of me and rose to his feet. Weeping, I backed into the wall. I knew I should run and call the hospital. I also knew that my father should not even be alive. I could see deeply inside his draining skull.

He staggered a few steps, gripped the edge of a bureau. The jars atop it rattled, tendrils stirred in yellowish fluid. "My God," father whispered, and looked at me. "I can see . . . things. Someplace . . . some other place . . ."

I sank to the floor, hugging my knees, still sobbing. My father tried to take another step, couldn't, slid down to sit on the floor, also, still staring agape into space. Blood was a soft continual pattering like rain on the floor and his legs.

"The air is all rippled, like it's hot. Or maybe it's under water. Those plants . . . it isn't the wind makes them move . . . so huge . . . and no—they aren't really plants . . ."

The bullet hadn't destroyed all those new tissues. No: somehow, even, its presence had given them more power. Perhaps it was the metal itself of the bullet, stimulating that tissue, interacting with the electrical charge in its cells. Or perhaps, in ruining so much of father's normal tissues, the bullet had given the new matter that remained the upper hand.

"The towers hurt my eyes . . . the lines," he went on. "There are things moving past the windows. White . . . pulpy. Starfish. And now they're looking out at me. More of them . . . noticing me. They can see me . . . see me watching them . . . dear God . . . looking at me . . . even now . . ."

We sat together thus for an indefinite time; it was hours, I know that. The blood began to congeal, turn to a black mask on father's face, cracking and flaking away around his mouth, the only part of him that moved (even his transfixed eyes did not blink), and crusted thick around his wound, which now only wept. He spoke incessantly of what he saw, I have no doubt, though after a while his words had become a gibberish that might be another language, or a muddle born of his ruined brain. There were only fragments of English, fragments of images. He made reference to, "the purple ooze, across the land . . . like a sea," and in a similar tone of terrible awe made mention of, "the great crater . . . big as a city . . ."

And at last, never again truly looking at me, my father ceased his discourse.

They called it a suicide, which of course it was, born of my mother's death, which is true. And policemen came. They took my father's books. The bottles. The obsidian skull with the third eye bored in its side . . .

I don't doubt that these men could tell me more stories, if drunk enough, of the things they have seen and collected in my hometown. For there is a force a work in Arkham, at work even when its cults have been arrested or driven out

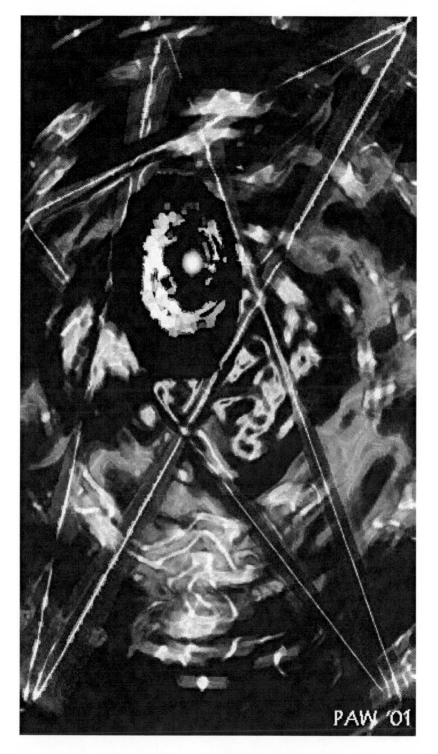

PAW '01

or perhaps even secretly killed. These men are our guardians. Their backs are walls . . . albeit flimsy ones. But the only ones we have.

I graduate this year from the academy, myself. And I will return to live, and serve, in Arkham.

I will do this for my parents.

And around my neck, like some sheriff's badge, I will wear the necklace my father gave me . . . the stone disk, with the star, with the eye, and the flame at its center.

THE FACE OF BAPHOMET

"Some say the worshiped image represented the face of Mohammed," said Rosier. "Others said that it was the face of a child, or a bearded man. This last might be why there are those today who believe it was, in fact, the Shroud of Turin the Templars were secretly revering."

"Interesting," muttered d'Urberville, though he did not reveal that he had heard the theory before.

D'Urberville's host, Basil Rosier, paced across the room holding his glass of wine before him like a candle. It was the oldest wine that had ever touched d'Urberville's palate, a treasure in itself. The bottle had come from an extensive collection of similarly ancient vessels, their glass cloudy under cataracts of dust. The wine collection was on the opposite end of these passages and rooms beneath Rosier's manor-house. The subterranean room they currently occupied was   the largest of these chambers. The ceiling was low, the walls of dark stone, but the air was not damp. It was kept diligently dry, so as to preserve the chamber's varied contents.

Rosier went on in the lofty tones of an historian lecturing a novice. "Some said this enshrined, mysterious object was the body of a hermaphrodite, or a phallus."

D'Urberville could not help but interrupt his host, though he kept his anger concealed. "The enemies of the Templars were obviously just trying to shock the Pope with such ideas."

"Were they?" Having reached the far wall, Rosier turned about, his smile a curved scimitar. "Or did they sense something closer to the truth? There's a pattern here. A phallus is a fertility symbol—naturally. Hermaphrodites have both sets of genitalia. 'Baphomet', the enemies of the Knights Templar called the image they worshiped. 'The Golden Calf', they called Baphomet. Baphomet is most commonly thought of as a horned demonic visage. I submit that the Golden Calf, the terrible Baphomet, was actually more akin to the Horned God of Celtic beliefs—a fertility god—than to the Satanic entity our good Pope Clement the Fifth envisioned."

"Why," d'Urberville asked quietly, even as he seethed behind his composed, even features, "would an order of disciplined warrior monks, charged with guarding the Holy Sepulcher of Solomon, having taken vows of poverty, chastity and humility, come to worship some heathen fertility idol?"

"They were in Holy Lands. A totally alien, exotic culture. They were exposed to strange things . . . and as insular a group as they were, strange, uh . . . habits . . . may have fermented amongst them."

"Prostrating themselves before some mysterious head that spoke to them and granted them strange powers? Rites where they spat three times on an image of *Christ*? Orgies of sodomy? Rituals where they stripped and kissed each other at the base of the spine, then on the navel, then on the lips?"

"You have to look no further than the college fraternities of your own United States, Mr. d'Urberville, to see how strange rites evolve within a secret society. And you have to look no further than your country's recent spate of priests charged with child molestation, rape and homosexuality, to see how a man who has taken a vow of chastity can delude himself into thinking he is still a proud servant of God, even as he is slipping his vows off with his cassock."

D'Urberville felt the blood drain from his body as surely as if it were absorbed through his feet into the cold stone floor. And he saw that bright scimitar in Rosier's face widen, edging past its expression of pompous showing-off to one of malicious delight. Yes, no matter how much d'Urberville had sought to hide his feelings, the older man had sniffed them out and was toying with them, savoring the taste of d'Urberville's anger, as he had savored the dusty wine.

"There are bad priests, as there are bad policemen, bad teachers, bad parents, bad politicians," d'Urberville replied, his voice as cold as his bloodless flesh. "But I contend that the Knights Templar were not bad men. Their only sin was that they amassed too much wealth in the Holy Lands, too much power. The Pope was jealous, intimidated. All the charges against these brave men—men dedicated to lives of charity, to Christ—were false. They were arrested, tortured and burned for no good, honest reason. They were martyrs."

Rosier sniffed his wine, tasted it, smacked his lips and then casually asked his American guest, "Tell me, d'Urberville, are you a Freemason?"

"No."

"I thought you might be of the order of Freemasons who have named themselves after the Knights Templar."

"I am not a Freemason."

That great grin, again. "But you *are* a d'Urberville, aren't you? That's an old name. It has the clashing metallic ring of the Crusades to it."

Rosier gestured around him at the furnishings and exhibits of this, his own buried museum, as secret a place as any Templar shrine. "I know old things." D'Urberville set his wine glass down on the edge of a table. As he straightened, meeting his host's sparkling eyes squarely, he confessed, "My family is descended from one of the hundred and forty knights burned by the order of Pope Clement."

"I see. So your great interest in the Templars, and your emotional investment in their reputation after nearly seven centuries, is well justified. Though I find it curious that any of those poor men who were burned alive would have left descendants . . . having taken a vow of chastity, as you point out."

D'Urberville thought Rosier might chuckle smugly then. Both seemed to hold themselves back, in the interest of good manners. "My father is the descendant of a brother of the knight of whom I speak. But his blood is still in my veins, just as much, however it found its way to me."

"And you should be proud. I understand that. And angry, as well. It wouldn't be the last time innocents were sacrificed, victims of false charges. Just look at your country's Salem case. Appalling." Rosier made an agonized face of sad disgust. "However, I myself feel that there is a truth to the legend of Baphomet. In fact, I know there is. And if you didn't believe there was something to learn of these truths, why did you seek me out? You heard I had certain relics in my possession, did you not?"

"Yes. But that doesn't ensure their authenticity. Even the Shroud is a brilliant and convincing fake, I'm sorry to say."

"Ah . . . but you're still curious to see my little . . . idol."

"As I would be curious to see a Holy Grail or an Ark of the Covenant. Much as I would totally disbelieve in their authenticity."

"You're a man of little faith."

"I'm a former priest," d'Urberville retorted, his voice for the first time conveying the anger he felt.

Rosier looked shocked and dismayed, though d'Urberville couldn't be sure if his exaggerated expression was a fake. "Oh, I'm sorry to insult you, my friend. Now I see your interest more clearly yet. But if it's not too rude . . . *former* priest?"

There was no longer need for—and d'Urberville had no more patience with—secrecy. "Yes. I'm no longer a priest. My superiors felt that I was too . . . obsessive, perhaps . . . about certain subjects. That I needed more discipline. But it was my own decision that I was unsuitable to go on. A regrettable decision. But I am not one of your perverse, deluded priests, Mr. Rosier. I never broke my vow of chastity while a priest and in fact I haven't broken it yet. I'm not a priest any more but I still uphold the principles to which I made vows, just as my ancestor did."

"You vowed to humility, then, as he did? But you have a lot of family pride, for all that."

"May I see this relic you supposedly own, or not?" d'Urberville snapped.

Rosier looked distressed again. "Please, Mr. d'Urberville, don't be so rude. Do you know I seldom allow anyone to see this relic, let alone even enter this room? Once *National Geographic* magazine learned of the relic in question, through a former friend of mine, and offered to pay me for an interview and photographs of said relic. I denied them access. I have never even allowed anyone to photograph it, in fact, or even sketch it . . . to reproduce the image of Baphomet in any way, just as the face of Mohammed is not to be reproduced. Not that Baphomet is, after all, Mohammed."

Rosier was right in one thing: d'Urberville had to swallow his pride. He forced his voice back to civil tones, cooled the molten heat out of his gaze. He took up his glass again, the act of sipping wine helping him to regain his composure. "I apologize for my behavior. I'm honored and appreciative that you would agree to let me see the idol."

Rosier came to the younger man's side and squeezed his arm like a dear comrade. "Oh, apology accepted. Come now, let's have our look, shall we? Let your eyes take in what no one in your family has viewed for over seven hundred years."

D'Urberville allowed his host to guide him across the chamber. "Where did you acquire this thing?"

"In the Middle East. I can't reveal more, except for this: I also acquired a rare book from the same source, a book written many years before the Templars, in the eighth century in Damascus by a man called Abdul Alhazred. It was this book that helped me understand and identify the countenance of Baphomet. The book is called the *Necronomicon.* Have you heard of it?"

"No."

"A pity. It's very enlightening. I'm sorry, though; I never show that to anyone. *Anyone . . .*"

There was a depression in the wall, almost a shallow alcove, to which Rosier directed his guest. D'Urberville had glanced at it numerous times already, suspecting that the image of Baphomet the Templars worshiped was there. His suspicions were now confirmed.

Standing framed in the arched depression was an oblong wooden cabinet which resembled nothing so much as a coffin, but with hinged double doors. The wood of the cabinet was old, but how old? Even if it dated to the time of the Templar's trials, it might be a fake concocted as evidence against them. But wouldn't it still be of interest even as a fake? In fact, d'Urberville preferred it that way. He *wanted* the relic to be a fake. Because if it wasn't . . . if the idol, whatever it was, should be authentic . . . but that was impossible. Only if Baphomet proved to be an image of Christ would d'Urberville believe his ancestor would have paid homage to it.

Rosier lit a candle on a small table to either side of the alcove, then flicked some switches on the nearby wall to extinguish all the electric lamps. He explained, "The image is faint and takes a while to discern. The lights bleach it out." He laid his fingers lightly on d'Urberville's arm. "Are you ready?"

D'Urberville felt a repulsion at the man's lingering touch, but maintained his control and didn't withdraw. "Please," he said.

Rosier removed his hand from d'Urberville, confronted the upright cabinet and unfastened the clasp at its front. D'Urberville found himself craning his neck to see over the other man's shoulder as he delicately swung both doors

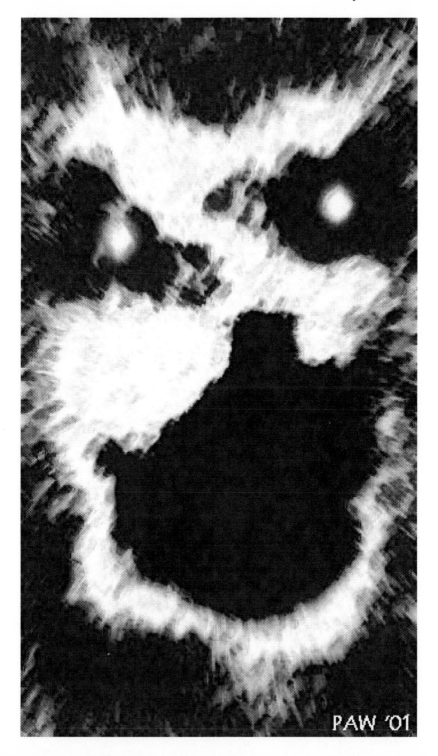

PAW '01

outwards on their hinges. Having unveiled the cabinet's interior, Rosier then stepped back behind d'Urberville to give his guest an unblocked view.

D'Urberville squinted, his brows knotting in intensity, and took a few steps closer to the cabinet . . . holding his breath, as if afraid the moisture in it would somehow stain or sully the allegedly ancient artifact within.

But it seemed to only be an oblong slab of tarnished metal, or a mirror now nearly opaque with the dull patina of age. A blank, featureless slab. The most he saw upon it was his own shadowy reflection, quavering in an eerie liquid way as the candlelight writhed. Was that the message and meaning, then: that Baphomet was personified by the face of its current beholder?

"What," he began, but then he saw that there *was* something there, and leaned closer yet. At face level, where he had thought he saw only his own reflection, there was a subtle image on the slab. A face, fainter and more vague even than the features of the Turin shroud. So faint that it didn't seem so much painted on the slab as buried inside it like the face of a man submerged in cloudy water, or frozen in a block of ice.

The most obvious feature of the obscure image was the ram-like horns above its head. But the rest . . . no wonder no two people had seemed to convey the same impression. A bearded man? Yes, he could imagine that. There did seem to be a beard to the face. A child? Perhaps—the face was slender and its eyes disproportionately large. But they were scarcely human. They were too dark, apparently without whites or irises.

Perhaps d'Urberville's eyes, in growing more accustomed to the gloom, were perceiving more details the longer he gazed on the painted image, but it seemed as if the image were darkening, growing clearer, less vague. He could see now that the beard wasn't of hair, but of thick entwined fibers almost like a nest of thin tendrils. And oddly, the clearer the image seemed to him, the less and less human it appeared, until d'Urberville found himself shuddering at the sight of it.

"Just as I thought," he muttered to the man behind him, but without taking his gaze off the visage. "A fake to discredit the Knights. A demon."

"Not a demon," Rosier replied, in a strange reverent whisper. "A *God*."

"God . . ."

"Baphomet . . . no. Not the correct name. Golden Calf? No. Black Goat is more correct. Alhazred's book taught me that, my good Father d'Urberville. The image is that of the Black Goat of the Woods with a Thousand Young. A fertility god, yes. But not Celtic. Much, much older than that. The Black Goat's name is Shub-Niggurath. Some call the Goat female, some male. A hermaphrodite . . . though more correctly, the Goat reproduces through parthenogenesis . . ."

D'Urberville heard all this, but his attention was focused more and more intently upon the image, almost as though the reason he could see it more clearly every moment was that he had been drawn into the cloudy water of the metal slab to join the face. The face no longer resembled a painting to him. It was too vivid for that. It was like a photograph, recorded on that strange alien metal. The slab seemed like a screen receiving a transmission of that horrible visage from some far, far away place and time. And plane.

Behind him, in soft seductive tones, Rosier went on, "Perhaps the Goat's influence over us is to procreate, to colonize, to be fertile—as it is. Perhaps that explains the orgies of the Knights amongst themselves. The mindless compulsion toward intercourse that you will see among animals of the same sex, caged together." A soft chuckle. "But despite the influence of Shub-Niggurath, they were able to at least resist breaking their vows with the opposite sex. However they were inspired, their rites bonded them. They broke old vows to forge new ones . . ."

No, those weren't ram horns curled above the hideous, otherworldly countenance after all, d'Urberville realized. They were coiled appendages, like tentacles.

"Whatever Shub-Niggurath wants from us, I can't be certain," Rosier confessed. "But we've devoted ourselves to learning. For generations, we've been striving toward that end. But our quest has not been easy. We've been persecuted terribly, as you yourself know. You thought me insensitive to the suffering of the Templars, but now you see I hid my affiliation from you as you did yours from me. Just as I lied about my acquisition of the idol. I did indeed find Athazred's book in the Middle East, but this treasure has been in my family for centuries." Rosier's tone earlier had been all posturing and performance, but now his words couldn't sound more heart-felt. "We've found it difficult to convert new members to our holy order. Men worthy to convert. But when I met you, when I suspected your sacred bloodline . . . it was like a gift."

D'Urberville's eyes were becoming strained, but he was unable to blink. Was it the guttering candlelight or could the tendrils of that beard be seething with movement like plants stirring at the bottom of the sea? Could those black emotionless pupils be glittering, reflecting ember-like   glints from the glowing candles? Could those two tentacles atop the head be flexing, as if to uncoil and reach out of the slab to him?

"Sir   d'Urberville," Rosier whispered. D'Urberville heard the rustle of clothing, the clink of a belt. "Turn and face me."

Without questioning, still without blinking, d'Urberville pivoted his body fully to face his host. Now the candlelight glittered in his own eyes. Now he knew why he had not been destined for the priesthood. At least not in that order. His destiny had been awaiting him here, all along.

Rosier had disrobed. His paunch was as heavy and pale as a satyr's. He held his arms out from his sides, as if offering himself as a sacrifice or sacrament.

He turned his back to d'Urberville.

And, like a trained acolyte, d'Urberville knelt and kissed the base of the man's spine. He remained on his knees while Rosier presented him his front. D'Urberville laid a kiss upon the man's navel, and then allowed Rosier to help him to his feet. Rosier embraced the younger man, who did not resist, and they pressed their lips together. As he kissed Rosier, d'Urberville felt tears trickle down his cheeks. They were not tears of self-horror or self-pity, but rather of joy, for after all these generations—after his family had known such disgrace and dishonor in its past—the name of d'Urberville had once again been initiated into the Order of the Knights Templar.

CELLS

"Dr. East, your wife has been calling for you."

"I know, Mrs. LeBlanc. I can hear her from here." Noticing how the private nurse was trying to peer curiously past him into his workshop, Carl East closed the door so that only his face was wedged in the crack. Mrs. LeBlanc softened slightly. His face was not the face of an apathetic, unconcerned man. Rather, he looked so drained of color and energy she might have believed that his wife's cancer was contagious. He seemed to be dying with her. It was no wonder he was apparently avoiding seeing her, now that the end was drawing close, now that Violet East was delirious with the cancer in her brain and morphine was being administered to alleviate the agony.

"It's difficult for you, I realize, but . . ."

"So many divorces, Mrs. LeBlanc. So many unhappy couples even when they do stay together. But my wife and I . . . we truly *love* each other. We've been married seventeen years, and we're still in love. She is my best friend, Mrs. LeBlanc. I've never been embarrassed to say that, even to my male friends. They've teased me. Laughed at me. But I think they're jealous, because they don't have that. Such a simple thing, to let someone close to you like that. But so few people will do it, for all our love songs and romance novels. And even when they do open themselves they sabotage it in so many ways. But we were *happy*. So happy. And we could have had so many more years. We're only in our forties. We could have had *decades*. Why does this have to happen to us, when we had what was so rare? Does that seem fair to you?"

"No sir . . . it doesn't. I guess you can call it irony."

"I call it evil. And I won't accept it."

The face wedged in the door looked odd—maybe frightening. Mrs. LeBlanc hesitated. She saw a computer monitor's glow behind Dr. East, heard a steady liquid burbling. "I know it's hard to accept these things, Dr. East, and it really isn't any of my business, but I think she needs you right now . . ."

"That's the drugs talking. And the pain. It isn't *her* She knows I have work to do in here. We discussed all this."

"It could be any time now." She was getting a bit irritated again. Work? What kind of work? He needed to wake up and go hold his wife's hand right now, help her on her way. If he didn't, he'd never forgive himself when he realized what he'd done. "Denial is normal, I know, but . . ."

"I don't deny that my wife is dying. I just deny that Death has a right to take her."

Mrs. LeBlanc thought it odd that a Beckham University biology professor should make death sound like an entity. "Look," she sighed, "I'd better get back to her."

"Please do, Mrs. LeBlanc. Please stay with her." The anger that had made East's face increasingly unsettling dispersed, and once more he simply looked exhausted by his tragedy. "Mrs. LeBlanc . . . do you believe in the afterlife?"

"Yes, sir. I . . . just don't know what it must be like."

East knew better than to believe her. She had no faith. Still, he told her, "My wife believes. She believes very strongly. And so do I. She got me to believing, despite the stance of those who do what I do. My wife is very widely read . . . and she introduced me to concepts of metaphysics my colleagues haven't even heard of, let alone subscribe to." East thought better of what he was revealing, and got to his point. "I believe there is a spirit, but that it's simply a scientific reality beyond the scope of contemporary science."

"I sure hope so, Dr. East. It sure would be nice."

He would tell her no more. "Thank you, Mrs. LeBlanc. Now, please go to her."

Nodding, the nurse turned back toward the house. East's workshop was contained within a converted stable adjacent to a vast barn she thought would make somebody a nice apartment, though she had never seen inside. On her way back across the cool night grass, she thought about what East had said. He was right; what he had with his wife was rare. She and her husband had just filed for divorce themselves.

*   *   *

He couldn't go up there. Couldn't see what she had become at the last. And he couldn't place the tank in the room with her, not with the nurse keeping constant vigil. He had explained this to Violet before—before she lost coherence—and she had understood. She had smiled to reassure him. "I'll come find the tank. I'll know where to look. And you don't have to be with me when I go, Carl, because I won't be gone long." She had had even more faith than he in this all along. Now she was crying out, but it was like Christ crucified and feeling forsaken. The suffering getting in the way. He only hoped that through the suffering, through the drugs, her subconscious, her will, her *spirit* held on to her conviction.

Christ had cried out. But Christ had come back.

"I don't want you to see me like that anyway," she had reassured him, then. She was down to ninety-six pounds, but the mass in the tank weighed one hundred and forty—the weight she had carried before. Well, minus twenty pounds.

It would seem a huge mass of protoplasm to anyone not familiar with the experiment. (He tried not to think of it as an experiment. That implied possible failure. This must not fail. It was, quite literally, a matter of life and death.) But East thought of the mass as tiny, compared with what he had grown and could have grown.

He had been inspired by a series of experiments by Dr. Phillip White of the Rockefeller Institute, had duplicated much of them in his workshop and later in the barn.

Like White, he had begun with a tiny wart of a growth taken from a tobacco plant. This, rather than the specialized cells of, say, a stem or a leaf. In a special solution of nutrients, he had allowed the cells to multiply, unhindered, unchecked. He dubbed the growth a "couch potato", since it only had to sit and grow obese, without work, with no specialized identity. Undifferentiated cells with no purpose or responsibility other than to eat, to grow . . .

The theoretical rate of multiplication for White's cells—and East's—was 10,000,000,000,000,000,000-fold over a forty week period. At this rate of growth, had White not cut away and disposed of the culture of cells, at the end of that forty weeks he would have ended up with a solid mass which would fill the solar system to its very rim.

Theoretically speaking, of course. And given the vast nourishment necessary.

But White had continued to dispose of most of the growth throughout the course of his experiments. East had followed suit; he was constantly pruning, slicing away, like a surgeon. Sometimes he imagined that he was cutting out Violet's cancer, and burning it. But every day it grew back, and he had to do it again . . .

Carl East had disposed of much of his growth. Though not as much as Dr. White had disposed of.

*   *   *

East lifted his head with a small gasp. After one vertiginous moment he remembered where he was. The workshop. Shortly after the nurse had left him he had put his head down on his arms at his desk, fatigued.

He was badly shaken from his dream. It had been awful. In it, it wasn't Violet's spirit which found a new home in the blank mass of cells, in its tank of nourishment awaiting some purpose as a canvas awaits paint. It was the cancer which took over the mass . . . becoming a 140-pound tumor. After all, wasn't that what the cancer wanted to do? Engulf and obliterate Violet entirely? And didn't its mindless will now seem to be stronger than her own?

He smoothed back his hair with his hands, his eyes falling on the spines of the books on their shelves above his desk. Some Violet had owned when he met her. Others they had sought out together, in preparation. Modern works by Colin Wilson, rare moldering texts by all but forgotten hands. Violet might once have been burned as a witch for possessing any one of these older tomes. What would East's fellow professors think if they knew he had spent as much money acquiring two volumes of the eleven-volume *Revelations of Glaaki* as they would spend on a vacation to Bermuda with their healthy wives? And what would they think if they saw what those pages contained, the madness purported to be history and science? Why, they might well wonder, was there a bookmark in the pages which told of the origins and conjuring—the growing—of something called a *shoggoth* . . . an amorphous aggregation of cells that could be telepathically molded by those who dared to use these creatures as slaves?

What would they think of the odd, Mayan-like tattoo Violet had copied from one of her books onto her belly, only last month? Vaguely East wondered what Mrs. LeBlanc must think of that strange spiraling design. Would she believe them both insane if he told her it was a doorway from which his wife would escape her poisoned flesh?

He rose from the desk. His dream had so unsettled him that he felt compelled to go look in on the tank . . .

The fluorescent lights of the barn came on with a hesitant flicker.

East was reassured to see things in order. He checked the tank for the tenth time that day. Inside its glass coffin, the culture was an oblong blob of pale dough. It didn't breathe. It didn't pulsate. But it was life, in its most primitive state. It awaited specialization. Transformation. It awaited the strong vision of the artist and her paints. If only there would be enough of Violet left to be that artist . . .

At least the mass wouldn't fight her for dominion of its body. It had no consciousness, no sense of self; indeed, no self. It *awaited* self.

East wandered the barn, smoking a cigarette. He peered into the other tanks and containers.

There were other masses. Some tiny. A few in tanks as large as the one containing Violet's clay. Some masses were larger. One of these was a huge mound, a white mountain of protoplasm, sitting in a puddle of solution in a child's plastic swimming pool. As he passed, he stroked its slick, smooth flesh. In a few other pools were somewhat smaller masses. Other experiments. But these were also spare parts. If Violet couldn't shape, sculpt, transform the designated lump of cells, maybe she could switch to another and try again. Or what if she did transform the mass, but it couldn't sustain its integrity? She might need to constantly switch to a fresh vehicle.

He hoped his wife would not have to live in one of these tanks, sit forever in one of these pools. No . . . she wouldn't have to. He mustn't let his faith falter.

The spirit existed. Persisted. So many already believed that when the body

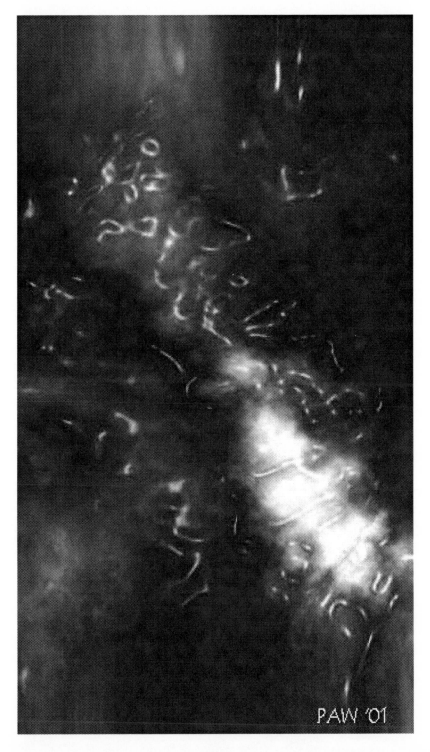

died, the spirit went on its own. But why shouldn't it have a new body to possess? One with no real life of its own to oust? A sort of reincarnation. Tibetan monks conjured up thought forms called *tulpas,* gave them life of their own. Why shouldn't Violet conjure herself in this pliable stuff of life from which all life had originated in the first place?

East heard her calling for him in the house, sobbed as he stood smoking his cigarette amongst his hulking, idiot crop.

*   *   *

The pounding at the workshop door was, in East's dream interpretation, the beat of a heart lurching violently to life. His ear was to his work bench as if to a cold chest listening for that throb. In his jolting awake he leapt to his feet, almost knocking back his chair. He rushed to the door, opened it to see the orange-pink of dawn glowing dimly around the head of Mrs. LeBlanc.

She was breathless. "Dr. East . . . I'm sorry. She's gone . . ."

"Gone?" He gawked at her, disoriented.

"I'm not sure when it happened. I fell asleep in my chair. She's very cold; it must have been a few hours ago, at least. I'm sorry, Dr. East, I'm so sorry. But it must have been peaceful, for me not to have heard anything . . ."

"Yes," East said, snapping his head to look at his wall, racks and shelves cluttered with the paraphernalia of science and his books on the occult and mysticism. Beyond that wall was the barn interior. "Thank you, Mrs. LeBlanc. Please make the appropriate calls now, will you?"

"Yes, sir, um . . . I will. But . . . don't you want to see her?"

"Not yet. Maybe later."

The nurse's eyes dropped to his fingers, gripping the door edge as if to burrow into the wood. In addition, the claw hand was humming with vibration. She said, "Yes, sir," and walked back across the sparkling morning dew, crushing and killing countless minute and primitive organisms whose passing went unnoticed and unmourned.

*   *   *

He burst into the barn. Slants of pink-gold light were beaming through a few gaps in the high wood walls. A bar of this light lay across the giant mound of cells in its child's pool, the rest of its flesh a cool shadowy blue. The tank was out of reach of the light, dark and obscure. Before going to it, East hit the lights . . . as if for the first time, the thought of seeing Violet lying in there naked, eyes open and waiting for him, terrified him. But even as he did so, he knew what he would see.

The dough was not bread The stone unchiseled. The canvas blank.

In its tank, the 140 pounds of tobacco plant wart slept serenely, dreamless.

How could he have ever believed? How had he ever deluded himself, found faith in his delusions?

The same way all those who dreamed of the spirit persisting, of heavens, deluded themselves. Out of denial, as Mrs. LeBlanc had said. Out of fear . . .

It all ended in the flesh. In the jail of the cells, without escape or chance of parole.

With a liberation of his full fury, with a long suppressed wail of loss and frustration, Carl East swept up a heavy spade from its nail in the barn wall and ran at the obese bathing mound first. The Lord of the Idiots. The Emperor of the Unknowing. Its flesh was slashed without bleeding under the thumping and whacking blows of the shovel. It didn't seem to mind dying.

East was soaked in sweat and hoarse by the time he turned on the tank. It was the last target he'd saved, and he hesitated. He hesitated. But then he struck. The glass shattered, the nutrient solution gushed free like liquor amnii . . . but this fetus had never formed.

Mrs. LeBlanc heard his cries, and the smashing, but was too afraid to go see what he was doing. She'd rather remain with the corpse.

*   *   *

Her cold flesh had been taken away. East laughed at himself, wagging his head. He nearly tipped the glass of vodka reaching for it. Finally, with Violet gone, he sat in the house. Finally he had held her hand, just as they were ready to take her. Once again Mrs. LeBlanc had been right; he should have come to her while she was calling for him. Now it was too late. She was gone forever. Even Mrs. LeBlanc was gone. Night was a mantle on his house and on what he once would have called his soul.

She must have been calling out for him to tell him the truth she had realized toward the end. That there were not going to be any miracles. Only the mindless mind of Nature could shape primal matter—not the ingenuity or will of humans. Nature was pragmatic; maybe that was the key. With humans, passion hindered everything.

There was a loud crash from outside the house. From the barn.

East stiffened. It was surely something he had attacked with the shovel, toppling further. Or maybe raccoons or skunks had gotten in there, now that it was night; he remembered having left the barn doors wide, no longer concerned with secrecy.

But another sound came, and East knew that no raccoon or skunk would be smashing things so loudly . . .

He rose from the sofa. Vandals, maybe? Kids, having seen the barn open? He moved into the kitchen, shut off the lights and peeked around the lace in the back door window. The barn door gaped darkly. No ghostly flashlights in that cavern. He took up his own flashlight—and a short sword of a bread knife. Violet's knife. She had been a wonderful cook. A gourmet. The foolish attention humans paid to such primitive functions as eating . . . and for what, in the end, all that effort, all that love? Only to lose it, only to die, only . . .

East hushed his babbling mind as he eased the back door open. The night was cool and still—poised. He stalked away from the house, feeling vulnerable away from it, under the yawning black sky. His ears strained ahead of him like dogs on leash, but he heard no further sounds coming from the . . .

"*Carl* . . ."

Oh, God.

East was spiked to his spot, transfixed from head to soles. It was Violet's voice. The same mournful sob of a cry he had heard last night. But now it came from the barn.

Part of him leaped up inside, elated. Part of him wanted to spin and bolt for the house. Caught between these extremes, he swayed, a sob of fear or hope or confusion snagged in his throat.

"*Caarrl,*" the voice moaned. The voice was louder than it had been last night, and deeper. Oddly strong and resonant. Almost a rumble across the damp grass to him. But it was Violet, without question. Violet.

East staggered forward, a smile flickering on the electrified muscles of his face . . . and yet he still gripped the bread knife and held it before him as he went.

"Violet," he said. "Violet," as he reached the dark mouth of the barn. He reached only his arm inside to paw for the lights. "Violet . . ."

For a moment before he hit the switch, his eyes made out shapes across the barn floor. The carnage of his fury; the shattered tanks, splintered shelves, the slaughtered giants too primitive to be either plant or amoeba but so large that he had barely chiseled them down. Dark blobs glowing so very dimly in the blue light from outside. And even as his finger tips found the switch, East saw several of the hulking mounds *move* . . .

At the revelation in the full light from overhead, East screamed. Not a cry. Not a shout. A scream . . .

The pale masses of primal flesh lay where he had left them, for the most part. They rested in the splinters of glass and wood on the floor. But the floor as he had left it had been awash in nutrient solution from the shattered tanks and overturned pools. Now it was dry, the spilled nourishment greedily *absorbed.*

A small mass twitched by his foot, but his eyes flicked horrified between several of the larger pallid blobs. From one—twisted in anguished knots—there protruded a slim, nearly skeletal arm which clawed at the floorboards in an attempt to pull itself along. An almost spherical mass nearer to him was smooth except for the outlines of bones pressing at its skin; humped vertebrae like the horny spine of a dinosaur, ribs like prison bars picked out in vivid relief.

The once inviting cradle of her pelvis was now some sharp and hateful animal skull yawning to tear through the flesh of another blob, this one with glass shards stuck in it. Somehow, several pseudopods like grotesque flippers slapped at the floor to draw this horror along.

A thumping drew East's streaming eyes to the greatest of his crop, still hulking despite his attack. Though rent and cleft by his blows, it loomed, and a rudimentary human leg hung from its side, stamping at the ground in an obscene convulsion.

"Ohh, God . . . oh, Violet . . . oh *God!*" East sobbed. It was the vodka, the vodka and insanity . . .

"Carl," Violet's voice rattled, to his side.

He dare not look dare not look . . .

He looked.

The 140-pound vessel he had set out to catch her soul. The clay for her to mold. The voice, of course, came from that. From the mockery of vocal cords shaped from that primordial matter.

He met Violet's eyes there. Not much else of her showed in that too white rubbery flesh. The light from above made her eyes dark skull socket pools, made pools under the jutting of her bony cheeks. Her mouth was a wide, gnashing orifice. It was a face wasted by cancer, this now her subconscious conception of herself. It was a face of suffering. The mouth worked, the eyes blinked. They were white like the flesh, no color left in them.

"Carl . . ." the deep, sepulchral voice groaned.

Had she started with the destination mass he had cultivated as her spirit's receptacle? Found it lying on the boards and taken it anyway . . . but then needed more cells to take full form, to duplicate the great complexity of her former body? Or had her spirit become confused in transit, sent forth as it was in the delirium of her pain? Had he acted prematurely, and in smashing his experiment, shattered her focus? Had he done this to her?

Or had the cancer in her brain had its own tenacity for life . . . also imposed its will in the making of this tormented sculpture? And might it continue to make its will known; its hunger?

"Caaarrl."

A number of the blobs had variations on those crude flippers, used them or a single distorted limb to drag themselves along, and East realized their intention. They were hopelessly attempting to converge, to meet. To unite. It was futile. Several blobs were already floundering against each other helplessly. It was good that they couldn't link. Their mass, united, would only result in one great monster in the place of these many.

East thought of the hypothetical monster of Dr. White. Growing to the orbit of Pluto, and beyond. In his mind, he saw these creatures drawing on more nutrients, growing without his diligent pruning and burning, dragging their bulks out into the world, a herd of cancerous titans, hungry . . . so hungry to *live*. A herd of gods. Idiot gods. He began to laugh . . . laugh and wag his head. Laugh and wag his head and shake with wrenching sobs that pummeled him inside.

"Carl," Violet moaned. Her face implored him from one blob, a beseeching arm reached for him from another. He stumbled back into the threshold, thinking that the creatures meant to seize him, engulf him, absorb him, grow larger and hungrier yet.

"Carl . . . kill me . . ."

"Yes," he sobbed.

"Kill me."

"I will. I will, darling."

The fear went out of him at those words, washed out of him in his tears, and with a purity of purpose, East went to the reaching hand and took hold of it. The fingers were cold but strong as they clasped his. He pulled the blob into the center of the floor . . . then went to push another of them closer. Another. The leg of the great hulk did its best to assist him in sliding itself along.

Last, the mass with her face. East avoided looking at it as he lifted the thing in his arms. Ignored her mouth as it worked in dry sobs against his chest. Gently, reverently, he set this creature down with the others.

He walked across the floor boards to where several cans of gasoline were lined up along the inner wall by the lawnmower. "I love you, darling," he choked, returning to splash the fluid across the hideous congregation. "Oh, God . . . I love you . . ."

She shook now with sobs herself, painful retches that made most of the fragments of her quiver and spasm, and with their combined bulk made the floor tremble. East could only bear it long enough to complete his task.

He poured the last of the second gasoline can over his own head and shoulders. Then he went to her, unafraid, and knelt down for her to gently enfold him. An arm from this mass wrapped around his back, most of a hand from that mass clutched at his sleeve. He met her eyes again, and though they appeared blind he felt their contact. He clasped himself against her for a few moments, both of them now hushed, strangely calmed, before he dug the lighter from his pocket.

He smiled against her white flesh, pressed his lips into it. This was not a tragedy, he realized. It was a revelation.

The spirit lived on. It could escape its cells, live free of them. But he had been wrong in trying to ground it in matter once more.

Now, they would escape those bonds together.

THE HOUSE ON THE PLAIN

The black ship lay steaming on the plain, more a globe than a ship, like a great spherical meteor which had magnetized to it a thousand odd-matched fragments of machinery, all of it now scorched black by the hurtling speeds which had dropped it here. But the ship was made more of ceramics than metal, and the baroque details of its shell all served their practical functions. Probes extended to sniff the air, to test the temperature, camera eyes panned, skeletal arms unfolded to dig into the bland colorless soil.

For it was a boring enough planet. The sky was a dull heavy platinum. The horizon was as flat as an ocean's, though there were no oceans on this unnamed world. While in orbit, the ship had scanned no life.

The temperature was moderate and the gravity Earth-like, but the air was thoroughly unbreathable, so the three humans who set out from the globe wore full protective suits and helmets, their suits uniformly black but the helmets individually colored—neon green, orange and yellow—to make the explorers identifiable to each other and to the other two who remained aboard, should communications fail. These three were the most vital instruments the globe had extended.

It was a drab landscape, as stated. There was barely even a breeze to stir the bone dust grit beneath their boots. It was this chilling salt-flat emptiness, in addition to the mind-shaking incongruity itself, that made the old wooden house looming before them all the more startling.

"It's a Victorian, I think," said J'nette over her helmet mike. She tipped her head back to gaze up at the third floor, evidently an attic level. The house seemed taller than it might have in a less desolate setting.

"It can't be Terran," chuckled Dennis, wagging his head. "It can't be. Seth, man, let's go back in and get some guns, huh?"

"No way, I told you."

"This could be a trap! Who knows what built this place! Somebody wants to entice us inside . . ."

"They'd fabricate a space craft or at least a contemporary structure."

"Not if they were observing Earth through a time lapse. Could be they think this *is* contemporary."

"Could be they built it as a trap back when it was contemporary," mused J'nette.

"The scans show no life," Seth, the expedition leader, reminded them both. "Not even inside."

"No life that our scans can *recognize*," Dennis advised.

"Whatever it is," J'nette commented, "it could use a paint job." She moved

forward toward the dilapidated structure but Seth caught her lightly by the elbow. She looked to him puzzledly.

"Denny," he muttered, "go back in the ship and bring me one hand gun."

*   *   *

J'nette was running her hand along the clapboards of the house, once apparently painted white but the wood now as bone-bare as the plain the house rested on like some great many-eyed cattle skull. "It isn't an illusion," she said. "Or else it's a better illusion than we thought."

Dennis was holding a device against the outside of the house, watching the small screen set into it. "My scan isn't hallucinating. It's real. And it's real wood." He turned his head to Seth. "There are no trees on this planet, boss."

Seth had been gazing in through a window. The glass of every window seemed intact but the shades were drawn in all the ground-floor windows except for this one. Too gloomy inside to see much; indistinct shadows, presumably furniture. He had been afraid, perhaps irrationally, that he would see one of the hunched shadows suddenly *move*. At Dennis' words he nodded as if distracted by other thoughts. The pistol was clipped on his belt and now he unsnapped the holster. "Let's go inside."

*   *   *

J'nette went about the spacious living room raising the shades, letting in the lifeless silvery light, while Dennis lifted a *TV Guide* from the cheap pressed-wood coffee table. Seth had picked up a remote control device and pointed it toward the blank screen of a television set. Nothing happened. Dennis glanced over. "No electricity, chief. They didn't own individual power cells then, but were all linked up to a municipal utility system."

Seth noticed the electrical cords snaking from the TV and ancient videotape recorder into a wall outlet. A lamp was plugged into this outlet also but nothing happened when he tried its switch. He wasn't surprised.

"Well, the house was already old before these things were added," J'nette observed, her pretty brown face pinched with intensity. She moved to a built-in bookcase, and plucked out volumes at random to check the copyright or printing date in their fronts. The most recent book she found was one from 1992, and most of them were older. Some *much* older. Titles in English, Latin and German. There were books on non-Euclidean geometry, "rubber-sheet" geometry, Klein bottles and Moebius strips and the studies that had made possible at last the traversal warpage that had brought their ship here through compressed folds of space, crossing distances that otherwise would be impossible for them to cover in mortal life spans.

But in addition to these scientific volumes there were those quite old books with odd titles, all of them apparently studies of mysticism and magic, witchcraft or something much darker. J'nette hefted one heavy tome and it fell open to a page where a sheet had been inserted as a book mark. Seth drew closer to look over her shoulder.

"Weird," he said, reading the scribbled incantations the owner of the book, of this house, had copied from the discolored pages. The incantations were modified, however, on the notebook sheet, altered and with new sections inserted. Geometric figures had also been inserted as illustrations, and some resembled the simplified diagrams of Klein bottles and worm holes Seth had studied in his academy days.

The book was replaced, the three drifted on into other rooms, pointing their flashlights and lifting shades. In the kitchen, J'nette knelt by a dog dish and a water bowl, the water long since evaporated.

Dennis gestured to the two doors in here. One, with lacy curtains over a window, obviously was a back way leading outside. The other probably led into the basement. He moved toward this one.

J'nette rose, approached Seth to show him something she had gathered from the floor. "Dog hairs, sir. We could make up a clone when we get back to base."

"We'd have a dog, all right, J'nette. But I don't think it could tell us much. Even if we find a hair from a human . . . we can't clone its memories."

"We could at least prove that he or she was a human. A human being from Earth."

"J'nette," Seth said, "I don't think that needs to be proven any more."

"Look," called Dennis, and the other two rushed to his side at the tone of his voice.

The cellar stairs seemed to disappear into the ash-like dirt of the plain after only several steps. As if the basement had flooded in sand.

"This house was displaced here," Seth breathed. "Transplanted here intact. Without so much as a window cracked or a cup knocked over in a cabinet."

"How?" Dennis chuckled, wagging his head again. "By whom? I don't see a traversal warp engine under the kitchen sink."

"Another way, but the same result. This house came from Earth before us. Before we'd even invented warp travel."

"You think the owner did it? Come on. Do you see any machines he might have built? Unless they were in the basement and got left back in the foundation on Earth a hundred years ago."

"Maybe he didn't use a machine," Seth half whispered.

"What?" Dennis had scrunched his face.

"The books in the parlor . . ."

"Oh. Right. He used magic . . ."

197

"One generation's magic is the science of the next."

"Hey," J'nette said. She had moved to the back door and opened it. The two men went to her.

"What are those?" Dennis asked. "Tree stumps?"

The trio stepped back onto the vast plain. The objects of their attention must have been previously hidden from their sight behind the house, they decided. When the globe had descended, they must have been too shocked at the house itself to take notice. Now they approached the tree stumps, as Dennis had called them.

They stood around the closest of the three. Dennis said, "No life here, huh?"

"They don't register as life," J'nette observed, pressing her hand scanner to the thing. "It must have been alive once." It did indeed resemble a tree stump even this close up, the stump of a very large tree, with a star-shaped deep opening in the top. The roots were thick and forked, trailing away into the dirt, the bark a glossy black and wrinkled, grooved, hard. Her scanner bit into the tough bark and collected a sample for more detailed study.

Dennis sighed, sat on the table-like top of the stump to gaze out across the plain. It taunted him with its mysterious emptiness, a mood so persuasive that the cryptical house seemed a crystallized personification of it. "Well, boss, maybe you're right. But I think some other force or intelligence reached out to Earth and dragged this house here."

"Why, though, a house that just happened to have books anticipating traversal warpage?"

Dennis had no further replies ready. They returned to the interior of the house, moved upstairs. There was a bedroom. Framed photographs on a bureau. Seth lifted one. A man with an intense face and thinning hair with his arm around the shoulders of a plain but warmly smiling woman. From a drawer, J'nette removed a scrapbook. The two men flanked her to peer at it also.

"James Ward," J'nette said. "That was his name."

School pictures. As a boy, Ward had looked no less intense. He had done well in school; pasted honor rolls cut from newspapers. Later pictures showed Ward enrolled in a university. Still later, photos of the woman from the framed picture in Seth's hand. Then, toward the end, an obituary for Margaret Ward, aged 42, dead from cancer back before they had a cure for it, obviously.

"This must have been their dog," J'nette noted, tapping a photo of a German Shepherd. "The one whose hairs I found."

"If Ward and the dog were teleported here with the house," Dennis observed, "they both would have died within minutes at the most. They wouldn't be able to breathe. Right?"

"Right . . ." said Seth.

"So where are the bodies?"

Now it was Seth who had no reply at hand. Across the landing was another bedroom, and they passed into this. There was no bed, however, the room having obviously been used by Ward as a study. Bookshelves overflowing, stacks piled on the floor. On the desk blotter was a notebook filled with more of the indecipherable nonsense that had filled the sheet in the old book on magic. Seth lifted an odd paper weight and turned it over in his gloved hands; black crystal with striations of red streaked through it. Symbols had been carved into its many faces.

"Check this," J'nette told him. He joined her and Dennis at the center of the room, where a pentagram or some such geometric figure had been burned into the otherwise lovely golden boards of the hardwood floor. Between the arms of the star were reproduced some of the symbols Seth recognized from the black crystal.

"I'm not much on twentieth-century religion," Dennis said, "but I'd say Mr. Ward was into some very unorthodox practices."

"Maybe he was just an explorer," Seth said softly. "Like us."

A ghostly white movement in the corner of his eye, and Seth was spinning about, his hand slapping to the gun holstered on his hip.

It was only the gauzy window curtains stirring subtly in a very mild breeze. This one window at the back of the house was open. He went to it idly to look down on the tree stumps.

"Jesus!" Seth gasped, as soon as he had parted the curtains with his hands.

The mummy was suspended in air just a few feet beyond the window. Its attitude suggested that this being had dove suicidally from the window, only to be frozen in mid-air. It was impossibly suspended. It faced away from him, but the hands and back of the head, with its scant hair, suggested mummification. But Seth didn't need to see the face to know that these were the unearthly remains of their host, James Ward.

Dennis and J'nette had crowded in beside him. J'nette said, "This is just too much! What the hell happened to this guy?"

"I don't think I wanna know," said Dennis.

"Hey," said Seth. "The tree stumps are gone."

Dennis leaned his head out the window, incredulous. The tree stumps were indeed gone, as if they had never been there. No depressions or covered mounds where they had been. There did appear to be, however, three broad trails all leading in to one center point . . . as if the three stumps had been dragged together to that central point. But then what? At that point there was nothing but the featureless flatness of the plain.

"Let's get back on the ship!" Dennis hissed, pulling inside hurriedly.

J'nette had found a folding measuring stick, perhaps having been used to map out the figure on the floor, and unfolded it so as to prod Ward's body. She could stir his clothing with it, but when she pushed at one of his hands it was so unyielding that the stick bowed.

Dennis yanked her away from the window. "Don't do that!"

"This could be a dangerous situation," Seth had to agree. "We'd better get back on the ship until we can run further tests and scans. We'll call station. They might even advise us to go orbital until further notice."

"I think we should do that anyway!"

They turned from the window, descended the creaking stairs, left the old house through the front door. All of them walked very briskly back to the globe . . . as if the very earth beneath their feet might open up and swallow them. Just before they had reached the ship, there came a beep in their headsets. Seth answered it. "Yes?"

"Chief," came the voice of Louise, aboard their craft, "you'd better get back in here quick."

"We're an our way now . . . what is it?"

"Just come look, please. Hurry."

The trio of explorers boarded, felt automatically safer sealed back inside this shelter of their own period. Removing only their garish helmets, they hastened to central command . . . and as they entered, froze in the doorway as if whatever force had seized hold of the body of James Ward had locked onto them as well.

Scan technician Louise, Sam their pilot and a panting German Shepherd looked up at the paralyzed trio. The dog, beautiful and healthy, was smiling black-lipped in the way dogs seemed to be able.

"He just walked into the room with us," said Sam. "Like he'd been on the ship with us the whole time."

"Friendly," Louise added, her hands stroking the animal.

Seth turned to gaze at the banks of monitor screens above the scan stations. The old house was there. Looming. In need of paint and some repair. Black eyes gazing back at him enigmatically.

"Magic," he whispered to himself.

THE FOURTH UTTERANCE

6:33 pm—3/01—Call #1

—UNAVAILABLE—

Cornelia switched her attention from the caller ID box to the answering machine directly beside it, both on the kitchen table beneath the wall-mounted telephone. A red digital "1" showed in the answering machine's little window.

She hadn't thought to look at either device until 1:45, even though she had gotten home from her second shift job before 12:30. Since she had bought a computer and gone online several months ago, she was more concerned with checking and replying to her email, which she had just finished doing. Tonight's offering: a humorous list of "The Top 10 Things That Women Can Do Better Than Men", sent by her mother; a work at home scheme; a story about a little girl with a brain tumor the size of a grapefruit (weren't *all* scary tumors the size of a grapefruit?), for some reason inoperable, which Cornelia was supposed to pass along to five people or presumably she'd grow a brain tumor as well; an email from her ex-boyfriend, Brian:

Cornelia,

I know you could probably shoot me right about now, but I really do care about you, and I always will. I'm . . .

DELETE.

She was sorry now she hadn't read the whole thing. Was it still in her trash can or would her email service have dumped that already? No—why read it? What was the point? The presence of his words inside that box was a mockery when her apartment rang hollow with the absence of his body. Ghost in the machine. He had deleted her from his life; insincere guilt did not soothe or comfort her, exonerate or redeem him. Would he send her one of those silly little animated email cards next?

DELETE.

Cornelia had shut off the computer and now, dressed in comfortable much-laundered pajamas, barefoot, her lank hair released from the tight ponytail that had constrained it all evening, she had gone to fix herself a late snack of microwave popcorn. A CD played softly in the other room (Sade's *Love Deluxe*; sad, dreamy post-midnight music). And while pouring herself a glass of soda, she had let her eyes drift to the two devices patiently, silently awaiting her attentions atop the kitchen table.

The one and only call, she saw, had been received at 6:33—when she'd been at work. UNAVAILABLE, the lead display read, in lieu of the caller's number. A bill collector? They were often listed that way, or as

ANONYMOUS CALL, and so when she was home Cornelia never picked up a call bearing either of those labels until she heard the message come over the answering machine (and if it was a bill collector, they usually didn't leave a message, anyway). She reached out and touched the PLAY button on the answering machine, expecting the few seconds of dead silence that would prove her theory correct.

But instead of silence, there was a voice. A youngish man, speaking softly and intimately so that the first image that sprang to Cornelia's mind was of lips brushing a mouthpiece:

"It's me. I'm sorry . . . I know I promised not to call . . ."

For one beat, Cornelia thought it was Brian, even though it sounded nothing like him. Her chest constricted.

". . . I know you don't want to see me. I can't blame you for being afraid of what I'm doing. I don't fault you for getting out. It was probably stupid of me not to stop . . . to just go on with it. Yeah—that's right: I finished it. Last night I put the stones in the four corners of the room. I drew the sign on each stone. I gave the fourth utterance of ascent. And . . . And . . . yeah. And it worked. It happened . . ."

Cornelia didn't know this voice. She didn't know what he was discussing. It was a wrong number. He had dialed a number similar to the one he wanted, no doubt . . .

". . . I looked all over the house for it. I thought it would be in the cellar, or the attic, for some reason. It was in the bathroom, of all places. In the corner behind the hamper. I could only see . . . fog. But it felt cold, when I moved the hamper and got close. And I thought I heard a sound in there, way back, far off—like monkeys, maybe. A sound like monkeys calling. But, sort of like . . . electronic sounding . . ."

Cornelia shot an angry look at the microwave, where her popcorn was noisily popping, the appliance annoyingly humming. She leaned her head down over the answering machine, holding her long hair away from her ear.

". . . It's still there now. But you know—after all my reading. After all this work. After losing you to get this far—I just can't bring myself to go into . . ."

"END OF MESSAGES", a robotic voice suddenly announced, cutting in. The intense young man was gone. The switch in voices, from emotional to mechanical, startled Cornelia, and she drew back.

The microwave stopped, and only one or two last kernels popped, the bag now swollen like some inoperable tumor.

What had the stranger been going on about? What had he been looking for in his house or apartment? What was it he had found in the bathroom (of all places)?

Cornelia played the message back again. It made no more sense to her the second time.

UNAVAILABLE. He had called from someplace where they didn't have caller ID, then. Without his number being displayed, she couldn't call him back to inform him that he'd whispered so intently to someone other than this person he had promised he would never call again.

Wasn't there some kind of feature called Call Trace? Yes . . . punch star, then a number. But what was the number? It was two-digit, right? She couldn't recall it; and anyway, would it be able to trace an "unavailable" call?

What did it matter? He was a stranger. But she had been drawn in, she had to admit, by his earnest-sounding emotion. The touch of bitter, regretful humor in his words. By the warm, dark sound of his voice. Here was a man who still loved the person he was calling. It was the woman who had broken off with him. He still wanted to be with her. How lucky she was, Cornelia thought. And what a fool she was.

Cornelia's eyes were growing moist. As if it were the young man's pain that moved her.

She touched a button. The robotic voice intoned, "MESSAGES DELETED."

* * *

What a long night it had been.

A new Brazilian coworker had flirted with her. He wasn't bad looking, but at the end of the shift Judi had told her he was married, with kids.

A long, long night, Cornelia thought, letting herself into her apartment. Not popcorn tonight, with its low dietary points. Ice cream. Ice cream for sure.

But before she went to the refrigerator. Before she checked her email. Before, even, she removed her coat, Cornelia glanced over at the kitchen table.

A red digital "1" on her answering machine. She stepped nearer to see the caller ID's display. It read:

8:43 pm—3/02—Call #1

—UNAVAILABLE—

Without even removing her woolen gloves, Cornelia depressed the button labeled PLAY on her answering machine.

Tonight, she recognized the voice. As if it were someone she knew.

"I didn't think you'd call me back. Then again, I hope I have the right number. I copied it out of your brother's book, very quickly, when he was out of the room. I'm sure that's enough to make you furious in itself . . .

"But I wish you'd talk to me. I wish . . ."

He sighed. Trailed off. A few seconds of silence. Hurry, Cornelia wordlessly urged him, before your time runs out.

"I still haven't gone through. I'm—just plain afraid. Those sounds in there. And it's so dark. And cold. Last night I could barely sleep, knowing it was in the house, just a few rooms away from me. I'm keeping the bathroom door shut, but I can't lock it from the outside. I should at least screw in an eye-hook latch or something. Humph—like that would stop anything that wanted to come through . . ."

Cornelia found herself unaccountably glancing up at her own bathroom, which opened off the kitchen. Unlit, murky inside. Since childhood she had had a fear of looking in the mirror and seeing someone standing behind her shoulder, only in the glass. A ghost. Something worse, perhaps . . .

The young man continued in his hushed, melancholy voice.

"You were right to get out. I should have listened. I took it too far. I really don't think I'm going to have the guts to go in there. I think . . . I really think I need to close it up again. That's what I'm going to have to do. I'm just afraid that if any of them see it from their side, they'll be a lot braver than I am. They'll want to come here. And not to learn. Not to explore. I don't even want to imagine what . . ."

"END OF MESSAGES."

"Bastard," Cornelia hissed under her breath at the robot.

Well, her man was in some kind of danger, then. But who were these people he feared? What had he done that might draw their attention to him?

Who am I kidding? Cornelia thought. *He's crazy. He's obviously crazy. Or on drugs. Or both.*

She played the message back again. And this time, having already listened to the words, she discerned another sound behind them. It lasted only a fraction of a second, and it came right before the tape allocated for his message ran out. Right before he said, ". . . imagine what . . ."

Cornelia played the tape a third time. Leaned so close to the machine that its sound became distorted, but at least she heard that funny little background sound again.

It was a distant squeal of high-pitched laughter. She guessed. From a child. But . . . maybe it had been a cat's drawn-out meow? A pet tropical bird, making an odd sound . . . trying to form words?

Monkeys calling . . . electronic sounding . . .

I'm letting his delusions become my delusions, Cornelia thought, disgusted at herself and the gooseflesh she'd raised on her arms. She deleted the message, removed her winter coat, and stepped into the bathroom to pee.

She put the light on quickly, however—not wanting to see the mirror in the dark.

* * *

The next night there were two messages left on her machine—like letters written by an old friend, a lover called away overseas, brimming with contents that ached to be opened.

The first message had come in at 11:43. The second at 11:45. Damn, Cornelia thought . . . damn. Why couldn't he have called just a little bit later? She would have been home to pick up at last . . .

Pick up and what? Tell him he had the wrong number? But then he'd stop calling, wouldn't he? Not if she asked him what was troubling him so. Not if she asked him if she—unlike his apathetic lover—could help him.

Cornelia squeezed her wool gloves into a ball, unsqueezed them, squeezed them, like a heart she was manually pumping. You're losing your mind, she told herself gravely.

But then her eyes returned to the twin heralds on her table. And she played the first message on the tape.

The whisper was softer, more intense than ever. It seemed to come through a blizzard of static, to make matters worse. Had he switched to a portable phone with a weak battery? Or was something interfering with the connection?

"Two of them came through tonight . . . I pray to God it was only two. I was in the bedroom. I stayed home all day—I don't dare go to work, to go out at all, with the doorway open like that. I was in the bedroom—" there was a pause here, and it made Cornelia's breath solidify in her throat, as if the caller had stopped to listen for something "—and I heard something like feet pattering in the kitchen. A sound like children giggling. I rushed out . . . without a weapon, like an idiot . . . and I saw them duck into the bathroom. It was just a second, just a flash . . . I'm not sure I could really describe them. But . . . but they were horrible. Dark purple, like they were—rotting. Their heads were huge, pulpy. Like sacks. Like they didn't have skulls. And their arms didn't have bones. They couldn't have had bones, the way they were moving. They might have been . . . tentacles . . ."

"My God," Cornelia barely mouthed.

"I'm sure they've been stealing my books . . . my papers. They're all gone. All of it. It has to be the Larvae. Carrying it all away—"

His sentence was severed. But the tape went on to the next message; this time he had immediately phoned back to continue. Being cut off the first time only seemed to heighten the tone of urgency in his voice.

"I can't remember the words to close the doorway! I have most of it, but I can't remember what sign to put on the second stone. And I can't remember the fourth utterance of descent! Please . . . Please . . . I know you're angry at me . . ."

He was almost in tears now. So was Cornelia. She didn't know why. Did she ache at having to listen to an agonized man go out of his mind? Or did she . . . believe him, somehow? Poor Cornelia. Always so gullible when it came to men. But listen to him! Listen to his sincere emotion!

". . . I need your help. I don't want you to come here—I don't want you to be in danger, too. But if you remember the things I'm forgetting, please help me! Just this one last time! I beg you, honey, I beg you!"

There was a distant crash behind his last words. Something knocked over in another room.

"I have to go!" he hissed.

"END OF MESSAGES."

No!" Cornelia said loudly, accusingly, to the traitorous, taunting machine. A tear coursed down her cheek. "No!" she sobbed, louder still.

He might call back yet. Right? It hadn't been that long ago. If he had called twice in one night, why not again?

She didn't check her email. Going online would give a caller the busy signal.

She drew a bath. Put on a CD. Made a cup of orange flavored tea. A headache was coming on, so she lay back in the tub with a wet face cloth folded over her eyes. But it was like being blindfolded—it was too dark. She didn't even want to shut her eyes. Not in the bathroom, of all places.

Her eyes traced suspicious cracks in the plaster of the ceiling she had never taken note of before, then slowly lowered to the corner of the room, just beyond the tub. They scanned sideways, across the toiletries and hair brushes piled atop her toilet tank. Something had crashed to the floor . . . something in his bathroom. Her eyes returned to the corner. At any moment, she expected to see it yawn open. To feel a frigid breath exhaled from that new opening, like the breath of a dead man. To hear horrible cries deep within the churning mists. To see eyes, perhaps, glinting out at her from between the tendrils of fog. If they even *had* eyes . . .

Even as she finally slipped into bed, at 3:10, she thought he might call her yet. That she would be awakened by the yearning cry of the phone.

Her sleep went undisturbed, however—except by dreams.

*   *   *

Just before she'd drifted off last night, Cornelia had decided to stay home from work the next day—to call in sick. This time she'd be here to receive his message when it came . . .

But in the light of day, she found herself unable to go through with it. When Brian had left her, only a week and a half ago, she had stayed out sick for two consecutive days. The company wouldn't put up with much more of that.

But at the end of the shift, when Brett—Cornelia's boss—asked her if she could stay an hour late tonight, she stammered her way out of it, claiming she had a headache.

And as soon as she unlocked the back door to her apartment she headed

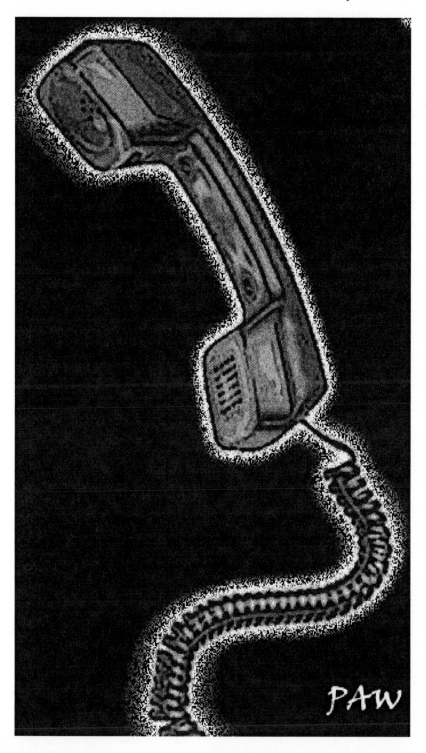

straight to the kitchen table . . .

The counter on her answering machine read 0.

Slowly she withdrew the finger that brushed the PLAY button.

Had he found the correct phone number, finally? Or had he given up on appealing to his former lover?

Unwilling to believe it was over, this little affair of hers with a man who didn't even know she was receiving his communications, Cornelia checked the caller ID's dim little window. It, too, showed no calls had been received.

Well, then. Well . . .

She took off her coat. Reluctantly trudged into her bedroom—where her computer waited for her like a paid lover—to check her email. She illogically hoped to find a message from her mysterious caller there. But . . . another chain letter. An animated email card from her mother. Not even anything from Brian. She looked at the contents of her email account's trash can. It was empty.

They got him, she thought in a small, droning interior voice. They got him . . .

"He's crazy!" she argued out loud. "You heard him! He's . . ."

Cornelia disconnected from the internet. What if he had tried to call while she was online?

"He won't call again!" she snapped. "Jesus! She doesn't care—he knows that now! So he gave up on her!"

From the kitchen, the shrill alert of her telephone.

Cornelia pushed her chair back so hard that it nearly toppled. She plunged into the living room, on into the kitchen. She had programmed the machine to start recording after four rings. She knew she would get to it in time to pick up the call herself . . .

But when she stood over the kitchen table, even though there were still two rings left to go, she found herself unable to take the receiver off the wall. She had to listen first. Screen her call. See if it was him. And even if it was—would she really be able to speak back to him at last?

Third ring . . .

A glance at the caller ID display. UNAVAILABLE. It might as well be his name.

Fourth ring.

"Hi," she heard her own recorded voice say. She hated her voice. Dark and gluey, it sounded—morose, sulky, self-pitying. Weak. Lonely. It sounded just like her, she thought. "I'm not able to come to the phone right now," she lied, so as to avoid bill collectors, so as to eavesdrop on desperate strangers, "but please leave a message after the beep and I'll try to get back to you."

The tape began to turn, to record . . .

Dead silence.

A bill collector? At one o'clock in the morning?

But then she heard a faint rustling noise. The subtle shifting of a body on the other end. A wet little sound like someone licking dry lips before speaking. But the static, worse than last night, might be fooling her. She might be hearing nothing at all . . .

And then the terrible noises began. They were animal cries of some kind, wild, deranged—deafening. Cornelia fell back from the table several steps, and clapped her hands over her ears. It was a cacophony. Voices filled with rage and glee. But they sounded like monkeys or tropical birds, whooping and shrieking, as if they were on fire. Banshee wails. The laughter of insane children with tumors like new brains crowding out their skulls.

"END OF MESSAGES."

Slowly, timidly, Cornelia lowered her hands from her ears. She heard the humming of her refrigerator directly behind her. And that was all.

Where had the calls been originating from? Several towns away? Another state?

She hoped, now, that he had lived very, very far away from her.

Tomorrow she would have her number changed. But for tonight . . . she took the phone off the hook.

She could only hope that it was the other woman—the nameless lover—and not her, not Cornelia, that tonight's call had been intended for.

Despite her own fear, however, she felt fresh tears well in her eyes. "I'm sorry," she said very quietly to the two small machines. Wishing she could be speaking the words into a mouthpiece instead. "I'm so sorry," she whispered. And she reached out to the answering machine once more.

"MESSAGES DELETED."

THE WRITING ON THE WALL

(Author's note: the following vignette appeared in the newsletter of the printing company I once worked for. It was supposed to be the second chapter in a comical series I was coerced into doing, called The History of Printing—*but darker impulses seized my mind. I'm not sure if a story featuring Mythos elements ever before appeared in a company newsletter . . . but said publication did have the decidedly Lovecraftian-sounding title of* The Nameless Newsletter.)

* * *

Last time we spoke of the use of Egyptian hieroglyphics as a major step in the history of the written word, the recording of language, and hence a prelude to printing. We also alluded to the theory that the pyramids and the plain of Giza were the first industrial park (the brain-child of that forgotten and very unpopular pharaoh, Immafartun). But with Halloween around the corner, we'll concentrate on the pyramids in more recent times, and on those who study the writing of the ancients, like the archeologist and hieroglyphist, Dr. Henry Paxton.

* * *

Paxton turned around . . .

He wanted to excitedly exclaim about the discovery he had just made, but then he remembered he was alone in the cellars of the pyramid. No one was there in the gloom of the tunnel behind him. The others waited above, outside, bored porters and tired assistants without his sense of dedication. How could they not be more enthusiastic? After all, no one had even suspected that these hidden chambers lay beneath the pyramid until Paxton had discovered them only a few days earlier.

He returned his attention to his latest discovery, moved the lantern closer and used a brush to sweep aside the dust of dreaming millenniums. He began to unveil a long series of hieroglyphs, carven in the stone blocks that formed this narrow corridor, which tapered into silent darkness at either end.

The figures in the hieroglyphics seemed more realistic, naturalistic than he was accustomed to. Normally they were more stylized. He recognized familiar symbols mixed in with others he had never encountered before. He had seen the scarab, but never the starfish with a human eye in its center. He had encountered the jackal-headed, baboon-headed and falcon-headed gods . . .

but what of this alien god, with a head like an octopus and wings rather like those of a bat?

As he moved along the low-ceilinged tunnel in an uncomfortable crouch to remain at the level of the pictographs, he cleared away more and more of what appeared to be some story or myth that was unfolding. It was stifling in the confines of the tunnel, so he swept a free hand under the wide brim of his rumpled and sweat-stained hat to wipe away a trickle of sweat.

The story in stone carvings seemed to begin with stylized rays of light piercing into a burial chamber, where there was a sarcophagus inscribed with mysterious symbols. In the next uncovered image, Paxton saw the sarcophagus lid was now open and a terrible figure was revealed   within . . . a skeletal mummy with a head like the remains of an octopus, withered tentacles where a human mouth should be.

The following panel showed the octopus-headed corpse having departed from its elaborate coffin, walking into a corridor of stone. Its body was bent forward, its bat wings were in tatters, its fingers spread like eagle's talons.

"Remarkable!" Paxton whispered under his breath. "Such a find." He dusted at the next picture. "Never seen anything like it! Never!"

Paxton stared at the next carving. It showed two figures. One was the resurrected bat-winged mummy, and it seemed to be sneaking up behind the other figure. A crouching figure. This crouching figure, carven in stone thousands of years earlier, somehow carried a modern lantern and worn a rumpled, wide-brimmed hat.

Paxton turned around . . .

CORPSE CANDLES

That the old man—apparently in his nineties—was still alive was miracle enough. That he was conscious and capable of intelligible speech was, to Grange, shocking. He had been told that when the fire department answered a neighbor's call about smoke billowing from the attic windows of the old man's house, and upon discovering his charred body on the floor—his hair and clothing entirely burned away—they had thought him dead. Until he groaned, and raked one man's leg with a hand like a blackened bird's claw.

"You know the first thing that went through my head?" this firefighter had related to Grange only an hour ago. "Spontaneous human combustion. I know, I know . . . but I'm telling you, the only thing burned in that attic was this guy. Even the old rug he fell on was barely scorched. There was a greasy kind of soot on the walls, but that came from him. Maybe it was spontaneous human combustion. Just, that in his case it didn't entirely do the job."

Grange didn't understand medicine, but knew there must be some good reason the elderly man's face was not entirely swathed in gauze. It had been difficult, upon entering the room, to conceal his revulsion. That hideous mask could not be the countenance of a human being. Grange had been told the body, covered in a sheet at least, was much worse. The frail little man's body barely tented the sheet; Grange had seen more substantial remains dug out of decades-old shallow graves.

"Mr. Brill, I'm Detective Grange . . ." he said, leaning a bit over the bed, expecting the old man's eyes to open. The nurse, before letting him in, had assured him Brill was awake. But when Brill replied, he still did not open his eyes, and Grange queasily wondered if his eyelids were fused shut, or if those orbs had turned to gelatin beneath them.

"Detective," Brill greeted him. "Sit down. Uh, have I done something wrong?"

Taking a seat at the bedside, Grange couldn't prevent himself from chuckling uncomfortably. "Well, setting yourself on fire is wrong, I guess, but I didn't come here to arrest you . . . just to find out what happened."

"I didn't set myself on fire," Brill told him. His voice was both an agonized rasp, and weirdly calm.

"So it wasn't intentional . . . That's a good thing. How did it happen? Were you smoking?"

"I told you—I didn't set myself on fire."

Grange took in the man's ruined profile for several beats. He was reminded of the fireman's talk of spontaneous human combustion. Stupid, he scolded himself. The old man was senile; of course he had set himself ablaze. He might not know how he had done it, but done it he surely had. Nevertheless Grange asked him again, "So how did it happen?"

There was a long pause. Life support equipment hissed, red numbers fluctuated on monitor screens as if flashing an encoded message. "It was my brother. Martin Brill. He did this to me."

"Your brother?" Grange sat forward. "Where is he? I was told you didn't have any family."

"He lives across town. On Pine Street, right on the outside of Eastborough Swamp."

"And he set you on fire? Purposely?"

A slight nod of a head like that of a peeling, unwrapped mummy, horribly contrasted against the pristine white pillows.

"Why?"

"We haven't spoken much in years. We had a falling out a long, long time ago. For a while we made up, and moved out here to Massachusetts together, but . . ." A cough painful even to hear. "We have . . . different philosophies." After a moment, Brill amended, "Different religions."

"So he came to your house and set you on fire? Where is he now?"

"He's home. But he never left his house to do this to me. He sent . . . something else to my house to do it for him."

Had the old man meant to say someone else? "Who was that?" he asked, wondering if this story were all a delusion born of pain, delirium, paranoia.

Again, just the hissing, the beeping, a rattling cart being pushed past the door. Then: "An elemental. A fire vampire. One of the minions of the god Martin worships."

Grange found himself sitting back in his chair, his hands untensing on his knees. Yes, the elderly man was delusional. Yes, he had to have unconsciously immolated himself. No . . . Grange did not believe that Brill's brother had set him ablaze . . . with or without the help of any "minion."

Still, he at least had to talk to this next of kin. At the very least, all feuding aside, he should know that his brother was probably not going to survive.

*   *   *

Before Grange sought out this Martin Brill on Pine Street, however, upon returning to Eastborough from the hospital in Worcester he first stopped at Edgar Brill's own home. He himself had not yet viewed the scene, had only spoken with the men who had sprayed the coal-like smoldering crisp of Brill's body, and the uniformed men who had initially responded to the call.

With Brill's own keys, Grange let himself into the now empty old house.

That the old man was an eccentric, strange even when he wasn't delirious with pain, was readily apparent. The squalor of the house was bad enough—

filthy clothing strewn about, food-encrusted dishes resting throughout the house, newspapers, magazines and books stacked precariously in each room to the point where some rooms had mere pathways through this landscape of paper mesas and plateaus. But this in itself was not surprising for an elderly person living by himself. It was, rather, the . . . décor . . . that mystified the small town detective.

One room's ceiling was painted black, for instance. Large eye-hooks had been screwed into the ceiling, and metal wire threaded through them, making a kind of hanging web . . . from the middle of which dangled an intricate contraption like a box kite, but much more elaborate, constructed of sticks and paper, that twirled gently in the breeze of Grange's movement. Odd symbols or markings on the various faces of the mobile revealed themselves as it turned in the displaced air.

In another room, in amongst an abundance of crumbling ancient books that filled a number of built-in shelves, Grange's eye was drawn to a biological specimen preserved for display in a greenish-tinted block of Lucite or some such substance. The frayed, grayish-pink matter in this block was not even remotely recognizable except as something organic. This wasn't some human organ, was it? On the top he noticed a narrow label, the typed ink very faint on the yellow paper. Grange had to take the object down from the shelf to read it. It read: *Saint Augustine, Florida, 1896.* Replacing the heavy block, Grange took note of a photograph cut from a book and tacked to the wall beside the bookshelf. A similar typed label was taped across its bottom. It appeared to show some blob-like rotting carcass washed ashore on a beach, obviously in Saint Augustine, Florida. A typed letter was tacked below the photo, and read simply: *Edgar, Here is that chunk I alluded to; methinks it was a Spawn of C———. Photo enclosed, as well. Best, S. Sargent.*

In other rooms, more photographs and cryptic correspondence, and articles clipped from newspapers and magazines such as National Geographic and Fate, adorned the walls, sometimes in great profusion, like a kind of patchwork wallpaper.

At last, Grange mounted a narrow, creaking staircase to the attic, passing through beams of late afternoon sunlight in which dust motes swarmed like plankton. The attic, which had once been a third floor apartment, was more of the same clutter, only worse. The walls had been stripped down to the plaster but never papered again except for more clippings. Halfway up the stairs, he had paused to read about a family plagued by poltergeist activity, including a profusion of mysterious fires. Just beyond the top the stairs, Grange paused to read from a lengthy article—very yellowed and crumbling, as it was dated 1971—written on the hundredth anniversary of the Great Chicago Fire.

Grange had never realized just what a horrific tragedy that had been, or how strangely widespread the fiery devastation had been all on that night of October 8, 1871. Tremendous fires had swept through Illinois, Indiana, Iowa, Minnesota, North and South Dakota, and Wisconsin. Twenty-four towns burned to charcoal, 2,000 lives lost. Of these, 1,500 had been lost in a 400 square mile area of Wisconsin. The town of Peshtigo, Wisconsin suffered the greatest violence, when monstrous windstorms of fire had descended from the sky with Biblical fury. One house had been lifted by the hellish winds one hundred feet into the air, there to erupt into flame. An eyewitness to the nightmare had written:

> *"In one awful instant a great flame shot up in the western heavens, and in countless fiery tongues struck downward into the village, piercing every object that stood in the town like a red-hot bolt . . . the flaming whirlwind swirled in an instant through the town. All heard the first inexplicable roar . . . while a few avow that the heavens opened and the fire rained down from above."*

"So much for a cow kicking over a lantern," Grange muttered. He read on . . . eerie details about the mysterious, often fickle behavior of the blazing tornado. One man had been found dead, but strangely untouched by the fire . . . and yet some coins in his pocket were partly fused from the heat. And another man was found alive, staggering along in a stupor, his hair and clothes seared away but an oddly carved musical instrument merged with the hand that clutched it. He had been mumbling repeatedly about something called Cthugha, which he blamed for the conflagration, and spoke of as an entity, leading those who found him to believe he was referring to some Indian god. The man, one Edgar Brill, had ended up in a sanitarium, his mind blasted.

Edgar Brill. So that explained the interest of Eastborough's Edgar Brill in this story. His grandfather, perhaps, for whom he had been named?

Grange sighed, straightened, barely able to take in the enormity of the horror described. He moved further into the attic, turning into a front room from which emanated a burnt smell.

The walls in here were indeed coated in a black soot, but other than that and the blackened scrap of rug on the floor, fire damage was not apparent. The room was unsettling enough without it.

It was a small room with slanted walls, again covered in clippings, most obscured by the soot but barely scorched. One photo drew Grange closer. It showed a man presenting an object before him in both hands. Was it a carved walking stick? Some primitive club? The end of it was bell shaped, so Grange concluded it was a musical instrument. The photo was labeled: *Rick's Lake, Wisconsin.* Wisconsin again. Was that, then, the musical instrument that had been fused to the earlier Edgar Brill's hand? If so, the photo was more recent than that.

Grange took in a kind of altar that had been set up at the end of the room, directly before its one window, and remembered what Brill had said about him and his brother practicing opposing religions. What could Edgar Brill's beliefs be, to account for this? The window had been masked off with thin black cardboard, from the center of which had been cut a five-armed star shape that vaguely had a human-like form. All the sunlight in the room poured through this rough figure . . . though to either side of it much smaller shapes, cut perhaps with an Exacto knife, let in a little more light. They were hard to make out . . . perhaps many-limbed insects or squid?

Grange removed a cloth from atop the table presumably used as an altar. There was a spiral-bound notebook there, an old leather-bound book written in German, and the musical instrument he had seen in that photo only moments before.

It was scorched black, and had to be the very instrument which Edgar Brill the elder had been carrying after the Peshtigo Horror, almost a hundred and thirty years ago. Grange lifted the heavy object in both hands, turning it to scrutinize its bizarre detail. The thing didn't seem to be of metal, or even wood . . . seemed more grown than carved. It had a segmented, bony appearance, like the straightened spinal column of some animal.

He set the instrument back down, paged through the journal. Grange was further convinced of Brill's senility—perhaps, even, insanity—by entries like, "Last night summoned the Messenger . . . heard His howling from the swamp. Martin, being closer to the swamp, must have had a restless night. Ha!" and, later: "Martin sent a letter. The usual ranting. That the great Faceless Messenger is too close to the world of men, sometimes moving amongst us as one of us, and draws the curious too close to knowledge of Those Who Wait Outside . . . that His works and movements are not truly in the best interest of those Outsiders. He again threatens to bring his god against me, to stop my communion with N———. He is a fool to think that he would survive such an onslaught himself. One can not predict or control the fire vampires beyond a certain point. And N——— and His servitors will let no harm come to me . . ."

Grange wagged his head, closed the journal. With his obsession with fire, it was not surprising that Brill had immolated himself. But now to go talk to the brother . . . and see if he was just as crazy.

As he began to descend from the attic, Grange thought he heard music—a kind of faint, high piping—coming from downstairs. He quickened his pace, oddly conscious of the gun holstered under his jacket.

By the time he had reached the ground floor, the distant music was fading away. He cracked the cellar door, peered down into damp-smelling blackness. Flicked the switch at the head of the stairs. It didn't work. Had the music truly seemed to have come from down here, when he reached the ground floor? No, he decided, it had to have come from outside. A kid practicing on a flute or recorder, or a radio somewhere. The house was as still as a tomb. Grange shut the basement door.

Before leaving, he decided to avail himself of Brill's bathroom. He found it, opened the lid of the toilet with the toe of his shoe, and began to unzip his fly . . . but paused at a soft hissing sound as if something were being dragged across the floor of the bathtub.

Swinging around, Grange tore aside the mildew-blackened curtain.

He saw the thing for only two instants, before it was whipped down the drain of the bathtub. A black eel or snake, it must have been. Grange was badly startled, and clawed at his holster, but the slithering thing was gone before he even had the snap off.

Yes, it had to have been a snake, though he had not seen its head, already in the drain. Black, with a lighter belly. But that the belly had been covered in grayish-pink disks like suckers was surely an illusion.

*   *   *

By the time Grange's car turned onto Pine Street and began crawling along it in search of the house of Martin Brill, evening had begun to fall. Grange remembered trick-or-treating along this row of old houses as a boy in the early sixties, remembered the delightful terror of having Eastborough Swamp looming vast, deep and dark on the opposite side of the street. Quicksand in there, the parents said. Coyotes, and snapping turtles large enough to take your hand off (he had once found a tiny baby, at least, and carried it into the swamp a short ways to set it free, it hissing at him all the while).

He glanced now at the thickly massed trees, blackly silhouetted with the summer sun sunk behind them, in between glancing at the houses in an effort to determine which might be Brill's (he wasn't listed in the phonebook; might Grange have accepted candy from him as a boy?). People had indeed disappeared in the swamp a number of times, their remains never found. There had also been talk of ghosts in the swamp, over the years: distant lights drifting through the trees, and in the back of Pine Grove Cemetery, which also bordered the swamp, reports of ball lightning flitting about. Will-o'-the-wisps, people called them, or jack-o'-lanterns, and the Welsh had dubbed them corpse candles. Grange had read up on the phenomenon one time, after hearing a variety of local reports. Swamp gas, that was all, he was told . . . but in some of the cases reported, as in many he read, the ball lightning seemed to move as if an intelligence directed it, as if it might be some ethereal but living creature.

The detective was eliminating houses by reading mailboxes, observing toys and new vans in driveways, when the large Victorian caught his eye; hulking, badly in need of paint, an obsolete TV antenna lying on its side like a giant insect poised on the roof, a tall chimney tottering dangerously, the lawn a miniature jungle, every window black, it was the twin of Edgar Brill's house, right down to the obviously sizable third story attic.

Grange pulled into the driveway. If there was a car, it was shut up in the garage. For a moment he sat in his own vehicle, staring up through the windshield at a three-eyed bay window projecting from that third story, as if he were reluctant—afraid, for some reason—to leave his enclosing shelter. But then, he cracked the door and stepped out onto the driveway.

He had gone only a few steps when his car radio squawked, calling to him specifically, and he went back to answer it. "Yeah; Grange," he said, leaning half inside.

The dispatcher told the detective that he had been asked to return to the hospital where Edgar Brill had been admitted. "The patient just passed away suddenly," the dispatcher related.

Suddenly? thought Grange. Hardly. He would have been surprised to see the poor eccentric old-timer last the week. And what good could he do there now that there was nothing else to gleam from the man? But he had been requested by the Worcester police themselves, and they must want to know how far he had gotten in the investigation on his end. Grange told the dispatcher he was on his way.

As he slipped back into the car, he glanced up again through the windshield at the dilapidated old edifice. Martin Brill would just have to wait a bit longer to learn of his brother's fate . . . and from what Grange had learned thus far, he might not even care.

Grange started his car, but hesitated in backing out, for he had heard a sound underneath the awakening of his engine. He thrust his head out the open window, and shut the motor off. Had it really been a distant sound like a flute playing . . . coming from the dense woods of Eastborough Swamp?

For nearly a minute he listened, but the sound did not resume; just the whirring music of summer insects. Dismissing the notion as his own imagination, he again started the car, and this time backed out onto Pine Street, headed off for Worcester.

* * *

When Grange turned into the hall and saw the nurse crying outside Edgar Brill's room, a quivering hand clamped over her mouth and two Worcester cops soothing her, he knew that Brill's death hadn't been quite so expected after all. And the smell . . .

And was there really a slight smoky haze in the air of the hallway?

Seeing him approach, one of the two uniformed boys hurried breathlessly forward to meet him. "You better come see this," he said as he came.

"What happened?"

"We're not sure. The doctors don't know. We think maybe Brill set himself on fire again somehow. But it was almost like the fire was never entirely out . . . still smoldering away inside him . . . until it just erupted again. But you better see for yourself . . ."

Grange continued down the corridor and halted in the threshold of Brill's room. It was close enough for him.

The walls were black with a greasy soot, though the sheets of the bed Brill lay in were barely scorched. Brill himself was another matter. A blackened stick figure, a mere skeleton crusted in peeling ash, his empty eye sockets still curling tendrils of smoke, his arms bent and reaching into the air above him like two denuded branches. In his mid-section, revealed by the sheets Brill must have kicked off in his agony, there was a gaping, smoking pit.

Grange took a step back into the hall, twisting to face the nurse. "What did you see?" he asked her.

"I . . . I was in his room, but my back was turned . . . only for a second." Her voice kept hitching, and she paused to suck back a sob. "I heard this . . . *whump* . . . and saw a flash, and when I turned around, he was screaming . . . moving . . . and this fire . . . this weird fire was coming out of his belly."

Grange nodded impassively, but inside he gave a shudder. He had once heard it said that in the past, if a body were not embalmed a puncture would sometimes be made in it and the leaking gases ignited to burn them away.

The nurse went on, "Then the fire . . . it like rose up out of him . . . like a ball, floating over his bed . . . then it just kind of exploded. There was a loud bang. But that was all . . . it was gone."

Grange continued nodding, remembering as he did so his research on "swamp gas," how alike this story was to so many cases of ball lightning, often so weirdly sentient in their movements, and frequently disappearing with a loud report. And he thought again of the house of Martin Brill, facing onto Eastborough Swamp, where so many ghostly lights had been witnessed over the years . . .

*　　*　　*

When Detective Grange had no success in getting Martin Brill to come to his door, he assumed the old man was hard of hearing, or had gone to bed. After all, night had now fallen. (He kept looking over his shoulder at the woods, but they remained solidly black.)

But the next day, when Brill again did not reply to his loud knocking, he called into the station and received permission from the chief himself to enter the premises to check on the old man's welfare. After all, there was no surviving family member to give consent or objection.

Grange found the front and back doors locked, but was able to dislodge a screen window on the ground floor and through that slipped into a gloomy living room, thick with dust and stillness and silence.

"Mr. Brill?" he called. And his eyes roved across the shelves heavy with books older than Brill himself, across the strange photographs, paintings and astronomical charts mounted on the walls. He saw a staircase in the room beyond, went to it, called up into the murk. "Mr. Brill?"

Grange ascended the loudly complaining stairs. On the second floor, no one. But he found another set of stairs . . . narrower . . . proceeding on into the attic . . .

He mounted them. Slowly. His heart seemed to be thumping from all his climbing. "Mr. Brill?"

In the room just off the stairs, he found him.

The elderly man sat in a chair before a bay window, the central window of which was open, the dusty curtains stirring in a welcome breeze. There were odd geometric patterns drawn on the white-painted walls. Star charts? If so, only one star in them had been labeled, if that were indeed the meaning of the word *Fomalhaut*.

Martin Brill was dead. His eyes bulged hideously in a face turned almost black—but not from burning. The man had apparently been strangled, for around his neck there were terrible marks. And in the midst of this bruising there were raw abraded circular scars in double rows . . . as if suckers had pressed into his flesh . . .

Grange shifted his gaze past the slumped, staring figure, out to the shadowed fringe of Eastborough Swamp, upon which the bay windows faced.

He waited to see a ghostly light moving through the trees. Waited to hear distant, frenzied piping. But there was neither. The brothers Brill were dead . . . and the trees of Eastborough Swamp merely whispered to him with mocking secrecy in the new cool breeze.

YOO HOO, CTHULHU

Up from Stygian depths—whatever that means
An inky-black dark murk devoid of sun beams
Looms a monolithic creature trailing gelatinous foam
If Cthulhu calls tell him that I'm not home.

When evil cults gather and passages are read
From the *Necronomicon* of the mad Arab Abdul Alhazred
And demons called forth from that nasty old book
If Cthulhu calls I'll leave my phone off the hook.

His age-old power makes me nervous
Better stick to my tape-recorded answering service
When up through fetid soil he's dug
If Cthulhu calls I'll pull the plug.

When monsters stir in slimy lairs
Disturb our sleep with hellish nightmares
When graveyard vapors start to misting
I'll change my number to a private listing.

When rusty-hinged crypt doors start to creak
And bat-things spread their wings on jagged rock peaks
When lost islands rise from the cold ocean deep
And the Great Old Ones grumble in their sleep.

When Dark Gods rise from endless night
Filled with healthy appetite
When Cthulhu awakens from his timeless slumber
In deepened voice: "Sorry, sir, you have the wrong number."

LOST SOUL

"*The Book of Awe*," read Andrea, in a mocking tone of great gravity.

Leaning over her shoulder to read the table of contents was easy for Meredith, who was as tall as Andrea was short in addition to being as dark-haired as Andrea was blond. Meredith's half-brother Leonard called her Lulu—after the character portrayed by the similarly bob-haired, similarly lovely Louise Brooks in the 1929 German film *Pandora's Box*. It was one of Meredith's favorite films.

Meredith had a number of secret nicknames for Andrea, her brother's girlfriend, with her profusion of blond hair pinned up over her head as if to give her height. "That blond troll" was one, and indicative of the others.

Meredith read from the table of contents aloud . . .

"'The Keys to Keys.'" She looked up at Leonard. "Huh?"

Standing apart from them, arms folded, he explained, "Keys meaning certain tones, a certain pitch, a certain sound that will create resonance, a special vibration. Like *ohm* . . . and Buddhist chants. It's not the words chanted, but the sound they make, especially repeated over and over. It's one of the ways in . . ."

Meredith returned her gaze to the text, but Andrea was paging ahead, then shutting the book to again take in its odd design. *The Book of Awe*—front and back covers and every page between—was triangular in shape rather than rectangular, bound along one of its three sides. Andrea scrunched her face at the book, held it up horizontally to view it from its side. "What could be stuck in there, Lenny? It's big. And it smells."

"I didn't want to pry those pages apart yet. I didn't wanna tear anything. They're stuck pretty good."

"Can I see the thing, please?" Meredith sighed in great weariness.

Andrea pushed the heavy volume into her hands. "Go for it."

Meredith inspected the book in a similar way but with a more composed expression. A group of pages about three quarters of the way through were adhered together by a black material like tar that had hardened but retained a tackiness. She shrugged lightly, flipped to the start of a chapter. "'The Geometry of Transcendence' . . . ha. Looks like trigonometry on acid."

"Another way to open doors. Certain bizarre geometric patterns . . . configurations . . . when reproduced precisely can bend the barriers between dimensions. The patterns have to be drawn in the corner of a room, and differently depending on the angles of the corner."

"Like drawing a witch's circle?" Andrea asked.

Meredith gave her an arched eyebrow, but Leonard said, "Something like that." He turned back to Meredith. "There are a number of ways to travel between dimensions. Some ways only involve astral exploration. Some involve dreams. But these ways here, the ones Marotta really gets into, involve full physical results . . ."

"And he got his information from that—*Necronomicon?*"

"Among other sources . . . yeah. *The Pnakotic Manuscripts, The Book of Dzyan . . . De Vermis Mysteriis, The Book of Thoth, Liber Ivonis* and *The Metal Book.* Your standard Book of the Month Club fare." Leonard smiled as he watched Meredith page further in, as if he himself were the proud author of the volume. But that man, Louis Marotta, had compiled *The Book of Awe* over twenty years before. And he had also disappeared without leaving a trace less than a year after that.

Leonard smiled more broadly when Andrea peered around Meredith's arm at the book and a moment later recoiled with a small gasp. She hadn't seen the illustrations before. Meredith showed no outward reaction upon discovering them, but shuddered once. She returned her attention to the stuck pages. They crackled at the gentle probing of her thumb in the crevice at their center. "Have you shined a light in here?"

"No. I just got the thing a few hours ago. But that's a good idea . . ."

"A better idea would be to just peel the thing open. I don't think it'll rip any pages."

"I have to look at it some more."

"Looks like something was purposely sealed in here, Len." The bulge at the center of the glued section was fairly large.

"I hardly think he would've glued something inside a book of such importance."

"How many copies did he have made?"

"Only six," Andrea spoke up. She worked for The Book Worm bookstore in Cambridge, old and rare books their specialty. Leonard had met her in that store last year, and she had helped him finally track down this damaged copy of *The Book of Awe.* It had been in the possession of Marotta's niece. She had obviously never cared to try prying the stuck pages apart, and it hadn't been hard to convince her to sell the book. She hadn't haggled for a higher price, either. But as cooperative as she'd been in letting Leonard have the volume, she hadn't been able to tell him much about her strange uncle. "Drugs," was about the extent of her description.

Meredith sat down with the deltoid book in her lap, became more engrossed. She found, in fact, that Marotta did suggest drugs as a way into other realms. Leonard lit a cigarette, turned his back to the women and stared into the corner of the room. His apartment was on the third floor. An attic loft. The ceiling slanted down to meet the floor along the sides of this, his bedroom. He had only a mattress for a bed, as he preferred, and he had always kept it in that corner before. But today he had slid the mattress against the opposite wall . . .

Andrea watched Meredith's lips silently form words from the text. She asked, "Do you honestly believe in this stuff, too?"

Meredith only glanced up at her emotionlessly before plunging her eyes back into the book parted open across her thighs.

*   *   *

Andrea was close to her family. Leonard was not even close to his own, but for Meredith. He did not accompany Andrea to Sunday dinner.

Meredith had come, and Leonard made her coffee in the kitchen while she sat down in the small parlor with the book. She called in to him, "You haven't cracked open the gummy part yet . . ."

"I know . . . I told you," he replied. From his cupboard he selected the heavy black mug with white marbling he knew was her favorite. "There's enough to read in there for now while I figure out what to do. Maybe a solvent that won't damage the . . ."

He heard the crackling rasp.

"Hey!" he said, and set the mug down heavily.

Then he heard something thud heavily to the floor. And on the tail of that, Meredith was crying out his name. Even as a child, she had never cried out to him before . . .

"Merry." He bolted for the central roan, and nearly collided with his sister in the threshold. Even in the seconds following her cry she had regained much of her composure, but she was still not his familiar Meredith. Her face was flushed, her neat bowl of hair had got ruffled, and her fingers were claws hooked into his forearms.

"What's going on? What did you do to my book?"

"Go look at it."

"What . . ."

"I think I found Louis Marotta."

Leonard pushed past her into the living room, and on the central rug he saw the book lying with its covers closed in the fall. He lifted it. Opened it to the crusted portion. And for the first time, he was able to easily peel the central crevice apart.

"Jesus," he muttered.

There was a withered, mummified human hand pressed in the book, in the center of a pool of that black material, which totally obscured the text on the two facing pages. The hardened ooze had not covered the hand, but was thicker and layered around the base of the wrist like melted and resolidified wax around the base of a candle. It seemed that the ooze had originated from inside the book. From this page. Either from the stump of the wrist . . . or . . .

"Blood?" Meredith asked.

"No. God . . ."

"What, for Chrissakes?"

Leonard didn't know a huge, odd grin had stretched upon his face. "This goop came from around the wrist. It came out of a hole . . ."

"A hole? In the book?"

"Not in the book, Merry. In our dimension . . ."

"Len . . ."

"*Look* at it!" He whirled to hold the book open under her nose. She recoiled slightly from the sight and the smell. "The hand isn't cut off, Merry. It just didn't go all the way in with the rest of him."

Excited by this discovery, less concerned about damage to pages already obviously ruined, Leonard peeled open more of the stuck pages. The ooze had only marred the edges of these. At last, a bit more carefully, he pulled free the page immediately following the one into which the hand was pressed. "Look at this!" He moved the page with the hand sprouting from its center open and shut away from the rest. "One page! One page in this book he turned into a door!"

"And that stuff came out."

"Maybe the ocean of another world. Or the air . . ."

It was as though a great void on the other side, a fluid limbo, had begun to pour through and congealed upon contact with this plane. Wouldn't it be funny, Meredith thought deliriously, if the hand had corked the hole accidentally, thus saving the earth—the universe?—from being totally consumed? Yeah, funny. Hilarious.

"Len. Len, you gotta get rid of it! That thing is too damn *dangerous* . . ."

He lifted his great grin to her. "What? What are you saying? *You* . . . afraid? Hey, do you know what we could learn from this?"

"Maybe what he learned. How to *die*."

"Whatever dangerous shit was written on that page is gone now. There are as many other doors as there are dimensions, and that's an infinite amount. We'll avoid the one he chose. Anyway, we know Marotta's motivations for making this book. Personal gain. Power. Immortality. All that good shit. But I'm not out for that, I'm not some power-hungry madman. Right? He got greedy . . ."

"So what the hell do *you* want?"

"What do I want? To learn, for God's sake! I can learn more from this book than I would've learned in a lifetime at Clark, or any other school in the world! Do you know what could be done with this thing? The places we could see? The races we could meet and learn from? The resources we could tap? We could save our whole damn planet with this thing! It's a link to all creation, all space and time and knowledge! This book *is* God!"

"Well who are you to think you can handle it? Turn it over to somebody else more capable, if you aren't out for the glory."

"Turn it over to who? Ahh, religious leaders? They'd destroy the thing! The government? They'd use it like Marotta, not to help the masses. No one's qualified. At least I've got the open mind to believe in its potential and treat it with the proper caution. Marotta didn't write the thing, he just pretty much was a researcher. A thief. He didn't respect the powers enough. I do."

"Len," Meredith sighed, "who are you kidding? You sound just like any damn delusional Messiah I ever heard of."

"You think I'm only out for myself? That must be you you're thinking of! I care about things . . ."

"Oh . . . that's cute. I'm only out for myself. Well, face it, bro . . . *you've* always been a poor little rich boy trying to show daddy you can be something important on your own. But you don't really wanna work at being important. You're really just an irresponsible lost soul looking for a few thrills to kill the time . . . just like me. If you stop trying to dramatize it all the time and just live it, it won't be so bad. Life is empty and boring and pointless. More learning and knowledge never changes that."

"So why did you help me look for the book? What made you so interested in finding it, too? Just for a cheap thrill?"

She pouted. "Sure. Why not? It was something to do.

"Something to *do*? You don't care about anything, do you?"

Meredith thought of a line from *Pandora's Box*. When the character Alwa asked Lulu, "Do you love me, Lulu?" she replied, "I? Never a soul!" Meredith had quoted that line herself, more than once.

But in answer to her brother's frustrated question now, Meredith only gave an enigmatic shrug, and lit up a fresh cigarette.

*   *   *

Meredith straddled Leonard, the curled ends of her bob swaying down to frame her white face and her breasts swaying down to fill his milking, stroking hands. He dreaded her seductions. He lived in secret, aching hunger for her seductions. He never instigated them. Every time she had to seduce him like the first, and he thought that was most of the appeal for her. His guilt, the squirming nervous reluctance in him when he saw one of her seductions nearing, must have filled her with an odd satisfaction. When it was done he swore never again. And waited for the next time . . .

"Going to show the midget the hand?"

"No. Not yet . . ."

"It was his right hand."

226

"Mm . . ."

"Most people just put leaves inside books." Meredith smiled down at him and undulated.

"Did you see how long the nails were? Very long . . ."

"Don't nails grow after death?"

"No . . . that's just the skin receding around them. Either he had long nails to begin with, or . . . he didn't die right away. He was trying to catch a hold and not be drawn in. And he got pinned that way. And maybe he stayed that way for a long time . . ."

"If he wanted to explore other dimensions so bad, why'd he fight going in?"

"Maybe that was one dimension he didn't want to go."

*   *   *

Meredith had gone. Andrea had returned. She found Leonard stripped to the waist and sweaty, crouched in the corner where his mattress had previously been. He was drawing designs in that corner, along the low ceiling where it slanted down toward the floor. She knelt by him and stroked his back while he referred to a diagram in the opened triagonal book and then took a measurement between two curves he had drawn.

"Did you make that ruler?" Andrea asked him.

"Had to; it's in Smyth's pyramid inch, a little off from the English inch. Smyth was Astronomer Royal for Scotland, found all kinds of interesting things in the measurements of the Great Pyramid. Marotta believed the pyramids were powerful centers for interdimensional travel."

"You're crazy, Lenny, you know that?"

"This is driving me crazy, trying to draw this. I've been at it for five and a half hours."

"It's hot in here . . . let's go for a walk, get some oxygen, how 'bout?"

"In a minute . . ."

"Almost done?"

"This configuration has a few last vital curves. I won't draw the last one in, though, until I'm ready to open the door . . ."

"Open the door, huh?"

Leonard twisted around to her with a tired smile. "Speaking of vital curves." He slid his arm about her waist, drew her closer for a kiss. "Mm." They embraced more tightly . . .

They ended up making love there in the corner, as if the mattress had never been moved, their clothing puddled around them. At one point Andrea glanced at a can of white paint by her head, asked about it. Leonard explained, "If I want to close the door fast, I have to obliterate the lines."

"Oh, of course . . . right."

*   *   *

He woke first, sat up to stare at her for a short while as she lay on her side bare on the bare floor, curled in a ball. She was sweet and dull—a refreshing contrast to his sister. Maybe it would be Andrea to help him break that hold. He only wished he loved her more. He wished he could lose himself so deeply in Andrea that Meredith would never find him . . .

He dragged his shirt off the back of a chair, dug cigarettes and lighter from its pocket. Then he contemplated the patterns he had woven web-like into the corner. Connect-the-dots to the secrets of the universe. Idly he took up his charcoal pencil, touched it to a nexus point in the strange anarchy of lines, curves, spirals. At this critical stage, could he switch channels, so to speak? Open different but related doors by varying the last lines? If he were to connect this point not to the curve running below it, but over here . . . to this nodal point to form a triangle. Yes—it was funny. Suddenly the whole drawing seemed to depend on this triangle one last stroke would create at its center. Even incomplete, the figure seemed to hum with its own vibrating energy . . . like the musical instrument . . . keys to keys . . . yes . . . a triangle . . .

He drew the pencil to that final point to complete the equation. He didn't even use his ruler, but the line flowed straight and smooth, and even as he reached the nodal point he wondered if he had really meant to do this or if he'd been groggy from sleep, or if it had been the imp of the perverse. Or . . . if something close behind the barrier had influenced his foggy mind . . .

When the pencil point touched the nodal point a hand reached out of the plaster of the slanted ceiling.

Leonard was alerted to its presence by Andrea's gurgle. He looked and saw her clawing at the hand where it had seized her throat. It was a man's left hand. But the flesh was plaster white . . . and covered in the charcoal lines and curves Leonard had drawn. They smudged slightly from Andrea's palms but the hand didn't vanish.

"Oh God!" Leonard cried, leaping to his feet and backing away. He wanted to flee the apartment. Go find Meredith. Meredith was strong . . . Meredith could . . .

Andrea's bare heels drummed and dug at the floor. Leonard forgot the paint. His reaction was more primitive. He tore into the kitchen, found a bread knife in a drawer. He could hear Andrea wheezing, rattling behind him. "Oh God," he whispered. He still wanted to flee . . . but he whirled back toward the bedroom . . .

Andrea was gone. "No!" he shouted, and began to sob in fury and terror. "Let her *go!* Oh Jesus . . . let her *go,* God damn you!"

The hand returned. It passed easily out of the wall, again the patterns drawn there stretching out across its forearm like a fluid tattoo, coiled around the fingers like black rings. Leonard's eyes followed the fingers in their stretching and clawing.

The long nails were raking the floor only inches from *The Book of Awe*.

Leonard fell to his knees before the hand, plunged the knife down. The blade slammed into the forearm. The hand fluttered like a dying bird and a black blood like ink spattered its white surface. The hand and arm withdrew.

A moment later Leonard was sitting alone on the floor of his loft apartment, naked, the book hugged against his chest in both arms, his clothing and Andrea's strewn around him. And he stared at the slanted wall, that black blood like ink spattered on it and a trickle drying from a point where the bread knife stuck out of the plaster.

*　　*　　*

When he could rise he phoned Meredith.

She came, dressed primarily in black as always. "I was hoping you'd get rid of that bimbo, Len, but couldn't you have used a more conventional method . . . instead of using her for a human guinea pig?"

"I didn't use her like that, God damn it! I didn't mean to open the door then!"

"So much for caution." They had gingerly stepped into the bedroom's threshold. The room smelled of paint.

"It didn't look like one coat was going to be enough, but it's gone," Leonard mumbled. "I should have used black paint, anyway . . ."

"But even painted over . . . isn't the pattern still present? Under the paint? Couldn't there still be a danger?"

"I don't know," he whispered.

"How long did you turn your back on this thing?"

"Just to call you. And to let you in just now."

"Okay . . . let's break some plaster out of the wall. Some nice big chunks. That should disrupt it pretty well, huh?"

"Good idea! Watch it . . . I'll get my tool box."

When Leonard returned he seemed reluctant to go near the wall again, so Meredith took a claw hammer from him, crept up to the corner, swung the hammer in a vicious arc and then danced back. She had expected a hand to lunge out and catch her by the wrist to stop her. One didn't. The first blow only made a dent, so she danced in again. Again. At last the wall was cracking. A few strands of the web had to have been severed, by now. Leonard sighed, and moved in with a linoleum knife he had taken up more as a weapon than to obliterate his drawing. Crouching together, they dug several large slabs of plaster free of the slats beneath. Meredith seemed to ignore the paint smudges and the chalky plaster dust on her clothing. She said, "This week on *This Old House* we'll be closing interdimensional portals . . ."

Leonard was so grateful for her presence, her strength. Meredith always knew how to take charge. Neither of their mothers or the father they shared had given them the love the movies and TV shows told them was normal, nurturing love. Meredith had almost been a mother to Leonard. Yes, he thought, she had . . . though she was the younger. She'd helped him get into school. Helped him when he dropped out. She was suffocating, dominating, as mothers could be, of course. Had he in turn been a replacement for their father, fulfilling some need daddy hadn't? Given certain aspects of their relationship, Leonard didn't want to imagine just what Meredith's paternal yearnings might be. At any rate, as often as he itched to be free of Meredith's gravity, right now he was close to tears at her comforting nearness . . .

Even as the voice behind them spoke Leonard had caught a peripheral movement and begun to twist toward it.

"Now you've trapped me here . . . with you," said Andrea.

Meredith spun on her heels. "Jesus!" She clutched at her brother's arm with her left hand, raised the hammer in her right fist. "Go away!"

"I just told you . . . I can't," said Andrea. "You've ruined the corner."

She stood in the doorway, blocking their escape from the room. Andrea had always had a husky voice, but it was unnaturally deep and raspy now. Her eyes were closed and remained that way, as though she were hypnotized, sleepwalking. Her hair, blond and permed, was still gathered up in a plume above her head. But her flesh was so much paler than the brother and sister remembered it. And she was still naked. And her naked pale flesh was covered in grids and curves, angles and spirals. They were the same patterns from the corner—under the paint there was no longer any drawing—but this was a contoured map, with mountains and valleys of flesh and bone.

Leonard watched her lift her small right hand to her face, spread the fingers, flex them. Though her eyes remained closed she seemed to be studying the hand, testing it. Then he realized why, even before she said it.

"It's been a while since I had use of my good hand."

"Marotta," Leonard breathed. "Oh God . . ."

"Where is my book, young man?" Andrea lowered her hand. "I'm flattered by your interest in me. Your friend here told me a lot . . . while she could. But now I have things to do and I need back what belongs to me."

The grid seemed to pulse and writhe on her, and now they saw why. Black pincered insects like earwigs had emerged from the centers of spirals, from intersections and nodal points, and were crawling along her body. None dropped off, or even strayed from the narrow black highways, but soon she was covered in a seething mass. Meredith repressed a gag and looked away. Leonard had begun to shake violently. His eyes strained out of their sockets and tears coursed down his face, leaving flesh-colored trails in the plaster dust that made his own face ghostly.

"Let Andrea go!"

"She isn't important."

"Let her go, God damn you, let her *go!*"

"She's already gone."

"You *bastard!*"

Meredith looked up in shock as Leonard leapt at the thing, swinging the linoleum knife down at its chest, one bare breast a spiral with the nipple at its center.

The knife disappeared into that pale flesh. Leonard's hand disappeared into that pale flesh. His arm. His shoulder. Andrea took his head in both her hands and pressed it between her breasts, cutting off his scream before it could come. His head vanished into the soft white flesh without leaving a ripple. She hadn't even flinched at his impact. His momentum had buried him half inside her, and she guided the rest, oblivious to Meredith's hysterical shrieking and the mad thrashing and kicking of Leonard's legs in the air. Andrea took one leg in each hand, guided them in. One shoe fell off a foot, thumped at her bare feet, then Leonard was gone.

"Now *I'm* a door," Andrea said to Meredith. "This is what your brother wanted, isn't it? Now you have a choice. *Shut up!* If the police come you'll be sorry!" the thing rasped.

"Oh God . . . oh God . . ."

"Now you have a choice. Find me the book, or you can join your brother."

"I'll find it, oh God, I'll find it . . . *please!*"

Andrea stepped to one side to let Meredith pass from the room. "Look for it."

"Please don't hurt me . . . I'll do anything . . . Please . . . I'll find it . . ." As she passed the creature it caught her elbow and smiled in her face, insects roving across its cute, slack features. Meredith swallowed a shriek, gagged on it.

"It's been a long time since I had a woman. A human woman. And such a lovely woman. You did say you'd do anything . . ."

"No! Please! Please!"

Andrea let go of her arm. "Find the book."

Meredith stumbled on into the parlor, shaking with sobs. Andrea shuffled behind stiffly. As Meredith searched in the drawers of Leonard's corner desk she blubbered, "What's going to happen to my brother? Let him out . . . if it wasn't for him you wouldn't be getting your book back."

"If you miss him so much you can come in here and join him.'

"No! Please let him come *back!*"

"Find that book."

It was atop the monitor of his computer, in the shadowed nook of his computer desk shelf. Meredith slid it out into her arms, pressed it against her breasts.

"Good girl." Andrea spread her arms. "Give it here."

"*Take it!*" Meredith screamed, and she leaped a step at the apparition, flinging the book by one corner squarely at its naked breasts. At this range she couldn't miss . . . and Andrea was too somnambulistic to dodge. She hoped.

Andrea didn't dodge. If anything, she spread her arms out farther. The triangular book struck her between the breasts . . . so hard that it lodged in the flesh deeply. It remained that way, half buried, for two beats. Andrea had not flinched, her peacefully shut lids did not quiver. But she smiled.

"Thank you," she said, in the rasp of Louis Marotta, the lost explorer.

The book was sucked abruptly fully into her, was gone. But its passing left a twisted, funnel-like hole. And into that hole were sucked the lines and curves and spirals of the web of her body, like a net being pulled rapidly through a small opening. It took only seconds. Then Andrea stood rigid and totally white, like a soft cold statue.

She fell forward an her face, and Meredith heard her cute nose crunch.

The door was gone. Marotta was gone.

Leonard was gone. She had made a mistake. She should have run with the book. But she had trapped him.

She felt as though a twin conjoined by tissues had been roughly hacked away. With a pitiful wail, she crumpled near the nude corpse of his girlfriend.

"You bitch!" Meredith sputtered, and reached over to pound her on the shoulder with the heel of her fist. "You had to find him that book, didn't you? *Didn't you?*"

She had never liked that brain-dead blond dwarf. Perched on their connecting membrane. Splitting it with her weight. *She* had taken him away. Meredith felt more jealous now than when they'd both been   alive . . .

But Leonard might still be. Right? Like Marotta had remained alive, all these years . . .

She could only hope that the two men were not in the same dimension.

*   *   *

She spoke to the people at The Book Worm. She spoke to the niece, Anna Marotta. Neither could help her . . .

But there were five more books. That was a lot. Five more of them . . . somewhere.

She heard that there might be a copy in San Francisco, where Marotta had lived before Boston. She took a plane. And on the plane she thought about the risks. The creatures that might be unleashed into this dimension. She remembered the insects swarming along Andrea's body, then sucked into the hole with the map like flies caught in a web. She didn't care if she let through great clouds of flying creatures like blood-drinking locusts. Didn't care if she let through insects that dwarfed mountains. Or let back into the world scores of greedy, hungry men like Marotta who had vanished over the years into one door or another . . .

Infinite dimensions, Leonard had told her. An infinite maze for her to search through . . .

But she would open those doors. One by one. With sound, and drugs. With symbols. And dream her way into them. And enter her flesh into them, if she had to . . .

He was out there. She felt the connection of an astral membrane. Twins, they had always been. Twins of different mothers.

When she found him, maybe then he'd believe that there were some things she cared about.

It would be a lot to go through, to show a person you cared, she thought aboard the plane.

But why not? It was something to do.

PAZUZU'S CHILDREN

They brought him a few dates and a piece of unleavened bread. His meager repast was not meant as punishment; it was all that could be scrounged, as yet, from the labyrinth's ruins. The man who told him this looked embarrassed as he explained it. This man's role of apologetic host was a curious contrast to his previous role; not an hour ago, the man had repeatedly burned the head of Lieutenant Gavin Hilliard's penis with the head of his cigarette.

Hilliard had read several books about Iraq, and he took his captors to be Yezidi, Devil worshipers. Some of them wore ponytails, and fancy little beards that looked like something actors might wear to look foreign and villainous in bad movies. The Yezidi never uttered any word that started with the sound *sh,* Hilliard remembered, because it was the sound which began the Arabic name of the Devil. He would have to listen for that. But there were things about his captors beyond their appearance that made him consider the possibility.

There was the strange brusque sign language they used as a kind of salute to each other, or to punctuate their speech occasionally. (Maybe in place of *sh* words?) And sometimes they didn't even seem to be speaking Arabic at all, but some tongue even more tangled to Hilliard's ears, who didn't speak Arabic but had at least gotten used to its sound.

And then there were the books. Hilliard's cell in this subterranean complex was carved out of solid rock, rock that had been hidden from the air beneath the sands of the Syrian Desert . . . all but for jutting fangs and talons of stone as if a behemoth had been buried there and fossilized. At first, from his plane, he had taken the natural spires to be the eroded towers of man-made ruins. The rock must be tough to stand up to the hellish blasting desert winds at all; it must have been an arduous process tunneling and building this honeycomb within it. The narrow hall outside his cell was lined in stone blocks, with an arched ceiling. Hilliard could see into it clearly when he was alone and approached the slot of a window in the iron door of his small room. Once he had looked out to see men scurrying down the hall, their arms laden with books. Old books, covered in dust and bits of rock, salvaged from one of the sections of these catacombs that had collapsed under Hilliard's attack.

One of the men transporting this ancient library had seen his eyes in the window, set down his burden, made a weird angry sign with his hand, and slammed shut the panel that covered the window slot. As if the American's eyes were not fit to gaze at these tomes, even with their covers closed.

And then there was the pendant his host/inquisitor wore. He had worn it when he brought Hilliard the dates and bread, and he wore it now as he returned to the cell. The man brought a friend this time, whose bizarre appearance might help support Hilliard's theory. This new man was weather-eroded as rock himself, entirely bald, his eyes so filmed in cataracts that they were white as cue balls in his skull. Around both eyes were spirals tattooed in blurred dark blue ink, filling the sockets and extending beyond his shaven eyebrows, so that his blind eyes rested at the center of these spirals like the molten centers of twin black galaxies.

The blind man sat down on a chair against the wall. The torturer gestured for Hilliard to sit down on the other chair in the room. He himself would stand. He was being the polite host again.

He lit a cigarette. Hilliard must have reacted; the man smiled and said, "I know, a nasty habit. I hope I don't have to share my cigarettes with you this visit."

"I told you," Hilliard croaked, his throat feeling coated in the dust of this place. "I don't know anything about why I was sent out here."

The inquisitor was still smiling, drew at his butt; it crackled, glowed brighter like a small glaring eye winking open. "You don't have to play Clint Eastwood, my friend. Your comrades aren't watching. No one will ever know what you tell me." He seemed amused by his own reference to the American film star, explained—though Hilliard didn't ask—"I've been to your country, you know. And England. Elsewhere. Meeting with brothers spread across this world, in dark corners like this." Crackle, ember glow. "I know you were just doing your job. A loyal follower does that, I fully understand. But don't make me do my job, Lieutenant. I have men who take pleasure in it, but it's far too crude for my tastes. I only meet with you myself because I can speak with you. If I deem you no longer worth speaking with, then you'll meet these men of mine I refer to. And we shouldn't let it get to that."

Hilliard sat up straighter, cleared his throat. He tried to appear strong, despite the tears that wound out of his left eye, which was swollen nearly shut from a blow by a rifle butt when his captors first found him in the desert. "You can't be torturing me. Even if you don't respect the laws of civilized people, you should at least realize that when my people see me like this it will only make them angrier at your country, and more supportive of Desert Storm."

The inquisitor chuckled, turned his back and began to slowly pace the cell as if he were its restless inhabitant. "You are brave, Lieutenant. But you would have to be, to pilot one of those planes. I, myself, abhor flying." He looked over his shoulder. "You have the American arrogance that you'll live forever. That you deserve to live forever. Neither is true." He stopped pacing. "Your people will never see your wounds, Lieutenant, because they will never know that you survived your plane's crash."

Hilliard stared out of his one good eye. He tried to swallow; the ball of saliva caught at the top of his throat.

The inquisitor went on, "I know; why then cooperate with me? Well, if you do, I promise you there will be no more pain. I will give you a drink. You will go peacefully to sleep like a drunken man. And you will dream forever. But if you are difficult with me . . . if you persist in your pompous American . . . ah, tough guy routine," pause, crackle, glow, "then I will skin you alive. Quite seriously. You will suffer in ways that make man's imaginings of hell seem merciful."

"Look . . . please," Hilliard began. "I . . . I have . . ." A strangled tiny sob cut off his own words and he sagged in his chair.

"Good. That's a good sign, my friend. You're growing humble already. Yes, I know, you have children, a wife, a dog, a little white fence." The inquisitor resumed his pacing. "I mentioned man's visions of hell before you interrupted me. I was going to ask you if you recognized my pendant. Hm? No?" He lifted it from his chest, halted in front of the Navy pilot. "Hm?" he persisted, until Hilliard looked up and wagged his head.

"A demon," he managed.

"This is a representation of Pazuzu. He was the Assyrian devil of the southwest wind. He sowed pestilence, disease . . . just as you bring death from the skies. You see his form is rather like a man's. Man's arrogance is not limited to America, I confess. Men all over have remade the gods in our own image. And also in the image of other life around us. Horns of a goat, snarl of a dog, claws of a bird. The wings are correct, roughly."

The grimacing monster that the man wore around his neck had double sets of wings. "The truth is obscured in time, but also hidden purposely, of course. Misdirection. You symbolize one thing by representing it as another. You call it Pazuzu, even when its name is similar but different and infinitely more sacred. You give it the head of a dog because you can't . . . or don't want to . . . imagine it more like the body of a devilfish. But even that description is a human's unimaginative—insufficient—comparison."

Hilliard glanced up at the blind man, who remained silent and seemed to be staring at him but couldn't possibly see through those ruined orbs. Some kind of priest, to give him a final absolution? Or curse?

The inquisitor paced once more, went on, "In the Louvre—I've seen it myself—they have a bronze Pazuzu from the seventh century. There is an inscription which says, 'I am Pazuzu, son of Hanpa; I am the king of the evil spirits of the air who come raging violently from the mountains.' Son of Hanpa; huh. Gods are not 'sons,' though Cth— though Pazuzu has children. And he is from far beyond earthly mountains. Far beyond this sphere. He is no spirit of earthly winds, but of the winds of *stars.*"

"Did anyone else but me survive?" Hilliard said.

The inquisitor slowly turned his head to regard his captive audience. Suddenly Hilliard regretted his bold interruption, but the Iraqi kept his tone

civil. "No. You are the only one, I'm afraid."

There had been five crewmen in each of the two Vikings that had been sent from the carrier *Eisenhower*. Both had delivered their deadly cargo, but once they did so the Vikings had no real means to defend themselves other than their maneuverability. The Vikings had fired flares that were meant to attract ground-to-air missiles away from the planes, but this tactic hadn't worked. Hilliard had never seen where the missiles could have come from, since from the air he had observed nothing at the target site but rocks jutting up from the desert sands. No guns, no structures, no men. Maybe it hadn't been missiles at all, but some devil worshipers' magic, he thought deliriously. All he knew was, his plane had been struck from behind, while the pilot of the other plane screamed something about an arm . . . look out for the arm . . .

"Since you seem eager to return to the subject at hand, let me ask you again," his host continued, still civil. "What did they say you were to bomb out here? What did they tell you about it?"

"Nothing. They gave us coordinates, that's all. They scrambled us   fast . . . like they had just found out the information and were acting on it as quickly as possible."

The torturer did an odd thing. He turned to look at the seated blind man, his galaxy eyes unblinking. And the old man nodded once. This seemed to satisfy the inquisitor. He asked Hilliard, "They said nothing to you about what we might be doing here? Nothing about our practices?"

"Nothing. They were very urgent, that's all I know. Bomb the rocks . . . that's all they told us. But we knew it was hush-hush. Something to keep quiet about. They got that across."

Again, the Iraqi looked to his elder. Again, the old one nodded. What, then—was he some human lie detector? Being blind, were his powers of hearing more keen (Hilliard had thought such ideas were a myth), so that he could detect the intonations of falsehood?

"Look," Hilliard said, "I won't say you tortured me. I give you my word of honor on the lives of my kids. I've cooperated with you all along. I don't know anything. Really, it will be better for you if you let me go. If they ever found out you'd killed me . . ."

"Shh." The inquisitor held a finger to his lips. So that sound wasn't forbidden to his sect after all. "You have been in a holy place. Though you do not comprehend them, you have seen things you should not see. You see the Inner Circle."

"But like you say, I don't understand it, so what can I tell people?"

"They must know some of it already," the inquisitor sighed, shrugging. "That's why they sent you. But I wonder if they know the full scope of things. The full scope of our jihad. They must think this is all about silly human politics. That Saddam wants oil, or land, the material things you godless

Westerners crave. Saddam is of the Inner Circle, Lieutenant. He is no Moslem. That is a young religion, a religion of mere men. It is his facade, like the name of Pazuzu. Saddam is the Man of the Blue Turban. The Man of the Apocalypse. He is a manifestation of the Faceless One. He is Nyarlathotep."

"I don't understand any of this," Hilliard sobbed abruptly, desperation electrifying his nerves. "I don't *want* to understand it . . . please don't tell me about it! Please just let me go . . ."

"You are very fortunate that I am offering you such a merciful death, Lieutenant. You destroyed many valuable grimoires, important objects . . . and you came very close to slaying one of Pazuzu's children. A being that we were to have unleashed upon your people. A being to make their conceptions of demons seem like fairy tales for children . . ."

A breathless man burst into the room then, and began babbling to the inquisitor incoherently. Hilliard had flinched sharply at the man's dramatic entrance, but grew even more alarmed at the look that came over the inquisitor's face at this news . . . especially when the inquisitor shot a narrow-eyed glance Hilliard's way.

The new man left, and the inquisitor bent to whisper in the blind man's ear. The old man nodded, his sightless gaze not wavering from Hilliard until he stood up and shuffled out of the cell, leaving the iron door open behind him.

"Come with me," the inquisitor said gruffly.

"Where are we going?"

"More of your friends are on their way. They'll be here soon. You should be happy, Lieutenant . . . they may have just saved your life. You're going to contact them. Tell them you're alive. Tell them to turn back." The man grinned and flicked his cigarette to the stone floor. "I know you'll do it. I said you were brave, but only superficially. You're a coward with no solid commitment, no real faith, no true loyalty to your God, your country, your kind. You don't understand the glory of true servitude. You will live, Lieutenant. For now. Until those who slumber awaken." He gestured. "Enough chat. Come on; we'd better be quick . . ."

Dazed by the revelation that he would live after having just absorbed the fact that he would die, Hilliard floated unsteadily to his feet. Should he trust this madman, this Devil worshiper who believed that demons—more so than chemical, biological or nuclear weapons—were the greatest threats his country had to offer? But what choice did he have? If this place took another bombing he knew the labyrinth would cave in completely. And he would be buried forever amongst these people, his skeleton one day indistinguishable from the rest.

He shuffled out of the cell as wearily as the old man, the inquisitor taking his arm. Together they walked the narrow tunnels of these catacombs, a few times stepping over fallen stones, skirting partially tumbled walls. Dust was still trickling down from the arched ceilings. Men ran past them carrying weapons, supplies, and more of the ancient books.

And then they turned a corner and stopped. A group of nearly a dozen men were ahead of them, blocking an intersection of several tunnels, at least one of these fully caved in. The men were dragging something large and heavy out of one tunnel that looked mostly collapsed, and carrying it toward the mouth of another tunnel. The object they carried was long as a tree trunk and just as thick, but flaccid, drooping from their arms heavily. At first, Hilliard took the black, slippery-looking object to be the carcass of an immense python. Some pet, living idol, mascot. The tapered forward end he took to be the snake's tail.

But then he saw that along the underside of the glistening black object were rows of suckers, much like those of an octopus . . . except that they were more diamond-shaped than circular, a translucent gray. And, impossibly, they seemed to be moving independently, their edges slowly opening and closing. Could this be the limb of some gigantic cephalopod? Did the men expect to drag the entire creature through these tunnels by just one arm? The entire animal must be impossibly gargantuan. Could this hive connect with some vast subterranean pool, out here in the middle of the desert?

Just then the last man clambered out of the partially collapsed tunnel, bringing up what proved to be—despite the fluctuating suckers—the severed end of the arm. The end was a ruined mess where a falling ceiling had torn it from its body. There was no blood, just a jagged wound in fibrous, stringy flesh, the meat white under the black skin. Dangling from the wound were a number of globe-like bladders or tumors, like obscene clusters of fruit, the largest the size of a beach ball. These globular organs were translucent and covered in webs of black veins. A sloshing sound came from the orbs, and was he imagining that shadowy dark shapes, vaguely human, fetus-like, were contained within them? Was the largest globe actually pulsing with movement, as if its occupant were restless to be born?

Hilliard heard a cry and jerked his head. The man at the front of the great limb had called out in fear as the pointed end wound itself around his neck. Another man moved forward, helped extricate the limb before it could cut off the man's air, held it in both hands as they continued toward the new corridor.

An anus-like pucker the pilot hadn't noticed before at the tip of the tentacle suddenly yawned wide into a straining toothless maw, but the man gripping this end maintained his hold. It was a good thing; the mouth had stretched wide enough to engulf . . .

. . . a man. And suddenly Hilliard understood the globes that hung from the shattered limb. Those figures inside the orbs were not fetuses growing . . . but men being dissolved into grotesque little dolls . . .

"It is a desecration that you see this," said the inquisitor. "A blasphemy that you will live to remember it. But we have no choice. See what you have done to this child of Pazuzu, Lieutenant? But he lives. He will regain his body, in time. But those planes have to be stopped, first."

The inquisitor dragged him forward again, and they moved around behind the great limb and the struggling men.

"My God," Hilliard whispered, glancing back over his shoulder.

"Sorry, it's too late for conversion; I don't think this god would have you. But how quickly one becomes a believer, eh, Lieutenant?"

They would not feed their own men to the creature, would they? Perhaps it was an honor to sacrifice oneself. "The glory of true servitude." Please let it be that, Hilliard thought. Please that . . . and not the other possibility.

That perhaps Hilliard hadn't been the only survivor of the two Vikings, after all.

They lost sight of the nightmare spectacle, turned a few more corners and stepped into a fairly large room. Atop a table rested a radio set. Men stood around the room with anxious faces, some gripping assault rifles. One of them was already holding a microphone out to Hilliard.

"Tell them you live," the inquisitor repeated. "You have my oath that you will be freed. No one will believe what you saw. Until the day comes when they see Pazuzu's children for themselves, of course. Whole. And Pazuzu himself, when the stars sit right. But go back to your wife and dog for now, Lieutenant. Tell your friends to turn back."

Hilliard staggered forward a few steps. Hesitated. Lifted his arm slowly, as if under water.

He pictured the Vikings in his mind, soaring on the desert winds. Small, yes, but steel. Angels of death . . . "spirits of the air who come raging violently" . . .

Coward, the inquisitor had called him. No loyalty to his kind . . .

A man wearing headphones gestured wildly, sputtered urgently. The inquisitor snapped, "They're getting nearer. Hurry, now!"

Hilliard accepted the microphone, moved it to his lips. He thumbed on the switch.

"Hello?" he croaked.

"Who is this?" crackled a voice that sounded as though it were filtered through a sand storm.

"Hit them!" Lieutenant Gavin Hilliard cried abruptly, finding his voice. "Hit them with everything you have! Hurry up!"

The inquisitor snarled something in Arabic and surged toward the American, to tear him away from the radio and speak into it himself. Other men rushed at him. Rifle barrels lifted . . .

And even as their hands found him, he coiled his own hand in the radio cord and with his right wrenched the microphone from the end of it.

And even as the microphone ripped free, Hilliard continued to shout hoarsely into it.

"Hit them!" he screamed. "For the love of G—"

THE BOARDED WINDOW

Alan used his trowel to poke at the thing in the rain gutter.

It resembled a dead baby bird; translucent, purple-pink flesh devoid of feathers, crooked limbs like rudimentary wings and legs. But it was as large as a full grown pigeon, or larger. A group of pigeons favored the roof of his mother's tall old house, sleeping in the cornices and in gaping holes in the eaves. He guessed it was one of those birds, dead and decomposing. Still, it didn't look long dead. And the mouth . . . he prodded the small limp carcass once more. The mouth looked more like it possessed lips than a beak.

Disgusted, Alan used the trowel to flip the animal over the side of the gutter to drop into the large trash barrel below.

He had decided to clean out his mother's rain gutters himself, since neither she nor he could afford hiring someone at the present. The gutters had become more like flower pots in the past few years since his father had passed away; lush green plants filled this one stretch of gutter, no doubt seeded there by the tall tree which grew along the side of the sorrowful-looking Victorian. Alan had borrowed a ladder from a friend, and brought up with him a number of small trash bags to be filled with the plants and the layer of debris they grew in. When each bag was full he meant to drop them down into the bucket.

But the discovery of the bird or flayed squirrel or whatever it might be had distracted him from his project. That, and the broken attic window.

The window was visible from the ground; it ran diagonally, filling a space between a higher and shorter level of the roof where the attic rose above the second story. It consisted of three square panes, none of which seemed able to slide or swing open. However, one of the panes was broken at the corner. From the ground Alan hadn't been able to see this, the plants in their trough helping to obscure the damage.

Another project. Alan sighed. Well, who else could help his mother tend to these things? For now he would simply go up into the attic and tape a piece of cardboard over the hole so that no pigeons or squirrels would get in there to make it their home.

He'd do that first. He hated heights, and now found he welcomed the chance to come down from the high ladder.

Before descending, however, he dared to lean closer to the window, near enough to touch it with his fingers if he had cared to stretch, which he didn't. He tried to see into the attic from here. He had played in it as a boy, despite his father forbidding him from going up there. It had been years since he'd really looked around in there. He was trying to imagine this diagonal window from the other side, in relation to his memories of the attic rooms. He found he couldn't picture it from the inside.

He couldn't see into the attic through it, either. The panes might have been painted black inside, for all he could tell. The most he could make out was his own curious face reflected in the dirty glass, staring back at him.

* * *

When Alan stepped up into the attic a small creature hopped behind a box of books, thrashing its upper limbs. He gasped, became a frozen pose framed in the threshold. Then he heard the cooing, and saw the white droppings on the floor boards. Damn pigeons; how had they got up in here? Why did his mother have to throw bread out for them and encourage them to congregate? When he came further into the attic he saw that a window in this end had been propped open with a board. Mother. She must have done that to let some air in while she was up here one time, and had forgotten to close it again. Alan sighed. He'd have to close it and catch each pigeon individually and carry them outside. Yet another project. Maybe he should just go home, he thought.

For now he left the window as it was, and moved into the darker end of the attic, where the walls angled closer together . . .

It was no wonder he couldn't see through the window from the outside. It was thoroughly boarded up on the inside. This also explained why he hadn't been able to recall the window from the inside from his boyhood; it had apparently been covered like this for many years.

Returning from the attic to borrow his father's old tool box from his mother, Alan first gave her hell about the pigeons up there, and then asked, "Why did Dad board up that slanted attic window? On this end of the house, up over the back door?"

"Oh, my father was the one who did that. Your father started to take the boards off once so the attic would get more light, but then he changed his mind and boarded it back up again."

"Well, why did Granddad board it up in the first place?"

"When your grandparents owned the house there was a big thunderstorm one time, and I guess a lightning bolt struck that window. I remember that night . . . I was about eight, I think. It was terrible. The whole house shook. I don't know what the lightning did to the window, though. Maybe it scorched the glass black or just cracked it." She shrugged.

"It isn't cracked. One piece is broken off, is all. Recently, too; I saw the broken pieces in the gutter."

"I don't know." She shrugged again.

"Well, I'm gonna pull the boards off. The attic is real dark down in that end and there's no electric lights. It could use a little sunlight."

His deceased father's tool box in hand, Alan returned to the back hall, climbed up past the second floor, up into the attic.

* * *

Alan pulled the uppermost board off first, using the back of a claw hammer. The first thought that struck him as he looked out through the glass was how quickly it had become dark. It was only five thirty in the afternoon, and here it was summer. Maybe a thunderstorm was brewing.

He glanced over his shoulder, into the opposite, roomier end of the attic. That end of the attic was awash in golden sunlight. Dust motes swam lazily in the slanting mellow beams.

Alan jerked around to gape at the diagonal window. After a moment of confused hesitation, he began to pry off the next board down. It was nailed thoroughly and he really had to lever and strain, splintering the wood, but at last it clattered at his feet.

The sky out there was almost entirely black, but closer to the horizon was streaked in startling reds and purple. Alan saw a distant cluster of birds or perhaps bats cross the bands of laser red.

Could that be an approaching storm, or was the earth more in shadow in that direction as the sun sank? It seemed far, far too great a contrast to be that. Strangely alarmed, Alan pried off the next board with several great jerks.

"Dear God," he breathed, stepping back from the window. He clutched the hammer tightly before him as a weapon or merely for reassurance that reality had not abandoned him without leaving some sort of hand hold.

The roofs of neighboring houses should be out there. Trees bushy between them, and familiar church steeples rising against a backdrop of gentle hills.

Should be . . .

Instead, the distant hills were jagged rocky peaks, ominous in the red glow of twilight. Red and purple light glistened on a lake or large pond in the distance, where he knew none should be. In the foreground there were weirdly gnarled and tangled trees, the closest ones showing him that their branches were thorny and leafless.

Alan wanted to scream, up there in that claustrophobic space, the ceiling close to touching his head, the walls slanting in toward him, dust coating his lungs. He wanted to turn and bolt from there. And yet, he was riveted. Mesmerized. Too afraid to move. Reality indeed was not as it seemed. If he moved, what terrible revelation might next yawn wide before him to engulf his sanity?

Without stepping nearer to the window or reaching to tear free the last board, he looked more closely out upon what could be seen at present. His eyes adjusted to the dark of the scene, and he decided he could make out a few rooftops here and there after all . . . amongst the thorny trees and across the dark lake. None of these houses or buildings had any windows lit, however, despite the deep gloom.

A breeze stirred the twisted trees; Alan felt it through the broken corner of window, and though the breeze was merely cool he shivered as though it were an arctic gust. He realized then that he could also hear this hallucination as well as feel it; he heard the scrape of those barbed-wire branches against one-another as the breeze stirred them. And there were the distant cries of birds, perhaps. Very faint . . . but he wished, from their odd child-like quality, that he could not hear them at all.

What had that lightning bolt done to this window?

It had to be a corresponding dimension he was looking out into. A parallel universe, an alternate interpretation of the same space. Somewhere far away but in this same space there was another old house with an attic, and it was as though he himself were now standing in the attic of that alien building gazing out. This idea so shook him that he had to look wildly around him to convince himself that he was still here in his mother's attic. But the sun still shone warmly at the opposite end. Nothing else had changed around him.

A bird flapped by out there, closer than the others had been. Its movements were unexplainably frightening, unnatural. Awkward or just too weirdly different. How could a creature without real wings fly? It was dark, but he had seen the creature well enough to know that it was identical to the one he had found in his mother's rain gutter.

Alan sought to comprehend how the creature he had discovered had blundered into his reality. The murmur of a pigeon behind him made him realize that in the doppelganger house, a window must have been left open also. The bird-thing had come into the alien house that way, and exited through the diagonal window. The attic window of that house must not be boarded, and thus permitted exit. But when the creature broke out through the glass to take to the sky again, it had entered into *his* dimension, and died, either from its injuries or because of the different conditions of Alan's world.

That meant that the window in the parallel house had been altered, also. Their views had become switched, traded. The alien window must look out, now, upon the more plentiful rooftops of his New England town. Distant church steeples, gentle hazy hills . . .

He had to board the window back up again. As his father had done, when he had discovered its secret.

Alan took new nails from the tool box, filled his pockets. He didn't want to near that window but he couldn't leave it like this for his mother to find. What if something else came through that broken hole? What if she stuck her hand through the hole to see what it looked like translated into the reality of that other realm?

Alan picked up one of the fallen boards, moved to set it back in place. Closer to the window now, and looking further down, he saw the dark face that was out there, peering in at him.

He cried out, dropped the board, tore desperately into the sunny end of the attic.

It was several minutes before he could go back. He smoked a cigarette, gazed at the dark window from a distance. At last, determined, he returned. He picked up the board, set it in place. He didn't look out there this time. He looked only at the grain of the board. Then of the next one. And on, until he had sealed that window closed for the third time in its history.

*   *   *

Outside the house, he mounted the ladder once again. Now it was actually becoming darker as evening approached in his world. He had found a can of black paint in his father's work shop, and had taped a brush to the end of a broken broom handle.

But when he reached the roof, he couldn't help but strain to gaze into the attic through the window once more.

He saw several things then. He wouldn't be able to reflect on all of them until later . . . but this time he could see inside.

The interior of that other attic, pretending it existed within his mother's house through the two-way trickery of the glass, glowed red not with dusk but with dawn. It was the rising sun, not the setting sun, that had streaked that alien sky. More light entered the parallel attic now than before, permitting him to see inside. It was not boards that had darkened the view earlier, but merely the pre-dawn gloom. The alien window had never been boarded.

But these were the realizations Alan made later, after he had painted the window panes black. At the moment he stared through the mysteriously altered glass, his mind registered only one thing.

And that was the face of the creature—the *being*—inside that attic, gazing out at him. It was the same dark face he had seen outside the window, before. When he had been inside his attic, it had been atop its ladder peeking in at him. And now that he was atop his ladder, it had changed places with him, and was inside its own attic.

As they locked eyes in that moment, the being lifted a board in place, meaning to nail it there. To shut out the terrifying visage it had witnessed.

That was when Alan began to paint . . . trying not to see the face as he did so.

Because the face was not human. Not remotely human. But more horrifying than this fact was Alan's realization that—despite its terrible distortions—that face was in effect his own.

WHAT WASHES ASHORE

Marsha was sorry she had wandered so far in this skull-drilling heat in a place she didn't know, which for all its bleakness didn't look known by any. The small houses were silvered from the salt air, warped and bloodless, rows of bleached skulls on display. She had wandered beyond the coffee shops and gift stores tacky or trendy, the miniature art galleries and the expensive little restaurants that crowded the more tourist-favored streets of this seaside town. Marsha didn't hold those bustling, colorful streets in disfavor, but this afternoon she had felt the need to be alone.

Well, the need to escape the anonymous crowds, at any rate; she was traveling alone to begin with. She took on these missionary-like missions to far-flung ally companies eagerly, welcomed the time away from her tiny office, her bosses, her co-workers. She normally stayed in a hotel in the course of these excursions, but a co-worker had a summer cottage here, a mere half hour's ride from the host company. It was quaint, humble, not actually within view of the ocean but that was fine with Marsha, who had never been the volley-ball type. She had been reluctant to accept, not wanting to feel obligated to friendship or worse with this male co-worker, but had decided it might be nice to have a cute little cottage all to herself.

Today her work was over; tomorrow she flew back home. This time was her own, and her own time was of the greatest importance. So she had set out on foot, in sneakers and blue jeans and a crisp new t-shirt, short red hair and big dark glasses, free of her sharp-edged dark suits and ant-black shoes. She had forsaken her rental car, stopped at a coffee shop along the way to buy a large ice coffee to take with her on an aimless walk . . .

She had turned into one less-peopled street, then into another less-peopled than that. And on, until there were no shops, just houses, closing in on narrow streets more like alleys. From a tiny cage-like screened porch, an old woman who looked headless with her upper body lost in shadow waved at Marsha dreamily. Marsha gave a little wave back. A dog, unseen, had growled at her from beneath another porch—she assumed, or perhaps behind a screened window—as she passed by.

But in this street, there were no old ladies, no dogs, no strewn bright and broken toys. The houses looked derelict, abandoned; the windows and doors of several were even boarded up. As Marsha started down this street, sweating now and wondering if she should turn back (her coffee was gone but she carried the cup with her, not wanting to litter), she took note of an old faded barber pole outside one of the boarded-up structures. And then her gaze traveled from this point to the window of another establishment, next door.

This one wasn't boarded up; a large shop window, dusty but unbroken, faced out into the arid street. What did its sign say? Was it a laundry? A few more half-hearted steps through the broiling air and Marsha could read it.

ALL WASHED UP.

She smiled faintly. That was for sure. Was it a joke—a comment on the state of this little sub-neighborhood? She drew closer to the glass, which blazed back the molten sun.

On display inside the shop window were tables and chairs and angled boxes spread with mostly sea shells, along with decorative bits of driftwood and a blistered buoy or two.

Sea shells. Marsha had been taught an enthusiasm for them by her mother, who had a fine, museum-quality collection. It was something that they had in common, something they had been able to talk about. They had never talked about much. ("She's cold, your mother," Brian had said.

"She's British. It's her reserve," Marsha had told him.

"Even British people can be passionate," he had countered. "Or there wouldn't be any more Brits brought into the world, if you catch my meaning." He said this last bit in his favorite, Monty Pythonish caricature of a British accent.

He meant it about me, more than my mother, Marsha reminded herself now. He thought I was cold. He told me so. "I never know what you're feeling." "Do you even love me?" "You never even smile, Marsha!" The guilt trip. The accusations. She had left it behind, now. And he had cried, tears and all. "You're like your mother, you know that?")

But they talked about sea shells, she and her mother, from when Marsha was a child. Her mother didn't stroke her hair, didn't giggle and nudge her. But Marsha liked to believe that the dry, formal genus and species names they both uttered were like an encrypted language of affection. The touching of bony surfaces, crusted rough or smooth as mother-of-pearl, were like caresses traded. She liked to believe . . .

Marsha craned her neck from side to side, attempting to look further into the shop, but it was charcoal gloom. The displays were filmed in dust. Could this place still be in business? If it was indeed open, could enough tourists stray far enough to make this "business" anything more than a hobby, like selling one's own preserves at a fair?

Marsha moved to the door, and tested its latch. It was unlocked. The door squealed open. No bells jingled.

She stood a moment in an early evening beam of slanting and gilded light, that swarmed with motes like churning plankton.

There was a table in the corner with a chair behind it . . . a few books stacked there, and a lamp that was unlit. Marsha looked there, first, to see if someone would be waiting for that rare, lost customer. But the impromptu desk was empty.

She eased the door shut guiltily behind her, wondering if she were trespassing. She saw no sign in the door announcing business hours. How could this shop not be defunct? Only the fact that the door had been unlocked—that, and the tempting array of shells—encouraged her to move deeper into the shadowy room.

There were tables in its center, and shelves and benches around its sides. There was a bookshelf with various titles on shells and the sea, and Marsha recognized a few that her mother and even herself owned. But the shells drew her, foremost. She might find a few things here for her own, long-neglected collection. More importantly, she might even find a few things here that her mother didn't own, that she could mail to her back home. They had lived half a country apart for six years now. Mailing a shell would be better than their brief telephone exchanges.

Marsha neared the closest of the center tables. There were shallow cardboard boxes with shells ranked inside them, the names of the shells either written on cards, or on the floors of the boxes themselves, or on stickers stuck to the shells. The prices looked very good. Even too good. Again, Marsha had the impression that the shop was defunct. Either that, or lost in a pocket of time long past.

The names of shells had always delighted her, and she relived that old nostalgic pleasure now. She lifted a lovely Imperial Harp into her palm, then set it delicately down again. There was one called an Eye of Judas. There was an abalone used as a bowl, and filled with numerous little spotted shells called Measled Cowries.

She wondered, not for the first time, if the huge Queen Conch with its smooth, vivid-pink lips had been so named for its lewd resemblance to a female's genitalia. Even considering it made Marsha embarrassed. Brian would have made a joke if she had suggested such a thing. Perhaps held the shell up to his mouth and flicked his tongue in it. And she would have chided him, or just ignored him, and he might have laughed or sulked and told her she had no sense of humor.

From atop an old bureau, she lifted a greenish Violet Spider Conch in its own box pillowed with cotton pads. There was an Arthritic Spider Conch, which looked like a dangerous creature that had become fossilized. The diseased-sounding Pustulated Triton. The appropriately leering Grinning Tun.

A loud thump, the rattle of glass, and Marsha was startled—dropped the shell she was presently holding, heard it clatter at her feet. Peripherally, she had seen something strike the glass in the shop's closed door.

At first she had thought it was a thrown toy, but in the tail of her eye she had seen the dark blur whiz back up out of sight. A bird, then, chasing insects

251

and colliding with the glass. Good thing it hadn't broken through. It had to be stunned pretty nicely. And now Marsha looked back at the improvised desk in the corner, then at a closed door which must lead further into the house. The loud sound had brought no one to the door, and though she had half-expected to see some old woman (who perhaps looked like her aging mother) now seated in that chair, there was no one.

Still a bit unnerved, Marsha stooped to retrieve the shell she had dropped. Thank God it had no brittle horns or such to snap off. As she gathered it into her hand, she noticed there were more boxes of shells pushed under the table and hidden by its draped yellowish cloth. Some boxes were stuffed with brittle newspaper, the shells practically heaped amongst that crumpled garble of old printed words. And one box had written on its side in bold black marker the words: SAD THINGS.

Marsha glanced up furtively, knelt closer, dragged the box out into view.

These were not shells, but other sorts of flotsam and jetsam, detritus of the sea. There was a dark blue beer bottle without a label, with a mummified sea horse corked inside it. There was a child's green plastic alphabet block. There was a naked baby doll with both eyes missing, as if fish had plucked them out, thinking they might be real. Marsha saw a child's glove knitted from dark green wool, and picked it out of the box.

There was something inside the glove. Hardness, jointed and articulated, inside each finger of the glove. Marsha immediately dropped it in horror.

And part of the interior slid out into view. It was not the skeletal hand of a drowned and dismembered child, but a long-dead crab, some of its legs inserted into the fingers and thumb of the glove.

In a sort of disgust born of nervousness, Marsha slid the box back under the table. As she did so, another markered message caught her eye. It said: BLOOD.

She dragged this box out. It had sea shells in it. Some she knew by name, some she didn't, but they were all labeled with stickers. And there seemed to be a theme.

There was a number of one kind of shell called the Bleeding Tooth. It was apt: on the lip of the shell there were several lightish bumps that looked like molars set into a vivid red patch like bloody gums.

Similarly, there were several specimens of a Blood-Mouth Conch, with its whole interior a bright red, though it wasn't as gruesome an image as the former shell.

Another Marsha extricated from the box was a Blood-Sucker Miter, which wasn't red, and the naming of which she didn't understand . . .

But then there was the entirely red Full-Blooded Tellin, an elongated clam in two smooth halves. Marsha thought it was beautiful. She was sure her mother would, too. She selected the nicest specimen of it she could find in the carton, and as she lifted it out she took note of another sort of shell. The only example of it in the container, Marsha picked it out for a closer view.

It was much more violently red than the Tellin. Though it was elongated like the Tellin, it was only smooth on the inside (as glassy red as nail polish), its outer halves being rough and horny. They flared like the folded wings of a dragon, and Marsha wondered if it might be something in the family of bivalves called the Wing Oysters . . .

She turned it over in her hands and read the sticker.

BLOOD WINGS.

Well, she'd been close. But the thing was, she'd never heard of such a shell.

That was it, then. Without a second look Marsha set down the Tellin, and rose with the Blood Wings. There was no price on the sticker. Humph. The Tellin had said two dollars. Marsha decided she would leave ten on the table in the corner, with a little note. It wasn't a common shell or she'd be aware of it, and so ten dollars—at least in this store—seemed fair. It wasn't like she was buying the ultra-rare Glory-of-the-Seas with a ten. It couldn't be too extremely rare, to be buried in a box under a table like that . . .

The first pen she chose from the table was dried up, but she got a second to give up enough pale ink for her to scrawl on a scrap of newspaper from the sixties. Then, she weighed the note and the ten dollar bill down with a dried starfish.

Marsha lifted her head just as she finished, her eyes fixed on that closed door to the rest of the little structure. Had she heard a sound from somewhere deeper in the house? A distant and muffled but heavy thud? It was the sound, she imagined unaccountably, an old person heavy with soft, dead weight might make if they fell out of bed to the floor.

Marsha turned to the outer door, and saw that the sun was very low, much lower than she would have thought it would be. Her eyes must have adjusted to the increasing dimness of the shop without her being conscious of it. She had lost track of the time in her absorption.

She hurried toward the door, beginning to sweat again though the air was cooling, and was half-way out when she thought she heard the squeal of hinges in the room behind her. But she told herself it was the squeal of the door she was exiting, and thankfully she was out in the empty street again, not even a car parked along it, as silent as the inside of the shop had been except for the metallic ringing of cicadas.

As she walked briskly away, she darted a look over her shoulder that flicked her coppery hair. The shop's molten window now gone obsidian black. And a figure behind the displays, peering out at her from the window, timidly or stealthily. She saw it only as a palish smudge before she looked away sharply.

She turned a corner down another, even narrower street. Then took a right. It was supposed to be a right, wasn't it?

The shell was rough, fanged, in her hand. It hurt her flesh, pressing into it. She stopped to slip it into the zippered fanny pack she was wearing, then looked up about her to get a hold on her bearings.

Marsha saw the first of the flying things drop down from the bruising sky like a huge, hovering bee. Because of how it flew, for a moment she took it to be a hummingbird. The metallic cicada tone was right in front of her now.

Her first instinct was to turn abruptly and walk away from it. Was it a bat? She was afraid it would tangle in her hair, even though she had heard such fears were a myth.

She glanced back over her shoulder as she walked briskly. She saw two of the blurred dark flying things now, floating after her through the lingering heat of the air. Marsha quickened her pace . . . and looking forward again, about to turn down yet another side street, she saw one of the flying animals emerge from it ahead of her. She came to a jarring halt, just as another and another creature appeared from the side street . . .

Marsha kept on going straight, then, now breaking into a trot, her heart like a fish drowning in air as it labored in the hot confines of her chest. The cicada buzz mounting, closing in on her, more suffocating than the heat. Another glance back. Now there were more than a dozen of the things, a black swarm, the two groups having converged. They were pursuing her, she knew. Drawn to her. And they weren't entirely black, she understood in that instant of looking behind her. There was an indistinct black body, with trailing feathers that she realized were actually more like the short, numerous tentacles of a nautilus. And the wings were not black, but red. Violently red. They moved too quickly for her to see them clearly, but she believed the wings were hard, and thorny. Rough on the outside, smooth as glossy nail polish on the inside.

She began to run as fast as she could. The street, unfamiliar now in the rushing gloom, made a T ahead. She started toward the left—but a flock of perhaps a dozen more of the buzzing animals began to pour from its mouth. Stumbling, she caught her balance and redirected herself down the right-hand branch of the T. Marsha's mind was blank with fear and her lungs were working too hard to spare sound, but she felt a tear drop from the edge of her jaw.

She realized she still had the empty coffee cup, half-crushed, in her hand; she had been too polite to leave it in the shop. She let it drop. She ran. Ran. Yet another turn in the bleak maze ahead. She took a chance and lunged into it . . . and thank God, there were none of those creatures. But she heard them behind her, their buzz-saw sound so loud now it might tear her eardrums, tear her mind.

Marsha felt the foremost creature pluck at her white t-shirt with its many black limbs, seeking purchase.

She wanted to scream then, cry for help from these many dark staring windows, half-blind with grime, their half-drawn shades like senile drooping eyelids.

The groping creature caught hold of the material. She felt other squirming fingers reaching for her, now.

Her pace was faltering as she forced herself through the lava-like air, her mind a vortex of terror and buzzing. And ahead of her, a familiar landmark at last . . .

. . . a barber pole, unturning. Next door, the sea shell shop, its sign ALL WASHED UP smiling at her in welcome. She had come full circle, and there were more and more of the flying animals seizing hold of her clothing . . . and, for the first time, her skin.

Her steps slowing, crumbling. She had to find shelter. Safety. In her mind, she pictured sharp little bird beaks within those nests of writhing arms.

Just ahead of her, the door to the shop opened, and a pallid figure filled the doorway. It was an elderly woman, large-bodied and wearing a white nightgown, and for an instant Marsha thought it was her mother. Her mother here to protect her. But for all the resemblance, this woman was grinning, and her mother wasn't one to grin. The woman was beckoning to her, and Marsha went to her . . . staggering, sobbing, the things snarled in her hair and fixing themselves to the flesh of her back, both through and inside the material of her crisp new t-shirt. She could feel blood running down her ribs, the small of her back . . .

. . . but the woman was grinning, and held her fleshy arms out in welcome, and Marsha stumbled into them with a sob of mindless gratitude. Immediately, the creatures fell away. The buzzing stopped.

She heard the door close with a squeal behind her, and she was folded into the woman's damp and chilly bosom, which smelled of the sea.

THE CELLAR GODS

— 1 —

Ng was beautiful. It was not that I was so lacking in prejudice toward those strange, silent tenants of the brick warehouse, not that I was unafraid of them when the rest of the town let their fear turn to rage. I was too weak to save the others, but it was a weakness that made me save her. It was simply this: that Ng was beautiful.

I still can't say, with any certainty, where she—they—came from. They were oriental, at least in physical resemblance. Even today, over fifty years later, with the world so much smaller, more intimate, with most its mysterious shadowed corners lit by the bland light of cathode rays, I have never learned of her origins. I have watched documentaries, pored over crumbling tomes and glossy *National Geographics*. A few hints—just broken shards of myth like fragments of ancient pottery, dinosaur bones that cannot be assembled; rumors of a place called Leng, and of a place called the Dreamlands which could be reached by shamans only, through astral projection, the ritual use of drugs, or death. Whether this was truly an actual place, on this plane or another, or merely a state of mind, one might not tell from these obliterated legends. But I think I know the truth.

The most Ng told me herself was that she came from 'the Cold Waste.' She was not as stocky and broad-faced as an Eskimo, though I might have believed some of the others to be that. Ng spoke broken English, as some of those mysterious laborers did, so that they might interact with the people of Eastborough to some limited, unavoidable extent. They had purchased a small brick warehouse composed of two stories and a basement, close to the train tracks, where freight was unloaded and carried into the building, or vice versa, though what lay inside those heavy wooden crates and sealed metal drums we never learned; at the time the warehouse was burned, it was found to be largely emptied. At least, that is what was said. If that vengeful little mob did in fact find such freight stored within, and opened it to reveal its secrets, then those contents were either so meaningless—or so horrible—that the information was never revealed.

Later, there was a tannery on that spot. It, too, burned, though the cause of that conflagration was a mystery. There is a retirement complex on the spot now, and the trains no longer use that stretch of track, so that it lies covered in the woods on the outskirts of Eastborough Swamp, into which some people have ventured and never returned, said to be swallowed in quicksand, or abducted by the UFOs teenagers have claimed to see, or done some evil by the ghosts of the thirty oriental laborers murdered on that night in 1944.

The war was not yet over; it was the time of Yellow Peril, not of New World Order. Not to excuse the actions of the clan who descended on that warehouse to murder those who worked and dwelled within. But I will say this: during the war, much was said to portray the Japanese as monsters, fiends, demons straight out of hell. We know now that the Japanese are only as vile as ourselves. But Ng's people—and yes, I still shudder to imagine their fates, and I wonder if Ng was not the only one of them capable of tenderness—well, if fragments and whispers are to be taken as more than just similar propaganda . . . then the things said about the Japanese might in their case be far more fitting.

I am an old man now, and I will never live in that retirement complex. How much of the delirium of its tenants, thought to be senility, might be caused by ghostly possession, poison vibrations, the stain of sins both brutally human and horribly alien? I, myself, would rather die in an alley.

I was twenty in 1944. My epilepsy, though mild, had kept me out of the war, and I was attending college in nearby Worcester, Massachusetts, pursuing a career in medicine. I felt fortunate then, but in retrospect I think I would have preferred to go to war; to have witnessed merely terrestrial horrors; just blood spilt, just flesh torn. Not dimensions rent, not the black belly of the cosmos incised and peeled back in dissection. But then . . . but then . . . I would never have known Ng.

- 2 -

I worked weekends in a small grocery, and had as much contact with the mysterious foreigners as anyone in town did. Ng had come in before, and I couldn't help but notice her. Her face was round, the lips of her small mouth full, her teeth—when she would politely, shyly smile—crooked but white and appealing. Her eyes with their oriental fold were neat slits as if cut in the smooth paper mask of her face, slits from out of which those eyes gazed with a dark sheen. Her hair was glossy and straight, usually gathered in a braid in back, but sometimes flowing free about her slight, girlish shoulders. Though my age, she was as small and slim as a child.

One day she entered the tiny market with a companion; briskly they selected the items on their list, then came to the counter. At once I noticed Ng's hand was crudely bandaged in a dirty white rag, this stained deeply with blood. "What happened to you?" I asked with straightforward concern, gesturing at her swaddled limb.

The young woman shrugged and averted her gaze with embarrassment. "Cut hand working."

"Well, you should have it looked after. Here, come around here. Don't be afraid; I'm going to school to become a doctor. Let me have a look at it . . . dress it properly, at least."

Ng threw a doubtful look at her companion, a stern-faced older woman I had also seen before, and who never smiled. She was all the more unappealing for the deep fissure of a scar which ran down the center of her forehead, even extending down the bridge of her nose, as if she had miraculously survived a catastrophic axe wound to the skull. The woman grunted unpleasantly, but I persisted boldly, taking the younger woman's slim forearm.

"Come around here . . . please. Don't be afraid . . ."

And so she did, the older woman reluctantly following, muttering in an alien tongue. In the back room I quickly washed my hands (afraid they would flee if I didn't act fast), then ran to fetch some tape and gauze from one of the narrow aisles. Ng allowed me to unwrap her small hand, and I cleaned it in the sink, lathering it between my own. As the blood both dry and fresh was scrubbed away, I saw that the wounding consisted of four nasty lacerations across the top of her hand, deep but not requiring stitches. I wondered what machinery she had caught her hand in; to me it looked like a panther had raked her with its claws, but I told myself her exotic appearance was making my imagination too fanciful.

I bandaged her hand properly, as promised, and told her, "Come back when it needs to be changed again, will you?"

She smiled, nodded . . . and to my honest surprise, did return, the next day, and alone.

So it began, with my kindness, and our touching, and her blood. I couldn't wait for the weekends; her lovely face was superimposed over the dusty text of my school books. Several weeks passed, and she managed to come in alone every Saturday and Sunday. Finally, one Sunday afternoon, as it was near my time to leave, I asked her if I could walk her home, or maybe to get some coffee. She was visibly hesitant, and I cursed my foolishness, but then she said, "Go your house? People see us coffee. They talk. Your people. *My* people . . ."

I wondered what my parents would say if I brought her home; I lived with them in their large old Victorian. But I was too excited to decline. So Ng waited until I closed up, and we stepped outside together into the biting February air, and there floating toward us like some apparition was the stern-faced woman with her cracked doll's head, extending a claw of a hand to Ng. Commanding her, come to fetch her.

Ng spoke defiantly in her native tongue, but the woman seized her roughly by the elbow and began dragging her off. I wanted to speak up, but was too timid, and Ng gave in, casting a sad look at me over her shoulder.

- 3 -

The next weekend there came a great snowstorm, a howling wrathful god of a blizzard that dumped thirty inches of heavy wet snow on Eastborough before it was spent. On such a night, one would expect even drunken brutes to remain in their warm homes. Instead, for whatever reasons led to the final decision, that was the night that seven men from the town set out with shotguns and cans of gasoline for the warehouse by the train tracks. Perhaps it was the way the deep snow transformed our familiar town into a savage, isolating, alien world that stirred their fears and restlessness beyond the point they could endure.

The first I learned of the incident was when—it being past midnight, and I the only one awake, pouring over a text book—I heard a faint rapping at my bedroom window. I expected it to be the scraping of a whipped tree branch, but parted the curtains nonetheless and started violently when I saw a dark face peering in at me. I had a flashlight by my bed in case we lost power, pointed it at the glass, and saw Ng's face hovering in the cold black beyond.

I let her in, of course, and took her into the basement so my parents wouldn't hear us converse. She obviously had dressed hurriedly, inadequately, and was next to frozen. I took a blanket from the laundry corner and wrapped it around her shoulders, toweled her hair dry myself.

"What are you doing here? How did you find me?" I whispered as I worked. And then I noticed the burnt smell about her. "What happened?"

"Grayeyes—" she said. It was the first time she called me that, and she never called me anything else. Later, she would admit that the color of my eyes— more gray than blue—had fascinated her, as hers had me.

"Men come to our place. Shoot boss. Make fire. Only Ng escape. They not see me, but if see me kill me. I must stay here. Please . . . please, Grayeyes." She touched my face. Ah, seductress! But it wasn't a charade, wasn't insincere. I took her hand from my face . . . but I continued to hold it in my own.

In the morning, I confessed to my parents that I had taken her in. Naturally, they were alarmed, unhappy, concerned that the band that had gutted the warehouse would seek her out, too. I convinced them that the marauders didn't know she survived, let alone here in our house. I pleaded, and at last they gave in. Ng would remain in the basement, however. There was a corner of the basement, away from the furnace, the water heater, the laundry area, on the other side of the stairs, where we stored boxes of Christmas decorations and the like. I carried what I could up to the attic to clear it out, and into that corner dragged our old sofa, which we kept down in the basement to sit and read on when doing the wash. This became Ng's bed, our cellar her refuge, her sanctuary.

It was difficult returning to school, several days later, leaving this stranger— however meek and seemingly harmless—alone with my parents. Especially as the details of the brutal attack began to circulate   . . . this, despite the fact that no one had been arrested in connection with it, yet. (And no one ever was, though three of the men said to have been responsible died unnatural deaths—two in automobile accidents, and one having been found in his garage as late as 1969, with his throat cut, strung upside-down from the ceiling.)

But the first day I rushed home from school to find all three of them alive and well. My mother had brought food down to Ng, who had only ventured upstairs to use the toilet and bathe. Ng smiled her crooked, sweet smile upon seeing me return, but my father drew me into the living room to whisper to me with a harshness born of nervousness.

"I heard some of what they saw in the warehouse . . . weird stuff. Animal bones hanging from the ceiling in the cellar, and symbols painted on the walls, and the weirdest thing: out of the cellar floor there was sticking these two big statues, just heads, coming right out of the dirt. Like the warehouse was built around them, but how could that be? They weren't dug up out of the floor by those people, either, and they were too big to have been dragged in there . . ."

"Statues of what?"

"Just heads, is all. Slanty-eyed heads. Old . . . real old."

- 4 -

It was again past midnight, the first time we made love; on that narrow musty sofa in the basement, my parents asleep in their comfortable large bed above us.

I still remember the feel, the smell, the taste of her flesh. In the intimate soft glow of her one lamp, it had a warm honey color. She was so tiny, delicate but not weak, her breasts with their brown nipples adolescent, her skin flawless and so smooth, so unlined, barely creased, showing no muscle definition and yet her limbs so slender, that she resembled a child or a doll, not yet fully formed. There was but the barest wisp of coarse hair at the meeting of her legs, her small strong legs that hitched around me, squeezed me, as she squeezed her eyes tightly shut and bared her crooked teeth as if in agony, but moaning so softly in pleasure, her black hair flowing silken over my arms, her arms wrapped desperately around me, as if she would never let me go.

It was the first of many such times, and my parents of course knew what was happening. Soon they never came down cellar without knocking first. The weeks passed. It was now spring. But Ng would not leave the house; she was convinced, and I could not really deny it, that the police knew who the killers were, and would not protect her as they protected them. She feared, as my family did, that our house would be attacked next if her presence came to light. And so, it became summer. We had so much more time together that I almost did not want to return to school that fall. But during the summer I helped my father transform our basement for Ng. We built a wall that divided off her room from the rest of the basement, starting just where the stairs descended, so that the entrance to her tiny apartment (compartment would be fairer) was concealed in the dark beneath the stairs. My father was not cheerful about his labors and the expense, but it didn't show in his work (or was it that his love for me, and pity for Ng, showed in his work?). We installed a toilet and a cramped shower stall in her corner, and I bought her a narrow child's bed. We boarded up the one small window in her room so she wouldn't be as nervous about using her lamp at night. I purchased a second hand bureau, and in Worcester I bought clothing for her; up to now she had been wearing some of my mother's things. (When first she came to my home she had only the clothes on her back, and some few possessions she had gathered into a burlap sack.) After a time we stopped wondering how long we might have to take these precautions; it became our way of life, as it had for the family of Anne Frank, hiding from their persecutors.

And so, years began to pass.

I became a doctor, a general practitioner, and converted rooms in the hulking Victorian to make my office and two examination rooms. My parents, good as always, all but moved to the second floor. After a time I could have bought my own house, and moved Ng into it, but she would not leave her place of asylum. I told her in Worcester she would not be so alien in the more heterogeneous throngs of the city, but still she passionately refused. One time when I became especially insistent, and grabbed her arm as if to drag her upstairs, where she hadn't ventured in months, she snatched up a steak knife from the small table I'd given her and pressed its tip under her own jaw. I let her go.

And so I never married, as the years continued by. I declined dates, and once heard it rumored I was disinclined toward my own sex. I felt like the Beast, keeping his Beauty hostage in his castle dungeon, except that she was my willing prisoner. As time turned reality to history, even folklore, some of the rumors about that night of the blizzard also took on a fairy tale quality . . .

One patient of mine was an elderly man who lived with his son, and who drank too much and constantly injured himself in falls and such. One afternoon, as I was treating him, he began to speak of that night. Naturally, I encouraged him, though I could plainly tell he was already drunk. And this is what he said he saw, peeking out his window into the wild storm.

"I heard a noise, and I looked out the window, and I seen this plow, I thought, moving through Parker's Meadow, where there's houses now. I thought, what the hell's a plow doing in that field? But as I watched it, I saw it wasn't any truck. It was some kind of big animal, I swear to   God . . . big and black, and it started nosing down into the snow, right there in the middle of the meadow, burrowing right down 'til in about fifteen minutes the damn thing was gone. And the snow covered up the spot, of course, and come spring

I went out there one day and there was no sign of the spot. But I saw that thing, whatever it was, and it must've come through the woods from Eastborough Swamp."

"What do you think it was?" I asked him, though I had already dismissed his story; I'd been hoping it was the killers he had seen, making a getaway. "What did it look like?"

"I didn't make it out well . . . but best I can say is it looked like a cow. Big cow, all black . . . but with no head. Just this thing where a head should be—a clump of little squirmy arms like . . . look like one of those sea anenome things. Maybe it was really hair blowing, horse's mane, I don't know . . . but didn't look like there was a head there, to me. And no horse I ever heard of buried itself out in the middle of a field . . ."

- 5 -

Over a decade had passed. One time, after we had the water heater replaced, the worker told us he thought we had rats in the walls. I told him I'd look into it.

Mother died of cancer in 1956. All my medical training, and I was helpless as I watched her succumb to her torture. Ng was hit as hard by this as my father and I, as my mother would frequently visit her, saw her in fact more often than I did, in my school years. I slept most nights in Ng's little bed with her, and she was my solace. Thus, I became almost panicked with concern when, just a year later, Ng herself became ill.

I say ill. I don't know, even today, how to fully explain what I came to witness.

The first symptom was that a dark brown line appeared on her forehead running vertically down to the bridge of her nose. Even before this line began to open into a bloodless furrow, several weeks later, I was reminded of Ng's stern-faced companion who had perished in the inferno.

When I asked her what this condition was, which had been manifested in that other woman and now in her, she was very evasive, grew impatient with me, showed rare anger. The most she would relate was, "My people have this, if chosen. I not want it, but must. Nothing you can do. It will be worse. Nothing you or any doctor can do. I sorry. I chosen."

I thought it must be some self-inflicted wound, some ritual scarring, but it never showed bleeding, never grew infected. When, months later, the wound appeared very deep and began to widen, I finally exploded, attempted to drag her upstairs, meaning to get her to a hospital. She fought me, bit me; it was horrible. Even when my father joined in we could not restrain her wild struggles. She fled back to her room, and used the bolt I had installed on the other side at her insistence. She refused to allow me entrance for over a week and I did not try to force her again.

Despite the terrible appearance of the wound, how it marred her former unmarked beauty, we continued to make love. Though, Ng insisted, in the dark, and I silently agreed that was best. She was still beautiful . . . but as a Renoir would be, if slashed by a knife down the middle.

I studied everything I could find on medical anomalies, rare afflictions, when not assuming it was something self-inflicted. There were cases of hare-lip in which a median fissure resulted in a cleft face effect, but Ng did not have a cleft palate, and this condition would have been present at birth. Again, congenital division of the nose, as observed by Thomas of Tours, would have been apparent at birth.

And what could I make, later, of the black mass that began to show inside the wound, once it had reached a shocking depth? The black matter was shiny, smooth, as of some kind of membrane, firm to the touch. Ng took to wrapping her head in a scarf, by then, refused further examination, though the wound still showed down to the middle of her nose. And was it possible, as it appeared, that as the wound widened it was subtly pushing her orbits farther apart? So it seemed to me: that her eyes, still lovely, were being pressed out to the sides of her face.

By the time a year had passed since the beginning of her deformity, she no longer permitted me to make love to her, even in the dark. She was ashamed of her appearance, to the point where she began covering her face entirely with a kind of hood she made, revealing only her eyes through slitted holes. Her shame finally made me decide that this could not be a self-inflicted injury. I no longer believed that she had mutilated, disfigured herself as part of her duty as one 'chosen.'"

By now one might wonder why I went on with this life; why I did not marry a woman of my own kind, without this poor creature's cursed existence. But despite the ravaging of her beauty, and the fact that we no longer were intimate—I loved her. As far as I was concerned, I already had a wife.

At her insistence, I made a hinged door within her door, low to the floor, so that I could pass food in to her without having to come inside. I dreaded this development, as I saw what was coming, but gave in to it fatalistically, as it seemed the natural progression for this unnatural relationship.

Another year passed, and I hadn't seen her face for all of that time. Most often I simply sat outside her room, on the cellar stairs, and spoke to her through the little open door. I brought her books. Her English improved, though she revealed no more about her people or her affliction, for that. One day, however, she permitted me entrance to her room, which I hadn't entered in months. I had been waiting for this chance; taken off guard, she was unable to stop me from tearing away her hood.

I fell back in shock and dismay, to witness the progression of her condition.

Ng's slanted eyes had been thrust so far apart that they were like those of a fish, nearly on the sides of her head. And the black mass now protruded out of that great gaping wound. Further, still black and smooth, it had sprouted small growths like the beginnings of rubbery little tendrils.

"Out, get out!" Ng screamed at me, turning away. When I gathered the strength to reach out for her, she whirled at me with a knife, this time pointed at me, and snarled, "Get out! Get out!"

I staggered out to the stairs, leaned against them, and wept, hearing the bolt slam home behind me. Was it a cancer, eating her alive from within? It must be that; I had read harrowing reports of epithelial carcinoma, a case of sarcoma of the nasal septum that in mere months had made a monster out of a boy of nineteen, spreading his eyes to the sides of his head, his nose one huge distended mass. I should have men come and help me force her out of the house, drug her so that I could get her to a hospital, if it wasn't too late to save her . . .

But I didn't do that. Why? Was it that after these many years, I couldn't imagine Ng leaving the house any more than she could? Was I afraid someone might take her away forever, even kill her? I think it was that, even then, somehow I knew there was no cause for her ailment recorded in any medical text book, that there were mysteries regarding her origins that were only hinted at in books too obscure, ancient or controversial to be respected by men of a scientific mind. Scientific, in the conventional sense. I thought again of the burrowing creature my elderly patient had described, the carven heads my father had heard were found in the dirt cellar of that old warehouse. And I thought of what I believed I'd seen, when I ripped Ng's hood away. That those tiny rubbery growths extending from her wound had seemed to be moving of their own volition, writhing in the air.

- 6 -

For weeks I returned to passing Ng's food through her little portal. And then, one morning, she did not answer my raps upon it. "Ng?" I called, thinking she was asleep. Louder: "Ng?" There was still no reply. I continued to rap, loudly. I called so loudly, in fact, that my father came downstairs to see what the matter was.

I banged the panel and shouted frantically. At last, in a grim tone, my father said, "I'll get a crowbar."

When he wedged the bar's blade between the apartment door and its frame, and then began to jerk at the bar to splinter the wood, I thought Ng would respond at last, crying out for us to stop. No protest came, however, and my father persisted, until—with a final heave against the lever—he burst open the door he had made.

I pushed past him into the threshold. And froze there. When he tried to move around me, I gave a strangled sob. "No . . . No . . . please don't."

But my father was strong, and wrenched me aside, yet he too froze, too afraid and in awe to cross that threshold.

Ng sat at her little table, back straight, one hand on its surface, where a sheet of paper lay. She was, as I had feared, dead. And although I had passed her a plate of supper only the evening before, it was as though she had sat dead at that table since the reign of the pharaohs. For she was little more than a mummy, little more than a skeleton, her long glossy hair turned gray and straggly. And her skull—her poor face, that I remembered smiling shyly at me in the market, a lifetime ago . . . its crooked teeth now a death's head rictus— was riven down the middle straight through the bone so that even the hole of her nose was a part of that yawning pit. Only the black of emptiness showed within, now.

Webs covered her; webs growing down from the ceiling, up from the table and floor, webs of peculiar thickness and a strange yellowish color. Again, as if she had sat here in this tomb of my making for an eternity.

I might have broken down into sobbing, consumed by grief alone, if that was all we had found. But my grief was mixed with a kind of terrified wonder . . .

At some point she had turned her cot on its side, laid it up against the wall, and shoved her bureau aside, all to make room for what took up nearly half of her tiny little apartment. And that was a great stone head, that would seem to have risen up from the floor, the cement of which was shattered around its thick neck. Sculpted from some black rock, it put me in mind of both the solemn heads of Easter Island (its ears were similarly long-lobed) and the Asian visages at Angkor-Wat. Its slant-eyed, blind-staring face was similarly shrouded in a caul of yellow web. How far down did it extend into the earth; was there an entire titan body beneath our house? If so, how many thousands of years had it waited to rise? Or had it risen not so much from beneath our world, but out of some other?

I noted that in the center of the statue's forehead there was a third blind, stone eye of sorts resting in a vertical opening.

"Jesus!" my father suddenly blurted, and he pushed me aside so violently that I fell. I saw him lunge between the table and the sculpture, holding the crowbar back like a harpoon he meant to jab into a whale's flank.

But the animal I saw scramble out from behind the great head, when I propped myself up on my elbows, was small. Black, rubbery, waddling awkwardly on two flipper-like feet, small as a human toddler. But it had no arms, and on its sides were pink gill slits that fluttered and wheezed, and it had no head . . . just a whipping mass of medusa-like feelers. It had only got a little closer to the door—horribly, lurching toward me—when father dashed back the other way and brought the crowbar swinging down upon it, again, again, until it fell with a terrible squeal. Father stopped clubbing it, skewered it straight through instead, and after it flopped convulsively for a few seconds the tiny monstrosity curled up like a fetus, and lay still.

Later, we burned the diminutive carcass in our yard.

I got to my feet, stared down at the thing in its pool of sap-thick clear ichor. Looked back up at the wide hole in the dried-out husk of Ng's body. In her cloak of yellow filaments, I was put in mind of the shell of an insect in a spider's web.

My eyes lifted to the boarded up window behind her. Mounted below the window was a contraption I had never seen in here before. I can only assume that she had possessed it all along, had spirited it away from the burning warehouse inside her bag of belongings. It was little more than a crystal lens the size of a shaving mirror, set in a tarnished metal frame which sprouted a few odd knobs and levers. She had wedged the prong of its base into a crack in the wall, so that the lens was on level with the window; in particular, I would find, with a small slit between two boards of the window which I feel she herself had widened a bit for the purpose.

Afraid to near the wall, and thus Ng's corpse, I had to steel myself . . . but I approached the lens, pushing through the ghastly, clinging webs. For even from across her room, and at an indirect angle, I thought I saw blurry movement in the glass.

If only I hadn't looked through it! But then, I wouldn't have been inspired to shatter that lens (with difficulty, using a hammer) afterwards. I can only hope that the telescope, as such it was, was not merely an instrument for viewing, but for summoning, as I suspected it to be. I can only hope that in smashing it, I prevented more of those Outsiders from coming here. It has been many years since that terrible day, and perhaps I was successful. But who knows what mysteries, what horrors, lurk behind the innocent facades of old houses, here in this haunted town, and in every town?

My first impression was that it was a magnifying glass, trained on several beetles or slugs . . . a sort of microscope. These creatures I observed in the grain of the wood boarding the window were hideous, and all the more so for their familiarity. For they were black rubbery things, loosely bovine in their general outline . . . their blocky forms moving with great slowness. Only the nests of tentacles moved quickly, these seeming to feed from the ground, perhaps on creatures as tiny to them as these things were to me.

The creatures—one in the foreground, two further back—moved across a jagged bed of irregular dark crystal. In the background there was a forbidding sky of molten orange and dark brown cloud.

I looked up from the lens sharply. The mysterious instrument was not trained on the wood, but on the sky outside, seen through the crack. And yet . . . and yet . . . the sky outside was blue and clear. What sky was this I was seeing?

I realized, of course, that it was the sky of some other world. Some world separated by space, perhaps dimension, perhaps dream.

And I also realized that those were not tiny, microscopic monstrosities (those things that resembled the creature my father had killed, except for that creature having been bipedal, as if mixed blasphemously with human genes) . . . they were, instead, immense beyond anything that had walked on Earth, or God willing, ever would. For it was not a bed of dark crystal they strode upon, and crushed beneath their bulk, and fed from . . . but a city, an alien city, as great in size as New York . . . greater . . . but no more protected, no less vulnerable, for all that.

The creature in the foreground lifted the nest of worms that was all it owned for a head, and seemed to gaze back at me through the glass. I backed away from it with a cry of terror, and swatted the instrument out of the wall with the sticky crowbar that I seized out of my father's hands.

Panting, tears streaming down my face, I again regarded the shell of what had been my lover. Then, finally, I noticed the sheet she had written on. It was, I saw, a final message to me.

That note was the only thing I removed from her room before I sealed it up. Yes, even now, decades past her death, Ng sits in her chair in her room below me, much as she had in life. Her presence gives me comfort, and sometimes I sit on the cellar stairs, and talk to her through the wall.

When I decided to entomb her there, I wondered what the next owner of the house would think if they ever tore out that wall and found her . . . and the colossal stone head. But shortly before I sealed the room, I discovered that the head was gone, presumably sunken back into the earth or other world that it had risen from, leaving only a broken place in the cement, like a wound clotted with dirt.

I still don't know for certain, entirely, what Ng meant by her note. But I think she was apologizing for having followed the call of her kind, for having attempted to perform her chosen duty, despite her feelings for me and my family. I don't think she really wanted to do what she did. I must believe that.

But I also think she was apologizing for causing me worry and pain, over the years. And it caused me more pain to think she might not have realized that I had no regrets about our relationship. That I had loved her deeply, and would have wanted no other wife.

To the end, she was cryptic. To the end, a mystery. My mystery.

For the note she had left me said only, "I am sorry, Grayeyes" —and no more.

The Taint of Lovecraft

by Stanley C. Sargent
Robert M. Price, Editor

DH

The second collection from the author of *Ancient Exhumations,*
Stanley C. Sargent, with wonderful illustrations and
featuring his novella, *Nyarlatophis, a Fable of Ancient Egypt.*
$20

THE TALES OF INSPECTOR LEGRASSE

H. P. LOVECRAFT & C. J. HENDERSON

Spawned from the classical horror-hunt of Inspector Legrasse,
these seven tales detail an epic confrontation between an
unprepared mankind and the horrors of the Cthulhu Mythos.
$20

THE LOVECRAFT CHRONICLES

PETER CANNON

From Peter Cannon, author of *Pulptime,*
Scream for Jeeves, and *Forever Azathoth and Other Horrors*
comes three new tales, alternate histories of the Old Gent.

$15

WALTER C. DEBILL, JR.

THE BLACK SUTRA

Nineteen tales of terrors from prehistory
encroaching on the modern world
from Walter C. DeBill, Jr.

$20

Lightning Source UK Ltd.
Milton Keynes UK
19 August 2009

142848UK00001B/192/A